Five Little Pigs

Agatha Christie is known throughout the world as the Queen of Crime. Her books have sold over a billion copies in English with another billion in 44 foreign languages. She is the most widely published author of all time and in any language, outsold only by the Bible and Shakespeare. She is the author of 80 crime novels and short story collections, 19 plays, and six novels written under the name of Mary Westmacott.

Agatha Christie's first novel, *The Mysterious Affair at Styles*, was written towards the end of the First World War, in which she served as a VAD. In it she created Hercule Poirot, the little Belgian detective who was destined to become the most popular detective in crime fiction since Sherlock Holmes. It was eventually published by The Bodley Head in 1920.

In 1926, after averaging a book a year, Agatha Christie wrote her masterpiece. *The Murder of Roger Ackroyd* was the first of her books to be published by Collins and marked the beginning of an author-publisher relationship which lasted for 50 years and well over 70 books. *The Murder of Roger Ackroyd* was also the first of Agatha Christie's books to be dramatised – under the name *Alibi* – and to have a successful run in London's West End. *The Mousetrap*, her most famous play of all, opened in 1952 and is the longest-running play in history.

Agatha Christie was made a Dame in 1971. She died in 1976, since when a number of books have been published posthumously: the bestselling novel *Sleeping Murder* appeared later that year, followed by her autobiography and the short story collections *Miss Marple's Final Cases*, *Problem at Pollensa Bay* and *While the Light Lasts*. In 1998 *Black Coffee* was the first of her plays to be novelised by another author, Charles Osborne.

AGATHA CHRISTIE

FIVE LITTLE PIGS

HarperCollinsPublishers

HarperCollins*Publishers*
77-85 Fulham Palace Road,
Hammersmith, London W6 8JB

This paperback edition 1994
9

Previously published in paperback by Fontana 1959
Reprinted thirty-two times

First published in Great Britain by
Collins 1943

ISBN 0 00 765950 4

Set in Plantin

Printed and bound in Great Britain by
Mackays of Chatham plc, Chatham, Kent

To Stephen Glanville

CONTENTS

INTRODUCTION

BOOK III

INTRODUCTION

Carla Lemarchant

Hercule Poirot looked with interest and appreciation at the young woman who was being ushered into the room.

There had been nothing distinctive in the letter she had written. It had been a mere request for an appointment, with no hint of what lay behind that request. It had been brief and business-like. Only the firmness of the handwriting had indicated that Carla Lemarchant was a young woman.

And now here she was in the flesh – a tall, slender young woman in the early twenties. The kind of young woman that one definitely looked at twice. Her clothes were good, an expensive well-cut coat and skirt and luxurious furs. Her head was well poised on her shoulders, she had a square brow, a sensitively cut nose and a determined chin. She looked very much alive. It was her aliveness, more than her beauty, which struck the predominant note.

Before her entrance, Hercule Poirot had been feeling old – now he felt rejuvenated – alive – keen!

As he came forward to greet her, he was aware of her dark grey eyes studying him attentively. She was very earnest in that scrutiny.

She sat down and accepted the cigarette that he offered her. After it was lit she sat for a minute or two smoking, still looking at him with that earnest, thoughtful gaze.

Poirot said gently:

'Yes, it has to be decided, does it not?'

She started. 'I beg your pardon?'

Her voice was attractive, with a faint, agreeable huskiness in it.

'You are making up your mind, are you not, whether I am a mere mountebank, or the man you need?'

She smiled. She said:

'Well, yes – something of that kind. You see, M. Poirot, you – you don't look exactly the way I pictured you.'

'And I am old, am I not? Older than you imagined?'

'Yes, that too.' She hesitated. 'I'm being frank, you see. I want – I've got to have – the best.'

'Rest assured,' said Hercule Poirot. 'I *am* the best!'

Carla said: 'You're not modest . . . All the same, I'm inclined to take you at your word.'

Poirot said placidly:

'One does not, you know, employ merely the muscles. I do not need to bend and measure the footprints and pick up the cigarette ends and examine the bent blades of grass. It is enough for me to sit back in my chair and *think*. It is this' – he tapped his egg-shaped head – '*this* that functions!'

'I know,' said Carla Lemarchant. 'That's why I've come to you. I want you, you see, to do something fantastic!'

'That,' said Hercule Poirot, 'promises well!'

He looked at her in encouragement.

Carla Lemarchant drew a deep breath.

'My name,' she said, 'isn't Carla. It's Caroline. The same as my mother's. I was called after her.' She paused. 'And though I've always gone by the name of Lemarchant – my real name is Crale.'

Hercule Poirot's forehead creased a moment perplexedly. He murmured: 'Crale – I seem to remember . . .'

She said:

'My father was a painter – rather a well-known painter. Some people say he was a great painter. *I* think he was.'

Hercule Poirot said: 'Amyas Crale?'

'Yes.' She paused, then she went on: 'And my mother, Caroline Crale, was tried for murdering him!'

'Aha,' said Hercule Poirot. 'I remember now – but only vaguely. I was abroad at the time. It was a long time ago.'

'Sixteen years,' said the girl.

Her face was very white now and her eyes two burning lights.

She said:

'Do you understand? *She was tried and convicted* . . . She wasn't hanged because they felt that there were extenuating circumstances – so the sentence was commuted to penal servitude for life. But she died only a year after the trial. You see? It's all over – done – finished with . . .'

Poirot said quietly: 'And so?'

The girl called Carla Lemarchant pressed her hands together. She spoke slowly and haltingly but with an odd, pointed emphasis.

She said:

'You've got to understand – exactly – where I come in. I was five years old at the time it – happened. Too young to know anything about it. I remember my mother and my father, of course, and I remember leaving home suddenly – being taken to the country. I remember the pigs and a nice fat farmer's wife – and everybody being very kind – and I remember, quite clearly, the funny way they used to look at me – everybody – a sort of furtive look. I knew, of course, children do, that there was something wrong – but I didn't know what.

'And then I went on a ship – it was exciting – it went on for days, and then I was in Canada and Uncle Simon met me, and I lived in Montreal with him and with Aunt Louise, and when I asked about Mummy and Daddy they said they'd be coming soon. And then – and then I think I forgot – only I sort of knew that they were dead without remembering any one actually telling me so. Because by that time, you see, I didn't think about them any more. I was very happy, you know. Uncle Simon and Aunt Louise were sweet to me, and I went to school and had a lot of friends, and I'd quite forgotten that I'd ever had another name, not Lemarchant. Aunt Louise, you see, told me that that was

11

my name in Canada and that seemed quite sensible to me at the time – it was just my Canadian name – but as I say I forgot in the end that I'd ever had any other.'

She flung up her defiant chin. She said:

'Look at me. You'd say – wouldn't you? if you met me: "There goes a girl who's got nothing to worry about!" I'm well off, I've got splendid health, I'm sufficiently good to look at, I can enjoy life. At twenty, there wasn't a girl anywhere I'd have changed places with.

'But already, you know, I'd begun to ask questions. About my own mother and father. Who they were and what they did? I'd have been bound to find out in the end –

'As it was, they told me the truth. When I was twenty-one. They had to then, because for one thing I came into my own money. And then, you see, there was the letter. The letter my mother left for me when she died.'

Her expression changed, dimmed. Her eyes were no longer two burning points, they were dark dim pools. She said:

'That's when I learnt the truth. That my mother had been convicted of murder. It was – rather horrible.'

She paused.

'There's something else I must tell you. I was engaged to be married. They said we must wait – that we couldn't be married until I was twenty-one. When I knew, I understood why.'

Poirot stirred and spoke for the first time. He said:

'And what was your fiancé's reaction?'

'John? John didn't care. He said it made no difference – not to him. He and I were John and Carla – and the past didn't matter.'

She leaned forward.

'We're still engaged. But all the same, you know, it *does* matter. It matters to me. And it matters to John too . . . It isn't the past that matters to us – it's the future.' She clenched her hands. 'We want children, you see. We both

12

want children. And we don't want to watch our children growing up and be afraid.'

Poirot said:

'Do you not realize that amongst every one's ancestors there has been violence and evil?'

'You don't understand. That's so, of course. But then, one doesn't usually know about it. We do. It's very near to us. And sometimes – I've seen John just look at me. Such a quick glance – just a flash. Supposing we were married and we'd quarrelled – and I saw him look at me and – and *wonder*?'

Hercule Poirot said: 'How was your father killed?'

Carla's voice came clear and firm.

'He was poisoned.'

Hercule Poirot said: 'I see.'

There was a silence.

Then the girl said in a calm, matter-of-fact voice:

'Thank goodness you're sensible. You see that it does matter – and what it involves. You don't try and patch it up and trot out consoling phrases.'

'I understand very well,' said Poirot. 'What I do not understand is what you want of *me*?'

Carla Lemarchant said simply:

'I want to marry John! And I mean to marry John! And I want to have at least two girls and two boys. And you're going to make that possible!'

'You mean – you want me to talk to your fiancé? Ah no, it is idiocy what I say there! It is something quite different that you are suggesting. Tell me what is in your mind.'

'Listen, M. Poirot. Get this – and get it clearly. I'm hiring you to investigate a case of murder.'

'Do you mean –?'

'Yes, I do mean. A case of murder is a case of murder whether it happened yesterday or sixteen years ago.'

'But my dear young lady –'

'Wait, M. Poirot. You haven't got it all yet. There's a very important point.'

13

'Yes?'

'My mother was innocent,' said Carla Lemarchant.

Hercule Poirot rubbed his nose. He murmured:

'Well, naturally – I comprehend that –'

'It isn't sentiment. There's her letter. She left it for me before she died. It was to be given to me when I was twenty-one. She left it for that one reason – that I should be quite sure. That's all that was in it. That she hadn't done it – that she was innocent – that I could be sure of that always.'

Hercule Poirot looked thoughtfully at the young vital face staring so earnestly at him. He said slowly:

'*Tout de même –*'

Carla smiled.

'No, mother wasn't like that! You're thinking that it might be a lie – a sentimental lie?' She leaned forward earnestly. 'Listen, M. Poirot, there are some things that children know quite well. I can remember my mother – a patchy remembrance, of course, but I remember quite well the *sort* of person she was. She didn't tell lies – kind lies. If a thing was going to hurt she always told you so. Dentists, or thorns in your finger – all that sort of thing. Truth was a – a natural impulse to her. I wasn't, I don't think, especially fond of her – but I trusted her. I *still* trust her! If she says she didn't kill my father then she didn't kill him! She wasn't the sort of person who would solemnly write down a lie when she knew she was dying.'

Slowly, almost reluctantly, Hercule Poirot bowed his head.

Carla went on.

'That's why it's all right for *me* marrying John. *I* know it's all right. *But he doesn't.* He feels that naturally I would think my mother was innocent. It's got to be cleared up, M. Poirot. And *you're* going to do it!'

Hercule Poirot said slowly:

'Granted that what you say is true, mademoiselle, sixteen years have gone by!'

Carla Lemarchant said: 'Oh! of course it's going to be *difficult*! Nobody but *you* could do it!'

Hercule Poirot's eyes twinkled slightly. He said:

'You give me the best butter – hein?'

Carla said:

'I've heard about you. The things you've done. The *way* you have done them. It's psychology that interests you, isn't it? Well, that doesn't change with time. The tangible things are gone – the cigarette-end and the footprints and the bent blades of grass. You can't look for those any more. But you can go over all the facts of the case, and perhaps talk to the people who were there at the time – they're all alive still – and then – and then, as you said just now, you can lie back in your chair and *think. And you'll know what really happened . . .*'

Hercule Poirot rose to his feet. One hand caressed his moustache. He said:

'Mademoiselle, I am honoured! I will justify your faith in me. I will investigate your case of murder. I will search back into the events of sixteen years ago and I will find out the truth.'

Carla got up. Her eyes were shining. But she only said: 'Good.'

Hercule Poirot shook an eloquent forefinger.

'One little moment. I have said I will find out the truth. I do not, you understand, have the bias. I do not accept your assurance of your mother's innocence. If she was guilty – *eh bien*, what then?'

Carla's proud head went back. She said:

'I'm her daughter. I want the *truth*!'

Hercule Poirot said:

'*En avant*, then. Though it is not that, that I should say. On the contrary. *En arrière . . .*'

BOOK I

CHAPTER I

Counsel for the Defence

'Do I remember the Crale case?' asked Sir Montague Depleach. 'Certainly I do. Remember it very well. Most attractive woman. But unbalanced, of course. No self-control.'

He glanced sideways at Poirot.

'What makes you ask me about it?'

'I am interested.'

'Not really tactful of you, my dear man,' said Depleach, showing his teeth in his sudden famous 'wolf's smile', which had been reputed to have such a terrifying effect upon witnesses. 'Not one of my successes, you know. I didn't get her off.'

'I know that.'

Sir Montague shrugged his shoulders. He said:

'Of course I hadn't quite as much experience then as I have now. All the same I think I did all that could humanly be done. One can't do much without *co-operation*. We *did* get it commuted to penal servitude. Provocation, you know. Lots of respectable wives and mothers got up a petition. There was a lot of sympathy for her.'

He leaned back stretching out his long legs. His face took on a judicial, appraising look.

'If she'd shot him, you know, or even knifed him – I'd have gone all out for manslaughter. But poison – no, you can't play tricks with that. It's tricky – very tricky.'

'What was the defence?' asked Hercule Poirot.

He knew because he had already read the newspaper files, but he saw no harm in playing the complete ignorant to Sir Montague.

'Oh, suicide. Only thing you *could* go for. But it didn't go

19

down well. Crale simply wasn't that kind of man! You never met him, I suppose? No? Well, he was a great blustering, vivid sort of chap. Great womanizer, beer drinker – all the rest of it. Went in for the lusts of the flesh and enjoyed them. You can't persuade a jury that a man like that is going to sit down and quietly do away with himself. It just doesn't fit. No, I was afraid I was up against a losing proposition from the first. And she wouldn't play up! I knew we'd lost as soon as she went into the box. No fight in her at all. But there it is – if you *don't* put your client into the box, the jury draw their own conclusions.'

Poirot said:

'Is that what you meant when you said just now that one cannot do much without co-operation?'

'Absolutely, my dear fellow. We're not magicians, you know. Half the battle is the impression the accused makes on the jury. I've known juries time and again bring in verdicts dead against the judge's summing up. "'E did it, all right" – that's the point of view. Or "*He* never did a thing like that – don't tell me!" Caroline Crale didn't even *try* to put up a fight.'

'Why was that?'

Sir Montague shrugged his shoulders.

'Don't ask me. Of course, she was fond of the fellow. Broke her all up when she came to and realized what she'd done. Don't believe she ever rallied from the shock.'

'So in your opinion she was guilty?'

Depleach looked rather startled. He said:

'Er – well, I thought we were taking that for granted.'

'Did she ever admit to you that she was guilty?'

Depleach looked shocked.

'Of course not – of course not. We have our code, you know. Innocence is always – er – assumed. If you're so interested it's a pity you can't get hold of old Mayhew. Mayhews were the solicitors who briefed me. Old Mayhew could have told you more than I can. But there – he's joined the great majority. There's young George Mayhew, of course, but he was only a boy at the time. It's a long time ago, you know.'

'Yes, I know. It is fortunate for me that you remember so much. You have a remarkable memory.'

Depleach looked pleased. He murmured:

'Oh well, one remembers the main headings, you know. Especially when it's a capital charge. And, of course, the Crale case got a lot of publicity from the press. Lot of sex interest and all that. The girl in the case was pretty striking. Hard-boiled piece of goods, I thought.'

'You will forgive me if I seem too insistent,' said Poirot, 'but I repeat once more, you had no doubt of Caroline Crale's guilt?'

Depleach shrugged his shoulders. He said:

'Frankly – as man to man – I don't think there's much doubt about it. Oh yes, she did it all right.'

'What was the evidence against her?'

'Very damning indeed. First of all there was motive. She and Crale had led a kind of cat and dog life for years – interminable rows. He was always getting mixed up with some woman or other. Couldn't help it. He was that kind of man. She stood it pretty well on the whole. Made allowances for him on the score of temperament – and the man really was a first-class painter, you know. His stuff's gone up enormously in price – enormously. Don't care for that style of painting myself – ugly forceful stuff, but it's *good* – no doubt of that.

'Well, as I say, there had been trouble about women from time to time. Mrs Crale wasn't the meek kind who suffers in silence. There were rows all right. But he always came back to her in the end. These affairs of his blew over. But this final affair was rather different. It was a girl, you see – and quite a young girl. She was only twenty.

'Elsa Greer, that was her name. She was the only daughter of some Yorkshire manufacturer. She'd got money

21

and determination, and she knew what she wanted. What she wanted was Amyas Crale. She got him to paint her – he didn't paint regular Society portraits, "Mrs Blinkety Blank in satin and pearls", but he painted figures. I don't know that most women would have cared to be painted by him – he didn't spare them! But he painted the Greer girl, and he ended by falling for her good and proper. He was getting on for forty, you know, and he'd been married a good many years. He was just ripe for making a fool of himself over some chit of a girl. Elsa Greer was the girl. He was crazy about her, and his idea was to get a divorce from his wife and marry Elsa.

'Caroline Crale wasn't standing for that. She threatened him. She was overheard by two people to say that if he didn't give the girl up she'd kill him. And she meant it all right! The day before it happened, they'd been having tea with a neighbour. He was by way of dabbling in herbs and home-brewed medicines. Amongst his patent brews was one of coniine – spotted hemlock. There was some talk about it and its deadly properties.

'The next day he noticed that half the contents of the bottle had gone. Got the wind up about it. They found an almost empty bottle of it in Mrs Crale's room, hidden away at the bottom of a drawer.'

Hercule Poirot moved uncomfortably. He said:

'Somebody else might have put it there.'

'Oh! She admitted to the police she'd taken it. Very unwise, of course, but she didn't have a solicitor to advise her at that stage. When they asked her about it, she admitted quite frankly that she had taken it.'

'For what reason?'

'She made out that she'd taken it with the idea of doing herself in. She couldn't explain how the bottle came to be empty – nor how it was that there were only her fingerprints on it. That part of it was pretty damaging. She contended, you see, that Amyas Crale had committed suicide. But if he'd taken the coniine from the bottle she'd hidden in her room, *his* fingerprints would have been on the bottle as well as hers.'

'It was given him in beer, was it not?'

'Yes. She got out the bottle from the refrigerator and took it down herself to where he was painting in the garden. She poured it out and gave it to him and watched him drink it. Every one went up to lunch and left him – he often didn't come in to meals. Afterwards she and the governess found him there dead. Her story was that the beer *she* gave him was all right. Our theory was that he suddenly felt so worried and remorseful that he slipped the poison in himself. All poppycock – he wasn't that kind of man! And the fingerprint evidence was the most damning of all.'

'They found her fingerprints on the bottle?'

'No, they didn't – they found only *his* – and they were phoney ones. She was alone with the body, you see, while the governess went to call up a doctor. And what she must have done was to wipe the bottle and glass and then press his fingers on them. She wanted to pretend, you see, that she'd never even handled the stuff. Well, that didn't work. Old Rudolph, who was prosecuting, had a lot of fun with that – proved quite definitely by demonstration in court that a man *couldn't* hold a bottle with his fingers in that position! Of course *we* did our best to prove that he *could* – that his hands would take up a contorted attitude when he was dying – but frankly our stuff wasn't very convincing.'

Hercule Poirot said:

'The coniine in the bottle must have been put there before she took it down to the garden.'

'There was no coniine in the bottle at all. Only in the glass.'

He paused – his large handsome face suddenly altered – he turned his head sharply. 'Hallo,' he said. 'Now then, Poirot, *what are you driving at*?'

Poirot said:

'*If* Caroline Crale was innocent, how did that coniine get into the beer? The defence said at the time that Amyas Crale himself put it there. But you say to me that that was in the highest degree unlikely – and for my part I agree with you. He was not that kind of man. Then, if Caroline Crale did not do it, *someone else did*.'

Depleach said with almost a splutter:

'Oh, damn it all, man, you can't flog a dead horse. It's all over and done with years ago. Of course she did it. You'd know that well enough if you'd seen her at the time. It was written all over her! I even fancy that the verdict was a relief to her. She wasn't frightened. No nerves at all. Just wanted to get through the trial and have it over. A very brave woman, really . . .'

'And yet,' said Hercule Poirot, 'when she died she left a letter to be given to her daughter in which she swore solemnly that she was innocent.'

'I dare say she did,' said Sir Montague Depleach. 'You or I would have done the same in her place.'

'Her daughter says she was not that kind of woman.'

'The daughter says – pah! What does *she* know about it? My dear Poirot, the daughter was a mere infant at the time of the trial. What was she – four – five? They changed her name and sent her out of England somewhere to some relatives. What can *she* know or remember?'

'Children know people very well sometimes.'

'Maybe they do. But that doesn't follow in this case. Naturally the girl wants to believe her mother didn't do it. Let her believe it. It doesn't do any harm.'

'But unfortunately she demands proof.'

'Proof that Caroline Crale didn't kill her husband?'

'Yes.'

'Well,' said Depleach. 'She won't get it.'

'You think not?'

The famous K.C. looked thoughtfully at his companion.

'I've always thought you were an honest man, Poirot.

24

What are you doing? Trying to make money by playing on a girl's natural affections?'

'You do not know the girl. She is an unusual girl. A girl of great force of character.'

'Yes, I should imagine the daughter of Amyas and Caroline Crale might be that. What does she want?'

'She wants the truth.'

'Hm – I'm afraid she'll find the truth unpalatable. Honestly, Poirot, I don't think there's any doubt about it. She killed him.'

'You will forgive me, my friend, but I must satisfy myself on that point.'

'Well, I don't know what more you can do. You can read up the newspaper accounts of the trial. Humphrey Rudolph appeared for the Crown. He's dead – let me see, who was his junior? Young Fogg, I think. Yes, Fogg. You can have a chat with him. And then there are the people who were there at the time. Don't suppose they'll enjoy your butting in and raking the whole thing up, but I dare say you'll get what you want out of them. You're a plausible devil.'

'Ah yes, the people concerned. That is very important. You remember, perhaps, who they were?'

Depleach considered.

'Let me see – it's a long time ago. There were only five people who were really in it, so to speak – I'm not counting the servants – a couple of faithful old things, scared-looking creatures – they didn't know anything about anything. No one could suspect them.'

'There are five people, you say. Tell me about them.'

'Well, there was Philip Blake. He was Crale's greatest friend – had known him all his life. He was staying in the house at the time. *He's* alive. I see him now and again on the links. Lives at St George's Hill. Stockbroker. Plays the markets and gets away with it. Successful man, running to fat a bit.'

'Yes. And who next?'

25

'Then there was Blake's elder brother. Country squire – stay at home sort of chap.'

A jingle ran through Poirot's head. He repressed it. He must *not* always be thinking of nursery rhymes. It seemed an obsession with him lately. And yet the jingle persisted.

'This little pig went to market, this little pig stayed at home . . . '

He murmured:

'He stayed at home – yes?'

'He's the fellow I was telling you about – messed about with drugs – and herbs – bit of a chemist. His hobby. What was his name now? Literary sort of name – I've got it. Meredith. Meredith Blake. Don't know whether he's alive or not.'

'And who next?'

'Next? Well, there's the cause of all the trouble. The girl in the case. Elsa Greer.'

'This little pig ate roast beef,' murmured Poirot.

Depleach stared at him.

'They've fed her meat all right,' he said. 'She's been a go-getter. She's had three husbands since then. In and out of the divorce court as easy as you please. And every time she makes a change, it's for the better. Lady Dittisham – that's who she is now. Open any *Tatler* and you're sure to find her.'

'And the other two?'

'There was the governess woman. I don't remember her name. Nice capable woman. Thompson – Jones – something like that. And there was the child. Caroline Crale's half sister. She must have been about fifteen. She's made rather a name for herself. Digs up things and goes trekking to the back of beyond. Warren – that's her name. Angela Warren. Rather an alarming young woman nowadays. I met her the other day.'

'She is not, then, the little pig who cried Wee Wee Wee . . . ?'

Sir Montague Depleach looked at him rather oddly. He said drily:

'She's had something to cry Wee-Wee about in her life! She's disfigured, you know. Got a bad scar down one side of her face. She – Oh well, you'll hear all about it, I dare say.'

Poirot stood up. He said:

'I thank you. You have been very kind. If Mrs Crale did *not* kill her husband –'

Depleach interrupted him:

'But she did, old boy, she did. Take my word for it.'

Poirot continued without taking any notice of the interruption.

'Then it seems logical to suppose that one of these five people must have done so.'

'One of them *could* have done it, I suppose,' said Depleach, doubtfully. 'But I don't see why any of them *should*. No reason at all! In fact, I'm quite sure none of them *did* do it. Do get this bee out of your bonnet, old boy!'

But Hercule Poirot only smiled and shook his head.

CHAPTER II

Counsel for the Prosecution

'Guilty as Hell,' said Mr Fogg succinctly.

Hercule Poirot looked meditatively at the thin clear-cut face of the barrister.

Quentin Fogg, K.C. was a very different type from Montague Depleach. Depleach had force, magnetism, an over-bearing and slightly bullying personality. He got his effects by a rapid and dramatic change of manner. Handsome, urbane, charming one minute – then an almost magical transformation, lips back, snarling smile – out for your blood.

Quentin Fogg was thin, pale, singularly lacking in what is called personality. His questions were quiet and un-emotional – but steadily persistent. If Depleach was like a rapier, Fogg was like an auger. He bored steadily. He had never reached spectacular fame, but he was known as a first-class man on law. He usually won his cases.

Hercule Poirot eyed him meditatively.

'So that,' he said, 'was how it struck you?'

Fogg nodded. He said:

'You should have seen her in the box. Old Humpie Rudolph (he was leading, you know) simply made mince-meat of her. Mincemeat!'

He paused and then said unexpectedly:

'On the whole, you know, it was rather too much of a good thing.'

'I am not sure,' said Hercule Poirot, 'that I quite under-stand you?'

Fogg drew his delicately marked brows together. His sensitive hand stroked his bare upper lip. He said:

'How shall I put it? It's a very English point of view.

"Shooting the sitting bird" describes it best. Is that intelligible to you?'

'It is, as you say, a very English point of view, but I think I understand you. In the Central Criminal Court, as on the playing fields of Eton, and in the hunting country, the Englishman likes the victim to have a sporting chance.'

'That's it, exactly. Well, in this case, the accused *didn't* have a chance. Humpie Rudolph did as he liked with her. It started with her examination by Depleach. She stood up there, you know – as docile as a little girl at a party, answering Depleach's questions with the answers she'd learnt off by heart. Quite docile, word perfect – and absolutely unconvincing! She'd been told what to say and she said it. It wasn't Depleach's fault. That old mountebank played his part perfectly – but in any scene that needs two actors, one alone can't carry it. She didn't play up to him. It made the worst possible effect on the jury. And then old Humpie got up. I expect you've seen him? He's a great loss. Hitching his gown up, swaying back on his feet – and then – straight off the mark!

'As I tell you, he made mincemeat of her! Led up to this and that – and she fell into the pitfall every time. He got her to admit the absurdities of her own statements, he got her to contradict herself, she floundered in deeper and deeper. And then he wound up with his usual stuff. Very compelling – very convinced: "I suggest to you, Mrs Crale, that this story of yours about stealing coniine in order to commit suicide is a tissue of falsehood. I suggest that you took it in order to administer it to your husband who was about to leave you for another woman, and that you *did* deliberately administer it to him." And she looked at him – such a pretty creature – graceful, delicate – and she said: "Oh, no – no, I didn't." It was the flattest thing you ever heard – the most unconvincing. I saw old Depleach squirm in his seat. He knew it was all up them.'

Fogg paused a minute – then he went on:

'And yet – I don't know. In some ways it was the cleverest thing she could have done! It appealed to chivalry – to that queer chivalry closely allied to blood sports which makes most foreigners think us such almighty humbugs! The jury felt – the whole court felt – that she hadn't got a chance. She couldn't even fight for herself. She certainly couldn't put up any kind of a show against a great big clever brute like old Humpie. That weak, unconvincing: "*Oh no – no, I didn't,*" it was pathetic – simply pathetic. She was done for!

'Yes, in a way, it was the best thing she could have done. The jury were only out just over half an hour. They brought her in: Guilty with a recommendation to mercy.

'Actually, you know, she made a good contrast to the other woman in the case. The girl. The jury were unsympathetic to *her* from the start. She never turned a hair. Very good looking, hard-boiled, modern. To the women in the court she stood for a type – type of the home-breaker. Homes weren't safe when girls like that were wandering abroad. Girls damn full of sex and contemptuous of the rights of wives and mothers. She didn't spare herself, I will say. She was honest. Admirably honest. She'd fallen in love with Amyas Crale and he with her, and she'd no scruples at all about taking him away from his wife and child.

'I admired her in a way. She had guts. Depleach put in some nasty stuff in cross-examination and she stood up well to it. But the court was unsympathetic. And the judge didn't like her. Old Avis, it was. Been a bit of a rip himself when young – but he's very hot on morality when he's presiding in his robes. His summing up against Caroline Crale was mildness itself. He couldn't deny the facts but he threw out pretty strong hints as to provocation and all that.'

Hercule Poirot asked:

'He did not support the suicide theory of the defence?'

Fogg shook his head.

'*That* never really had a leg to stand upon. Mind you, I don't say Depleach didn't do his best with it. He was magnificent. He painted a most moving picture of a great-hearted, pleasure-loving, temperamental man, suddenly overtaken by a passion for a lovely young girl, conscience stricken, yet unable to resist. Then his recoil, his disgust with himself, his remorse for the way he was treating his wife and child and his sudden decision to end it all! The honourable way out. I can tell you, it was a most moving performance; Depleach's voice brought tears to your eyes. You saw the poor wretch torn by his passions and his essential decency. The effect was terrific. Only – when it was all over – and the spell was broken, you couldn't quite square that mythical figure with Amyas Crale. Everybody knew too much about Crale. He wasn't at all that kind of man. And Depleach hadn't been able to get hold of any evidence to show that he was. I should say Crale came as near as possible to being a man without even a rudimentary conscience. He was a ruthless, selfish, good-tempered happy egoist. Any ethics he had would have applied to painting. He wouldn't, I'm convinced, have painted a sloppy, bad picture – no matter what the inducement. But for the rest, he was a full-blooded man and he loved life – he had a zest for it. Suicide? Not he!'

'Not, perhaps, a very good defence to have chosen?'

Fogg shrugged his thin shoulders. He said:

'What else was there? Couldn't sit back and plead that there was no case for the jury – that the prosecution had got to prove their case against the accused. There was a great deal too much proof. She'd handled the poison – admitted pinching it, in fact. There was means, motive, opportunity – everything.'

'One might have attempted to show that these things were artificially arranged?'

Fog said bluntly:

'She admitted most of them. And, in any case, it's too far-fetched. You're implying, I presume, that somebody else murdered him and fixed it up to look as though she had done it.'

31

'You think that quite untenable?'

Fogg said slowly:

'I'm afraid I do. You're suggesting the mysterious X. Where do we look for him?'

Poirot said:

'Obviously in a close circle. There were five people, were there not, who *could* have been concerned?'

'Five? Let me see. There was the old duffer who messed about with his herb brewing. A dangerous hobby – but an amiable creature. Vague sort of person. Don't see him as X. There was the girl – she might have polished off Caroline, but certainly not Amyas. Then there was the stockbroker – Crale's best friend. That's popular in detective stories, but I don't believe in it in real life. There's no one else – oh yes, the kid sister, but one doesn't seriously consider her. That's four.'

Hercule Poirot said:

'You forget the governess.'

'Yes, that's true. Wretched people, governesses, one never does remember them. I do recall her dimly though. Middle-aged, plain, competent. I suppose a psychologist would say that she had a guilty passion for Crale and therefore killed him. The repressed spinster! It's no good – I just don't believe it. As far as my dim remembrance goes she wasn't the neurotic type.'

'It is a long time ago.'

'Fifteen or sixteen years, I suppose. Yes, quite that. You can't expect my memories of the case to be very acute.'

Hercule Poirot said:

'But on the contrary, you remember it amazingly well. That astounds me. You can see it, can you not? When you talk the picture is there before your eyes.'

Fogg said slowly:

'Yes, you're right – I do see it – quite plainly.'

Poirot said:

'It would interest me, my friend, very much, if you would tell me *why?*'

'Why?' Fogg considered the question. His thin intellectual face was alert – interested. 'Yes, now *why?*'

Poirot asked:

'*What* do you see so plainly? The witnesses? The counsel? The judge? The accused standing in the dock?'

Fogg said quietly:

'That's the reason, of course! You've put your finger on it. I shall always see *her* . . . Funny thing, romance. She had the quality of it. I don't know if she was really beautiful . . . She wasn't very young – tired looking – circles under her eyes. But it all centered round her. The interest – the drama. And yet, half the time, *she wasn't there*. She'd gone away somewhere, quite far away – just left her body there, quiescent, attentive, with the little polite smile on her lips. She was all half tones, you know, lights and shades. And yet, with it all, she was more alive than the other – that girl with the perfect body, and the beautiful face, and the crude young strength. I admired Elsa Greer because she had guts, because she could fight, because she stood up to her tormentors and never quailed! But I admired Caroline Crale because she didn't fight, because she retreated into her world of half lights and shadows. She was never defeated because she never gave battle.'

He paused:

'I'm only sure of one thing. She loved the man she killed. Loved him so much that half of her died with him . . .'

Mr Fogg, K.C., paused and polished his glasses.

'Dear me,' he said. 'I seem to be saying some very strange things! I was quite a young man at the time, you know. Just an ambitious youngster. These things make an impression. But all the same I'm sure that Caroline Crale was a very remarkable woman. I shall never forget her. No – I shall never forget her . . .'

CHAPTER III

The Young Solicitor

George Mayhew was cautious and non-committal.

He remembered the case, of course, but not at all clearly. His father had been in charge – he himself had been only nineteen at the time.

Yes, the case had made a great stir. Because of Crale being such a well-known man. His pictures were very fine – very fine indeed. Two of them were in the Tate. Not that that meant anything.

M. Poirot would excuse him, but he didn't see quite what M. Poirot's interest was in the matter. Oh, the *daughter*! Really? Indeed? Canada? He had always heard it was New Zealand.

George Mayhew became less rigid. He unbent.

A shocking thing in a girl's life. He had the deepest sympathy for her. Really it would have been better if she had never learned the truth. Still, it was no use saying that *now*.

She wanted to know? Yes, but what *was* there to know? There were the reports of the trial, of course. He himself didn't really know anything.

No, he was afraid there wasn't much doubt as to Mrs Crale's being guilty. There was a certain amount of excuse for her. These artists – difficult people to live with. With Crale, he understood, it had always been some woman or other.

And she herself had probably been the possessive type of woman. Unable to accept facts. Nowadays she'd simply have divorced him and got over it. He added cautiously:

'Let me see – er – Lady Dittisham, I believe, was the girl in the case.'

Poirot said that he believed that that was so.

'The newspapers bring it up from time to time,' said Mayhew. 'She's been in the divorce court a good deal. She's a very rich woman, as I expect you know. She was married to that explorer fellow before Dittisham. She's always more or less in the public eye. The kind of woman who likes notoriety, I should imagine.'

'Or possibly a hero worshipper,' suggested Poirot.

The idea was upsetting to George Mayhew. He accepted it dubiously.

'Well, possibly – yes, I suppose that might be so.'

He seemed to be turning the idea over in his mind.

Poirot said:

'Had your firm acted for Mrs Crale for a long period of years?'

George Mayhew shook his head.

'On the contrary. Jonathan and Jonathan were the Crale solicitors. Under the circumstances, however, Mr Jonathan felt that he could not very well act for Mrs Crale, and he arranged with us – with my father – to take over her case. You would do well, I think, M. Poirot, to arrange a meeting with old Mr Jonathan. He has retired from active work – he is over seventy – but he knew the Crale family intimately, and he could tell you far more than I can. Indeed, I myself can tell you nothing at all. I was a boy at the time. I don't think I was even in court.'

Poirot rose and George Mayhew, rising too, added:

'You might like to have a word with Edmunds, our managing clerk. He was with the firm then and took a great interest in the case.'

Edmunds was a man of slow speech. His eyes gleamed with legal caution. He took his time in sizing up Poirot before he let himself be betrayed into speech. He said:

'Ay, I mind the Crale case.'

He added severely: 'It was a disgraceful business.'

His shrewd eyes rested appraisingly on Hercule Poirot. He said:

'It's a long time since to be raking things up again.'

'A court verdict is not always an ending.'

Edmunds's square head nodded slowly.

'I'd not say that you weren't in the right of it there.'

Hercule Poirot went on: 'Mrs Crale left a daughter.'

'Ay, I mind there was a child. Sent abroad to relatives, was she not?'

Poirot went on:

'That daughter believes firmly in her mother's innocence.'

The huge bushy eyebrows of Mr Edmunds rose.

'That's the way of it, is it?'

Poirot asked:

'Is there anything you can tell me to support that belief?'

Edmunds reflected. Then, slowly, he shook his head:

'I could not conscientiously say there was. I admired Mrs Crale. Whatever else she was, she was a lady! Not like the other. A hussy – no more, no less. Bold as brass! Jumped-up trash – that's what *she* was – and showed it! Mrs Crale was quality.'

'But none the less a murderess?'

Edmunds frowned. He said, with more spontaneity than he had yet shown:

'That's what I used to ask myself, day after day. Sitting there in the dock so calm and gentle. "I'll not believe it," I used to say to myself. But, if you take my meaning, Mr Poirot, there wasn't anything else to believe. That hemlock didn't get into Mr Crale's beer by accident. It was put there. And if Mrs Crale didn't put it there, who did?'

'That is the question,' said Poirot. 'Who did?'

Again those shrewd old eyes searched his face.

'So that's your idea?' said Mr Edmunds.

'What do you think yourself?'

There was a pause before the officer answered. Then he said:

'There was nothing that pointed that way – nothing at all.'

Poirot said:

'You were in court during the hearing of the case?'

'Every day.'

'You heard the witnesses give evidence?'

'I did.'

'Did anything strike you about them – any abnormality, any insincerity?'

Edmunds said bluntly:

'Was one of them lying, do you mean? Had one of them a reason to wish Mr Crale dead? If you'll excuse me, Mr Poirot, that's a very *melodramatic* idea.'

'At least consider it,' Poirot urged.

He watched the shrewd face, the screwed-up, thoughtful eyes. Slowly, regretfully, Edmunds shook his head.

'That Miss Greer,' he said, 'she was bitter enough, *and* vindictive! I'd say she overstepped the mark in a good deal she said, but it was Mr Crale alive she wanted. He was no use to her dead. She wanted Mrs Crale hanged all right – but that was because death had snatched her man away from her. Like a baulked tigress she was! But, as I say, it was Mr Crale alive she'd wanted. Mr Philip Blake, *he* was against Mrs Crale too. Prejudiced. Got his knife into her whenever he could. But I'd say he was honest according to his lights. He'd been Mr Crale's great friend. His brother, Mr Meredith Blake – a bad witness he was – vague, hesitating – never seemed sure of his answers. I've seen many witnesses like that. Look as though they're lying when all the time they're telling the truth. Didn't want to say anything more than he could help, Mr Meredith Blake didn't. Counsel got all the more out of him on that account. One of these quiet gentlemen who get easily flustered. The governess now, she stood up well to them. Didn't waste words and answered pat and to the point. You couldn't have told, listening to her, which side she was on. Got all her wits about her, she

37

had. The brisk kind.' He paused. 'Knew a lot more than she ever let on about the whole thing, I shouldn't wonder.'

'I, too, should not wonder,' said Hercule Poirot.

He looked sharply at the wrinkled, shrewd face of Mr Alfred Edmunds. It was quite bland and impassive. But Hercule Poirot wondered if he had been vouchsafed a hint.

CHAPTER IV

The Old Solicitor

Mr Caleb Jonathan lived in Essex. After a courteous exchange of letters, Poirot received an invitation, almost royal in its character, to dine and sleep. The old gentleman was decidedly a character. After the insipidity of young George Mayhew, Mr Jonathan was like a glass of his own vintage port.

He had his own methods of approach to a subject, and it was not until well on towards midnight, when sipping a glass of fragrant old brandy, that Mr Jonathan really unbent. In oriental fashion he had appreciated Hercule Poirot's courteous refusal to rush him in any way. Now, in his own good time, he was willing to elaborate the theme of the Crale family.

'Our firm, of course, has known many generations of the Crales. I knew Amyas Crale and his father, Richard Crale, and I can remember Enoch Crale – the grandfather. Country squires, all of them, thought more of horses than human beings. They rode straight, liked women, and had no truck with ideas. They distrusted ideas. But Richard Crale's wife was cram full of ideas – more ideas than sense. She was poetical and musical – she played the harp, you know. She enjoyed poor health and looked very picturesque on her sofa. She was an admirer of Kingsley. That's why she called her son Amyas. His father scoffed at the name – but he gave in.

'Amyas Crale profited by his mixed inheritance. He got his artistic trend from his weakly mother, and his driving power and ruthless egoism from his father. All the Crales were egoists. They never by any chance saw any point of view but their own.'

Tapping with a delicate finger on the arm of his chair, the old man shot a shrewd glance at Poirot.

'Correct me if I am wrong, M. Poirot, but I think you are interested in – character, shall we say?'

Poirot replied.

'That, to me, is the principal interest of all my cases.'

'I can conceive of it. To get under the skin, as it were, of your criminal. How interesting. How absorbing. Our firm, of course, have never had a criminal practice. We should not have been competent to act for Mrs Crale, even if taste had allowed. Mayhews, however, were a very adequate firm. They briefed Depleach – they didn't perhaps show much imagination there – still, he was very expensive and, of course, exceedingly dramatic! What they hadn't the wits to see was that Caroline would never play up in the way he wanted her to. She wasn't a dramatic woman.'

'What was she?' asked Poirot. 'It is that that I am chiefly anxious to know.'

'Yes, yes – of course. How did she come to do what she did? That is the really vital question. I knew her, you know, before she married. Caroline Spalding, she was. A turbulent unhappy creature. Very alive. Her mother was left a widow early in life and Caroline was devoted to her mother. Then the mother married again – there was another child. Yes – yes, very sad, very painful. These young, ardent, adolescent jealousies.'

'She was jealous?'

'Passionately so. There was a regrettable incident. Poor child, she blamed herself bitterly afterwards. But you know, M. Poirot, these things happen. There is an inability to put on the brakes. It comes – it comes with maturity.'

Poirot said:

'What happened?'

'She struck the child – the baby – flung a paperweight at her. The child lost the sight of one eye and was permanently disfigured.'

Mr Jonathan sighed. He said:

'You can imagine the effect a simple question on that point had at the trial.'

He shook his head:

'It gave the impression that Caroline Crale was a woman of ungovernable temper. That was not true. No, that was not true.'

He paused and then resumed:

'Caroline Spalding came often to stay at Alderbury. She rode well, and was keen. Richard Crale was fond of her. She waited on Mrs Crale and was deft and gentle – Mrs Crale also liked her. The girl was not happy at home. She was happy at Alderbury. Diana Crale, Amyas's sister, and she were by way of being friends. Philip and Meredith Blake, boys from the adjoining estate, were frequently at Alderbury. Philip was always a nasty, money-grubbing little brute. I must confess I have always had a distaste for him. But I am told that he tells a very good story and that he has the reputation of being a staunch friend. Meredith was what my contemporaries used to call Namby Pamby. Liked botany and butterflies and observing birds and beasts. Nature study they call it nowadays. Ah, dear – all the young people were a disappointment to their parents. None of them ran true to type – huntin', shootin', fishin'. Meredith preferred watching birds and animals to shooting or hunting them, Philip definitely preferred town to country and went into the business of money-making. Diana married a fellow who wasn't a gentleman – one of the temporary officers in the war. And Amyas, strong, handsome, virile Amyas, blossomed into being a painter, of all things in the world. It's my opinion that Richard Crale died of the shock.

'And in due course Amyas married Caroline Spalding. They'd always fought and sparred, but it was a love match all right. They were both crazy about each other. And they continued to care. But Amyas was like all the Crales, a ruthless egoist. He loved Caroline but he never once considered her in any way. He did as he pleased. It's my opinion that he was as fond of her as he could be of anybody – but she came a long way behind his art. That came first. And I should say at no time did his art give place to a woman. He had affairs with women – they stimulated him – but he left them high and dry when he'd finished with them. He wasn't a sentimental man, nor a romantic one. And he wasn't entirely a sensualist either. The only woman he cared a button for was his own wife. And because she knew that she put up with a lot. He was a very fine painter, you know. She realized that, and respected it. He chased off in his amorous pursuits and came back again – usually with a picture to show for it.

'It might have gone on like that if it hadn't come to Elsa Greer. Elsa Greer –'

Mr Jonathan shook his head.

Poirot said: 'What of Elsa Greer?'

Mr Jonathan said unexpectedly:

'Poor child. Poor child.'

Poirot said: 'So you feel like that about her?'

Jonathan said:

'Maybe it is because I am an old man, but I find, M. Poirot, that there is something about the defencelessness of youth that moves me to tears. Youth is so vulnerable. It is so ruthless – so sure. So generous and so demanding.'

Getting up, he crossed to the bookcase. Taking out a volume he opened it, turned the pages, and then read out:

> '"If that thy bent of love be honourable,
> The purpose marriage, send me word tomorrow
> By one that I'll procure to come to thee,
> Where and what time thou wilt perform the rite,
> And all my fortunes at thy foot I'll lay,
> And follow thee my lord throughout the world."'

'There speaks love allied to youth, in Juliet's words. No reticence, no holding back, no so-called maiden modesty. It is the courage, the insistence, the ruthless force of youth. Shakespeare knew youth. Juliet singles out Romeo. Desdemona claims Othello. They have no doubts, the young, no fear, no pride.'

Poirot said thoughtfully:

'So to you Elsa Greer spoke in the words of Juliet?'

'Yes. She was a spoiled child of fortune – young, lovely, rich. She found her mate and claimed him – no young Romeo, a married, middle-aged painter. Elsa Greer had no code to restrain her, she had the code of modernity. "*Take what you want – we shall only live once!*"

He sighed, leaned back, and again tapped gently on the arm of his chair.

'A predatory Juliet. Young, ruthless, but horribly vulnerable! Staking everything on the one audacious throw. And seemingly she won . . . and then – at the last moment – death steps in – and the living, ardent, joyous Elsa died also. There was left only a vindictive, cold, hard woman, hating with all her soul the woman whose hand had done this thing.'

His voice changed:

'Dear, dear. Pray forgive this little lapse into melodrama. A crude young woman – with a crude outlook on life. Not, I think, an interesting character. *Rose white youth, passionate, pale*, etc. Take that away and what remains? Only a somewhat mediocre young woman seeking for another life-sized hero to put on an empty pedestal.'

Poirot said:

'If Amyas Crale had not been a famous painter –'

Mr Jonathan agreed quickly. He said:

'Quite – quite. You have taken the point admirably. The Elsas of this world are hero-worshippers. A man must have *done* something, must be somebody . . . Caroline Crale, now, could have recognized quality in a bank clerk or an insurance agent! Caroline loved Amyas Crale the man, not Amyas Crale the painter. Caroline Crale was not crude – Elsa Greer was.'

He added:

'But she was young and beautiful and to my mind infinitely pathetic.'

Hercule Poirot went to bed thoughtful. He was fascinated by the problem of personality.

To Edmunds, the clerk, Elsa Greer was a hussy, no more, no less.

To old Mr Jonathan she was the eternal Juliet.

And Caroline Crale?

Each person had seen her differently. Montague Depleach had despised her as a defeatist – a quitter. To young Fogg she had represented Romance. Edmunds saw her simply as a 'lady'. Mr Jonathan had called her a stormy, turbulent creature.

How would he, Hercule Poirot, have seen her?

On the answer to that question depended, he felt, the success of his quest.

So far, not one of the people he had seen had doubted that whatever else she was, Caroline Crale was also a murderess.

CHAPTER V

The Police Superintendent

Ex-Superintendent Hale pulled thoughtfully at his pipe.

He said: .

'This is a funny fancy of yours, M. Poirot.'

'It is, perhaps, a little unusual,' Poirot agreed cautiously.

'You see,' said Hale, 'it's all such a long time ago.'

Hercule Poirot foresaw that he was going to get a little tired of that particular phrase. He said mildly:

'That adds to the difficulty, of course.'

'Raking up the past,' mused the other. 'If there were an *object* in it, now . . .'

'There is an object.'

'What is it?'

'One can enjoy the pursuit of truth for its own sake. I do. And you must not forget the young lady.'

Hale nodded.

'Yes, I see *her* side of it. But – you'll excuse me, M. Poirot – you're an ingenious man. You could cook her up a tale.'

Poirot replied:

'You do not know the young lady.'

'Oh, come now – a man of your experience!'

Poirot drew himself up.

'I may be, *mon cher*, an artistic and competent liar – you seem to think so. But it is not my idea of ethical conduct. I have my standards.'

'Sorry, M. Poirot. I didn't mean to hurt your feelings. But it would be all in a good cause, so to speak.'

'Oh I wonder, would it really?'

Hale said slowly:

'It's tough luck on a happy innocent girl who's just going to get married to find that her mother was a murderess. If I were you I'd go to her and say that, after all, suicide was what it was. Say the case was mishandled by Depleach. Say that there's no doubt in *your* mind that Crale poisoned himself!'

'But there is every doubt in my mind! I do not believe for one minute that Crale poisoned himself. Do you consider it even reasonably possible yourself?'

Slowly Hale shook his head.

'You see? No, it is the truth I must have – not a plausible – or not very plausible – lie.'

Hale turned and looked at Poirot. His square rather red face grew a little redder and even appeared to get a little squarer. He said:

'You talk about the *truth*. I'd like to make it plain to you that we think we *got* the truth in the Crale case.'

Poirot said quickly:

'That pronouncement from you means a great deal. I know you for what you are, an honest and capable man. Now tell me this, was there no doubt at any time in your mind as to the guilt of Mrs Crale?'

The Superintendent's answer came promptly.

'No doubt at all, M. Poirot. The circumstances pointed to her straight away, and every single fact that we uncovered supported that view.'

'You can give me an outline of the evidence against her?'

'I can. When I received your letter I looked up the case.' He picked up a small notebook. 'I've jotted down all the salient facts here.'

'Thank you, my friend. I am all eagerness to hear.'

Hale cleared his throat. A slight official intonation made itself heard in his voice.

He said:

'At two forty-five on the afternoon of September 18th, Inspector Conway was rung up by Dr Andrew Faussett. Dr Faussett stated that Mr Amyas Crale of Alderbury had died suddenly and that in consequence of the circumstances of that death and also of a statement made to him by a Mr Blake, a guest staying in the house, he considered that it was a case for the police.

'Inspector Conway, in company with a sergeant and the police surgeon, came over to Alderbury straight away. Dr Faussett was there and took him to where the body of Mr Crale had not been disturbed.

'Mr Crale had been painting in a small enclosed garden, known as the Battery garden, from the fact that it overlooked the sea, and had some miniature cannon placed in embattlements. It was situated at about four minutes' walk from the house. Mr Crale had not come up to the house for lunch as he wanted to get certain effects of light on the stone – and the sun would have been wrong for this later. He had, therefore, remained alone in the Battery garden, painting. This was stated not to be an unusual occurrence. Mr Crale took very little notice of meal times. Sometimes a sandwich would be sent down to him, but more often he preferred to remain undisturbed. The last people to see him alive were Miss Elsa Greer (staying in the house) and Mr Meredith Blake (a near neighbour). These two went up together to the house and went with the rest of the household in to lunch. After lunch, coffee was served on the terrace. Mrs Crale finished drinking her coffee and then observed that she would "go down and see how Amyas was getting on." Miss Cecilia Williams, governess, got up and accompanied her. She was looking for a pullover belonging to her pupil, Miss Angela Warren, sister of Mrs Crale, which the latter had mislaid and she thought it possible it might have been left down on the beach.

'These two started off together. The path led downwards, through some woods, until it emerged at the door leading into the Battery garden. You could either go into the Battery garden or you could continue on the same path, which led down to the seashore.

Miss Williams continued on down and Mrs Crale went

into the Battery garden. Almost at once, however, Mrs Crale screamed and Miss Williams hurried back. Mr Crale was reclining on a seat and he was dead.

At Mrs Crale's urgent request Miss Williams left the Battery garden and hurried up to the house to telephone for a doctor. On her way, however, she met Mr Meredith Blake and entrusted her errand to him, herself returning to Mrs Crale whom she felt might be in need of someone. Dr Faussett arrived on the scene a quarter of an hour later. He saw at once that Mr Crale had been dead for some time – he placed the probable time of death at between one and two o'clock. There was nothing to show what had caused death. There was no sign of any wound and Mr Crale's attitude was a perfectly natural one. Nevertheless Dr Faussett, who was well acquainted with Mr Crale's state of health, and who knew positively that there was no disease or weakness of any kind, was inclined to take a grave view of the situation. It was at this point that Mr Philip Blake made a certain statement to Dr Faussett.'

Superintendent Hale paused, drew a deep breath and passed, as it were, to Chapter Two.

'Subsequently Mr Blake repeated this statement to Inspector Conway. It was to this effect. He had that morning received a telephone message from his brother, Mr Meredith Blake (who lived at Handcross Manor, a mile and a half away). Mr Meredith Blake was an amateur chemist – or perhaps herbalist would describe it best. On entering his laboratory that morning, Mr Meredith Blake had been startled to note that a bottle containing a preparation of hemlock, which had been quite full the day before, was now nearly empty. Worried and alarmed by this fact he had rung up his brother to ask his advice as to what he should do about it. Mr Philip Blake had urged his brother to come over to Alderbury at once and they would talk the matter over. He himself walked part way to meet his brother and they had come up to the house together. They had come to no decision as to what course to adopt and had left the matter in order to consult again after lunch.

'As a result of further inquiries, Inspector Conway ascertained the following facts: On the preceding afternoon five people had walked over from Alderbury to tea at Handcross Manor. There were Mr and Mrs Crale, Miss Angela Warren, Miss Elsa Greer and Mr Philip Blake. During the time spent there, Mr Meredith Blake had given quite a dissertation on his hobby and had taken the party into his little laboratory and "shown them round". In the course of this tour, he had mentioned certain specific drugs – one of which was coniine, the active principle of the spotted hemlock. He had explained its properties, had lamented the fact that it had now disappeared from the Pharmacopœia and boasted that he had known small doses of it to be very efficacious in whooping cough and asthma. Later he had mentioned its lethal properties and had actually read to his guests some passage from a Greek author describing its effects.'

Superintendent Hale paused, refilled his pipe and passed on to Chapter Three.

'Colonel Frere, the Chief Constable, put the case into my hands. The result of the autopsy put the matter beyond any doubt. Coniine, I understand, leaves no definite postmortem appearances, but the doctors knew what to look for, and an ample amount of the drug was recovered. The doctor was of the opinion that it had been administered two or three hours before death. In front of Mr Crale, on the table, there had been an empty glass and an empty beer bottle. The dregs of both were analysed. There was no coniine in the bottle, but there was in the glass. I made inquiries and learned that although a case of beer and glasses were kept in a small summerhouse in the Battery garden in case Mr Crale should feel thirsty when painting, on this particular morning Mrs Crale had brought down from the house a bottle of freshly iced beer. Mr Crale was busy painting when she arrived and Miss Greer was posing for him, sitting on one of the battlements.

'Mrs Crale opened the beer, poured it out and put the glass into her husband's hand as he was standing before the easel. He tossed it off in one draught – a habit of his, I learned. Then he made a grimace, set down the glass on the table, and said: "Everything tastes foul to me today!" Miss Greer upon that laughed and said, "Liver!" Mr Crale said: "Well, at any rate it was *cold*."'

Hale paused. Poirot said:

'At what time did this take place?'

'At about a quarter-past eleven. Mr Crale continued to paint. According to Miss Greer, he later complained of stiffness in the limbs and grumbled that he must have got a touch of rheumatism. But he was the type of man who hates to admit to illness of any kind, and he undoubtedly tried not to admit that he was feeling ill. His irritable demand that he should be left alone and the others go up to lunch was quite characteristic of the man, I should say.'

Poirot nodded.

Hale continued.

'So Crale was left alone in the Battery garden. No doubt he dropped down on the seat and relaxed as soon as he was alone. Muscular paralysis would then set in. No help was at hand, and death supervened.'

Again Poirot nodded.

Hale said:

'Well, I proceeded according to routine. There wasn't much difficulty in getting down to the facts. On the preceding day there had been a set-to between Mrs Crale and Miss Greer. The latter had pretty insolently described some change in the arrangement of the furniture "when I am living here." Mrs Crale took her up, and said, "What do you mean? When *you* are living here." Miss Greer replied: "Don't pretend you don't know what I mean, Caroline. You're just like an ostrich that buries its head in the sand.

You know perfectly well that Amyas and I care for each other and are going to be married." Mrs Crale said: "I know nothing of the kind." Miss Greer then said: "Well, you know it now." Whereupon, it seems, Mrs Crale turned to her husband who had just come into the room and said: "Is it true, Amyas, that you are going to marry Elsa?"'

Poirot said with interest:

'And what did Mr Crale say to that?'

'Apparently he turned on Miss Greer and shouted at her: "What the devil do you mean by blurting that out? Haven't you got the sense to hold your tongue?"'

'Miss Greer said: "I think Caroline ought to recognize the truth."

'Mrs Crale said to her husband: "Is it true, Amyas?"

'He wouldn't look at her, it seems, turned his face away and mumbled something.

'She said: "Speak out. I've got to know." Whereupon he said:

'"Oh, it's true enough – but I don't want to discuss it now."

'Then he flounced out of the room again and Miss Greer said:

'"You see!" and went on – with something about its being no good for Mrs Crale to adopt a dog-in-the-manger attitude about it. They must all behave like rational people. She herself hoped that Caroline and Amyas would always remain good friends.'

'And what did Mrs Crale say to that?' asked Poirot curiously.

'According to the witnesses she laughed. She said: "Over my dead body, Elsa." She went to the door and Miss Greer called after her: "What do you mean?" Mrs Crale looked back and said: "I'll kill Amyas before I give him up to *you*."'

Hale paused.

'Pretty damning – eh?'

'Yes.' Poirot seemed thoughtful. 'Who overheard this scene?'

'Miss Williams was in the room and Philip Blake. Very awkward for them.'

'Their accounts of the scene agree?'

'Near enough – you never got two witnesses to remember a thing exactly alike. *You* know that just as well as I do, M. Poirot.'

Poirot nodded. He said thoughtfully:

'Yes, it will be interesting to see –' He stopped with the sentence unfinished.

Hale went on: 'I instituted a search of the house. In Mrs Crale's bedroom I found in a bottom drawer, tucked away underneath some winter stockings, a small bottle labelled jasmine scent. It was empty. I fingerprinted it. The only prints on it were those of Mrs Crale. On analysis it was found to contain faint traces of oil of jasmine, and a strong solution of coniine hydrobromide.

'I cautioned Mrs Crale and showed her the bottle. She replied readily. She had, she said, been in a very unhappy state of mind. After listening to Mr Meredith Blake's description of the drug she had slipped back to the laboratory, had emptied out a bottle of jasmine scent which was in her bag and had filled the bottle up with coniine solution. I asked her why she had done this and she said: "I don't want to speak of certain things more than I can help, but I had received a bad shock. My husband was proposing to leave me for another woman. If that was so, I didn't want to live. That is why I took it."'

Hale paused.

Poirot said: 'After all – it is likely enough.'

'Perhaps, M. Poirot. But it doesn't square with what she was overheard to say. And then there was a further scene on the following morning. Mr Philip Blake overheard a portion of it. Miss Greer overheard a different portion of it. It took place in the library between Mr and Mrs Crale. Mr Blake was in the hall and caught a fragment or two. Miss Greer was sitting outside near the open library window and heard a good deal more.'

'And what did they hear?'

'Mr Blake heard Mrs Crale say: "You and your women. I'd like to kill you. Some day I will kill you."'

'No mention of suicide?'

'Exactly. None at all. No words like "If you do this thing, I'll kill *myself*." Miss Greer's evidence was much the same. According to her, Mr Crale said: "Do try and be reasonable about this, Caroline. I'm fond of you and will always wish you well – you and the child. But I'm going to marry Elsa. We've always agreed to leave each other free." Mrs Crale answered to that: "Very well, don't say I haven't warned you." He said: "What do you mean?" And she said: "I mean that I love you and I'm not going to lose you. I'd rather kill you than let you go to that girl."'

Poirot made a slight gesture.

'It occurs to me,' he murmured, 'that Miss Greer was singularly unwise to raise this issue? Mrs Crale could easily have refused her husband a divorce.'

'We had some evidence bearing on that point,' said Hale. 'Mrs Crale, it seems, confided partly in Mr Meredith Blake. He was an old and trusted friend. He was very distressed and managed to get a word with Mr Crale about it. This, I may say, was on the preceding afternoon. Mr Blake remonstrated delicately with his friend, said how distressed he would be if the marriage between Mr and Mrs Crale was to break up so disastrously. He also stressed the point that Miss Greer was a very young girl and that it was a very serious thing to drag a young girl through the divorce court. To this Mr Crale replied, with a chuckle (callous sort of brute he must have been): "That isn't Elsa's idea at all. *She* isn't going to appear. We shall fix it up in the usual way."'

Poirot said: 'Therefore even more imprudent of Miss Greer to have broken out the way she did.'

Superintendent Hale said:

'Oh, you know what women are! Have to get at each other's throats. It must have been a difficult situation anyhow. I can't understand Mr Crale allowing it to happen. According to Mr Meredith Blake he wanted to finish his picture. Does that make sense to you?'

'Yes, my friend, I think it does.'

'It doesn't to me. The man was asking for trouble!'

'He was probaby seriously annoyed with his young woman for breaking out the way she did.'

'Oh, he was. Meredith Blake said so. If he had to finish the picture I don't see why he couldn't have taken some photographs and worked from them. I know a chap – does watercolours of places – *he* does that.'

Poirot shook his head.

'No – I can understand Crale the artist. You must realize, my friend, that at that moment, probably, his picture was all that mattered to Crale. However much he wanted to marry the girl, the picture came first. That's why he hoped to get through her visit without its coming to an open issue. The girl, of course, didn't see it that way. With women, love always comes first.'

'Don't I know it?' said Superintendent Hale with feeling.

'Men,' continued Poirot, 'and especially artists – are different.'

'Art!' said the Superintendent with scorn. 'All this talk about *Art*! I never *have* understood it and I never shall! You should have seen that picture Crale was painting. All lopsided. He'd made the girl look as though she'd got toothache, and the battlements were all cock-eyed. Unpleasant looking, the whole thing. I couldn't get it out of my mind for a long time afterwards. I even dreamt about it. And what's more it affected my eyesight – I began to see battlements and walls and things all out of drawing. Yes, and women too!'

Poirot smiled. He said:

'Although you do not know it, you are paying a tribute to the greatness of Amyas Crale's art.'

'Nonsense. Why can't a painter paint something nice and

cheerful to look at? Why go out of your way to look for ugliness?'

'Some of us, *mon cher*, see beauty in curious places.'

'The girl was a good looker, all right,' said Hale. 'Lots of make-up and next to no clothes on. It isn't decent the way these girls go about. And that was sixteen years ago, mind you. Nowadays one wouldn't think anything of it. But then – well, it shocked me. Trousers and one of those canvas shirts, open at the neck – and not another thing, I should say!'

'You seem to remember these points very well,' murmured Poirot slyly.

Superintendent Hale blushed. 'I'm just passing on the impression I got,' he said austerely.

'Quite – quite,' said Poirot soothingly. He went on:

'So it would seem that the principal witnesses against Mrs Crale were Philip Blake and Elsa Greer?'

'Yes. Vehement, they were, both of them. But the governess was called by the prosecution too, and what she said carried more weight than the other two. She was on Mrs Crale's side entirely, you see. Up in arms for her. But she was an honest woman and gave her evidence truthfully without trying to minimize it in any way.'

'And Meredith Blake?'

'He was very distressed by the whole thing, poor gentleman. As well he might be! Blamed himself for his drug brewing – and the coroner blamed him for it too. Coniine and AE Salts comes under Schedule I of the Poisons Acts. He came in for some pretty sharp censure. He was a friend of both parties, and it hit him very hard – besides being the kind of county gentleman who shrinks from notoriety and being in the public eye.'

'Did not Mrs Crale's young sister give evidence?'

'No. It wasn't necessary. She wasn't there when Mrs Crale threatened her husband, and there was nothing she could tell us that we couldn't get from someone else equally well. She saw Mrs Crale go to the refrigerator and get the iced beer out and, of course, the Defence could have subpœnaed her to say that Mrs Crale took it straight down without tampering with it in any way. But that point wasn't relevant because we never claimed that the coniine was in the beer bottle.'

'How did she manage to put it in the glass with those two looking on?'

'Well, first of all, they weren't looking on. That is to say, Mr Crale was painting – looking at his canvas and at the sitter. And Miss Greer was posed, sitting with her back almost to where Mrs Crale was standing, and her eyes looking over Mr Crale's shoulder.'

Poirot nodded.

'As I say neither of the two was looking at Mrs Crale. She had the stuff in one of those pipette things – one used to fill fountain pens with them. We found it crushed to splinters on the path up to the house.'

Poirot murmured:

'You have an answer to everything.'

'Well, come now, M. Poirot! Without prejudice. *She* threatens to kill him. *She* takes the stuff from the laboratory. The empty bottle is found in *her* room and *nobody has handled it but her*. She deliberately takes down iced beer to him – a funny thing, anyway, when you realize that they weren't on speaking terms –'

'A very curious thing. I had already remarked on it.'

'Yes. Bit of a give away. *Why* was she so amiable all of a sudden? He complains of the taste of the stuff – and coniine *has* a nasty taste. She arranges to find the body and she sends the other woman off to telephone. Why? So that she can wipe that bottle and glass and then press *his* fingers on it. After that she can pipe up and say that it was remorse and that he committed suicide. A likely story.'

'It was certainly not very well imagined.'

'No. If you ask me she didn't take the trouble to *think*.

She was so eaten up with hate and jealousy. All she thought of was doing him in. And then, when it's over, when she sees him there dead – well, *then*, I should say, she suddenly comes to herself and realizes that what she's done is murder – and that you get hanged for murder. And desperately she goes bald-headed for the only thing she can think of – which is suicide.'

Poirot said:

'It is very sound what you say there – yes. Her mind might work that way.'

'In a way it was a premeditated crime and in a way it wasn't,' said Hale. 'I don't believe she really thought it out, you know. Just went on with it blindly.'

Poirot murmured:

'I wonder . . .'

Hale looked at him curiously. He said:

'Have I convinced you, M. Poirot, that it was a straight-forward case?'

'Almost. Not quite. There are one or two peculiar points . . .!'

'Can you suggest an alternative solution – that will hold water?'

Poirot said:

'What were the movements of the other people on that morning?'

'We went into them, I can assure you. We checked up on everybody. Nobody had what you could call an alibi – you can't have with poisoning. Why, there's nothing to prevent a would-be murderer from handing his victim some poison in a capsule the day before, telling him it's a specific cure for indigestion and he must take it before lunch – and then going away to the other end of England.'

'But you don't think that happened in this case?'

'Mr Crale didn't suffer from indigestion. And in any case I can't see that kind of thing happening. It's true that Mr Meredith Blake was given to recommending quack nos-

57

trums of his own concocting, but I don't see Mr Crale trying any of them. And if he did he'd probably talk and joke about it. Besides, why *should* Mr Meredith Blake want to kill Mr Crale? Everything goes to show that he was on very good terms with him. They all were. Mr Philip Blake was his best friend. Miss Greer was in love with him. Miss Williams disapproved of him, I imagine, very strongly – but moral disapprobation doesn't lead to poisoning. Little Miss Warren scrapped with him a lot, she was at a tiresome age – just off to school, I believe, but he was quite fond of her and she of him. She was treated, you know, with particular tenderness and consideration in that house. You may have heard why. She was badly injured when she was a child – injured by Mrs Crale in a kind of maniacal fit of rage. That rather shows, doesn't it, that she was a pretty uncontrolled sort of person? To go for a child – and maim her for life!'

'It might show,' said Poirot thoughtfully, 'that Angela Warren had good reason to bear a grudge against Caroline Crale.'

'Perhaps – but not against Amyas Crale. And anyway Mrs Crale was devoted to her young sister – gave her a home when her parents died, and, as I say, treated her with special affection – spoiled her badly, so they say. The girl was obviously fond of Mrs Crale. She was kept away from the trial and sheltered from it all as far as possible – Mrs Crale was very insistent about that, I believe. But the girl was terribly upset and longed to be taken to see her sister in prison. Caroline Crale wouldn't agree. She said that sort of thing might injure a girl's mentality for life. She arranged for her to go to school abroad.'

He added:

'Miss Warren's turned out a very distinguished woman. Traveller to weird places. Lectures at the Royal Geographical – all that sort of thing.'

'And no one remembers the trial?'

'Well, it's a different name for one thing. They hadn't

even the same maiden name. They had the same mother but different fathers. Mrs Crale's name was Spalding.'

'This Miss Williams, was she the child's governess, or Angela Warren's?'

'Angela's. There was a nurse for the child – but she used to do a few little lessons with Miss Williams every day, I believe.'

'Where was the child at the time?'

'She'd gone with the nurse to pay a visit to her grandmother. A Lady Tressillian. A widow lady who'd lost her own two little girls and who was devoted to this kid.'

Poirot nodded. 'I see.'

Hale continued:

'As to the movements of the other people on the day of the murder, I can give them to you.

'Miss Greer sat on the terrace near the library window after breakfast. There, as I say, she overheard the quarrel between Crale and his wife. After that she accompanied Crale down to the Battery and sat for him until lunch time with a couple of breaks to ease her muscles.

'Philip Blake was in the house after breakfast, and overheard part of the quarrel. After Crale and Miss Greer went off, he read the paper until his brother telephoned him. Thereupon he went down to the shore to meet his brother. They walked together up the path again past the Battery garden. Miss Greer had just gone up to the house to fetch a pullover as she felt chilly and Mrs Crale was with her husband discussing arrangements for Angela's departure to school.'

'Ah, an amicable interview.'

'Well, no, not amicable. Crale was fairly shouting at her, I understand. Annoyed at being bothered with domestic details. I suppose she wanted to get things straightened up if there *was* going to be a break.'

Poirot nodded.

Hale went on:

'The two brothers exchanged a few words with Amyas Crale. Then Miss Greer reappeared and took up her position, and Crale picked up his brush again, obviously wanting to get rid of them. They took the hint and went up to the house. It was when they were at the Battery, by the way, that Amyas Crale complained all the beer down there was hot and his wife promised to send him down some iced beer.'

'Aha!'

'Exactly – Aha! Sweet as sugar she was about it. They went up to the house and sat on the terrace outside. Mrs Crale and Angela Warren brought them out beer there.

'Later, Angela Warren went down to bathe and Philip Blake went with her.

'Meredith Blake went down to a clearing with a seat just above the Battery garden. He could just see Miss Greer as she posed on the battlements and could hear her voice and Crale's as they talked. He sat there and thought over the coniine business. He was still very worried about it and didn't know quite what to do. Elsa Greer saw him and waved her hand to him. When the bell went for lunch he came down to the Battery and Elsa Greer and he went back to the house together. He noticed then that Crale was looking, as he put it, very queer, but he didn't really think anything of it at the time. Crale was the kind of man who is never ill – and so one didn't imagine he would be. On the other hand, he *did* have moods of fury and despondency according as to whether his painting was not going as he liked it. On those occasions one left him alone and said as little as possible to him. That's what these two did on this occasion.

'As to the others, the servants were busy with housework and cooking lunch. Miss Williams was in the schoolroom part of the morning correcting some exercise books. Afterwards she took some household mending to the terrace. Angela Warren spent most of the morning wandering about the garden, climbing trees and eating things – you know what a girl of fifteen is! Plums, sour apples, hard pears, etc. After she came back to the house and, as I say, went down with Philip Blake to the beach and had a bathe before lunch.'

Superintendent Hale paused:

'Now then,' he said belligerently, 'do you find anything phoney about that?'

Poirot said: 'Nothing at all.'

'Well, then!'

The two words expressed volumes.

'But all the same,' said Hercule Poirot. 'I am going to satisfy myself. I –'

'What are you going to do?'

'I am going to visit these five people – and from each one I am going to get his or her own story.'

Superintendent Hale sighed with a deep melancholy.

He said:

'Man, you're nuts! None of their stories are going to agree! Don't you grasp that elementary fact? No two people remember a thing in the same order anyway. And after all this time! Why, you'll hear five accounts of five separate murders!'

'That,' said Poirot, 'is what I am counting upon. It will be very instructive.'

CHAPTER VI

This Little Pig Went to Market

Philip Blake was recognizably like the description given of him by Montague Depleach. A prosperous, shrewd, jovial-looking man – slightly running to fat.

Hercule Poirot had timed his appointment for half-past six on a Saturday afternoon. Philip Blake had just finished his eighteen holes, and he had been on his game – winning a fiver from his opponent. He was in the mood to be friendly and expansive.

Hercule Poirot explained himself and his errand. On this occasion at least he showed no undue passion for unsullied truth. It was a question, Blake gathered, of a series of books dealing with famous crimes.

Philip Blake frowned. He said:

'Good Lord, why make up these things?'

Hercule Poirot shrugged his shoulders. He was at his most foreign today. He was out to be despised but patronized.

He murmured:

'It is the public. They eat it up – yes, eat it up.'

'Ghouls,' said Philip Blake.

But he said it good-humouredly – not with the fastidiousness and the distaste that a more sensitive man might have displayed.

Hercule Poirot said with a shrug of the shoulders:

'It is human nature. You and I, Mr Blake, who know the world, have no illusions about our fellow human beings. Not bad people, most of them, but certainly not to be idealized.'

Blake said heartily:

'I've parted with my illusions long ago.'

'Instead, you tell a very good story, so I have been told.'

'Ah!' Blake's eyes twinkled. 'Heard this one?'

Poirot's laugh came at the right place. It was not an edifying story, but it was funny.

Philip Blake lay back in his chair, his muscles relaxed, his eyes creased with good humour.

Hercule Poirot thought suddenly that he looked rather like a contented pig.

A pig. *This little pig went to market* . . .

What was he like, this man, this Philip Blake? A man, it would seem, without cares. Prosperous, contented. No remorseful thoughts, no uneasy twinges of conscience from the past, no haunting memories here. No, a well-fed pig who had gone to market – and fetched the full market price . . .

But once, perhaps, there had been more to Philip Blake. He must have been, when young, a handsome man. Eyes always a shade too small, a fraction too near together, perhaps – but otherwise a well made, well set up young man. How old was he now? At a guess between fifty and sixty. Nearing forty, then, at the time of Crale's death. Less stultified, then, less sunk in the gratifications of the minute. Asking more of life, perhaps, and receiving less . . .

Poirot murmured as a mere catch-phrase:

'You comprehend my position.'

'No, really, you know, I'm hanged if I do.' The stockbroker sat upright again, his glance was once more shrewd. 'Why *you*? You're not a writer?'

'Not precisely – no. Actually I am a detective.'

The modesty of this remark had probably not been equalled before in Poirot's conversation.

'Of course you are. We all know that. The famous Hercule Poirot!'

But his tone held a subtly mocking note. Intrinsically, Philip Blake was too much of an Englishman to take the pretensions of a foreigner seriously.

To his cronies he would have said:

'Quaint little mountebank. Oh well, I expect his stuff goes down with the women all right.'

And although that derisive patronizing attitude was exactly the one which Hercule Poirot had aimed at inducing, nevertheless he found himself annoyed by it.

This man, this successful man of affairs, was unimpressed by Hercule Poirot! It was a scandal.

'I am gratified,' said Poirot untruly, 'that I am so well known to you. My success, let me tell you, has been founded on the psychology – the eternal *why*? of human behaviour. That, M. Blake, is what interests the world in crime today. It used to be romance. Famous crimes were retold from one angle only – the love-story connected with them. Nowadays it is very different. People read with interest that Dr Crippen murdered his wife because she was a big bouncing woman and he was little and insignificant and therefore she made him feel inferior. They read of some famous woman criminal that she killed because she'd been snubbed by her father when she was three years old. It is, as I say, the *why* of crime that interests nowadays.'

Philip Blake said, with a slight yawn:

'The why of most crimes is obvious enough, I should say. Usually money.'

Poirot cried:

'Ah, but my dear sir, the why must never be obvious. That is the whole point!'

'And that's where *you* come in?'

'And that, as you say, is where I come in! It is proposed to rewrite the stories of certain bygone crimes – from the psychological angle. Psychology in crime, it is my speciality. I have accepted the commission.'

Philip Blake grinned.

'Pretty lucrative, I suppose?'

'I hope so – I certainly hope so.'

'Congratulations. Now, perhaps, you'll tell me where *I* come in?'

64

'Most certainly. The Crale case, Monsieur.'

Phillip Blake did not look startled. But he looked thoughtful. He said:

'Yes, of course, the Crale case . . .'

Hercule Poirot said anxiously:

'It is not displeasing to you, Mr Blake?'

'Oh, as to that.' Philip Blake shrugged his shoulders. 'It's no use resenting a thing that you've no power to stop. The trial of Caroline Crale is public property. Any one can go ahead and write it up. It's no use *my* objecting. In a way – I don't mind telling you – I do dislike it a good deal. Amyas Crale was one of my best friends. I'm sorry the whole unsavoury business has to be raked up again. But these things happen.'

'You are a philosopher, Mr Blake.'

'No, no. I just know enough not to start kicking against the pricks. I dare say you'll do it less offensively than many others.'

'I hope, at least, to write with delicacy and good taste,' said Poirot.

Philip Blake gave a loud guffaw but without any real amusement. 'Makes me chuckle to hear you say that.'

'I assure you, Mr Blake, I am really interested. It is not just a matter of money with me. I genuinely want to re-create the past, to feel and see the events that took place, to see behind the obvious and to visualize the thoughts and feelings of the actors in the drama.'

Philip Blake said:

'I don't know that there was much subtlety about it. It was a pretty obvious business. Crude female jealousy, that was all there was to it.'

'It would interest me enormously, Mr Blake, if I could have your own reactions to the affair.'

Philip Blake said with sudden heat, his face deepening in colour.

'Reactions! Reactions! Don't speak so pedantically. I

didn't just stand there and react! You don't seem to understand that my friend – *my friend*, I tell you, had been killed – poisoned! And that if I'd acted quicker I could have saved him.'

'How do you make that out, Mr Blake?'

'Like this. I take it that you've already read up the facts of the case?' Poirot nodded. 'Very well. Now on that morning my brother Meredith called me up. He was in a pretty good stew. One of his Hell brews was missing – and it was a fairly deadly Hell brew. What did I do? I told him to come along and we'd talk it over. Decide what was best to be done. "Decide what was best." It beats me now how I could have been such a hesitating fool! I ought to have realized that there was no time to lose. I ought to have gone to Amyas straight away and warned him. I ought to have said: "Caroline's pinched one of Meredith's patent poisons, and you and Elsa had better look out for yourselves."'

Blake got up. He strode up and down in his excitement.

'Good God, man. Do you suppose I haven't gone over it in my mind again and again? I *knew*. I had the chance to save him – and I dallied about – waiting for Meredith! Why hadn't I the sense to realize that Caroline wasn't going to have any qualms or hesitancies. She'd taken that stuff to use – and, by God, she'd used it at the very first opportunity. She wouldn't wait till Meredith discovered his loss. I knew – of course I knew – that Amyas was in deadly danger – and I did nothing!'

'I think you reproach yourself unduly, Monsieur. You had not much time –'

The other interrupted him:

'Time? I had plenty of time. Any amount of courses open to me. I could have gone to Amyas, as I say – but there was the chance, of course, that he wouldn't believe me. Amyas wasn't the sort of man who'd believe easily in his own danger. He'd have scoffed at the notion. And he never thoroughly understood the sort of devil Caroline was. But I could have gone to her. I could have said: "I know what you're up to. I know what you're planning to do. But if Amyas or Elsa die of coniine poisoning, you'll be hanged by your neck!" That would have stopped her. Or I might have rung up the police. Oh! there were things that could have been done – and instead, I let myself be influenced by Meredith's slow, cautious methods. "We must be sure – talk it over – make quite certain who could have taken it . . .' Damned old fool – never made a quick decision in his life! A good thing for him he was the eldest son and has an estate to live on. If he'd ever tried to *make* money he'd have lost every penny he had.'

Poirot asked:

'You had no doubt yourself who had taken the poison?'

'Of course not. I knew at once it must be Caroline. You see, I knew Caroline very well.'

Poirot said:

'That is very interesting. I want to know, Mr Blake, what kind of a woman Caroline Crale was?'

Philip Blake said sharply:

'She wasn't the injured innocent people thought she was at the time of the trial!'

'What was she, then?'

Blake sat down again. He said seriously:

'Would you really like to know?'

'I would like to know very much indeed.'

'Caroline was a rotter. She was a rotter through and through. Mind you, she had charm. She had that kind of sweetness of manner that deceives people utterly. She had a frail, helpless look about her that appealed to people's chivalry. Sometimes, when I've read a bit of history, I think Mary Queen of Scots must have been a bit like her. Always sweet and unfortunate and magnetic – and actually a cold calculating woman, a scheming woman who planned the murder of Darnley and got away with it. Caroline was like that – a cold, calculating planner. And she had a wicked temper.

'I don't know whether they've told you – it isn't a vital point of the trial, but it shows her up – what she did to her baby sister? She was jealous, you know. Her mother had married again, and all the notice and affection went to little Angela. Caroline couldn't stand that. She tried to kill the baby with a crowbar – smash its head in. Luckily the blow wasn't fatal. But it was a pretty ghastly thing to do.'

'Yes, indeed.'

'Well, that was the real Caroline. She had to be first. That was the thing she simply could not stand – not being first. And there was a cold, egotistical devil in her that was capable of being stirred to murderous lengths.

'She appeared impulsive, you know, but she was really calculating. When she stayed at Alderbury as a girl, she gave us all the once over and made her plans. She'd no money of her own. I was never in the running – a younger son with his way to make. (Funny, that, I could probably buy up Meredith and Crale, if he'd lived, nowadays!) She considered Meredith for a bit, but she finally fixed on Amyas. Amyas would have Alderbury, and though he wouldn't have much money with it, she realized that his talent as a painter was something quite out of the way. She gambled on his being not only a genius but a financial success as well.

'And she won. Recognition came to Amyas early. He wasn't a fashionable painter exactly – but his genius was recognized and his pictures were bought. Have you seen any of his paintings? There's one here. Come and look at it.'

He led the way into the dining-room and pointed to the left-hand wall.

'There you are. That's Amyas.'

Poirot looked in silence. It came to him with fresh amazement that a man could so imbue a conventional subject with his own particular magic. A vase of roses on a polished mahogany table. That hoary old set-piece. How then did Amyas Crale contrive to make his roses flame and burn with a riotous almost obscene life. The polished wood of the table trembled and took on sentient life. How explain the excitement the picture roused? For it was exciting. The proportions of the table would have distressed Superintendent Hale, he would have complained that no known roses were precisely of that shape or colour. And afterwards he would have gone about wondering vaguely why the roses he saw were unsatisfactory, and round mahogany tables would have annoyed him for no known reason.

Poirot gave a little sigh.

He murmured:

'Yes – it is all there.'

Blake led the way back. He mumbled:

'Never have understood anything about art myself. Don't know why I like looking at that thing so much, but I do. It's – oh, damn it all, it's *good*.'

Poirot nodded emphatically.

Blake offered his guest a cigarette and lit one himself. He said:

'And that's the man – the man who painted those roses – the man who painted the "Woman with a Cocktail Shaker" – the man who painted that amazing painful "Nativity", *that's* the man who was cut short in his prime, deprived of his vivid forceful life all because of a vindictive mean-natured woman!'

He paused:

'You'll say that I'm bitter – that I'm unduly prejudiced against Caroline. She *had* charm – I've felt it. But I knew – I always knew – the real woman behind. And that woman, M. Poirot, was evil. She was cruel and malignant and a grabber!'

'And yet it has been told me that Mrs Crale put up with many hard things in her married life?'

'Yes, and didn't she let everybody know about it! Always the martyr! Poor old Amyas. His married life was one long hell – or rather it would have been if it hadn't been for his exceptional quality. His art, you see – he always had that. It was an escape. When he was painting he didn't care, he shook off Caroline and her nagging and all the ceaseless rows and quarrels. They were endless, you know. Not a week passed without a thundering row over one thing or another. *She* enjoyed it. Having rows stimulated her, I believe. It was an outlet. She could say all the hard bitter stinging things she wanted to say. She'd positively purr after one of those set-tos – go off looking as sleek and well-fed as a cat. But it took it out of *him*. *He* wanted peace – rest – a quiet life. Of course a man like that ought never to marry – he isn't out for domesticity. A man like Crale should have affairs but no binding ties. They're bound to chafe him.'

'He confided in you?'

'Well – he knew that I was a pretty devoted pal. He let me see things. He didn't complain. He wasn't that kind of man. Sometimes he'd say, "Damn all women." Or he'd say, "Never get married, old boy. Wait for hell till after this life."'

'You knew about his attachment to Miss Greer?'

'Oh yes – at least I saw it coming on. He told me he'd met a marvellous girl. She was different, he said, from anything or any one he'd ever met before. Not that I paid much attention to that. Amyas was always meeting one woman or other who was "different". Usually a month later he'd stare at you if you mentioned them, and wonder who you were talking about! But this Elsa Greer really was different. I realized that when I came down to Alderbury to stay. She'd got him, you know, hooked him good and proper. The poor mutt fairly ate out of her hand.'

'You did not like Elsa Greer either?'

'No, I didn't like her. She was definitely a predatory creature. She, too, wanted to own Crale body and soul. But I think, all the same, that she'd have been better for him than Caroline. She might conceivably have let him alone once she was sure of him. Or she might have got tired of him and moved on to someone else. The best thing for Amyas would have been to be quite free of female entanglements.'

'But that, it would seem, was not to his taste?'

Philip Blake said with a sigh:

'The damned fool was always getting himself involved with some woman or other. And yet, in a way, women really meant very little to him. The only two women who really made any impression on him at all in his life were Caroline and Elsa.'

Poirot said:

'Was he fond of the child?'

'Angela? Oh! we all liked Angela. She was such a sport. She was always game for anything. What a life she led that wretched governess of hers. Yes, Amyas liked Angela all right – but sometimes she went too far and then he used to get really mad with her – and then Caroline would step in – Caro was always on Angela's side and that would finish Amyas altogether. He hated it when Caro sided with Angela against him. There was a bit of jealousy all round, you know. Amyas was jealous of the way Caro always put Angela first and would do anything for her. And Angela was jealous of Amyas and rebelled against his overbearing ways. It was his decision that she should go to school that autumn, and she was furious about it. Not, I think, because she didn't like the idea of school, she really rather wanted to go, I believe – but it was Amyas's high-handed way of settling it all offhand that infuriated her. She played all sorts of tricks on him in revenge. Once she put ten slugs in his bed. On the whole, I think Amyas was right. It was time she got some discipline. Miss Williams was very efficient, but even she confessed that Angela was getting too much for her.'

He paused. Poirot said:

'When I asked if Amyas was fond of the child – I referred to his own child, his daughter?'

'Oh, you mean little Carla? Yes, she was a great pet. He

71

enjoyed playing with her when he was in the mood. But his affection for her wouldn't have deterred him from marrying Elsa, if that's what you mean. He hadn't *that* kind of feeling for her.'

'Was Caroline Crale very devoted to the child?'

A kind of spasm contorted Philip's face. He said:

'I can't say that she wasn't a good mother. No, I can't say that. It's the one thing –'

'Yes, Mr Blake?'

Philip said slowly and painfully:

'It's the one thing I really – regret – in this affair. The thought of that child. Such a tragic background to her young life. They sent her abroad to Amyas's cousin and her husband. I hope – I sincerely hope – they managed to keep the truth from her.'

Poirot shook his head. He said:

'The truth, Mr Blake, has a habit of making itself known. Even after many years.'

The stockbroker murmured: 'I wonder.'

Poirot went on:

'In the interests of truth, Mr Blake, I am going to ask you to do something.'

'What is it?'

'I am going to beg that you will write me out an exact account of what happened on those days at Alderbury. That is to say, I am going to ask you to write me out a full account of the murder and its attendant circumstances.'

'But, my dear fellow, after all this time? I should be hopelessly inaccurate.'

'Not necessarily.'

'Surely.'

'No, for one thing, with the passage of time, the mind retains a hold on essentials and rejects superficial matters.'

'Ho! You mean a mere broad outline?'

'Not at all. I mean a detailed conscientious account of each event as it occurred, and every conversation you can remember.'

'And supposing I remember them wrong?'

'You can give the wording at least to the best of your reflection. There may be gaps, but that cannot be helped.'

Blake looked at him curiously.

'But what's the idea? The police files will give you the whole thing far more accurately.'

'No, Mr Blake. We are speaking now from the psychological point of view. I do not want bare *facts*. *I want your own selections of facts*. Time and your memory are responsible for that selection. There may have been things done, words spoken, that I should seek for in vain in the police files. Things and words that you never mentioned because, maybe, you judged them irrelevant, or because you preferred not to repeat them.'

Blake said sharply:

'Is this account of mine for publication?'

'Certainly not. It is for my eye only. To assist me to draw my own deductions.'

'And you won't quote from it without my consent?'

'Certainly not.'

'Hm,' said Philip Blake. 'I'm a very busy man, M. Poirot.'

'I appreciate that there will be time and trouble involved. I should be happy to agree to a – reasonable fee.'

There was a moment's pause. Then Philip Blake said suddenly:

'No, if I do it – I'll do it for nothing.'

'And you will do it?'

Philip said warningly:

'Remember, I can't vouch for the accuracy of my memory.'

'That is perfectly understood.'

'Then I think,' said Philip Blake, 'that I should *like* to do it. I feel I owe it – in a way – to Amyas Crale.'

CHAPTER VII

This Little Pig Stayed at Home

Hercule Poirot was not a man to neglect details.

His advance towards Meredith Blake was carefully thought out. Meredith Blake was, he already felt sure, a very different proposition from Philip Blake. Rush tactics would not succeed here. The assault must be leisurely.

Hercule Poirot knew that there was only one way to penetrate the stronghold. He must approach Meredith Blake with the proper credentials. Those credentials must be social, not professional. Fortunately, in the course of his career, Hercule Poirot had made friends in many counties. Devonshire was no exception. He sat down to review what resources he had in Devonshire. As a result he discovered two people who were acquaintances or friends of Mr Meredith Blake. He descended upon him therefore armed with two letters, one from Lady Mary Lytton-Gore, a gentle widow lady of restricted means, the most retiring of creatures; and the other from a retired Admiral, whose family had been settled in the county for four generations.

Meredith Blake received Poirot in a state of some perplexity.

As he had often felt lately, things were not what they used to be. Dash it all, private detectives used to be private detectives – fellows you got to guard wedding presents at country receptions, fellows you went to – rather shame-facedly – when there was some dirty business afoot and you'd got to get the hang of it.

But here was Lady Mary Lytton-Gore writing: 'Hercule Poirot is a very old and valued friend of mine. Please do all you can to help him, won't you?' And Mary Lytton-Gore wasn't – no, decidedly she wasn't – the sort of woman you associate with private detectives and all that they stand for. And Admiral Cronshaw wrote: 'Very good chap – absolutely sound. Grateful if you will do what you can for him. Most entertaining fellow, can tell you lots of good stories.'

And now here was the man himself. Really a most impossible person – the wrong clothes – button boots! – an incredible moustache! Not his – Meredith Blake's – kind of fellow at all. Didn't look as though he'd ever hunted or shot – or even played a decent game. A foreigner.

Slightly amused, Hercule Poirot read accurately these thoughts passing through the other's head.

He had felt his own interest rising considerably as the train brought him into the West Country. He would see now, with his own eyes, the actual place where these long past events happened.

It was here, at Handcross Manor, that two young brothers had lived and gone over to Alderbury and joked and played tennis and fraternized with a young Amyas Crale and a girl called Caroline. It was from here that Meredith had started out to Alderbury on that fatal morning. That had been sixteen years ago. Hercule Poirot looked with interest at the man who was confronting him with somewhat uneasy politeness.

Very much what he had expected. Meredith Blake resembled superficially every other English country gentleman of straitened means and outdoor tastes.

A shabby old coat of Harris tweed, a weather-beaten, pleasant, middle-aged face with somewhat faded blue eyes, a weak mouth, half hidden by a rather straggly moustache. Poirot found Meredith Blake a great contrast to his brother. He had a hesitating manner, his mental processes were obviously leisurely. It was as though his tempo had slowed down with the years just as his brother's had been accelerated.

As Poirot had already guessed, he was a man whom you

could not hurry. The leisurely life of the English countryside was in his bones.

He looked, the detective thought, a good deal older than his brother, though, from what Mr Jonathan had said, it would seem that only a couple of years separated them.

Hercule Poirot prided himself on knowing how to handle an 'old school tie'. It was no moment for trying to seem English. No, one must be a foreigner – frankly a foreigner – and be magnanimously forgiven for the fact. 'Of course, these foreigners don't quite know the ropes. *Will* shake hands at breakfast. Still, a decent fellow really . . .'

Poirot set about creating this impression of himself. The two men talked, cautiously, of Lady Mary Lytton-Gore and of Admiral Cronshaw. Other names were mentioned. Fortunately Poirot knew someone's cousin and had met somebody else's sister-in-law. He could see a kind of warmth dawning in the Squire's eye. The fellow seemed to know the right people.

Gracefully, insidiously, Poirot slid into the purpose of his visit. He was quick to counteract the inevitable recoil. This book was, alas! going to be written. Miss Crale – Miss Lemarchant, as she was now called – was anxious for him to exercise a judicious editorship. The facts, unfortunately, were public property. But much could be done in their presentation to avoid wounding susceptibilities. Poirot murmured that before now he had been able to use discreet influence to avoid certain purple passages in a book of memoirs.

Meredith Blake flushed angrily. His hand shook a little as he filled a pipe. He said, a slight stammer in his voice:

'It's – it's g-ghoulish the way they dig these things up. S-sixteen years ago. Why can't they let it be?'

Poirot shrugged his shoulders. He said:

'I agree with you. But what will you? There is a demand for such things. And any one is at liberty to reconstruct a proved crime and to comment on it.'

'Seems disgraceful to me.'

Poirot murmured:

'Alas – we do not live in a delicate age . . . You would be surprised, Mr Blake, if you knew the unpleasant publications I had succeeded in – shall we say – softening. I am anxious to do all I can to save Miss Crale's feeling in the matter.'

Meredith Blake murmured: 'Little Carla! That child! A grown-up woman. One can hardly believe it.'

'I know. Time flies swiftly, does it not?'

Meredith Blake sighed. He said: 'Too quickly.'

Poirot said:

'As you will have seen in the letter I handed you from Miss Crale, she is very anxious to know everything possible about the sad events of the past.'

Meredith Blake said with a touch of irritation:

'Why? Why rake up everything again? How much better to let it all be forgotten.'

'You say that, Mr Blake, because you know all the past too well. Miss Crale, remember, knows nothing. That is to say she knows only the story as she has learnt it from the official accounts.'

Meredith Blake winced. He said:

'Yes, I forgot. Poor child. What a detestable position for her. The shock of learning the truth. And then – those soulless, callous reports of the trial.'

'The truth,' said Hercule Poirot, 'can never be done justice to in a mere legal recital. It is the things that are left out that are the things that matter. The emotions, the feelings – the characters of the actors in the drama. The extenuating circumstances –'

He paused and the other man spoke eagerly like an actor who had received his cue.

'Extenuating circumstances! That's just it. If ever there were extenuating circumstances, there were in this case. Amyas Crale was an old friend – his family and mine had been friends for generations, but one has to admit that his conduct was, frankly, outrageous. He was an artist, of course, and presumably that explains it. But there it is – he allowed a most extraordinary set of affairs to arise. The position was one that no ordinary decent man could have contemplated for a moment.'

Hercule Poirot said:

'I am interested that you should say that. It had puzzled me, that situation. Not so does a well-bred man, a man of the world, go about his affairs.'

Blake's thin, hesitating face had lit up with animation. He said:

'Yes, but the whole point is that Amyas never was an ordinary man! He was a painter, you see, and with him painting came first – really sometimes in the most extraordinary way! I don't understand these so-called artistic people myself – never have. I understood Crale a little because, of course, I'd known him all my life. His people were the same sort as my people. And in many ways Crale ran true to type – it was only where art came in that he didn't conform to the usual standards. He wasn't, you see, an amateur in any way. He was first-class – really first-class. Some people say he's a genius. They may be right. But as a result, he was always what I should describe as unbalanced. When he was painting a picture – nothing else mattered, nothing could be allowed to get in the way. He was like a man in a dream. Completely obsessed by what he was doing. Not till the canvas was finished did he come out of this absorption and start to pick up the threads of ordinary life again.'

He looked questioningly at Poirot and the latter nodded.

'You understand, I see. Well, that explains, I think, why this particular situation arose. He was in love with this girl. He wanted to marry her. He was prepared to leave his wife and child for her. But he'd started painting her down here, and he wanted to finish that picture. Nothing else mattered to him. He didn't *see* anything else. And the fact that the situation was a perfectly impossible one for the two women concerned, doesn't seem to have occurred to him.'

'Did either of them understand his point of view?'

'Oh yes – in a way. Elsa did, I suppose. She was terrifically enthusiastic about his painting. But it was a difficult position for her – naturally. And as for Caroline –'

He stopped. Poirot said:

'For Caroline – yes, indeed.'

Meredith Blake said, speaking with a little difficulty:

'Caroline – I had always – well, I had always been very fond of Caroline. There was a time when – when I hoped to marry her. But that was soon nipped in the bud. Still, I remained, if I may say so, devoted to – to her service.'

Poirot nodded thoughtfully. That slightly old-fashioned phrase expressed, he felt, the man before him very typically. Meredith Blake was the kind of man who would devote himself readily to a romantic and honourable devotion. He would serve his lady faithfully and without hope of reward. Yes, it was all very much in character.

He said, carefully weighing the words:

'You must have resented this – attitude – on *her* behalf?'

'I did. Oh, I did. I – I actually remonstrated with Crale on the subject.'

'When was this?'

'Actually the day before – before it all happened. They came over to tea here, you know. I got Crale aside and I – I put it to him. I even said, I remember, that it wasn't fair on either of them.'

'Ah, you said that?'

'Yes. I didn't think – you see, that he *realized*.'

'Possibly not.'

'I said to him that it was putting Caroline in a perfectly unendurable position. If he meant to marry this girl, he ought not to have her staying in the house and – well – more or less flaunt her in Caroline's face. It was, I said, an unendurable insult.'

Poirot asked curiously: 'What did he answer?'

Meredith Blake replied with distaste:

'He said: "Caroline must lump it."'

Hercule Poirot's eyebrows rose.

'Not,' he said, 'a very sympathetic reply.'

'I thought it abominable. I lost my temper. I said that no doubt, not caring for his wife, he didn't mind how much he made her suffer, but what, I said, about the girl? Hadn't he realized it was a pretty rotten position for *her*? His reply to that was that Elsa must lump it too!

'Then he went on: "You don't seem to understand, Meredith, that this thing I'm painting is the best thing I've done. It's *good*, I tell you. And a couple of jealous quarrelling women aren't going to upset it – no, by hell, they're not."

'It was hopeless talking to him. I said he seemed to have taken leave of all ordinary decency. Painting, I said, wasn't everything. He interrupted there. He said: "Ah, but it is to *me*."

'I was still very angry. I said it was perfectly disgraceful the way he had always treated Caroline. She had had a miserable life with him. He said he knew that and he was sorry about it. Sorry! He said: "I know, Merry, you don't believe that – but it's the truth. I've given Caroline the hell of a life and she's been a saint about it. But she did know, I think, what she might be letting herself in for. I told her candidly the sort of damnable egoistic, loose-living kind of chap I was."

'I put it to him then very strongly that he ought not to break up his married life. There was the child to be considered and everything. I said that I could understand that a girl like Elsa could bowl a man over, but that even for her sake he ought to break off the whole thing. She was very young. She was going into this bald-headed, but she might regret it bitterly afterwards. I said couldn't he pull himself together, make a clean break and go back to his wife?'

'And what did he say?'

Blake said: 'He just looked – embarrassed. He patted me on the shoulder and said: "You're a good chap, Merry. But you're too sentimental. You wait till the picture's finished and you'll admit that I was right."

'I said: "Damn your picture." And he grinned and said all the neurotic women in England couldn't do that. Then I said that it would have been more decent to have kept the whole thing from Caroline until after the picture was finished. He said that that wasn't *his* fault. It was Elsa who had insisted on spilling the beans. I said, Why? And he said that she had had some idea that it wasn't straight otherwise. She wanted everything to be clear and above board. Well, of course, in a way, one could understand that and respect the girl for it. However badly she was behaving, she did at least want to be honest.'

'A lot of additional pain and grief is caused by honesty,' remarked Hercule Poirot.

Meredith Blake looked at him doubtfully. He did not quite like the sentiment. He sighed:

'It was a – a most unhappy time for us all.'

'The only person who does not seem to have been affected by it was Amyas Crale,' said Poirot.

'And why? Because he was a rank egoist. I remember him now. Grinning at me as he went off saying: "Don't worry, Merry. Everything's going to pan out all right!"'

'The incurable optimist,' murmured Poirot.

Meredith Blake said:

'He was the kind of man who didn't take women seriously. *I* could have told him that Caroline was desperate.'

'Did she tell you so?'

'Not in so many words. But I shall always see her face as it was that afternoon. White and strained with a kind of desperate gaiety. She talked and laughed a lot. But her eyes – there was a kind of anguished grief in them that was the

81

most moving thing I have ever known. Such a gentle creature, too.'

Hercule Poirot looked at him for a minute or two without speaking. Clearly the man in front of him felt no incongruity in speaking thus of a woman who on the day after had deliberately killed her husband.

Meredith Blake went on. He had by now quite overcome his first suspicious hostility. Hercule Poirot had the gift of listening. To men such as Meredith Blake, the reliving of the past has a definite attraction. He spoke now almost more to himself than to his guest.

'I ought to have suspected something, I suppose. It was Caroline who turned the conversation to – to my little hobby. It was, I must confess, an enthusiasm of mine. The old English herbalists, you know, are a very interesting study. There are so many plants that were formerly used in medicine and which have now disappeared from the official Pharmacopœia. And it's astonishing, really, how a simple decoction of something or other will really work wonders. No need for doctors half the time. The French understand these things – some of their *tisanes* are first rate.' He was well away now on his hobby.

'Dandelion tea, for instance; marvellous stuff. And a decoction of hips – I saw the other day somewhere that that's coming into fashion with the medical profession again. Oh yes, I must confess, I got a lot of pleasure out of my brews. Gathering the plants at the right time, drying them – macerating them – all the rest of it. I've even dropped to superstition sometimes and gathered my roots at the full of the moon or whatever it was the ancients advised. On that day I gave my guests, I remember, a special disquisition on the spotted hemlock. It flowers biennially. You gather the fruits when they're ripening, just before they turn yellow. Coniine, you know, is a drug that's dropped out – I don't believe there's any official preparation of it in the last Pharmacopœia – but I've proved the usefulness of it in whooping cough – and in asthma too, for that matter –'

'You talked of all this in your laboratory?'

'Yes, I showed them round – explained the various drugs to them – valerian and the way it attracts cats – one sniff at that was enough for them! Then they asked about deadly nightshade and I told them about belladonna and atropine. They were very much interested.'

'They? What is comprised in that word?'

Meredith Blake looked faintly surprised as though he had forgotten that his listener had no first-hand knowledge of the scene.

'Oh, the whole party. Let me see, Philip was there and Amyas, and Caroline, of course. Angela. And Elsa Greer.'

'That was all?'

'Yes – I think so. Yes, I am sure of it,' Blake looked at him curiously. 'Who else should there be?'

'I thought perhaps the governess –'

'Oh, I see. No, she wasn't there that afternoon. I believe I've forgotten her name now. Nice women. Took her duties very seriously. Angela worried her a good deal I think.'

'Why was that?'

'Well, she was a nice kid, but she was inclined to run wild. Always up to something or other. Put a slug or something down Amyas's back one day when he was hard at work painting. He went up in smoke. Cursed her up and down dale. It was after that that he insisted on this school idea.'

'Sending her to school?'

'Yes. I don't mean he wasn't fond of her, but he found her a bit of a nuisance sometimes. And I think – I've always thought –'

'Yes?'

'That he was a bit jealous. Caroline, you see, was a slave to Angela. In a way, perhaps, Angela came first with her – and Amyas didn't like that. There was a reason for it of course. I won't go into that, but –'

Poirot interrupted.

'The reason being that Caroline Crale reproached herself for an action that had disfigured the girl?'

Blake exclaimed: 'Oh, you know that? I wasn't going to mention it. All over and done with. But yes, that was the cause of her attitude I think. She always seemed to feel that there was nothing too much she could do – to make up, as it were.'

Poirot nodded thoughtfully. He asked:

'And Angela? Did she bear a grudge against her half sister?'

'Oh no, don't run away with that idea. Angela was devoted to Caroline. She never gave that old business a thought, I'm sure. It was just Caroline who couldn't forgive herself.'

'Did Angela take kindly to the idea of boarding school?'

'No, she didn't. She was furious with Amyas. Caroline took her side, but Amyas had absolutely made his mind up about it. In spite of a hot temper, Amyas was an easy man in most respects, but when he really got his back up, everyone had to give in. Both Caroline and Angela knuckled under.'

'She was to go to school – when?'

'The autumn term – they were getting her kit together, I remember. I suppose, if it hadn't been for the tragedy, she would have gone off a few days later. There was some talk of her packing on the morning of that day.'

Poirot said: 'And the governess?'

'What do you mean – the governess?'

'How did she like the idea? It deprived her of a job, did it not?'

'Yes – well, I suppose it did in a way. Little Carla used to do a few lessons, but of course she was only – what? Six or thereabouts. She had a nurse. They wouldn't have kept Miss Williams on for her. Yes, that's the name – Williams. Funny how things come back to you when you talk them over.'

'Yes, indeed. You are back now, are you not, in the past?

You relive the scenes – the words that people said, their gestures – the expressions on their faces?'

Meredith Blake said slowly:

'In a way – yes . . . But there are gaps, you know . . . Great chunks missed out. I remember, for instance, the shock it was to me when I first learned that Amyas was going to leave Caroline – but I can't remember whether it was he who told me or Elsa. I do remember arguing with Elsa on the subject – trying to show her, I mean, that it was a pretty rotten thing to do. And she only laughed at me in that cool way of hers and said I was old fashioned. Well, I dare say I *am* old fashioned, but I still think I was right. Amyas had a wife and child – he ought to have stuck to them.'

'But Miss Greer thought that point of view out of date?'

'Yes. Mind you, sixteen years ago, divorce wasn't looked on quite so much as a matter of course as it is now. But Elsa was the kind of girl who went in for being modern. Her point of view was that when two people weren't happy together it was better to make a break. She said that Amyas and Caroline never stopped having rows and that it was far better for the child that she shouldn't be brought up in an atmosphere of disharmony.'

'And her argument did not impress you?'

Meredith Blake said slowly:

'I felt, all the time, that she didn't really know what she was talking about. She was rattling these things off – things she'd read in books or heard from her friends – it was like a parrot. She was – it's a queer thing to say – pathetic somehow. So young and so self-confident.' He paused. 'There is something about youth, M. Poirot, that is – that can be – terribly moving.'

Hercule Poirot said, looking at him with some interest: 'I know what you mean . . .'

Blake went on, speaking more to himself than to Poirot.

'That's partly, I think, why I tackled Crale. He was nearly twenty years older than the girl. It didn't seem fair.'

Poirot murmured:

'Alas – how seldom one makes any effect. When a person has determined on a certain course – it is not easy to turn them from it.'

Meredith Blake said:

'That is true enough.' His tone was a shade bitter. 'I certainly did no good by my interference. But then, I am not a very convincing person. I never have been.'

Poirot threw him a quick glance. He read into that slight acerbity of tone the dissatisfaction of a sensitive man with his own lack of personality. And he acknowledged to himself the truth of what Blake had just said. Meredith Blake was not the man to persuade any one into or out of any course. His well-meaning attempts would always be set aside – indulgently usually, without anger, but definitely set aside. They would not carry weight. He was essentially an ineffective man.

Poirot said, with an appearance of changing a painful subject: 'You still have your laboratory of medicines and cordials, yes?'

'No.'

The word came sharply – with an almost anguished rapidity Meridith Blake said, his face flushing:

'I abandoned the whole thing – dismantled it. I couldn't go on with it – how could I? – after what had happened. The whole thing, you see, might have been said to be *my* fault.'

'No, no, Mr Blake, you are too sensitive.'

'But don't you see? If I hadn't collected those damned drugs? If I hadn't laid stress on them – boasted about them – forced them on those people's notice that afternoon? But I never thought – I never dreamed – how could I –'

'How indeed.'

'But I went bumbling on about them. Pleased with my little bit of knowledge. Blind, conceited fool. I pointed out that damned coniine. I even, fool that I was, took them back into the library and read them out that passage from the

Phaedo describing Socrates' death. A beautiful piece of writing – I've always admired it. But it's haunted me ever since.'

Poirot said:

'Did they find any fingerprints on the coniine bottle?'

'Hers.'

'Caroline Crale's?'

'Yes.'

'Not yours?'

'No. I didn't handle the bottle, you see. Only pointed to it.'

'But at the same time, surely, you had handled it?'

'Oh, of course, but I gave the bottles a periodic dusting from time to time – I never allowed the servants in there, of course – and I had done that about four or five days previously.'

'You kept the room locked up?'

'Invariably.'

'When did Caroline Crale take the coniine from the bottle?'

Meredith Blake replied reluctantly:

'She was the last to leave the room. I called her, I remember, and she came hurrying out. Her cheeks were just a little pink – and her eyes wide and excited. Oh, God, I can see her now.'

Poirot said: 'Did you have any conversation with her at all that afternoon? I mean by that, did you discuss the situation as between her and her husband at all?'

Blake said slowly in a low voice:

'Not directly. She was looking as I've told you – very upset. I said to her at a moment when we were more or less by ourselves: "Is anything the matter, my dear?" She said: "Everything's the matter . . ." I wish you could have heard the desperation in her voice. Those words were the absolute literal truth. There's no getting away from it – Amyas Crale was Caroline's whole world. She said, "Everything's gone –

finished. I'm finished, Meredith." And then she laughed and turned to the others and was suddenly wildly and very unnaturally gay.'

Hercule Poirot nodded his head slowly. He looked very like a china mandarin. He said:

'Yes – I see – it was like that . . .'

Meredith Blake pounded suddenly with his fist. His voice rose. It was almost a shout.

'And I'll tell you this M. Poirot – when Caroline Crale said at the trial that she took the stuff for herself, I'll swear she was speaking the truth! There was no thought in her mind of murder at that time. I swear there wasn't. That came later.'

Hercule Poirot asked:

'Are you sure that it *did* come later?'

Blake stared. He said:

'I beg your pardon? I don't quite understand –'

Poirot said:

'I ask you whether you are sure that the thought of murder ever did come? Are you perfectly convinced in your own mind that Caroline Crale did deliberately commit murder?'

Meredith Blake's breath came unevenly. He said: 'But if not – if not – are you suggesting an – well, accident of some kind?'

'Not necessarily.'

'That's a very extraordinary thing to say?'

'Is it? You have called Caroline Crale a gentle creature. Do gentle creatures commit murder?'

'She was a gentle creature – but all the same – well, there were very violent quarrels, you know.'

'Not such a gentle creature, then?'

'But she *was* – Oh, how difficult these things are to explain.'

'I am trying to understand.'

'Caroline had a quick tongue – a vehement way of

speaking. She might say "I hate you. I wish you were dead."
But it wouldn't mean – it wouldn't entail – *action*.'

'So in your opinion, it was highly uncharacteristic of Mrs
Crale to commit murder?'

'You have the most extraordinary ways of putting things,
M. Poirot. I can only say that – yes – it does seem to me
uncharacteristic of her. I can only explain it by realizing that
the provocation was extreme. She adored her husband.
Under those circumstances a woman might – well – kill.'

Poirot nodded. 'Yes, I agree . . .'

'I was dumbfounded at first. I didn't feel it *could* be true.
And it wasn't true – if you know what I mean – it wasn't the
real Caroline who did that.'

'But you are quite sure that – in the legal sense – Caroline
Crale did do it?'

Again Meredith Blake stared at him.

'My dear man – if she didn't –'

'Well, if she didn't?'

'I can't imagine any alternative solution. Accident?
Surely impossible.'

'Quite impossible, I should say.'

'And I can't believe in the suicide theory. It had to be
brought forward, but it was quite unconvincing to any one
who knew Crale.'

'Quite.'

'So what remains?' asked Meredith Blake.

Poirot said coolly: 'There remains the possibility of
Amyas Crale having been killed by somebody else.'

'But that's absurd!'

'You think so?'

'I'm sure of it. Who would have wanted to kill him? Who
could have killed him?'

'You are more likely to know than I am.'

'But you don't seriously believe –'

'Perhaps not. It interests me to examine the possibility.
Give it your serious consideration. Tell me what you think.'

Meredith stared at him for a minute or two. Then he lowered his eyes. After a minute or two he shook his head. He said:

'I can't imagine *any* possible alternative. I should like to do so. If there were any reason for suspecting anybody else I would readily believe Caroline innocent. I don't want to think she did it. I couldn't believe it at first. But who else is there? Who else was there. Philip? Crale's best friend. Elsa? Ridiculous. Myself? Do I look like a murderer? A respectable governess? A couple of old faithful servants? Perhaps you'd suggest that the child Angela did it? No, M. Poirot, there's *no* alternative. *Nobody* could have killed Amyas Crale but his wife. But he drove her to it. And so, in a way, it was suicide after all, I suppose.'

'Meaning that he died by the result of his own actions, though not by his own hand?'

'Yes, it's a fanciful point of view, perhaps. But – well – cause and effect, you know.'

Hercule Poirot said:

'Have you ever reflected, Mr Blake, that the reason for murder is nearly always to be found by a study of the person murdered?'

'I hadn't exactly – yes, I suppose I see what you mean.'

Poirot said:

'Until you know exactly *what sort of a person the victim was*, you cannot begin to see the circumstances of a crime clearly.'

He added:

'That is what I am seeking for – and what you and your brother have helped to give me – a reconstruction of the man Amyas Crale.'

Meredith Blake passed the main point of the remark over. His attention had been attracted by a single word. He said quickly:

'Philip?'

'Yes.'

'You have talked with him also?'

'Certainly.'

Meredith Blake said sharply:

'You should have come to me first.'

Smiling a little, Poirot made a courteous gesture.

'According to the laws of primogenitude, that is so,' he said. 'I am aware that you are the elder. But you comprehend that as your brother lives near London, it was easier to visit him first.'

Meredith Blake was still frowning. He pulled uneasily at his lip. He repeated:

'You should have come to me first.'

This time, Poirot did not answer. He waited. And presently Meredith Blake went on:

'Philip,' he said, 'is prejudiced.'

'Yes?'

'As a matter of fact he's a mass of prejudices – always has been.' He shot a quick uneasy glance at Poirot. 'He'll have tried to put you against Caroline.'

'Does that matter, so long – after?'

Meredith Blake gave a sharp sigh.

'I know. I forget that it's so long ago – that it's all over. Caroline is beyond being harmed. But all the same I shouldn't like you to get a false impression.'

'And you think your brother might give me a false impression?'

'Frankly, I do. You see, there was always a certain – how shall I put it? – antagonism between him and Caroline.'

'Why?'

The question seemed to irritate Blake. He said:

'Why? How should I know *why*? These things are so. Philip always crabbed her whenever he could. He was annoyed, I think, when Amyas married her. He never went near them for over a year. And yet Amyas was almost his best friend. That was the reason really, I suppose. He didn't feel that any woman was good enough. And he probably felt that Caroline's influence would spoil their friendship.'

'And did it?'

'No, of course it didn't. Amyas was always just as fond of Philip – right up to the end. Used to twit him with being a money grabber and with growing a corporation and being a Philistine generally. Philip didn't care. He just used to grin and say it was a good thing Amyas had one respectable friend.'

'How did your brother react to the Elsa Greer affair?'

'Do you know, I find it rather difficult to say. His attitude wasn't really easy to define. He was annoyed, I think, with Amyas for making a fool of himself over the girl. He said more than once that it wouldn't work and that Amyas would live to regret it. At the same time I have a feeling – yes, very definitely I have a feeling that he was just faintly pleased at seeing Caroline let down.'

Poirot's eyebrows rose. He said:

'He really felt like that?'

'Oh, don't misunderstand me. I wouldn't go further than to say that I believe that feeling was at the back of his mind. I don't know that he ever quite realized himself that that is what he felt. Philip and I have nothing much in common, but there is a link, you know, between people of the same blood. One brother often knows what the other brother is thinking.'

'And after the tragedy?'

Meredith Blake shook his head. A spasm of pain crossed his face. He said:

'Poor Phil. He was terribly cut up. Just broken up by it. He'd always been devoted to Amyas, you see. There was an element of hero worship about it, I think. Amyas Crale and I are the same age. Philip was two years younger. And he looked up to Amyas always. Yes – it was a great blow to him. He was – he was terribly bitter against Caroline.'

'He, at least, had no doubts, then?'

Meredith Blake said:

'None of us had any doubts . . .'

There was a silence. Then Blake said with the irritable plaintiveness of a weak man:

'It was all over – forgotten – and now *you* come – raking it all up . . .'

'Not I. Caroline Crale.'

Meredith stared at him: '*Caroline?* What do you mean?'

Poirot said, watching him:

'Caroline Crale the second.'

Meredith's face relaxed.

'Ah yes, the child. Little Carla. I – I misunderstood you for a moment.'

'You thought I meant the original Caroline Crale? You thought that it was she who would not – how shall I say it – rest easy in her grave?'

Meredith Blake shivered.

'Don't, man.'

'You know that she wrote to her daughter – the last words she ever wrote – that she was innocent?'

Meredith stared at him. He said – and his voice sounded utterly incredulous:

'Caroline wrote *that?*'

'Yes.'

Poirot paused and said:

'It surprises you?'

'It would surprise you if you'd seen her in court. Poor, hunted, defenceless creature. Not even struggling.'

'A defeatist?'

'No, no. She wasn't that. It was, I think, the knowledge that she'd killed the man she loved – or I thought it was that.'

'You are not so sure now?'

'To write a thing like that – solemnly – when she was dying.'

Poirot suggested:

'A pious lie, perhaps.'

'Perhaps.' But Meredith was dubious. 'That's not – that's not like Caroline . . .'

Hercule Poirot nodded. Carla Lemarchant had said that. Carla had only a child's obstinate memory. But Meredith Blake had known Caroline well. It was the first confirmation Poirot had got that Carla's belief was to be depended upon.

Meredith Blake looked up at him. He said slowly:

'If – *if* Caroline was innocent – why, the whole thing's madness! I don't see – any other possible solution . . .'

He turned sharply on Poirot.

'And you? What do you think?'

There was a silence.

'As yet,' said Poirot at last, 'I think nothing. I collect only the impressions. What Caroline Crale was like. What Amyas Crale was like. What the other people who were there at the time were like. What happened exactly on those two days. *That* is what I need. To go over the facts laboriously one by one. Your brother is going to help me there. He is sending me an account of the events as he remembers them.'

Meredith Blake said sharply:

'You won't get much from that. Philip's a busy man. Things slip his memory once they're past and done with. Probably he'll remember things all wrong.'

'There will be gaps, of course. I realize that.'

'I tell you what –' Meredith paused abruptly, then went on, reddening a little as he spoke. 'If you like, I – I could do the same. I mean, it would be a kind of check, wouldn't it?'

Hercule Poirot said warmly:

'It would be most valuable. An idea of the first excellence!'

'Right. I will. I've got some old diaries somewhere. Mind you,' he laughed awkwardly. 'I'm not much of a hand at literary language. Even my spelling's not too good. You – you won't expect too much?'

'Ah, it is not the style I demand. Just a plain recital of everything you can remember. What every one said, how they looked – just what happened. Never mind if it doesn't seem relevant. It all helps with the atmosphere, so to speak.'

'Yes, I can see that. It must be difficult visualizing people and places you have never seen.'

Poirot nodded.

'There is another thing I wanted to ask you. Alderbury is the adjoining property to this, is it not? Would it be possible to go there – to see with my own eyes where the tragedy occurred?'

Meredith Blake said slowly:

'I can take you over there right away. But, of course, it is a good deal changed.'

'It has not been built over?'

'No, thank goodness – not quite so bad as that. But it's a kind of hostel now – it was bought by some society. Hordes of young people come down to it in the summer, and of course all the rooms have been cut up and partitioned into cubicles, and the grounds have been altered a good deal.'

'You must reconstruct it for me by your explanations.'

'I'll do my best. I wish you could have seen it in the old days. It was one of the loveliest properties I know.'

He led the way out through the window and began walking down a slope of lawn.

'Who was responsible for selling it?'

'The executors on behalf of the child. Everything Crale had came to her. He hadn't made a will, so I imagine that it would be divided automatically between his wife and the child. Caroline's will left what she had to the child also.'

'Nothing to her half-sister?'

'Angela had a certain amount of money of her own left her by her father.'

Poirot nodded. 'I see.'

Then he uttered an exclamation:

'But where is it that you take me? This is the seashore ahead of us!'

'Ah, I must explain our geography to you. You'll see for

yourself in a minute. There's a creek, you see, Camel Creek, they call it, runs inland – looks almost like a river mouth, but it isn't – it's just sea. To get to Alderbury by land you have to go right inland and round the creek, but the shortest way from one house to the other is to row across this narrow bit of the creek. Alderbury is just opposite – there, you can see the house through the trees.'

They had come out on a little beach. Opposite them was a wooded headland and a white house could just be distinguished high up amongst the trees.

Two boats were drawn up on the beach. Meredith Blake, with Poirot's somewhat awkward assistance, dragged one of them down to the water and presently they were rowing across to the other side.

'We always went this way in the old days,' Meredith explained. 'Unless, of course, there was a storm or it was raining, and then we'd take the car. But it's nearly three miles if you go round that way.'

He ran the boat neatly alongside a stone quay on the other side. He cast a disparaging eye on a collection of wooden huts and some concrete terraces.

'All new, this. Used to be a boathouse – tumbledown old place – and nothing else. And one walked along the shore and bathed off those rocks over there.'

He assisted his guest to alight, made fast the boat, and led the way up a steep path.

'Don't suppose we'll meet any one,' he said over his shoulder. 'Nobody here in April – except for Easter. Doesn't matter if we do. I'm on good terms with my neighbours. Sun's glorious today. Might be summer. It was a wonderful day then. More like July than September. Brilliant sun – but a chilly little wind.'

The path came out of the trees and skirted an outcrop of rock. Meredith pointed up with his hand.

'That's what they called the Battery. We're more or less underneath it now – skirting round it.'

They plunged into trees again and then the path took another sharp turn and they emerged by a door set in a high wall. The path itself continued to zigzag upwards, but Meredith opened the door and the two men passed through it.

For a moment Poirot was dazzled coming in from the shade outside. The Battery was an artificially cleared plateau with battlements set with cannon. It gave one the impression of overhanging the sea. There were trees above it and behind it, but on the sea side there was nothing but the dazzling blue water below.

'Attractive spot,' said Meredith. He nodded contemptuously towards a kind of pavilion set back against the back wall. 'That wasn't there, of course – only an old tumbledown shed where Amyas kept his painting muck and some bottled beer and a few deck chairs. It wasn't concreted then, either. There used to be a bench and a table – painted iron ones. That was all. Still – it hasn't changed much.'

His voice held an unsteady note.

Poirot said: 'And it was here that it happened?'

Meredith nodded.

'The bench was there – up against the shed. He was sprawled on that. He used to sprawl there sometimes when he was painting – just fling himself down and stare and stare – and then suddenly up he'd jump and start laying the paint on the canvas like mad.'

He paused.

'That's why, you know, he looked – almost natural. As though he might be asleep – just have dropped off. But his eyes were open – and he'd – just stiffened up. Stuff sort of paralyses you, you know. There isn't any pain . . . I've – I've always been glad of that . . .'

Poirot asked a thing that he already knew.

'Who found him?'

'She did. Caroline. After lunch. I and Elsa, I suppose, were the last ones to see him alive. It must have been coming on then. He – looked queer. I'd rather not talk about it. I'll write it to you. Easier that way.'

He turned abruptly and went out of the Battery. Poirot followed him without speaking.

The two men went on up the zigzag path. At a higher level than the Battery there was another small plateau. It was over-shadowed with trees and there was a bench there and a table.

Meredith said:

'They haven't changed this much. But the bench used not to be Ye Olde Rustic. It was just a painted iron business. A bit hard for sitting, but a lovely view.'

Poirot agreed. Through a framework of trees one looked down over the Battery to the creek mouth.

'I sat up here part of the morning,' Meredith explained. 'Trees weren't quite so overgrown then. One could see the battlements of the Battery quite plainly. That's where Elsa was posing, you know. Sitting on one with her head twisted round.'

He gave a slight twitch of his shoulders.

'Trees grow faster than one thinks,' he muttered. 'Oh well, suppose I'm getting old. Come on up to the house.'

They continued to follow the path till it emerged near the house. It had been a fine old house, Georgian in style. It had been added to and on a green lawn near it were set some fifty little wooden bathing hutches.

'Young men sleep there, girls in the house,' Meredith explained. 'I don't suppose there's anything you want to see here. All the rooms have been cut about. Used to be a little conservatory tacked on here. These people have built a loggia. Oh well – I suppose they enjoy their holidays. Can't keep everything as it used to be – more's the pity.'

He turned away abruptly.

'We'll go down another way. It – it all comes back to me, you know. Ghosts. Ghosts everywhere.'

They returned to the quay by a somewhat longer and

more rambling route. Neither of them spoke. Poirot respected his companion's mood.

When they reached Handcross Manor once more, Meredith Blake said abruptly:

'I bought that picture, you know. The one that Amyas was painting. I just couldn't stand the idea of its being sold for – well – publicity value – a lot of dirty-minded brutes gaping at it. It was a fine piece of work. Amyas said it was the best thing he'd ever done. I shouldn't be surprised if he was right. It was practically finished. He only wanted to work on it another day or so. Would – would you care to see it?'

Hercule Poirot said quickly: 'Yes, indeed.'

Blake led the way across the hall and took a key from his pocket. He unlocked a door and they went into a fair-sized, dusty smelling room. It was closely shuttered. Blake went across to the windows and opened the wooden shutters. Then, with a little difficulty, he flung up a window and a breath of fragrant spring air came wafting into the room.

Meredith said: 'That's better.'

He stood by the window inhaling the air and Poirot joined him. There was no need to ask what the room had been. The shelves were empty but there were marks upon them where bottles had stood. Against one wall was some derelict chemical apparatus and a sink. The room was thick in dust.

Meredith Blake was looking out of the window. He said:

'How easily it all comes back. Standing here, smelling the jasmine – and talking – talking – like the damned fool I was – about my precious potions and distillations!'

Absently, Poirot stretched a hand through the window. He pulled off a spray of jasmine leaves just breaking from their woody stem.

Meredith Blake moved resolutely across the floor. On the wall was a picture covered with a dust sheet. He jerked the dust sheet away.

Poirot caught his breath. He had seen so far, four pictures

of Amyas Crale's: two at the Tate, one at a London dealer's, one, the still life of roses. But now he was looking at what the artist himself had called his best picture, and Poirot realized at once what a superb artist the man had been.

The painting had an old superficial smoothness. At first sight it might have been a poster, so seemingly crude were its contrasts. A girl, a girl in a canary-yellow shirt and dark-blue slacks, sitting on a grey wall in full sunlight against a background of violent blue sea. Just the kind of subject for a poster.

But the first appearance was deceptive; there was a subtle distortion – an amazing brilliance and clarity in the light. And the girl –

Yes, here was life. All there was, all there could be of life, of youth, of sheer blazing vitality. The face was alive and the eyes . . .

So much life! Such passionate youth! That, then, was what Amyas Crale had seen in Elsa Greer, which had made him blind and deaf to the gentle creature, his wife. Elsa *was* life. Elsa was youth.

A superb, slim, straight creature, arrogant, her head turned, her eyes insolent with triumph. Looking at you, watching you – waiting . . .

Hercule Poirot spread out his hands. He said:

'It is a great – yes, it is great –'

Meredith Blake said, a catch in his voice:

'She was so young –'

Poirot nodded. He thought to himself.

'What do most people mean when they say that? *So young*. Something innocent, something appealing, something helpless. But youth is not that! Youth is crude, youth is strong, youth is powerful – yes, and cruel! And one thing more – youth is vulnerable.'

He followed his host to the door. His interest was quickened now in Elsa Greer whom he was to visit next. What would the years have done to that passionate, triumphant crude child?

He looked back at the picture.

Those eyes. Watching him . . . watching him . . . Telling him something . . .

Supposing he couldn't understand what they were telling him? Would the real woman be able to tell him? Or were those eyes saying something that the real woman did not know?

Such arrogance, such triumphant anticipation.

And then Death had stepped in and taken the prey out of those eager, clutching young hands . . .

And the light had gone out of those passionately anticipating eyes. What were the eyes of Elsa Greer like now?

He went out of the room with one last look.

He thought: 'She was too much alive.'

He felt – a little – frightened . . .

CHAPTER VIII

This Little Pig Had Roast Beef

The house in Brook Street had Darwin tulips in the window boxes. Inside the hall a great vase of white lilac sent eddies of perfume towards the open front door.

A middle-aged butler relieved Poirot of his hat and stick. A footman appeared to take them and the butler murmured deferentially:

'Will you come this way, sir?'

Poirot followed him along the hall and down three steps. A door was opened, the butler pronounced his name with every syllable correct.

Then the door closed behind him and a tall thin man got up from a chair by the fire and came towards him.

Lord Dittisham was a man just under forty. He was not only a Peer of the Realm, he was a poet. Two of his fantastical poetic dramas had been staged at vast expense and had had a *succès d'estime*. His forehead was rather prominent, his chin was eager, and his eyes and his mouth unexpectedly beautiful.

He said:

'Sit down, M. Poirot.'

Poirot sat down and accepted a cigarette from his host. Lord Dittisham shut the box, struck a match and held it for Poirot to light his cigarette, then he himself sat down and looked thoughtfully at his visitor.

Then he said:

'It is my wife you have come to see, I know.'

Poirot answered:

'Lady Dittisham was so kind as to give me an appointment.'

'Yes.'

There was a pause. Poirot hazarded:

'You do not, I hope, object, Lord Dittisham?'

The thin dreamy face was transformed by a sudden quick smile.

'The objections of husbands, M. Poirot, are never taken seriously in these days.'

'Then you do object?'

'No. I cannot say that. But I am, I must confess it, a little fearful of the effect upon my wife. Let me be quite frank. A great many years ago, when my wife was only a young girl, she passed through a terrible ordeal. She has, I hope, recovered from the shock. I have come to believe that she has forgotten it. Now you appear and necessarily your questions will reawaken these old memories.'

'It is regrettable,' said Hercule Poirot politely.

'I do not know quite what the result will be.'

'I can only assure you, Lord Dittisham, that I shall be as discreet as possible, and do all I can not to distress Lady Dittisham. She is, no doubt, of a delicate and nervous temperament.'

Then, suddenly and surprisingly, the other laughed. He said:

'Elsa? Elsa's as strong as a horse!'

'Then –' Poirot paused diplomatically. The situation intrigued him.

Lord Dittisham said:

'My wife is equal to any amount of shocks. I wonder if you know her reason for seeing you?'

Poirot replied placidly: 'Curiosity?'

A kind of respect showed in the other man's eyes.

'Ah, you realize that?'

Poirot said:

'It is inevitable. Women will *always* see a private detective! Men will tell him to go to the devil.'

'Some women might tell him to go to the devil too.'

'After they have seen him – not before.'

'Perhaps.' Lord Dittisham paused. 'What is the idea behind this book?'

Hercule Poirot shrugged his shoulders.

'One resurrects the old tunes, the old stage turns, the old costumes. One resurrects, too, the old murders.'

'Faugh!' said Lord Dittisham.

'Faugh! If you like. But you will not alter human nature by saying Faugh. Murder is a drama. The desire for drama is very strong in the human race.'

Lord Dittisham murmured:

'I know – I know . . .'

'So you see,' said Poirot, 'the book will be written. It is my part to make sure that there shall be no gross misstatements, no tampering with the known facts.'

'The facts are public property I should have thought.'

'Yes. But not the interpretation of them.'

Dittisham said sharply:

'Just what do you mean by that, M. Poirot?'

'My dear Lord Dittisham, there are many ways of regarding, for instance, a historical fact. Take an example: many books have been written on your Mary Queen of Scots, representing her as a martyr, as an unprincipled and wanton woman, as a rather simple-minded saint, as a murderess and an intriguer, or again as a victim of circumstance and fate! One can take one's choice.'

'And in this case? Crale was killed by his wife – that is, of course, undisputed. At the trial my wife came in for some, in my opinion, undeserved calumny. She had to be smuggled out of court afterwards. Public opinion was very hostile to her.'

'The English,' said Poirot, 'are a very moral people.'

Lord Dittisham said: 'Confound them, they are!'

He added – looking at Poirot: 'And you?'

'Me,' said Poirot. 'I lead a very moral life. That is not quite the same thing as having moral ideas.'

Lord Dittisham said:

'I've wondered sometimes what this Mrs Crale was really like. All this injured wife business – I've a feeling there was something *behind* that.'

'Your wife might know,' agreed Poirot.

'My wife,' said Lord Dittisham, 'has never mentioned the case once.'

Poirot looked at him with quickened interest. He said:

'Ah, I begin to see –'

The other said sharply:

'What do you see?'

Poirot replied with a bow:

'The creative imagination of the poet . . .'

Lord Dittisham rose and rang the bell. He said brusquely:

'My wife will be waiting for you.'

The door opened.

'You rang, my lord?'

'Take M. Poirot up to her ladyship.'

Up two flights of stairs, feet sinking into soft pile carpets. Subdued flood lighting. Money, money everywhere. Of taste, not so much. There had been a sombre austerity in Lord Dittisham's room. But here, in the house, there was only a solid lavishness. The best. Not necessarily the showiest, or the most startling. Merely 'expense no object', allied to a lack of imagination.

Poirot said to himself: 'Roast beef? Yes, roast beef!'

It was not a large room into which he was shown. The big drawing-room was on the first floor. This was the personal sitting-room of the mistress of the house and the mistress of the house was standing against the mantelpiece as Poirot was announced and shown in.

A phrase leapt into his startled mind and refused to be driven out.

She died young . . .

That was his thought as he looked at Elsa Dittisham who had been Elsa Greer.

He would never have recognized her from the picture Meredith Blake had shown him. That had been, above all, a picture of youth, a picture of vitality. Here there was no youth – there might never have been youth. And yet he realized, as he had not realized from Crale's picture, that Elsa was beautiful. Yes, it was a very beautiful woman who came forward to meet him. And certainly not old. After all, what was she? Not more than thirty-six now if she had been twenty at the time of the tragedy. Her black hair was perfectly arranged round her shapely head, her features were almost classic, her make-up was exquisite.

He felt a strange pang. It was, perhaps, the fault of old Mr Jonathan, speaking of Juliet . . . No Juliet here – unless perhaps one could imagine Juliet a survivor – living on, deprived of Romeo . . . Was it not an essential part of Juliet's make-up that she should die young?

Elsa Greer had been left alive . . .

She was greeting him in a level rather monotonous voice.

'I am so interested, M. Poirot. Sit down and tell me what you want me to do?'

He thought:

'But she isn't interested. Nothing interests her.'

Big grey eyes – like dead lakes.

Poirot became, as was his way, a little obviously foreign.

He exclaimed:

'I am confused, madame, veritably I am confused.'

'Oh no, why?'

'Because I realize that this – this reconstruction of a past drama must be excessively painful to you!'

She looked amused. Yes, it was amusement. Quite genuine amusement.

She said:

'I suppose my husband put that idea into your head? He saw you when you arrived. Of course he doesn't understand in the least. He never has. I'm not at all the sensitive sort of person he imagines I am.'

The amusement was still in her voice. She said:

'My father, you know, was a mill hand. He worked his way up and made a fortune. You don't do that if you're thin-skinned. I'm the same.'

Poirot thought to himself: Yes, that is true. A thin-skinned person would not have come to stay in Caroline Crale's house.

Lady Dittisham said:

'What is it you want me to do?'

'You are sure, madame, that to go over the past would not be painful to you?'

She considered a minute, and it struck Poirot suddenly that Lady Dittisham was a very frank woman. She might lie from necessity but never from choice.

Elsa Dittisham said slowly:

'No, not *painful*. In a way, I wish it were.'

'Why?'

She said impatiently:

'It's so stupid never to feel anything . . .'

And Hercule Poirot thought:

'Yes, Elsa Greer is dead . . .'

Aloud he said:

'At all events, Lady Dittisham, it makes my task very much easier.'

She said cheerfully:

'What do you want to know?'

'Have you a good memory, madame?'

'Reasonably good, I think.'

'And you are sure it will not pain you to go over those days in detail?'

'It won't pain me at all. Things can only pain you when they are happening.'

'It is so with some people, I know.'

Lady Dittisham said:

'That's what Edward – my husband – can't understand. He thinks the trial and all that was a terrible ordeal for me.'

'Was it not?'

Elsa Dittisham said:

'No, I enjoyed it.' There was a reflective satisfied quality in her voice. She went on: 'God, how that old brute Depleach went for me. He's a devil, if you like. I enjoyed fighting him. He didn't get me down.'

She looked at Poirot with a smile.

'I hope I'm not upsetting your illusions. A girl of twenty, I ought to have been prostrated, I suppose – agonized with shame or something. I wasn't. I didn't care what they said to me. I only wanted one thing.'

'What?'

'To get her hanged, of course,' said Elsa Dittisham.

He noticed her hands – beautiful hands but with long curving nails. Predatory hands.

She said:

'You're thinking me vindictive? So I am vindictive – to .any one who has injured me. That woman was to my mind the lowest kind of woman there is. She knew that Amyas cared for me – that he was going to leave her and she killed him so that *I* shouldn't have him.'

She looked across at Poirot.

'Don't you think that's pretty mean?'

'You do not understand or sympathize with jealousy?'

'No, I don't think I do. If you've lost, you've lost. If you can't keep your husband, let him go with a good grace. It's possessiveness I don't understand.'

'You might have understood it if you had ever married him.'

'I don't think so. We weren't –' She smiled suddenly at Poirot. Her smile was, he felt, a little frightening. It was so far removed from any real feeling. 'I'd like you to get this right,' she said. 'Don't think that Amyas Crale seduced an innocent young girl. It wasn't like that at all! Of the two of us, *I* was responsible. I met him at a party and I fell for him – I knew I'd got to have him –'

A travesty – a grotesque travesty but –

And all my fortunes at thy foot I'll lay
And follow thee, my lord, throughout the world . . .

'Although he was married?'

'Trespassers will be prosecuted? It takes more than a printed notice to keep you from reality. If he was unhappy with his wife and could be happy with me, then why not? We've only one life to live.'

'But it has been said he was happy with his wife.'

Elsa shook her head.

'No. They quarrelled like cat and dog. She nagged at him. She was – oh, she was a horrible woman!'

She got up and lit a cigarette. She said with a little smile:

'Probably I'm unfair to her. But I really *do* think she was rather hateful.'

Poirot said slowly: 'It was a great tragedy.'

'Yes, it was a great tragedy.' She turned on him suddenly, into the dead monotonous weariness of her face something came quiveringly alive.

'It killed *me*, do you understand? It killed me. Ever since there's been nothing – nothing at all.' Her voice dropped. 'Emptiness!' She waved her hands impatiently. 'Like a stuffed fish in a glass case!'

'Did Amyas Crale mean so much to you?'

She nodded. It was a queer confiding little nod – oddly pathetic. She said:

'I think I've always had a single-track mind.' She mused sombrely. 'I suppose – really – one ought to put a knife into oneself – like Juliet. But – but to do that is to acknowledge that you're done for – that life's beaten you.'

'And instead?'

'There ought to be everything – just the same – once one has got over it. I *did* get over it. It didn't mean anything to me any more. I thought I'd go on to the next thing.'

Yes, the next thing. Poirot saw her plainly trying so hard to fulfil that crude determination. Saw her beautiful and rich, seductive to men, seeking with greedy predatory hands to fill up a life that was empty. Hero worship – a marriage to a famous aviator – then an explorer, that big giant of a man, Arnold Stevenson – possibly not unlike Amyas Crale physically – a reversion to the creative arts: Dittisham!

Elsa Dittisham said:

'I've never been a hypocrite! There's a Spanish proverb I've always liked. *Take what you want and pay for it, says God*. Well, I've done that. I've taken what I wanted – but I've always been willing to pay the price.'

Hercule Poirot said:

'What you do not understand is that there are things that cannot be bought.'

She stared at him. She said:

'I don't mean just money.'

Poirot said:

'No, no, I understand what you mean. But it is not everything in life that has its ticket, so much. There are things that are *not for sale*.'

'Nonsense!'

He smiled very faintly. In her voice was the arrogance of the successful mill hand who had risen to riches.

Hercule Poirot felt a sudden wave of pity. He looked at the ageless, smooth face, the weary eyes, and he remembered the girl whom Amyas Crale had painted . . .

Elsa Dittisham said:

'Tell me all about this book. What is the purpose of it? Whose idea is it?'

'Oh! my dear lady, what other purpose is there but to serve up yesterday's sensation with today's sauce.'

'But *you're* not a writer?'

'No, I am an expert on crime.'

'You mean they consult you on crime books?'

'Not always. In this case, I have a commission.'

'From whom?'

'I am – what do you say – vetting this publication on behalf of an interested party.'

'What party?'

'Miss Carla Lemarchant.'

'Who is she?'

'She is the daughter of Amyas and Caroline Crale.'

Elsa stared for a minute. Then she said:

'Oh, of course, there *was* a child. I remember. I suppose she's grown up now?'

'Yes, she is twenty-one.'

'What is she like?'

'She is tall and dark and, I think, beautiful. And she has courage and personality.'

Elsa said thoughtfully:

'I should like to see her.'

'She might not care to see you.'

Elsa looked surprised.

'Why? Oh, I see. But what nonsense! She can't possibly remember anything about it. She can't have been more than six.'

'She knows that her mother was tried for her father's murder.'

'And she thinks it's my fault?'

'It is a possible interpretation.'

Elsa shrugged her shoulders. She said:

'How stupid! If Caroline had behaved like a reasonable human being –'

'So you take no responsibility?'

'Why should I? *I've* nothing to be ashamed of. I loved him. I would have made him happy.' She looked across at Poirot. Her face broke up – suddenly, incredibly, he saw the girl of the picture. She said: 'If I could make you see. If you could see it from my side. If you knew –'

Poirot leaned forward.

'But that is what I want. See, Mr Philip Blake who was there at the time, he is writing me a meticulous account of everything that happened. Mr Meredith Blake the same. Now if you –'

Elsa Dittisham took a deep breath. She said contemptuously:

'Those two! Philip was always stupid. Meredith used to trot round after Caroline – but he was quite a dear. But you won't have *any* real idea from *their* accounts.'

He watched her, saw the animation rising in her eyes, saw a living woman take shape from a dead one. She said quickly and almost fiercely:

'Would you like the *truth*? Oh, not for publication. But just for yourself –'

'I will undertake not to publish without your consent.'

'I'd like to write down the truth . . .' She was silent a minute or two, thinking. He saw the smooth hardness of her cheeks falter and take on a younger curve, he saw life ebbing into her as the past claimed her again.

'To go back – to write it all down . . . To show you what she was –'

Her eyes flashed. Her breast heaved passionately.

'She killed him. She killed Amyas. Amyas who wanted to live – who enjoyed living. Hate oughtn't to be stronger than love – but her hate was. And my hate for her is – I hate her – I hate her – I hate her . . .'

She came across to him. She stooped, her hand clutched at his sleeve. She said urgently:

'You must understand – you *must* – how we felt about each other. Amyas and I, I mean. There's something – I'll show you.'

She whirled across the room. She was unlocking a little desk, pulling out a drawer concealed inside a pigeon hole.

Then she was back. In her hand was a creased letter, the ink faded. She thrust it on him and Poirot had a sudden poignant memory of a child he had known who had thrust on him one of her treasures – a special shell picked up on the seashore and zealously guarded. Just so had that child stood back and watched him. Proud, afraid, keenly critical of his reception of her treasure.

He unfolded the faded sheets.

Elsa – you wonderful child! There never was anything as beautiful. And yet I'm afraid – I'm too old – a middle-aged, ugly tempered devil with no stability in me. Don't trust me, don't believe in me – I'm no good – apart from my work. The best of me is in that. There, don't say you haven't been warned.

Hell, my lovely – I'm going to have you all the same. I'd go to the devil for you and you know it. And I'll paint a picture of you that will make the fat-headed world hold its sides and gasp! I'm crazy about you – I can't sleep – I can't eat. Elsa – Elsa – Elsa – I'm yours for ever – yours till death. Amyas.

Sixteen years ago. Faded ink, crumbling paper. But the words still alive – still vibrating . . .

He looked across at the woman to whom they had been written.

But it was no longer a woman at whom he looked.

It was a young girl in love.

He thought again of Juliet . . .

CHAPTER IX

This Little Pig Had None

'May I ask why, M. Poirot?'

Hercule Poirot considered his answer to the question. He was aware of a pair of very shrewd grey eyes watching him out of the small wizened face.

He had climbed to the top floor of the bare building and knocked on the door of No. 584 Gillespie Buildings, which had come into existence to provide what were called 'flatlets' for working women.

Here, in a small cubic space, existed Miss Cecilia Williams, in a room that was bedroom, sitting-room, dining-room, and, by judicious use of the gas ring, kitchen – a kind of cubby hole attached to it contined a quarter-length bath and the usual offices.

Meagre though these surroundings might be, Miss Williams had contrived to impress upon them her stamp of personality.

The walls were distempered an ascetic pale grey, and various reproductions hung upon them. Dante meeting Beatrice on a bridge – and that picture once described by a child as a 'blind girl sitting on an orange and called, I don't know why, "Hope".' There were also two water colours of Venice and a sepia copy of Botticelli's 'Primavera'. On the top of the low chest of drawers were a large quantity of faded photographs, mostly, by their style of hairdressing, dating from twenty to thirty years ago.

The square of carpet was threadbare, the furniture battered and of poor quality. It was clear to Hercule Poirot that Cecilia Williams lived very near the bone. There was no roast beef here. This was the little pig that had none.

Clear, incisive and insistent, the voice of Miss Williams repeated its demand.

'You want my recollections of the Crale case? May I ask why?'

It had been said of Hercule Poirot by some of his friends and associates, at moments when he has maddened them most, that he prefers lies to truth and will go out of his way to gain his ends by means of elaborate false statements, rather than trust to the simple truth.

But in this case his decision was quickly made. Hercule Poirot did not come of that class of Belgian or French children who have had an English governess, but he reacted as simply and inevitably as various small boys who had been asked in their time: 'Did you brush your teeth this morning, Harold (or Richard or Anthony)?' They considered fleetingly the possibility of a lie and instantly rejected it, replying miserably, 'No, Miss Williams.'

For Miss Williams had what every successful child educator must have, that mysterious quality – authority! When Miss Williams said 'Go up and wash your hands, Joan,' or 'I expect you to read this chapter on the Elizabethan poets and be able to answer my questions on it,' she was invariably obeyed. It had never entered Miss Williams' head that she would not be obeyed.

So in this case Hercule Poirot proffered no specious explanation of a book to be written on bygone crimes. Instead he narrated simply the circumstances in which Carla Lemarchant had sought him out.

The small, elderly lady in the neat shabby dress listened attentively.

She said:

'It interests me very much to have news of that child – to know how she has turned out.'

'She is a very charming and attractive young woman, with plenty of courage and a mind of her own.'

'Good,' said Miss Williams briefly.

'And she is, I may say, a very persistent person. She is not a person whom it is easy to refuse or put off.'

The ex-governess nodded thoughtfully. She asked:

'Is she artistic?'

115

'I think not.'

Miss Williams said drily:

'That's one thing to be thankful for!'

The tone of the remark left Miss Williams' views as to artists in no doubt whatever.

She added:

'From your account of her I should imagine that she takes after her mother rather than after her father.'

'Very possibly. That you can tell me when you have seen her. You would like to see her?'

'I should like to see her very much indeed. It is always interesting to see how a child you have known has developed.'

'She was, I suppose, very young when you last saw her?'

'She was five and a half. A very charming child – a little over-quiet, perhaps. Thoughtful. Given to playing her own little games and not inviting outside co-operation. Natural and unspoilt.'

Poirot said:

'It was fortunate she was so young.'

'Yes, indeed. Had she been older the shock of the tragedy might have had a very bad effect.'

'Nevertheless,' said Poirot, 'one feels that there *was* a handicap – however little the child understood or was allowed to know, there would have been an atmosphere of mystery and evasion and an abrupt uprooting. These things are not good for a child.'

Miss Williams replied thoughtfully:

'They may have been less harmful than you think.'

Poirot said:

'Before we leave the subject of Carla Lemarchant – little Carla Crale that was, there is something I would like to ask you. If any one can explain it, I think you can.'

'Yes?'

Her voice was inquiring, non-commital.

Poirot waved his hands in an effort to express his meaning.

'There is a something – a *nuance* I cannot define – but it

116

seems to me always that the child, when I mention her, is not given her full representational value. When I mention her, the response comes always with a vague surprise, as though the person to whom I speak had forgotten altogether that there *was* a child. Now surely, Mademoiselle, that is not natural? A child, under these circumstances, is a person of importance, not in herself, but as a pivotal point. Amyas Crale may have had reasons for abandoning his wife – or for not abandoning her. But in the usual break-up of a marriage the child forms a very important point. But here the child seems to count for very little. That seems to me – strange.'

Miss Williams said quickly:

'You have put your finger on a vital point, M. Poirot. You are quite right. And that is partly why I said what I did just now – that Carla's transportation to different surroundings might have been in some respects a good thing for her. When she was older, you see, she might have suffered from a certain lack in her home life.'

She leaned forward and spoke slowly and carefully.

'Naturally, in the course of my work, I have seen a good many aspects of the parent and child problem. Many children, *most* children, I should say, suffer from over-attention on the part of their parents. There is too much love, too much watching over the child. It is uneasily conscious of this brooding, and seeks to free itself, to get away and be unobserved. With an only child that is particularly the case, and of course mothers are the worst offenders. The result on the marriage is often unfortunate. The husband resents coming second, seeks consolation – or rather flattery and attention – elsewhere, and a divorce results sooner or later. The best thing for a child, I am convinced, is to have what I should term healthy neglect on the part of both its parents. This happens naturally enough in the case of a large family of children and very little money. They are overlooked because the mother has literally no time to occupy herself with them. They realize quite well that she is

117

fond of them, but they are not worried by too many manifestations of the fact.

'But there is another aspect. One does occasionally find a husband and wife who are so all-sufficient to each other, so wrapped up in each other, that the child of the marriage hardly seems very real to either of them. And in those circumstances I think a child comes to resent that fact, to feel defrauded and left out in the cold. You understand that I am not speaking of *neglect* in any way. Mrs Crale, for instance, was what is termed an excellent mother, always careful of Carla's welfare, of her health – playing with her at the right times and always kind and gay. But for all that, Mrs Crale was really completely wrapped up in her husband. She existed, one might say, only in him and for him.' Miss Williams paused a minute and then said quietly: 'That, I think, is the justification for what she eventually did.'

Hercule Poirot said:

'You mean that they were more like lovers than like husband and wife?'

Miss Williams, with a slight frown of distaste for foreign phraseology, said:

'You could certainly put it that way.'

'He was devoted to her as she was to him?'

'They were a devoted couple. But he, of course, was a man.'

Miss Williams contrived to put into that last word a wholly Victorian significance.

'Men –' said Miss Williams, and stopped.

As a rich property owner says 'Bolsheviks' – as an earnest Communist says 'Capitalists!' – as a good housewife says 'Blackbeetles' – so did Miss Williams say 'Men!'

From her spinster's, governess's life, there rose up a blast of fierce feminism. Nobody hearing her speak could doubt that to Miss Williams Men were the Enemy!

Poirot said: 'You hold no brief for men?'

She answered drily:

'Men have the best of this world. I hope that it will not always be so.'

Hercule Poirot eyed her speculatively. He could quite easily visualize Miss Williams methodically and efficiently padlocking herself to a railing, and later hunger-striking with resolute endurance. Leaving the general for the particular, he said:

'You did not like Amyas Crale?'

'I certainly did not like Mr Crale. Nor did I approve of him. If I were his wife I should have left him. There are things that no woman should put up with.'

'But Mrs Crale did put up with them?'

'Yes.'

'You thought she was wrong?'

'Yes, I do. A woman should have a certain respect for herself and not submit to humiliation.'

'Did you ever say anything of that kind to Mrs Crale?'

'Certainly not. It was not my place to do so. I was engaged to educate Angela, not to offer unasked advice to Mrs Crale. To do so would have been most impertinent.'

'You liked Mrs Crale?'

'I was very fond of Mrs Crale.' The efficient voice softened, held warmth and feeling. 'Very fond of her and very sorry for her.'

'And your pupil – Angela Warren?'

'She was a most interesting girl – one of the most interesting pupils I have had. A really good brain. Undisciplined, quick-tempered, most difficult to manage in many ways, but really a very fine character.'

She paused and then went on:

'I always hoped that she would accomplish something worth while. And she has! You have read her book – on the Sahara? And she excavated those very interesting tombs in the Fayum! Yes, I am proud of Angela. I was not at Alderbury very long – two years and a half – but I always

119

cherish the belief that I helped to stimulate her mind and encourage her taste for archæology.'

Poirot murmured: 'I understand that it was decided to continue her education by sending her to school. You must have resented that decision.'

'Not at all, M. Poirot. I thoroughly concurred with it.'

She paused and went:

'Let me make the matter clear to you. Angela was a dear girl – really a very dear girl – warm-hearted and impulsive – but she was also what I call a difficult girl. That is, she was at a difficult age. There is always a moment where a girl feels unsure of herself – neither child nor woman. At one minute Angela would be sensible and mature – quite grown up, in fact – but a minute later she would relapse into being a hoydenish child – playing mischievous tricks and being rude and losing her temper. Girls, you know, *feel* difficult at that age – they are terribly sensitive. Everything that is said to them they resent. They are annoyed at being treated like a child and then they suddenly feel shy at being treated like adults. Angela was in that state. She had fits of temper, would suddenly resent teasing and flare out – and then she would be sulky for days at a time, sitting about and frowning – then again she would be in wild spirits, climbing trees, rushing about with the garden boys, refusing to submit to any kind of authority.'

Miss Williams paused and went on:

'When a girl gets to that stage, school is very helpful. She needs the stimulation of other minds – that, and the wholesome discipline of a community, help her to become a reasonable member of society. Angela's home conditions were not what I would have called ideal. Mrs Crale spoiled her, for one thing. Angela had only to appeal to her and Mrs Crale always backed her up. The result was that Angela considered she had first claim upon her sister's time and attention, and it was in these moods of hers that she used to clash with Mr Crale. Mr Crale naturally thought that *he* should come first – and intended to do so. He was really very fond of the girl – they were good companions and used to spar together quite amiably, but there were times when Mr Crale used suddenly to resent Mrs Crale's preoccupation with Angela. Like all men, he was a spoilt child; he expected everybody to make a fuss of *him*. Then he and Angela used to have a real set-to – and very often Mrs Crale would take Angela's side. Then he would be furious. On the other hand, if *she* supported *him*, Angela would be furious. It was on these occasions that Angela used to revert to childish ways and play some spiteful trick on him. He had a habit of tossing off his drinks and she once put a lot of salt into his drink. The whole thing, of course, acted as an emetic, and he was inarticulate with fury. But what really brought things to a head was when she put a lot of slugs into his bed. He had a queer aversion for slugs. He lost his temper completely and said that the girl had got to be sent away to school. He wasn't going to put up with all this petty nonsense any more. Angela was terribly upset – though actually she had once or twice expressed a wish herself to go to a boarding school – but she chose to make a huge grievance of it. Mrs Crale didn't want her to go but allowed herself to be persuaded – largely owing, I think, to what I said to her on the subject. I pointed out to her that it would be greatly to Angela's advantage, and that I thought it would really be a great benefit to the girl. So it was settled that she should go to Helston – a very fine school on the south coast – in the autumn term. But Mrs Crale was still unhappy about it all those holidays. And Angela kept up a grudge against Mr Crale whenever she remembered. It wasn't really serious, you understand, M. Poirot, but it made a kind of undercurrent that summer to – well – to everything *else* that was going on.'

Poirot said: 'Meaning – Elsa Greer?'

Miss Williams said sharply:

'Exactly.' And shut her lips very tight after the word.

'What was your opinion of Elsa Greer?'

'I had no opinion of her at all. A thoroughly unprincipled young woman.'

'She was very young.'

'Old enough to know better. I can see no excuse for her – none at all.'

'She fell in love with him, I suppose –'

Miss Williams interrupted with a snort.

'Fell in love with him indeed. I should hope, M. Poirot, that whatever our feelings, we can keep them in decent control. And we can certainly control our actions. That girl had absolutely no morals of any kind. It meant nothing to her that Mr Crale was a married man. She was absolutely shameless about it all – cool and determined. Possibly she may have been badly brought up – but that's the only excuse I can find for her.'

'Mr Crale's death must have been a terrible shock to her.'

'Oh, it was. And she herself was entirely to blame for it. I don't go as far as condoning murder, but all the same, M. Poirot, if ever a woman was driven to breaking point, that woman was Caroline Crale. I tell you frankly, there were moments when I would have liked to murder them both myself. Flaunting the girl in his wife's face, listening to her having to put up with the girl's insolence – and she *was* insolent, M. Poirot. Oh no, Amyas Crale deserved what he got. No man should treat his wife as he did and not be punished for it. His death was a just retribution.'

Hercule Poirot said: 'You feel strongly . . .'

The small woman looked at him with those indomitable grey eyes. She said:

'I feel *very strongly* about the marriage tie. Unless it is respected and upheld, a country degenerates. Mrs Crale was a devoted and faithful wife. Her husband deliberately flouted her and introduced his mistress into her home. As I say, he deserved what he got. He goaded her past endurance and I, for one, do not blame her for what she did.'

Poirot said slowly: 'He acted very badly – that I admit – but he was a great artist, remember.'

Miss Williams gave a terrific snort.

'Oh yes, I know. That's always the excuse nowadays. An artist! An excuse for every kind of loose living, for drunkenness, for brawling, for infidelity. And what kind of an artist was Mr Crale, when all is said and done? It may be the fashion to admire his pictures for a few years. But they won't last. Why, he couldn't even draw! His perspective was terrible! Even his anatomy was quite incorrect. I know something of what I am talking about, M. Poirot. I studied painting for a time, as a girl, in Florence, and to any one who knows and appreciates the great masters, these daubs of Mr Crale's are really ludicrous. Just splashing a few colours about on the canvas – no construction – no careful drawing. No,' she shook her head, 'don't ask me to admire Mr Crale's painting.'

'Two of them are in the Tate Gallery,' Poirot reminded her.

Miss Williams sniffed.

'Possibly. So is one of Mr Epstein's statues, I believe.'

Poirot perceived that, according to Miss Williams, the last word had been said. He abandoned the subject of art.

He said:

'You were with Mrs Crale when she found the body?'

'Yes. She and I went down from the house together after lunch. Angela had left her pullover on the beach after bathing, or else in the boat. She was always very careless about her things. I parted from Mrs Crale at the door of the Battery garden, but she called me back almost at once. I believe Mr Crale had been dead over an hour. He was sprawled on the bench near his easel.'

'Was she terribly upset at the discovery?'

'What exactly do you mean by that, M. Poirot?'

'I am asking you what your impressions were at the time.'

'Oh, I see. Yes, she seemed to me quite dazed. She sent

me off to telephone for the doctor. After all, we couldn't be absolutely sure he was dead – it might have been a cataleptic seizure.'

'Did she suggest such a possibility?'

'I don't remember.'

'And you went and telephoned?'

Miss William's tone was dry and brusque.

'I had gone half up the path when I met Mr Meredith Blake. I entrusted my errand to him and returned to Mrs Crale. I thought, you see, she might have collapsed – and men are no good in a matter of that kind.'

'And had she collapsed?'

Miss Williams said drily:

'Mrs Crale was quite in command of herself. She was quite different from Miss Greer, who made a hysterical and very unpleasant scene.'

'What kind of a scene?'

'She tried to attack Mrs Crale.'

'You mean she realized that Mrs Crale was responsible for Mr Crale's death?'

Miss Williams considered for a moment or two.

'No, she could hardly be sure of that. That – er – terrible suspicion had not yet arisen. Miss Greer just screamed out: "It's all your doing, Caroline. You killed him. It's all your fault." She did not actually say "You've poisoned him," but I think there is no doubt that she thought so.'

'And Mrs Crale?'

Miss Williams moved restlessly.

'Must we be hypocritical, M. Poirot? I cannot tell you what Mrs Crale really felt or thought at that moment. Whether it was horror at what she had done –'

'Did it seem like that?'

'N-no, n-no, I can't say it did. Stunned, yes – and, I think, frightened. Yes, I am sure, frightened. But that is natural enough.'

Hercule Poirot said in a dissatisfied tone:

'Yes, perhaps that is natural enough . . . What view did she adopt officially as to her husband's death?'

'Suicide. She said, very definitely from the first, that it must be. suicide.'

'Did she say the same when she was talking to you privately, or did she put forward any other theory.'

'No. She – she – took pains to impress upon me that it must be suicide.'

Miss Williams sounded embarrassed.

'And what did you say to that?'

'Really, M. Poirot, does it matter *what* I said?'

'Yes, I think it does.'

'I don't see why –'

But as though his expectant silence hypnotized her, she said reluctantly:

'I think I said: "Certainly, Mrs Crale. It must have been suicide."'

'Did you believe your own words?'

Miss Williams raised her head. She said firmly:

'No, I did not. But please understand, M. Poirot, that I was entirely on Mrs Crale's side, if you like to put it that way. My sympathies were with her, not with the police.'

'You would have liked to have seen her acquitted?'

Miss Williams said defiantly:

'Yes, I would.'

Poirot said:

'Then you are in sympathy with her daughter's feelings?'

'I have every sympathy with Carla.'

'Would you have any objection to writing out for me a detailed account of the tragedy?'

'You mean for her to read?'

'Yes.'

Miss Williams said slowly:

'No, I have no objection. She is quite. determined to go into the matter, is she?'

'Yes. I dare say it would have been preferable if the truth had been kept from her –'

Miss Williams interrupted him:

'No. It is always better to face the truth. It is no use evading unhappiness by tampering with facts. Carla has had a shock learning the truth – now she wants to know exactly how the tragedy came about. That seems to me the right attitude for a brave young woman to take. Once she knows all about it she will be able to forget it again and go on with the business of living her own life.'

'Perhaps you are right,' said Poirot.

'I'm quite sure I'm right.'

'But you see, there is more to it than that. She not only wants to know – she wants to prove her mother innocent.'

Miss Williams said: 'Poor child.'

'That is what you say, is it?'

Miss Williams said:

'I see now why you said that it might be better if she had never known. All the same, I think it is best as it is. To wish to find her mother innocent is a natural hope – and hard though the actual revelation may be, I think from what you say of her that Carla is brave enough to learn the truth and not flinch from it.'

'You are sure it *is* the truth?'

'I don't understand you?'

'You see no loophole for believing that Mrs Crale was innocent?'

'I don't think that possibility has ever been seriously considered.'

'And yet she herself clung to the theory of suicide?'

Miss Williams said drily:

'The poor woman had to say *something*.'

'Do you know that when Mrs Crale was dying she left a letter for her daughter in which she solemnly swears that she is innocent?'

Miss Williams stared.

'That was very wrong of her,' she said sharply.

'You think so?'

'Yes, I do. Oh, I dare say you are a sentimentalist like most men –'

Poirot interrupted indignantly:

'I am *not* a sentimentalist.'

'But there is such a thing as false sentiment. Why write that, a lie; at such a solemn moment? To spare your child pain? Yes, many women would do that. But I should not have thought it of Mrs Crale. She was a brave woman and a truthful woman. I should have thought it far more like her to have told her daughter not to judge.'

Poirot said with slight exasperation:

'You will not even consider then the possibility that what Caroline Crale wrote was the truth?'

'Certainly not!'

'And yet you profess to have loved her?'

'I did love her. I had a great affection and deep sympathy for her.'

'Well, then –'

Miss Williams looked at him in a very odd way.

'You don't understand, M. Poirot. It doesn't matter my saying this now – so long afterwards. You see, I happen to *know* that Caroline Crale was guilty!'

'*What?*'

'It's true. Whether I did right in withholding what I knew at the time I cannot be sure – but I *did* withhold it. But you must take it from me, quite definitely, that I *know* Caroline Crale was guilty . . .'

CHAPTER X

This Little Pig Cried 'Wee Wee Wee'

Angela Warren's flat overlooked Regent's Park. Here, on this spring day, a soft air wafted in through the open window and one might have had the illusion that one was in the country if it had not been for the steady menacing roar of the traffic passing below.

Poirot turned from the window as the door opened and Angela Warren came into the room.

It was not the first time he had seen her. He had availed himself of the opportunity to attend a lecture she had given at the Royal Geographical. It had been, he considered, an excellent lecture. Dry, perhaps, from the view of popular appeal. Miss Warren had an excellent delivery, she neither paused nor hesitated for a word. She did not repeat herself. The tones of her voice were clear and not unmelodious. She made no concessions to romantic appeal or love of adventure. There was very little human interest in the lecture. It was an admirable recital of concise facts, adequately illustrated by excellent slides, and with intelligent deductions from the facts recited. Dry, precise, clear, lucid, highly technical.

The soul of Hercule Poirot approved. Here, he considered, was an orderly mind.

Now that he saw her at close quarters he realized that Angela Warren might easily have been a very handsome woman. Her features were regular, though severe. She had finely marked dark brows, clear intelligent brown eyes, a fine pale skin. She had very square shoulders and a slightly mannish walk.

There was certainly about her no suggestion of the little pig who cries 'Wee Wee.' But on the right cheek, disfiguring and puckering the skin, was that healed scar. The right eye was slightly distorted, the corner pulled downwards by it but no one would have realized that the sight of that eye was destroyed. It seemed to Hercule Poirot almost certain that she had lived with her disability so long that she was now completely unconscious of it. And it occurred to him that of the five people in whom he had become interested as a result of his investigations, those who might have been said to start with the fullest advantages were not those who had actually wrested the most success and happiness from life. Elsa, who might have been said to start with all advantages – youth, beauty, riches – had done worst. She was like a flower overtaken by untimely frost – still in bud – but without life. Cecilia Williams, to outward appearances, had no assets of which to boast. Nevertheless, to Poirot's eye, there was no despondency there and no sense of failure. Miss Williams's life had been interesting to her – she was still interested in people and events. She had that enormous mental and moral advantage of a strict Victorian upbringing denied to us in these days – she had done her duty in that station of life to which it had pleased God to call her, and that assurance encased her in an armour impregnable to the slings and darts of envy, discontent and regret. She had her memories, her small pleasures, made possible by stringent economies, and sufficient health and vigour to enable her still to be interested in life.

Now, in Angela Warren – that young creature handicapped by disfigurement and its consequent humiliation, Poirot believed he saw a spirit strengthened by its necessary fight for confidence and assurance. The undisciplined schoolgirl had given place to a vital and forceful woman, a woman of considerable mental power and gifted with abundant energy to accomplish ambitious purposes. She was a woman, Poirot felt sure, both happy and successful. Her life was full and vivid and eminently enjoyable.

She was not, incidentally, the type of woman that Poirot really liked. Though admiring the clear-cut precision of her mind, she had just a sufficient *nuance* of the *femme formidable* about her to alarm him as a mere man. His taste had always been for the flamboyant and extravagant.

With Angela Warren it was easy to come to the point of his visit. There was no subterfuge. He merely recounted Carla Lemarchant's interview with him.

Angela Warren's severe face lighted up appreciatively.

'Little Carla? She is over here? I would like to see her so much.'

'You have not kept in touch with her?'

'Hardly as much as I should have done. I was a schoolgirl at the time she went to Canada, and I realized, of course, that in a year or two she would have forgotten us. Of late years, an occasional present at Christmas has been the only link between us. I imagined that she would, by now, be completely immersed in the Canadian atmosphere and that her future would lie over there. Better so, in the circumstances.'

Poirot said: 'One might think so, certainly. A change of name – a change of scene. A new life. But it was not to be so easy as that.'

And he then told of Carla's engagement, the discovery she had made upon coming of age and her motives in coming to England.

Angela Warren listened quietly, her disfigured cheek resting on one hand. She betrayed no emotion during the recital, but as Poirot finished, she said quietly:

'Good for Carla.'

Poirot was startled. It was the first time that he had met with this reaction. He said:

'You approve, Miss Warren?'

'Certainly. I wish her every success. Anything I can do to help, I will. I feel guilty, you know, that I haven't attempted anything myself.'

'Then you think that there is a possibility that she is right in her views.'

Angela Warren said sharply:

'Of course she's right. Caroline didn't do it. I've always known that.'

Hercule Poirot murmured:

'You surprise me very much indeed, mademoiselle. Everybody else I have spoken to –'

She cut in sharply:

'You mustn't go by that. I've no doubt that the circumstantial evidence is overwhelming. My own conviction is based on knowledge – knowledge of my sister. I just know quite simply and definitely that Caro *couldn't* have killed any one.'

'Can one say that with certainty of any human creature?'

'Probably not in most cases. I agree that the human animal is full of curious surprises. But in Caroline's case there were special reasons – reasons which I have a better chance of appreciating than any one else could.'

She touched her damaged cheek.

'You see this? You've probably heard about it?' Poirot nodded. 'Caroline did that. That's why I'm sure – I *know* – that she didn't do murder.'

'It would not be a convincing argument to most people.'

'No, it would be the opposite. It was actually used in that way, I believe. As evidence that Caroline had a violent and ungovernable temper! Because she had injured me as a baby, learned men argued that she would be equally capable of poisoning an unfaithful husband.'

Poirot said:

'I, at least, appreciated the difference. A sudden fit of ungovernable rage does not lead you to first abstract a poison and then use it deliberately on the following day.'

Angela Warren waved an impatient hand.

'That's not what I mean at all. I must try and make it plain to you. Supposing that you are a person normally

131

affectionate and of kindly disposition – but that you are also liable to intense jealousy. And supposing that during the years of your life when control is most difficult, you do, in a fit of rage, come near to committing what is, in effect, murder. Think of the awful shock, the horror, the remorse that seizes upon you. To a sensitive person, like Caroline, that horror and remorse will never quite leave you. It never left her. I don't suppose I was consciously aware of it at the time, but looking back I recognize it perfectly. Caro was haunted, continually haunted, by the fact that she had injured me. That knowledge never left her in peace. It coloured all her actions. It explained her attitude to me. Nothing was too good for me. In her eyes, I must always come first. Half the quarrels she had with Amyas were on my account. I was inclined to be jealous of him and played all kinds of tricks on him. I pinched cat stuff to put in his drink, and once I put a hedgehog in his bed. But Caroline was always on my side.'

Miss Warren paused, then she went on:

'It was very bad for me, of course. I got horribly spoilt. But that's neither here nor there. We're discussing the effect on Caroline. The result of that impulse to violence was a life-long abhorrence of any further act of the same kind. Caro was always watching herself, always in fear that something of that kind might happen again. And she took her own ways of guarding against it. One of these ways was a great extravagance of language. She felt (and I think, psychologically quite truly) that if she were violent enough in speech she would have no temptation to violence in action. She found by experience that the method worked. That's why I've heard Caro say things like "I'd like to cut so and so in pieces and boil him slowly in oil." And she'd say to me, or to Amyas, "If you go on annoying me I shall murder you." In the same way she quarrelled easily and violently. She recognized, I think, the impulse to violence that there was in her nature, and she deliberately gave it an outlet that way. She and Amyas used to have the most fantastic and lurid quarrels.'

Hercule Poirot nodded.

'Yes, there was evidence of that. They quarrelled like cat and dog, it was said.'

Angela Warren said:

'Exactly. That's what is so stupid and misleading about evidence. Of course Caro and Amyas quarrelled! Of course they said bitter and outrageous and cruel things to each other! What nobody appreciates is that they *enjoyed* quarrelling. But they did! Amyas enjoyed it too. They were that kind of couple. They both of them liked drama and emotional scenes. Most men don't. They like peace. But Amyas was an artist. He liked shouting and threatening and generally being outrageous. It was like letting off steam to him. He was the kind of man who when he loses his collar stud bellows the house down. It sounds very odd, I know, but living that way with continual rows and makings-up was Amyas's and Caroline's idea of fun!'

She made an impatient gesture.

'If they'd only not hustled me away and let me give evidence, I'd have told them that.' Then she shrugged her shoulders. 'But I don't suppose they would have believed me. And anyway then it wouldn't have been as clear in my mind as it is now. It was the kind of thing I knew but hadn't thought about and certainly had never dreamed of putting into words.'

She looked across at Poirot.

'You do see what I mean?'

He nodded vigorously.

'I see perfectly – and I realize the absolute rightness of what you have said. There are people to whom agreement is monotony. They require the stimulant of dissension to create drama in their lives.'

'Exactly.'

'May I ask you, Miss Warren, what were your own feelings at the time?'

Angela Warren sighed.

'Mostly bewilderment and helplessness, I think. It seemed a fantastic nightmare. Caroline was arrested very soon – about three days afterwards, I think. I can still remember my indignation, my dumb fury – and, of course, my childish faith that it was just a silly mistake, that it would be all right. Caro was chiefly perturbed about *me* – she wanted me kept right away from it all as far as possible. She got Miss Williams to take me away to some relations almost at once. The police had no objection. And then, when it was decided that my evidence would not be needed, arrangements were made for me to go to school abroad.

'I hated going, of course. But it was explained to me that Caro had me terribly on her mind and that the only way I could help her was by going.'

She paused. Then she said:

'So I went to Munich. I was there when – when the verdict was given. They never let me go to see Caro. Caro wouldn't have it. That's the only time, I think, when she failed in understanding.'

'You cannot be sure of that, Miss Warren. To visit someone dearly loved in a prison might make a terrible impression on a young sensitive girl.'

'Possibly.'

Angela Warren got up. She said:

'After the verdict, when she had been condemned, my sister wrote me a letter. I have never shown it to any one. I think I ought to show it to you now. It may help you to understand the kind of person Caroline was. If you like you may take it to show to Carla also.'

She went to the door, then turning back she said:

'Come with me. There is a portrait of Caroline in my room.'

For a second time, Poirot stood gazing up at a portrait.

As a painting, Caroline Crale's portrait was mediocre. But Poirot looked at it with interest – it was not its artistic value that interested him.

He saw a long oval face, a gracious line of jaw and a sweet, slightly timid expression. It was a face uncertain of itself, emotional, with a withdrawn hidden beauty. It lacked the forcefulness and vitality of her daughter's face – that energy and joy of life Carla Lemarchant had doubtless inherited from her father. This was a less positive creature. Yet, looking at the painted face, Hercule Poirot understood why an imaginative man like Quentin Fogg had not been able to forget her.

Angela Warren stood at his side again – a letter in her hand.

She said quietly:

'Now that you have seen what she was like – read her letter.'

He unfolded it carefully and read what Caroline Crale had written sixteen years ago.

My darling little Angela,

You will hear bad news and you will grieve, but what I want to impress upon you is that it is all all right. I have never told you lies and I don't now when I say that I am actually happy – that I feel an essential rightness and a peace that I have never known before. It's all right, darling, it's all right. Don't look back and regret and grieve for me – go on with your life and succeed. You can, I know. It's all, all right, darling, and I'm going to Amyas. I haven't the least doubt that we shall be together. I couldn't have lived without him . . . Do this one thing for me – be happy. I've told you – I'm happy. One has to pay one's debts. It's lovely to feel peaceful.

> *Your loving sister,*
>
> *Caro*

Hercule Poirot read it through twice. Then he handed it back. He said:

'That is a very beautiful letter, mademoiselle – and a very remarkable one. A *very* remarkable one.'

'Caroline,' said Angela Warren, 'was a very remarkable person.'

'Yes, an unusual mind . . . You take it that this letter indicates innocence?'

'Of course it does!'

'It does not say so explicitly.'

'Because Caro would know that I'd never dream of her being guilty!'

'Perhaps – perhaps . . . But it might be taken another way. In the sense that she was guilty and that in expiating her crime she will find peace.'

It fitted in, he thought, with the description of her in court. And he experienced in this moment the strongest doubts he had yet felt of the course to which he had committed himself. Everything so far had pointed unswervingly to Caroline Crale's guilt. Now, even her own words testified against her.

On the other side was only the unshaken conviction of Angela Warren. Angela had known her well, undoubtedly, but might not her certainty be the fanatical loyalty of an adolescent girl, up in arms for a dearly loved sister?

As though she had read his thoughts Angela Warren said:

'No, M. Poirot – I *know* Caroline wasn't guilty.'

Poirot said briskly:

'The Bon Dieu knows I do not want to shake you on that point. But let us be practical. You say your sister was not guilty. Very well, then, *what really happened*?'

Angela nodded thoughtfully. She said:

'That is difficult, I agree. I suppose that, as Caroline said, Amyas committed suicide.'

'Is that likely from what you know of his character?'

'Very unlikely.'

'But you do not say, as in the first case, that you *know* it is impossible?'

'No, because, as I said just now, most people *do* do impossible things – that is to say things that seem out of

136

character. But I presume, if you know them intimately, it wouldn't be out of character.'

'You knew your brother-in-law well?'

'Yes, but not like I knew Caro. It seems to me quite fantastic that Amyas should have killed himself – but I suppose he *could* have done so. In fact, he *must* have done so.'

'You cannot see any other explanation?'

Angela accepted the suggestion calmly, but not without a certain stirring of interest.

'Oh, I see what you mean . . . I've never really considered that possibility. You mean one of the other people killed him? That it was a deliberate cold-blooded murder . . .'

'It might have been, might it not?'

'Yes, it might have been . . . But it certainly seems very unlikely.'

'More unlikely than suicide?'

'That's difficult to say . . . On the face of it, there was no reason for suspecting anybody else. There isn't now when I look back . . .'

'All the same, let us consider the possibility. Who of those intimately concerned would you say was – shall we say – the most likely person?'

'Let me think. Well, I didn't kill him. And the Elsa creature certainly didn't. She was mad with rage when he died. Who else was there? Meredith Blake? He was always very devoted to Caroline, quite a tame cat about the house. I suppose that *might* give him a motive in a way. In a book he might have wanted to get Amyas out of the way so that he himself could marry Caroline. But he could have achieved that just as well by letting Amyas go off with Elsa and then in due time consoling Caroline. Besides I really can't *see* Meredith as a murderer. Too mild and too cautious. Who else was there?'

Poirot suggested: 'Miss Williams? Philip Blake?'

Angela's grave face relaxed into a smile for a minute.

'Miss Williams? One can't really make oneself believe that one's governess could commit a murder! Miss Williams was always so unyielding and so full of rectitude.'

She paused a minute and then went on:

'She was devoted to Caroline, of course. Would have done anything for her. And she hated Amyas. She was a great feminist and disliked men. Is that enough for murder? Surely not.'

'It would hardly seem so,' agreed Poirot.

Angela went on:

'Philip Blake?' She was silent for some few moments. Then she said quietly: 'I think, you know, if we're just talking of *likelihoods, he's* the most likely person.'

Poirot said:

'You interest me very much, Miss Warren. May I ask why you say that?'

'Nothing at all definite. But from what I remember of him, I should say he was a person of rather limited imagination.'

'And a limited imagination predisposes you to murder?'

'It might lead you to take a crude way of settling your difficulties. Men of that type get a certain satisfaction from action of some kind or other. Murder is a very crude business, don't you think so?'

'Yes – I think you are right . . . It is definitely a point of view, that. But all the same, Miss Warren, there must be more to it than that. What motive could Philip Blake possibly have had?'

Angela Warren did not answer at once. She stood frowning down at the floor.

Hercule Poirot said:

'He was Amyas Crale's best friend, was he not?'

She nodded.

'But there is something in your mind, Miss Warren. Something that you have not yet told me. Were the two men rivals, perhaps, over the girl – over Elsa?'

Angela Warren shook her head.

'Oh, no, not Phillip.'

'What is there then?'

Angela Warren said slowly:

'Do you know the way that things suddenly come back to you – after years perhaps. I'll explain what I mean. Somebody told me a story once, when I was eleven. I saw no point in that story whatsoever. It didn't worry me – it just passed straight over my head. I don't believe I ever, as they say, thought of it again. But about two years ago, sitting in the stalls at a revue, that story came back to me, and I was so surprised that I actually said aloud, "Oh, *now* I see the point of that silly story about the rice pudding." And yet there had been no direct allusion on the same lines – only some fun sailing rather near the wind.'

Poirot said: 'I understand what you mean, mademoiselle.'

'Then you will understand what I am going to tell you. I was once staying at a hotel. As I walked along a passage, one of the bedroom doors opened and a woman I knew came out. It was not her bedroom – and she registered the fact plainly on her face when she saw me.

'*And I knew then the meaning of the expression I had once seen on Caroline's face when at Alderbury she came out of Philip Blake's room one night.*'

She leant forward, stopping Poirot's words.

'I had no idea at the *time*, you understand. I *knew* things – girls of the age I was usually do – but I didn't connect them with reality. Caroline coming out of Philip Blake's bedroom was just Caroline coming out of Philip Blake's bedroom to me. It might have been Miss Williams's room or my room. But what I *did* notice was the expression on her face – a queer expression that I didn't know and couldn't understand. I didn't understand it until, as I have told you, the night in Paris when I saw that same expression on another woman's face.'

Poirot said slowly:

'But what you tell me, Miss Warren, is sufficiently astonishing. From Philip Blake himself I got the impression that he disliked your sister and always had done so.'

Angela said:

'I know. I can't explain it but there it is.'

Poirot nodded slowly. Already, in his interview with Philip Blake, he had felt vaguely that something did not ring true. That overdone animosity against Caroline – it had not, somehow, been natural.

And the words and phrases from his conversation with Meredith Blake came back to him. 'Very upset when Amyas married – did not go near them for over a year . . .'

Had Philip, then, always been in love with Caroline? And had his love, when she chose Amyas, turned to bitterness and hate?

Yes, Philip had been too vehement – too biased. Poirot visualized him thoughtfully – the cheerful prosperous man with his golf and his comfortable house. What had Philip Blake really felt sixteen years ago.

Angela Warren was speaking.

'I don't understand it. You see, I've no experience in love affairs – they haven't come my way. I've told you this for what it's worth in case – in case it might have a bearing on what happened.'

BOOK II

(Covering letter received with manuscript)

Dear M. Poirot,

I am fulfilling my promise and herewith find enclosed an account of the events relating to the death of Amyas Crale. After such a lapse of time I am bound to point out that my memories may not be strictly accurate, but I have put down what occurred to the best of my recollection.

Yours truly,

Philip Blake

NOTES ON PROGRESS OF EVENTS LEADING UP TO MURDER OF AMYAS CRALE ON SEPT., 19 . . .

My friendship with deceased dates back to a very early period. His home and mine were next door to each other in the country, and our families were friends. Amyas Crale was a little over two years older than I was. We played together as boys, in the holidays, though we were not at the same school.

From the point of view of my long knowledge of the man I feel myself particularly qualified to testify as to his character and general outlook on life. And I will say this straight away – to any one who knew Amyas Crale well – the notion of his committing suicide is quite ridiculous. Crale would *never* have taken his own life. He was far too fond of living! The contention of the defence at the trial that Crale was obsessed by conscience, and took poison in a fit of remorse, is utterly absurd to any one who knew the man. Crale, I should say, had very little conscience, and certainly not a morbid one. Moreover, he and his wife were on bad terms,

143

and I don't think he would have had any scruples about breaking up what was, to him, a very unsatisfactory married life. He was prepared to look after her financial welfare and that of the child of the marriage, and I am sure would have done so generously. He was a very generous man – and altogether a warm-hearted and lovable person. Not only was he a great painter, but he was a man whose friends were devoted to him. As far as I know he had no enemies.

I had also known Caroline Crale for many years. I knew her before her marriage, when she used to come and stay at Alderbury. She was then a somewhat neurotic girl, subject to uncontrollable outbursts of temper, not without attraction, but unquestionably a difficult person to live with.

She showed her devotion to Amyas almost immediately. He, I do not think, was really very much in love with her. But they were frequently thrown together – she was, as I say, attractive, and they eventually became engaged. Amyas Crale's best friends were rather apprehensive about the marriage, as they felt that Caroline was quite unsuited to him.

This caused a certain amount of strain in the first few years between Crale's wife and Crale's friends, but Amyas was a loyal friend and was not disposed to give up his old friends at the bidding of his wife. After a few years, he and I were on the same old terms and I was a frequent visitor at Alderbury. I may add that I stood godfather to the little girl, Carla. This proves, I think, that Amyas considered me his best friend, and it gives me authority to speak for a man who can no longer speak for himself.

To come to the actual events of which I have been asked to write, I arrived down at Alderbury (so I see by an old diary) five days before the crime. That is, on Sept. 13th. I was conscious at once of a certain tension in the atmosphere. There was also staying in the house Miss Elsa Greer whom Amyas was painting at the time.

It was the first time I had seen Miss Greer in the flesh, but I had been aware of her existence for some time. Amyas had raved about her to me a month previously. He had met, he said, a marvellous girl. He talked about her so enthusiastically that I said to him jokingly: 'Be careful, old boy, or you'll be losing your head again.' He told me not to be a bloody fool. He was painting the girl; he'd no personal interest in her. I said: 'Tell that to the marines! I've heard you say that before.' He said: 'This time it's different'; to which I answered somewhat cynically: 'It always is!' Amyas then looked quite worried and anxious. He said: 'You don't understand. She's just a girl. Not much more than a child.' He added that she had very modern views and was absolutely free from old-fashioned prejudices. He said: 'She's honest and natural and absolutely fearless!'

I thought to myself, though I didn't say so, that Amyas had certainly got it badly this time. A few weeks later I heard comments from other people. It was said that the 'Greer girl was absolutely infatuated.' Somebody else said that it was a bit thick of Amyas considering how young the girl was, whereupon somebody else sniggered and said that Elsa Greer knew her way about all right. Further remarks were that the girl was rolling in money and had always got everything she wanted, and also that 'she was the one who was making most of the running.' There was a question as to what Crale's wife thought about it – and the significant reply that she must be used to that sort of thing by now, to which someone demurred by saying they'd heard that she was jealous as hell and led Crale such an impossible life that any man would be justified in having a fling from time to time.

I mention all this because I think it is important that the state of affairs before I got down there should be fully realized.

I was interested to see the girl – she was remarkably good-looking and very attractive – and I was, I must admit,

145

maliciously amused to note that Caroline was cutting up very rough indeed.

Amyas Crale himself was less light-hearted than usual. Though to any one who did not know him well, his manner would have appeared much as usual, I who knew him so intimately noted at once various signs of strain, uncertain temper, fits of moody abstraction, general irritability of manner.

Although he was always inclined to be moody when painting, the picture he was at work upon did not account entirely for the strain he showed. He was pleased to see me and said as soon as we were alone: 'Thank goodness you've turned up, Phil. Living in a house with four women is enough to send any man clean off his chump. Between them all they'll send me into a lunatic asylum.'

It was certainly an uncomfortable atmosphere. Caroline, as I said, was obviously cutting up rough about the whole thing. In a polite, well-bred way, she was ruder to Elsa than one would believe possible – without a single actually offensive word. Elsa herself was openly and flagrantly rude to Caroline. She was top dog and she knew it – and no scruples of good breeding restrained her from overt bad manners. The result was that Crale spent most of his time scrapping with the girl Angela when he wasn't painting. They were usually on affectionate terms, though they teased and fought a good deal. But on this occasion there was an edge in everything Amyas said or did, and the two of them really lost their tempers with each other. The fourth member of the party was the governess. 'A sour-faced hag,' Amyas called her. 'She hates me like poison. Sits there with her lips set together, disapproving of me without stopping.'

It was then that he said:

'God damn all women! If a man is to have any peace he must steer clear of women!'

'You oughtn't to have married,' I said. 'You're the sort of man who ought to have kept clear of domestic ties.'

He replied that it was too late to talk about that now. He added that no doubt Caroline would be only too glad to get rid of him. That was the first indication I had that something unusual was in the wind.

I said: 'What's all this? Is this business with the lovely Elsa serious then?' He said with a sort of groan:

'She *is* lovely, isn't she? Sometimes I wish I'd never seen her.'

I said: 'Look here, old boy, you must take a hold on yourself. You don't want to get tied up with any more women.' He looked at me and laughed. He said: 'It's all very well for you to talk. I can't let women alone – simply can't do it – and if I could, they wouldn't let me alone!' Then he shrugged those great shoulders of his, grinned at me and said: 'Oh well, it will all pan out in the end, I expect. And you must admit the picture is good?'

He was referring to the portrait he was doing of Elsa, and although I had very little technical knowledge of painting, even I could see that it was going to be a work of especial power.

Whilst he was painting, Amyas was a different man. Although he would growl, groan, frown, swear extravagantly, and sometimes hurl his brushes away, he was really intensely happy.

It was only when he came back to the house for meals that the hostile atmosphere between the women got him down. That hostility came to a head on Sept. 17th. We had had an embarrassing lunch. Elsa had been particularly – really, I think *insolent* is the only word for it! She had ignored Caroline pointedly, persistently addressing the conversation to Amyas as though he and she were alone in the room. Caroline had talked lightly and gaily to the rest of us, cleverly contriving so that several perfectly innocent-sounding remarks should have a sting. She hadn't got Elsa Greer's scornful honesty – with Caroline every thing was oblique, suggested rather than said.

147

Things came to a head after lunch in the drawing-room just as we were finishing coffee. I had commented on a carved head in highly polished beechwood – a very curious thing, and Caroline said: 'That is the work of a young Norwegian sculptor. Amyas and I admire his work very much. We hope to go and see him next summer.' That calm assumption of possession was too much for Elsa. She was never one to let a challenge pass. She waited a minute or two and then she spoke in her clear, rather over-emphasized voice. She said: 'This would be a lovely room if it was properly fixed. It's got far too much furniture in it. When I'm living here I shall take all the rubbish out and just leave one or two good pieces. And I shall have copper-coloured curtains, I think – so that the setting sun will just catch them through that big western window.' She turned to me and said. 'Don't you think that would be rather lovely?'

I didn't have time to answer. Caroline spoke, and her voice was soft and silky and what I can only describe as dangerous. She said:

'Are you thinking of buying this place, Elsa?'

Elsa said: 'It won't be necessary for me to buy it.'

Caroline said: 'What do you mean?' And there was no softness in her voice now. It was hard and metallic. Elsa laughed. She said: 'Must we pretend? Come now, Caroline, you know very well what I mean!'

Caroline said: 'I've no idea.'

Elsa said to that: 'Don't be such an ostrich. It's no good pretending you don't see and know all about it. Amyas and I care for each other. This isn't your home. It's his. And after we're married I shall live here with him!'

Caroline said: 'I think you're crazy.'

Elsa said: 'Oh no, I'm not, my dear, and you know it. It would be much simpler if we were honest with each other. Amyas and I love each other – you've seen that clearly enough. There's only one decent thing for you to do. You've got to give him his freedom.'

148

Caroline said: 'I don't believe a word of what you are saying.'

But her voice was unconvincing. Elsa had got under her guard all right.

And at that minute Amyas Crale came into the room and Elsa said with a laugh:

'If you don't believe me, ask him.'

And Caroline said: 'I will.'

She didn't pause at all. She said:

'Amyas, Elsa says you want to marry her. Is this true?'

Poor Amyas. I felt sorry for him. It makes a man feel a fool to have a scene of that kind forced upon him. He went crimson and started blustering. He turned on Elsa and asked her why the devil she couldn't have held her tongue?

Caroline said: 'Then it *is* true?'

He didn't say anything, just stood there passing his finger round inside the neck of his shirt. He used to do that as a kid when he got into a jam of any kind. He said – and he tried to make the words sound dignified and authoritative – and of course couldn't manage it, poor devil:

'I don't want to discuss it.'

Caroline said: 'But we're going to discuss it!'

Elsa chipped in and said:

'I think it's only fair to Caroline that she should be told.'

Caroline said, very quietly:

'Is it true, Amyas?'

He looked a bit ashamed of himself. Men do when women pin them down in a corner.

She said:

'Answer me, please. I've got to know.'

He flung up his head then – rather the way a bull does in the bull-ring. He snapped out:

'It's true enough – but I don't want to discuss it now.'

And he turned and strode out of the room. I went after him. I didn't want to be left with the women. I caught up with him on the terrace. He was swearing. I never knew a man swear more heartily. Then he raved:

149

'Why couldn't she hold her tongue? Why the devil couldn't she hold her tongue? Now the fat's in the fire. And I've got to finish that picture – do you hear, Phil? It's the best thing I've done. The best thing I've ever done in my *life*. And a couple of damn' fool women want to muck it up between them!'

Then he calmed down a little and said women had no sense of proportion.

I couldn't help smiling a little. I said:

'Well, dash it all, old boy, you have brought this on yourself.'

'Don't I know it,' he said, and groaned. Then he added: 'But you must admit, Phil, that a man couldn't be blamed for losing his head about her. Even Caroline ought to understand that.'

I asked him what would happen if Caroline got her back up and refused to give him a divorce.

But by now he had gone off into a fit of abstraction. I repeated the remark and he said absently:

'Caroline would never be vindictive. You don't understand, old boy.'

'There's the child,' I pointed out.

He took me by the arm.

'Phil, old boy, you mean well – but don't go on croaking like a raven. I can manage my affairs. Everything will turn out all right. You'll see if it doesn't.'

That was Amyas all over – an absolutely unjustified optimist. He said now, cheerfully:

'To hell with the whole pack of them!'

I don't know whether we would have said anything more, but a few minutes later Caroline swept out on the terrace. She'd got a hat on, a queer, flopping, dark-brown hat, rather attractive.

She said in an absolutely ordinary, every-day voice:

'Take off that paint-stained coat, Amyas. We're going over to Meredith's to tea – don't you remember?'

He stared, stammered a bit as he said:

'Oh, I'd forgotten. Yes, of c-c-course we are.'

She said:

'Then go and try and make yourself look less like a rag-and-bone man.'

Although her voice was quite natural, she didn't look at him. She moved over towards a bed of dahlias and began picking off some of the overblown flowers.

Amyas turned round slowly and went into the house.

Caroline talked to me. She talked a good deal. About the chances of the weather lasting. And whether there might be mackerel about, and if so Amyas and Angela and I might like to go fishing. She was really amazing. I've got to hand it to her.

But I think, myself, that that showed the sort of woman she was. She had enormous strength of will and complete command over herself. I don't know whether she'd made up her mind to kill him then – but I shouldn't be surprised. And she was capable of making her plans carefully and unemotionally, with an absolutely clear and ruthless mind.

Caroline Crale was a very dangerous woman. I ought to have realized then that she wasn't prepared to take this thing lying down. But like a fool I thought that she had made up her mind to accept the inevitable – or else possibly she thought that if she carried on exactly as usual Amyas might change his mind.

Presently the others came out. Elsa looking defiant – but at the same time triumphant. Caroline took no notice of her. Angela really saved the situation. She came out arguing with Miss Williams that she wasn't going to change her skirt for any one. It was quite all right – good enough for darling old Meredith anyway – *he* never noticed anything.

We got off at last. Caroline walked with Angela. And I walked with Amyas. And Elsa walked by herself – smiling.

I didn't admire her myself – too violent a type – but I have to admit that she looked incredibly beautiful that afternoon. Women do when they've got what they want.

I can't remember the events of that afternoon clearly at all.

It's all blurred. I remember old Merry coming out to meet us. I think we walked round the garden first. I remember having a long discussion with Angela about the training of terriers for ratting. She ate an incredible lot of apples, and tried to persuade me to do so too.

When we got back to the house, tea was going on under the big cedar tree. Merry, I remember, was looking very upset. I suppose either Caroline or Amyas had told him something. He was looking doubtfully at Caroline, and then he stared at Elsa. The old boy looked thoroughly worried. Of course Caroline liked to have Meredith on a string more or less, the devoted, platonic friend who would never, never go too far. She was that kind of woman.

After tea Meredith had a hurried word with me. He said:

'Look here, Phil, Amyas *can't* do this thing!'

I said:

'Make no mistake, he's going to do it.'

'He can't leave his wife and child and go off with this girl. He's years older than she is. She can't be more than eighteen.'

I said to him that Miss Greer was a fully sophisticated twenty.

He said: 'Anyway, that's under age. She can't know what she's doing.'

Poor old Meredith. Always the chivalrous pukka sahib. I said:

'Don't worry, old boy. *She* knows what she's doing, *and* she likes it!'

That's all we had the chance of saying. I thought to myself that probably Merry felt disturbed at the thought of Caroline being a deserted wife. Once the divorce was through she might expect her faithful Dobbin to marry her. I had an idea that hopeless devotion was really far more in his line. I must confess that that side of it amused me.

Curiously enough I remember very little about our visit to Meredith's stink room. He enjoyed showing people his hobby. Personally I always found it very boring. I suppose I was in there with the rest of them when he gave a dissertation on the efficacy of coniine, but I don't remember it. And I didn't see Caroline pinch the stuff. As I've said, she was a very adroit woman. I do remember Meredith reading aloud the passage from Plato describing Socrates' death. Very boring I thought it. Classics always did bore me.

There's nothing much more I can remember about that day. Amyas and Angela had a first-class row, I know, and the rest of us rather welcomed it. It avoided other difficulties. Angela rushed off to bed with a final vituperative outburst. She said A, she'd pay him out. B, she wished he were dead. C, she hoped he'd die of leprosy, it would serve him right. D, she wished a sausage would stick to his nose, like in the fairy story, and never come off. When she'd gone we all laughed, we couldn't help it, it was such a funny mixture.

Caroline went up to bed immediately afterwards. Miss Williams disappeared after her pupil. Amyas and Elsa went off together into the garden. It was clear that I wasn't wanted. I went for a stroll by myself. It was a lovely night.

I came down late the following morning. There was no one in the dining-room. Funny the things you do remember. I remember the taste of the kidneys and bacon I ate quite well. They were very good kidneys. Devilled.

Afterwards I wandered out looking for everybody. I went outside, didn't see anybody, smoked a cigarette, encountered Miss Williams running about looking for Angela, who had played truant as usual when she ought to have been mending a torn frock. I went back into the hall and realized that Amyas and Caroline were having a set-to in the library. They were talking very loud. I heard her say:

'You and your women! I'd like to kill you. Some day I will kill you.' Amyas said: 'Don't be a fool, Caroline.' And she said: 'I mean it, Amyas.'

Well, I didn't want to overhear any more. I went out

again. I wandered along the terrace the other way and came across Elsa.

She was sitting on one of the long seats. The seat was directly under the library window, and the window was open. I should imagine that there wasn't much she had missed of what was going on inside. When she saw me she got up as cool as a cucumber and came towards me. She was smiling. She took my arm and said:

'Isn't it a lovely morning?'

It was a lovely morning for her all right! Rather a cruel girl. No, I think merely honest and lacking in imagination. What she wanted herself was the only thing that she could see.

We'd been standing on the terrace talking for about five minutes, when I heard the library door bang and Amyas Crale came out. He was very red in the face.

He caught hold of Elsa unceremoniously by the shoulder.

He said: 'Come on, time for you to sit. I want to get on with that picture.'

She said: 'All right. I'll just go up and get a pullover. There's a chilly wind.'

She went into the house.

I wondered if Amyas would say anything to me, but he didn't say much. Just: 'These women!'

I said: 'Cheer up, old boy.'

Then we neither of us said anything till Elsa came out of the house again.

They went off together down to the Battery garden. I went into the house. Caroline was standing in the hall. I don't think she even noticed me. It was a way of hers at times. She'd seem to go right away – to get inside herself as it were. She just murmured something. Not to me – to herself. I just caught the words:

'It's too cruel . . .'

That's what she said. Then she walked past me and upstairs, still without seeming to see me – just like a person intent on some inner vision. I think myself (I've no authority for saying this, you understand) that she went up to get the stuff, and that it was then she decided to do what she did do.

And just at that moment the telephone rang. In some houses one would wait for the servants to answer it, but I was so often at Alderbury that I acted more or less as one of the family. I picked up the receiver.

It was my brother Meredith's voice that answered. He was very upset. He explained that he had been into his laboratory and that the coniine bottle was half-empty.

I don't need to go again over all the things I know now I ought to have done. The thing was so startling and I was foolish enough to be taken aback. Meredith was dithering a good bit at the other end. I heard someone on the stairs, and I just told him sharply to come over at once.

I myself went down to meet him. In case you don't know the lay of the land, the shortest way from one estate to the other was by rowing across a small creek. I went down the path to where the boats were kept by a small jetty. To do so I passed under the wall of the Battery garden. I could hear Elsa and Amyas talking as he painted. They sounded very cheerful and carefree. Amyas said it was an amazingly hot day (so it was very hot for September), and Elsa said that sitting where she was, poised on the battlements, there was a cold wind blowing in from the sea. And then she said: 'I'm horribly stiff from posing. Can't I have a rest, darling?' And I heard Amyas cry out: 'Not on your life. Stick it. You're a tough girl. And this is going good, I tell you.' I heard Elsa say, 'Brute' and laugh, as I went out of earshot.

Meredith was just rowing himself across from the other side. I waited for him. He tied up the boat and came up the steps. He was looking very white and worried. He said to me:

'Your head's better than mine, Philip. What ought I to do? That stuff's dangerous.'

155

I said: 'Are you absolutely sure about this?' Meredith, you see, was always a rather vague kind of chap. Perhaps that's why I didn't take it as seriously as I ought to have done. And he said he was quite sure. The bottle had been full yesterday afternoon.

I said: 'And you've absolutely *no* idea who pinched it?'

He said none whatever and asked me what *I* thought. Could it have been one of the servants? I said I supposed it might have been, but it seemed unlikely to me. He always kept the door locked, didn't he? Always, he said, and then began a rigmarole about having found the window a few inches open at the bottom. Someone might have got in that way.

'A chance burglar?' I asked sceptically. 'It seems to me, Meredith, that there are some very nasty possibilities.'

He said what did I really think? And I said, if he was sure he wasn't making a mistake, that probably Caroline had taken it to poison Elsa with – or that alternatively Elsa had taken it to get Caroline out of the way and straighten the path of true love.

Meredith twittered a bit. He said it was absurd and melodramatic and couldn't be true. I said: 'Well, the stuff's gone. What's *your* explanation?' He hadn't any, of course. Actually thought just as I did, but didn't want to face the fact.

He said again: 'What are we to do?'

I said, damned fool that I was: 'We must think it over carefully. Either you'd better announce your loss, straight out when everybody's there, or else you'd better get Caroline alone and tax her with it. If you're convinced *she's* nothing to do with it, adopt the same tactics for Elsa.' He said: 'A girl like that! She couldn't have taken it.' I said I wouldn't put it past her.

We were walking up to the house as we talked. After that last remark of mine neither of us spoke for some few seconds. We were rounding the Battery garden again and I heard Caroline's voice.

I thought perhaps a three-handed row was going on, but

actually it was Angela that they were discussing. Caroline was protesting. She said: 'It's very hard on the girl.' And Amyas made some impatient rejoinder. Then the door to the garden opened just as we came abreast of it. Amyas looked a little taken aback at seeing us. Caroline was just coming out. She said: 'Hallo, Meredith. We've been discussing the question of Angela's going to school. I'm not at all sure it's the right thing for her.' Amyas said: 'Don't fuss about the girl. She'll be all right. Good riddance.'

Just then Elsa came running down the path from the house. She had some sort of scarlet jumper in her hand. Amyas growled:

'Come along. Get back into the pose. I don't want to waste time.'

He went back to where his easel was standing. I noticed that he staggered a bit and I wondered if he had been drinking. A man might easily be excused for doing so with all the fuss and the scenes.

He grumbled.

'The beer here is red hot. Why can't we keep some ice down here?'

And Caroline Crale said:

'I'll send you down some beer just off the ice.'

Amyas grunted out:

'Thanks.'

Then Caroline shut the door of the Battery garden and came up with us to the house. We sat down on the terrace and she went into the house. About five minutes later Angela came along with a couple of bottles of beer and some glasses. It was a hot day and we were glad to see it. As we were drinking it Caroline passed us. She was carrying another bottle and said she would take it down to Amyas. Meredith said he'd go, but she was quite firm that she'd go herself. I thought – fool that I was – that it was just her jealousy. She couldn't stand those two being alone down there. That was what had taken her down there once already with the weak pretext of arguing about Angela's departure.

·She went off down that zigzag path – and Meredith and I watched her go. We'd still not decided anything, and now Angela clamoured that I should come bathing with her. It seemed impossible to get Meredith alone. I just said to him: 'After lunch.' And he nodded.

Then I went off bathing with Angela. We had a good swim – across the creek and back, and then we lay out on the rocks sunbathing. Angela was a bit taciturn and that suited me. I made up my mind that directly after lunch I'd take Caroline aside and accuse her point-blank of having stolen the stuff. No use letting Meredith do it – he'd be too weak. No, I'd tax her with it outright. After that she'd have to give it back, or even if she didn't she wouldn't dare use it. I was pretty sure it must be her on thinking things over. Elsa was far too sensible and hard-boiled a young woman to risk tampering with poisons. She had a hard head and would take care of her own skin. Caroline was made of more dangerous stuff – unbalanced, carried away by impulses and definitely neurotic. And still, you know, at the back of my mind was the feeling that Meredith *might* have made a mistake. Or some servant might have been poking about in there and spilt the stuff and then not dared to own up. You see, poison seems such a melodramatic thing – you can't believe in it.

Not till it happens.

It was quite late when I looked at my watch, and Angela and I fairly raced up to lunch. They were just sitting down – all but Amyas, who had remained down in the Battery painting. Quite a normal thing for him to do – and privately I thought him very wise to elect to do it today. Lunch was likely to have been an awkward meal.

We had coffee on the terrace. I wish I could remember better how Caroline looked and acted. She didn't seem excited in any way. Quiet and rather sad is my impression. What a devil that woman was!

For it is a devilish thing to do, to poison a man in cold

blood. If there had been a revolver about and she caught it up and shot him – well, that might have been understandable. But this cold, deliberate, vindictive poisoning. . . . And so calm and collected.

She got up and said she'd take his coffee to him in the most natural way possible. And yet she knew – she must have known – that by now she'd find him dead. Miss Williams went with her. I don't remember if that was at Caroline's suggestion or not. I rather think it was.

The two women went off together. Meredith strolled away shortly afterwards. I was just making an excuse to go after him, when he came running up the path again. His face was grey. He gasped out:

'We must get a doctor – quick – Amyas –'

I sprang up.

'Is he ill – dying?'

Meredith said:

'I'm afraid he's dead . . .'

We'd forgotten Elsa for the minute. But she let out a sudden cry. It was like the wail of a banshee.

She cried:

'Dead? Dead? . . .' And then she ran. I didn't know any one could move like that – like a deer – like a stricken thing. And like an avenging Fury, too.

Meredith panted out:

'Go after her. I'll telephone. Go after her. You don't know what she'll do.'

I did go after her – and it's as well I did. She might quite easily have killed Caroline. I've never seen such grief and such frenzied hate. All the veneer of refinement and education was stripped off. You could see her father and her father's mother and father had been millhands. Deprived of her lover, she was just elemental woman. She'd have clawed Caroline's face, torn her hair, hurled her over the parapet if she could. She thought for some reason or other that Caroline had knifed him. She'd got it all wrong – naturally.

I held her off, and then Miss Williams took charge. She was good, I must say. She got Elsa to control herself in under a minute – told her she'd got to be quiet and that we couldn't have this noise and violence going on. She was a tartar, that woman. But she did the trick. Elsa was quiet – just stood there gasping and trembling.

As for Caroline, so far as I am concerned, the mask was right off. She stood there perfectly quiet – you might have said dazed. But she wasn't dazed. It was her eyes gave her away. They were watchful – fully aware and quietly watchful. She'd begun, I suppose, to be afraid . . .

I went up to her and spoke to her. I said it quite low. I don't think either of the two women overheard.

I said:

'You damned murderess, you've killed my best friend.'

She shrank back. She said:

'No – oh no – he – he did it himself . . ,'

I looked her full in the eyes. I said:

'You can tell that story – to the police.'

She did – and they didn't believe her.

End of Philip Blake's Statement.

Dear M. Poirot,

As I promised you, I have set down in writing an account of all I can remember relating to the tragic events that happened sixteen years ago. First of all I would like to say that I have thought over carefully all you said to me at our recent meeting. And on reflection I am more convinced than I was before that it is in the highest degree unlikely that Caroline Crale poisoned her husband. It always seemed incongruous, but the absence of any other explanation and her own attitude led me to follow, sheep-like, the opinion of other people and to say with them – that if she didn't do it, what explanation could there be?

Since seeing you I have reflected very carefully on the alternative solution presented at the time and brought forward by the defence at the trial. That is, that Amyas Crale took his own life. Although from what I knew of him that solution seemed quite fantastic at the time, I now see fit to modify my opinion. To begin with, and highly significant, is the fact that Caroline believed it. If we are now to take it that that charming and gentle lady was unjustly convicted, then her own frequently reiterated belief must carry great weight. She knew Amyas better than anyone else. If *she* thought suicide possible, then suicide *must* have been possible in spite of the scepticism of his friends.

I will advance the theory, therefore, that there was in Amyas Crale some core of conscience, some undercurrent of remorse and even despair at the excesses to which his temperament led him, of which only his wife was aware. This, I think, is a not impossible supposition. He may have shown that side of himself only to her. Though it is inconsistent with anything I ever heard him say, yet it is nevertheless a truth that in most men there is some unsuspected and

161

inconsistent streak which often comes as a surprise to people who have known them intimately. A respected and austere man is discovered to have had a coarser side to his life hidden. A vulgar money-maker has, perhaps, a secret appreciation of some delicate work of art. Hard and ruthless people have been convicted of unsuspected hidden kindnesses. Generous and jovial men have been shown to have a mean and cruel side to them.

So it may be that in Amyas Crale there ran a strain of morbid self-accusation, and that the more he blustered out his egoism and his right to do as he pleased, the more strongly that secret conscience of his worked. It is improbable, on the face of it, but I now believe that it must have been so. And I repeat again, Caroline herself held steadfastly to that view. That, I repeat, is significant!

And now to examine *facts*, or rather my memory of facts, in the light of that new belief.

I think that I might with relevance include here a conversation I held with Caroline some weeks before the actual tragedy. It was during Elsa Greer's first visit to Alderbury.

Caroline, as I have told you, was aware of my deep affection and friendship for her. I was, therefore, the person in whom she could most easily confide. She had not been looking very happy. Nevertheless I was surprised when she suddenly asked me one day whether I thought Amyas really cared very much for this girl he had brought down.

I said: 'He's interested in painting her. You know what Amyas is.'

She shook her head and said:

'No, he's in love with her.'

'Well – perhaps a little.'

'A great deal, I think.'

I said: 'She is unusually attractive, I admit. And we both know that Amyas is susceptible. But you must know by now, my dear, that Amyas really only cares for one person – and that is you. He has these infatuations – but they don't last. You are the one person to him, and though he behaves badly, it does not really affect his feeling for you.'

Caroline said: 'That is what I always used to think.'

'Believe me, Caro,' I said. 'It is so.'

She said: 'But this time, Merry, I'm afraid. That girl is so – so terribly sincere. She's so young – and so intense. I've a feeling that this time – it's serious.'

I said: 'But the very fact that she is so young and, as you say, so sincere, will protect her. On the whole, women are fair game to Amyas, but in the case of a girl like this it will be different.'

She said: 'Yes, that's what I'm afraid of – it will be different.'

And she went on. 'I'm thirty-four, you know, Merry. And we've been married ten years. In looks I can't hold a candle to this Elsa child, and I know it.'

I said: 'But you know, Caroline, you *know* – that Amyas is really devoted to you?'

She said to that: 'Does one ever know with men?' And then she laughed a little ruefully and said: 'I'm a very primitive woman, Merry. I'd like to take a hatchet to that girl.'

I told her that the child probably didn't understand in the least what she was doing. She had a great admiration and hero-worship for Amyas, and she probably didn't realize at all that Amyas was falling in love with her.

Caroline just said to me:

'Dear Merry!' and began to talk about the garden. I hoped that she was not going to worry any more about the matter.

Shortly afterwards, Elsa went back to London. Amyas was away too for several weeks. I had really forgotten all about the business. And then I heard that Elsa was back again at Alderbury in order that Amyas might finish the picture.

I was a little disturbed by the news. But Caroline, when I

saw her, was not in a communicative mood. She seemed quite her usual self – not worried or upset in any way. I imagined that everything was all right.

That's why it was such a shock to me to learn how far the thing had gone.

I have told you of my conversations with Crale and with Elsa. I had no opportunity of talking to Caroline. We were only able to exchange those few words about which I have already told you.

I can see her face now, the wide dark eyes and the restrained emotion. I can still hear her voice as she said:

'Everything's finished . . .'

I can't describe to you the infinite desolation she conveyed in those words. They were a literal statement of truth. With Amyas's defection, everything was finished for her. That, I am convinced, was why she took the coniine. It was a way out. A way suggested to her by my stupid dissertation on the drug. And the passage I read from the Phædo gives a gracious picture of death.

Here is my present belief. She took the coniine, resolved to end her own life when Amyas left her. He may have seen her take it – or he may have discovered that she had it later.

That discovery acted upon him with terrific force. He was horrified at what his actions had led her to contemplate. But notwithstanding his horror and remorse, he still felt himself incapable of giving up Elsa. I can understand that. Any one who had fallen in love with her would find it almost impossible to tear himself away.

He could not envisage life without Elsa. He realized that Caroline could not live without him. He decided there was only one way out – to use the coniine himself.

And the manner in which he did it might be characteristic of the man, I think. His painting was the dearest thing in life to him. He chose to die literally with his brush in his hand. And the last thing his eyes would see was the face of the girl he loved so desperately. He might have thought, too, that his death would be the best thing for her . . .

I admit that this theory leaves certain curious facts unexplained. Why, for instance, were only Caroline's fingerprints found on the empty coniine bottle. I suggest that after Amyas had handled it, all prints got smudged or rubbed off by the soft piles of stuffs that were lying over the bottle and that, after his death, Caroline handled it to see if any one had touched it. Surely that is possible and plausible? As to the evidence about the fingerprints on the beer bottle, the witnesses for the defence were of opinion that a man's hand *might* be distorted after taking poison and so could manage to grasp a beer bottle in a wholly unnatural way.

One other thing remains to be explained. Caroline's own attitude throughout the trial. But I think I have now seen the cause for that. It was *she who actually took the poison from my laboratory*. It was *her* determination to do away with herself that impelled her husband to take his own life instead. Surely it is not unreasonable to suppose that in a morbid excess of responsibility she considered herself responsible for his death – that she persuaded herself that she *was* guilty of murder – though not the kind of murder of which she was being accused?

I think all that could be so. And if that is the case, then surely it will be easy for you to persuade little Carla of the fact? And she can marry her young man and rest contented that the only thing of which her mother was guilty was an impulse (no more) to take her own life.

All this, alas, is not what you asked me for – which was an account of the happenings as I remember them. Let me now repair that omission. I have already told you fully what happened on the day preceding Amyas's death. We now come to the day itself.

I had slept very badly – worried by the disastrous turn of events for my friends. After a long wakeful period whilst I vainly tried to think of something helpful I could do to avert the catastrophe, I fell into a heavy sleep about six a.m. The bringing of my early tea did not awaken me, and I finally woke up heavy-headed and unrefreshed about half-past nine. It was shortly after that that I thought I heard movements in the room below me, which was the room I used as a laboratory.

I may say here that actually the sounds were probably caused by a cat getting in. I found the window-sash raised a little way as it had carelessly been left from the day before. It was just wide enough to admit the passage of a cat. I merely mention the sounds to explain how I came to enter the laboratory.

I went in there as soon as I had dressed, and looking along the shelves I noticed that the bottle containing the preparation of coniine was slightly out of line with the rest. Having had my eye drawn to it in this way, I was startled to see that a considerable quantity of it had gone. The bottle had been nearly full the day before – now it was nearly empty.

I shut and locked the window and went out, locking the door behind me. I was considerably upset and also bewildered. When startled, my mental processes are, I am afraid, somewhat slow.

I was first disturbed, then apprehensive, and finally definitely alarmed. I questioned the household, and they all denied having entered the laboratory at all. I thought things over a little while longer, and then decided to ring up my brother and get his advice.

Philip was quicker than I was. He saw the seriousness of my discovery, and urged me to come over at once and consult with him.

I went out, encountering Miss Williams, who had come across from the other side to look for a truant pupil. I assured her that I had not seen Angela and that she had not been to the house.

I think that Miss Williams noticed there was something

amiss. She looked at me rather curiously. I had no intention, however, of telling her what had happened. I suggested she should try the kitchen garden – Angela had a favourite apple tree there – and I myself hurried down to the shore and rowed myself across to the Alderbury side.

My brother was already there waiting for me.

We walked up to the house together by the way you and I went the other day. Having seen the topography you can understand that in passing underneath the wall of the Battery garden we were bound to overhear anything being said inside it.

Beyond the fact that Caroline and Amyas were engaged in a disagreement of some kind, I did not pay much attention to what was said.

Certainly I overheard no threat of any kind uttered by Caroline. The subject of discussion was Angela, and I presume Caroline was pleading for a respite from the fiat of school. Amyas, however, was adamant, shouting out irritably that it was all settled, he'd see to her packing.

The door of the Battery opened just as we drew abreast of it, and Caroline came out. She looked disturbed – but not unduly so. She smiled rather absently at me, and said they had been discussing Angela. Elsa came down the path at that minute, and as Amyas clearly wanted to get on with the sitting without interruption from us, we went on up the path.

Philip blamed himself severely afterwards for the fact that we did not take immediate action. But I myself cannot see it the same way. We had no earthly right to assume that such a thing as murder was being contemplated. (Moreover I now believe that it was *not* contemplated.) It was clear that we should have to adopt *some* course of action, but I still maintain that we were right to talk the matter over carefully first. It was necessary to find the right thing to do – and once or twice I found myself wondering if I had not after all made a mistake. Had the bottle really been full the day before as I thought? I am not one of those people (like my brother Philip) who can be cock-sure of everything. One's memory does play tricks on one. How often, for instance, one is convinced one has put an article in a certain place, later to find that you have put it somewhere quite different. The more I tried to recall the state of the bottle on the preceding afternoon, the more uncertain and doubtful I became. This was very annoying to Philip, who began completely to lose patience with me.

We were not able to continue our discussion at the time, and tacitly agreed to postpone it until after lunch. (I may say that I was always free to drop in for lunch at Alderbury if I chose.)

Later, Angela and Caroline brought us beer. I asked Angela what she had been up to playing truant, and told her Miss Williams was on the warpath, and she said she had been bathing – and added that she didn't see why she should have to mend her horrible old skirt when she was going to have all new things to go to school with.

Since there seemed no chance of further talk with Philip alone, and since I was really anxious to think things out by myself, I wandered off down the path towards the Battery. Just above the Battery, as I showed you, there is a clearing in the trees where there used to be an old bench. I sat there smoking and thinking, and watching Elsa as she sat posing for Amyas.

I shall always think of her as she was that day. Rigid in the pose, with her yellow shirt and dark-blue trousers and a red pullover slung round her shoulders for warmth.

Her face was so alight with life and health and radiance. And that gay voice of hers reciting plans for the future.

This sounds as though I was eavesdropping, but that is not so. I was perfectly visible to Elsa. Both she and Amyas knew I was there. She waved her hand at me and called up that Amyas was a perfect bear that morning – he wouldn't let her rest. She was stiff and aching all over.

Amyas growled out that she wasn't as stiff as he was. He was stiff all over – muscular rheumatism. Elsa said mockingly: 'Poor old man!' And he said she'd be taking on a creaking invalid.

It shocked me, you know, their lighthearted acquiescence in their future together whilst they were causing so much suffering. And yet I couldn't hold it against her. She was so young, so confident, so very much in love. And she didn't really know what she was doing. She didn't understand suffering. She just assumed with the naïve confidence of a child that Caroline would be 'all right', that 'she'd soon get over it.' She saw nothing, you see, but herself and Amyas – happy together. She'd already told me my point of view was old-fashioned. She had no doubts, no qualms – no pity either. But can one expect pity from radiant youth? It is an older, wiser emotion.

They didn't talk very much, of course. No painter wants to be chattering when he is working. Perhaps every ten minutes or so Elsa would make an observation and Amyas would grunt a reply. Once she said:

'I think you're right about Spain. That's the first place we'll go to. And you must take me to see a bullfight. It must be wonderful. Only I'd like the bull to kill the man – not the other way about. I understand how Roman women felt when they saw a man die. Men aren't much, but animals are splendid.'

I suppose she was rather like an animal herself – young and primitive and with nothing yet of man's sad experience and doubtful wisdom. I don't believe Elsa had begun to *think* – she only *felt*. But she was very much alive – more alive than any person I have ever known . . .

That was the last time I saw her radiant and assured – on top of the world. Fey is the word for it, isn't it?

The bell sounded for lunch, and I got up and went down the path and in at the Battery door, and Elsa joined me. It was dazzlingly bright there coming in out of the shady trees.

I could hardly see. Amyas was sprawled back on the seat, his arms flung out. He was staring at the picture. I've so often seen him like that. How was I to know that already the poison was working, stiffening him as he sat?

He so hated and resented illness. He would never own to it. I dare say he thought he had got a touch of the sun – the symptoms are much the same – but he'd be the last person to complain about it.

Elsa said:

'He won't come up to lunch.'

Privately I thought he was wise. I said:

'So long, then.'

He moved his eyes from the picture until they rested on me. There was a queer – how shall I describe it – it looked like malevolence. A kind of malevolent glare.

Naturally I didn't understand it then – if his picture wasn't going as he liked he often looked quite murderous. I thought *that* was what it was. He made a sort of grunting sound.

Neither Elsa nor I saw anything unusual in him – just artistic temperament.

So we left him there and she and I went up to the house laughing and talking. If she'd known, poor child, that she'd never see him alive again . . . Oh, well, thank God she didn't. She was able to be happy a little longer.

Caroline was quite normal at lunch – a little preoccupied; nothing more. And doesn't that show that she had nothing to do with it? She *couldn't* have been such an actress.

She and the governess went down afterwards and found him. I met Miss Williams as she came up. She told me to telephone a doctor and went back to Caroline.

That poor child – Elsa, I mean! She had that frantic unrestrained grief that a child has. They can't believe that life can do these things to them. Caroline was quite calm. Yes, she was quite calm. She was able, of course, to control herself better than Elsa. She didn't seem remorseful – then.

Just said he must have done it himself. And we couldn't believe that. Elsa burst out and accused her to her face.

Of course she may have realized, already, that she herself would be suspected. Yes, that probably explains her manner.

Philip was quite convinced that she *had* done it.

The governess was a great help and standby. She made Elsa lie down and gave her a sedative, and she kept Angela out of the way when the police came. Yes, she was a tower of strength, that woman.

The whole thing became a nightmare. The police searching the house and asking questions, and then the reporters, swarming about the place like flies and clicking cameras and wanting interviews with members of the family.

A nightmare, the whole thing . . .

It's a nightmare, after all these years. Please God, once you've convinced little Carla what really happened, we can forget it all and never remember it again.

Amyas *must* have committed suicide – however unlikely it seems.

End of Meredith Blake's Narrative.

171

I have set down here the full story of my meeting with Amyas Crale, up to the time of his tragic death.

I saw him first at a studio party. He was standing, I remember, by a window, and I saw him as I came in at the door. I asked who he was. Someone said: 'That's Crale, the painter.' I said at once that I'd like to meet him.

We talked on that occasion for perhaps ten minutes. When any one makes the impression on you that Amyas Crale made on me, it's hopeless to attempt to describe them. If I say that when I saw Amyas Crale, everybody else seemed to grow very small and fade away, that expresses it as well as anything can.

Immediately after that meeting I went to look at as many of his pictures as I could. He had a show on in Bond Street at the moment, and there was one of his pictures in Manchester and one in Leeds and two in public galleries in London. I went to see them all. Then I met him again. I said: 'I've been to see all your pictures. I think they're wonderful.'

He just looked amused. He said:

'Who said you were any judge of painting? I don't believe you know anything about it.'

I said: 'Perhaps not. But they are marvellous, all the same.'

He grinned at me and said: 'Don't be a gushing little fool.'

I said: 'I'm not. I want you to paint me.'

Crale said: 'If you've any sense at all, you'll realize that I don't paint portraits of pretty women.'

I said: 'It needn't be a portrait and I'm not a pretty woman.'

He looked at me then as though he'd begun to see me. He said: 'No, perhaps you're not.'

I said: 'Will you paint me then?'

He studied me for some time with his head on one side. Then he said: 'You're a strange child, aren't you?'

I said: 'I'm quite rich, you know. I can afford to pay well for it.'

He said: 'Why are you so anxious for me to paint you?'

I said: 'Because I want it!'

He said: 'Is that a reason?'

And I said: 'Yes, I always get what I want.'

He said then: 'Oh, my poor child, how young you are!'

I said: 'Will you paint me?'

He took me by the shoulders and turned me towards the light and looked me over. Then he stood away from me a little. I stood quite still, waiting.

He said: 'I've sometimes wanted to paint a flight of impossibly-coloured Australian Maccaws alighting on St Paul's Cathedral. If I painted you against a nice traditional bit of outdoor landscape, I believe I'd get exactly the same result.'

I said: 'Then you will paint me?'

He said: 'You're one of the loveliest, crudest, most flamboyant bits of exotic colouring I've ever seen. I'll paint you!'

I said: 'Then that's settled.'

He went on: 'But I'll warn you, Elsa Greer. If I do paint you, I shall probably make love to you.'

I said: 'I hope you will . . .'

I said it quite steadily and quietly. I heard him catch his breath, and I saw the look that came into his eyes.

You see, it was as sudden as all that.

A day or two later we met again. He told me that he wanted me to come down to Devonshire – he'd got the very place there that he wanted for a background. He said:

'I'm married, you know. And I'm very fond of my wife.'

I said if he was fond of her she must be very nice.

He said she was extremely nice. 'In fact,' he said, 'she's quite adorable – and I adore her. So put that in your pipe, young Elsa, and smoke it.'

I told him that I quite understood.

He began the picture a week later. Caroline Crale welcomed me very pleasantly. She didn't like me much –

but, after all, why should she? Amyas was very circumspect. He never said a word to me that his wife couldn't have overheard, and I was quite polite and formal to him. Underneath, though, we both knew.

After ten days he told me I was to go back to London.

I said: 'The picture isn't finished.'

He said: 'It's barely begun. The truth is, I can't paint you, Elsa.'

I said: 'Why?'

He said: 'You know well enough why, Elsa. And that's why you've got to clear out. I can't think about the painting – I can't think about anything but you.'

We were in the Battery garden. It was a hot sunny day. There were birds and humming bees. It ought to have been very happy and peaceful. But it didn't feel like that. It felt – somehow – tragic. As though – as though what was going to happen was already mirrored there.

I knew it would be no good my going back to London, but I said: 'Very well, I'll go if you say so.'

Amyas said: 'Good girl.'

So I went. I didn't write to him.

He held out for ten days and then he came. He was so thin and haggard and miserable that it shocked me.

He said: 'I warned you, Elsa. Don't say I didn't warn you.'

I said: 'I've been waiting for you. I knew you'd come.'

He gave a sort of groan and said: 'There are things that are too strong for any man. I can't eat or sleep or rest for wanting you.'

I said I knew that and that it was the same with me, and had been from the first moment I'd seen him. It was Fate and it was no use struggling against it.

He said: 'You haven't struggled much, have you, Elsa?' And I said I hadn't struggled at all.

He said he wished I wasn't so young, and I said that didn't matter. I suppose I might say that for the next few weeks we were very happy. But happiness isn't quite the word. It was something deeper and more frightening than that.

174 .

We were made for each other and we'd found each other – and we both knew we'd got to be together always.

But something else happened, too. The unfinished picture began to haunt Amyas. He said to me: 'Damned funny, I couldn't paint you before – you yourself got in the way of it. But I *want* to paint you, Elsa. I want to paint you so that that picture will be the finest thing I've ever done. I'm itching and aching now to get at my brushes to see you sitting there on that hoary old chestnut of a battlement wall with the conventional blue sea and the decorous English trees – and you – you – sitting there like a discordant shriek of triumph.'

He said: 'And I've got to paint you that way! And I can't be fussed and bothered while I'm doing it. When the picture's finished I'll tell Caroline the truth and we'll get the whole messy business cleared up.'

I said: 'Will Caroline make a fuss about divorcing you?'

He said he didn't think so. But you never knew with women.

I said I was sorry if she was going to be upset, but after all, I said, these things did happen.

He said: 'Very nice and reasonable, Elsa. But Caroline isn't reasonable, never has been reasonable, and certainly isn't going to feel reasonable. She loves me, you know.'

I said I understood that, but if she loved him, she'd put his happiness first, and at any rate she wouldn't want to keep him if he wanted to be free.

He said: 'Life can't really be solved by admirable maxims out of modern literature. Nature's red in tooth and claw, remember.'

I said: 'Surely we are all civilized people nowadays?' and Amyas laughed. He said: 'Civilized people my foot! Caroline would probably like to take a hatchet to you. She might do it too. Don't you realize, Elsa, that she's going to suffer – *suffer*? Don't you know what suffering means?'

I said: 'Then don't tell her.'

He said: 'No. The break's got to come. You've got to belong to me properly, Elsa. Before all the world. Openly mine.'

I said: 'Suppose she won't divorce you?'

He said: 'I'm not afraid of that.'

I said: 'What are you afraid of then?'

And then he said slowly: 'I don't know . . .'

You see, he knew Caroline. I didn't.

If I'd had any idea . . .

We went down again to Alderbury. Things were difficult this time. Caroline had got suspicious. I didn't like it – I didn't like it – I didn't like it a bit. I've always hated deceit and concealment. I thought we ought to tell her. Amyas wouldn't hear of it.

The funny part of it was that he didn't really care at all. In spite of being fond of Caroline and not wanting to hurt her, he just didn't care about the honesty or dishonesty of it all. He was painting with a kind of frenzy, and nothing else mattered. I hadn't seen him in one of his working spells before. I realized now what a really great genius he was. It was natural for him to be so carried away that all the ordinary decencies didn't matter. But it was different for me. I was in a horrible position. Caroline resented me – and quite rightly. The only thing to put the position quite straight was to be honest and tell her the truth.

But all Amyas would say was that he wasn't going to be bothered with scenes and fusses until he'd finished the picture. I said there probably wouldn't be a scene. Caroline would have too much dignity and pride for that.

I said: 'I want to be honest about it all. We've *got* to be honest!'

Amyas said: 'To hell with honesty. I'm painting a picture, damn it.'

I did see his point of view, but he wouldn't see mine.

And in the end I broke down. Caroline had been talking of some plan she and Amyas were going to carry out next autumn. She talked about it quite confidently. And I suddenly felt it was too abominable, what we were doing – letting her go on like this – and perhaps, too, I was angry, because she was really being very unpleasant to me in a clever sort of way that one couldn't take hold of.

And so I came out with the truth. In a way, I still think I was right. Though, of course, I wouldn't have done it if I'd had the faintest idea what was to come of it.

The clash came right away. Amyas was furious with me, but he had to admit that what I had said was true.

I didn't understand Caroline at all. We all went over to Meredith Blake's to tea, and Caroline played up marvellously – talking and laughing. Like a fool, I thought she was taking it well. It was awkward my not being able to leave the house, but Amyas would have gone up in smoke if I had. I thought perhaps Caroline would go. It would have made it much easier for us if she had.

I didn't see her take the coniine. I want to be honest so I think that it's just possible that she may have taken it as she said she did, with the idea of suicide in her mind.

But I don't *really* think so. I think she was one of those intensely jealous and possessive women who won't let go of anything that they think belongs to them. Amyas was her property. I think she was quite prepared to kill him rather than to let him go – completely and finally – to another woman. I think she made up her mind, right away, to kill him. And I think that Meredith's happening to discuss coniine so freely just gave her the means to do what she'd already made up her mind to do. She was a very bitter and revengeful woman – vindictive. Amyas knew all along that she was dangerous. I didn't.

The next morning she had a final showdown with Amyas. I heard most of it from the outside on the terrace. He was splendid – very patient and calm. He implored her to be reasonable. He said he was very fond of her and the child and always would be. He'd do everything he could do to assure their future. Then he hardened up and said: 'But understand this. I'm damned well going to marry Elsa – and nothing shall stop me. You and I always agreed to leave each other free. These things happen.'

Caroline said to him: 'Do as you please. I've warned you.'

Her voice was very quiet, but there was a queer note in it.

Amyas said: 'What do you mean, Caroline?'

She said: 'You're mine and *I don't mean to let you go.* Sooner than let you go to that girl *I'll kill you* . . .'

Just at that minute, Philip Blake came along the terrace. I got up and went to meet him. I didn't want him to overhear.

Presently Amyas came out and said it was time to get on with the picture. We went down together to the Battery. He didn't say much. Just said that Caroline was cutting up rough – but for God's sake not to talk about it. He wanted to concentrate on what he was doing. Another day, he said, would about finish the picture.

He said: 'And it'll be the best thing I've ever done, Elsa, even if it is paid for in blood and tears.'

A little later I went up to the house to get a pullover. There was a chilly wind blowing. When I came back again Caroline was there. I suppose she had come down to make one last appeal. Philip and Meredith Blake were there too.

It was then that Amyas said he was thirsty and wanted a drink. He said there was beer but it wasn't iced.

Caroline said she'd send him down some iced beer. She said it quite naturally in an almost friendly tone. She was an actress, that woman. She must have known then what she meant to do.

She brought it down about ten minutes later. Amyas was painting. She poured it out and set the glass down beside him. Neither of us were watching her. Amyas was intent on what he was doing and I had to keep the pose.

Amyas drank it down the way he always drank beer, just pouring it down his throat in one draught. Then he made a face and said it tasted foul – but at any rate it was cold.

And even then, when he said that, no suspicion entered my head, I just laughed and said: 'Liver.'

When she'd seen him drink it Caroline went away.

It must have been about forty minutes later that Amyas complained of stiffness and pains. He said he thought he must have got a touch of muscular rheumatism. Amyas was always intolerant of any ailment and he didn't like being fussed over. After saying that he turned it off with a light: 'Old age, I suppose. You've taken on a creaking old man, Elsa.' I played up to him. But I noticed that his legs moved stiffly and queerly and that he grimaced once or twice. I never dreamt that it wasn't rheumatism. Presently he drew the bench along and sat sprawled on that, occasionally stretching up to put a touch of paint here and there on the canvas. He used to do that sometimes when he was painting. Just sit staring at me and then the canvas. Sometimes he'd do it for half an hour at a time. So I didn't think it specially queer.

We heard the bell go for lunch, and he said he wasn't coming up. He'd stay where he was and he didn't want anything. That wasn't unusual either, and it would be easier for him than facing Caroline at the table.

He was talking in rather a queer way – grunting out his words. But he sometimes did that when he was dissatisfied with the progress of the picture.

Meredith Blake came in to fetch me. He spoke to Amyas, but Amyas only grunted at him.

We went up to the house together and left him there. We left him there – to die alone. I'd never seen much illness – I didn't know much about it – I thought Amyas was just in a painter's mood. If I'd known – if I'd realized – perhaps a doctor could have saved him . . . Oh God, why didn't I – it's no good thinking of that now. I was a blind fool. A blind, stupid fool.

There isn't much more to tell.

Caroline and the governess went down there after lunch.

179

Meredith followed them. Presently he came running up. He told us Amyas was dead.

Then I knew! Knew, I mean, that it was Caroline. I still didn't think of poison. I thought she'd gone down that minute and either shot him or stabbed him.

I wanted to get at her – to kill her . . .

How *could* she do it? How *could* she? He was so alive, so full of life and vigour. To put all that out – to make him limp and cold. Just so that I shouldn't have him.

Horrible woman . . .

Horrible, scornful, cruel, vindictive woman . . .

I hate her. I still hate her.

They didn't even hang her.

They ought to have hanged her . . .

Even hanging was too good for her . . .

I hate her . . . I hate her . . . I hate her . . .

End of Lady Dittisham's Narrative.

Dear M. Poirot,

I am sending you an account of those events in September, 19 . . . actually witnessed by myself.

I have been absolutely frank and have kept nothing back. You may show it to Carla Crale. It may pain her, but I have always been a believer in truth. Palliatives are harmful. One must have the courage to face reality. Without that courage, life is meaningless. The people who do us most harm are the people who shield us from reality.

Believe me, yours sincerely,
Cecilia Williams

My name is Cecilia Williams. I was engaged by Mrs Crale as governess to her half-sister Angela Warren, in 19 . . . I was then forty-eight.

I took up my duties at Alderbury, a very beautiful estate in south Devon which had belonged to Mr Crale's family for many generations. I knew that Mr Crale was a well-known painter, but I did not meet him until I took up residence at Alderbury.

The household consisted of Mr and Mrs Crale, Angela Warren (then a girl of thirteen), and three servants, all of whom had been with the family many years.

I found my pupil an interesting and promising character. She had very marked abilities and it was a pleasure to teach her. She was somewhat wild and undisciplined, but these faults arose mainly through high spirits, and I have always preferred my girls to show spirit. An excess of vitality can be trained and guided into paths of real usefulness and achievement.

On the whole, I found Angela amenable to discipline. She had been somewhat spoiled – mainly by Mrs Crale, who was far too indulgent where she was concerned. Mr Crale's influence was, I considered, unwise. He indulged her absurdly one day, and was unnecessarily peremptory on another occasion. He was very much a man of moods – possibly owing to what is styled the artistic temperament.

I have never seen, myself, why the possession of artistic ability should be supposed to excuse a man from a decent exercise of self-control. I did not myself admire Mr Crale's paintings. The drawing seemed to me faulty and the colouring exaggerated, but naturally I was not called upon to express any opinion on these matters.

I soon formed a deep attachment to Mrs Crale. I admired her character and her fortitude in the difficulties of her life. Mr Crale was not a faithful husband, and I think that that fact was the source of much pain to her. A stronger-minded woman would have left him, but Mrs Crale never seemed to contemplate such a course. She endured his infidelities and forgave him for them – but I may say that she did not take them meekly. She remonstrated – and with spirit!

It was said at the trial that they led a cat and dog life. I would not go as far as that – Mrs Crale had too much dignity for that term to apply, but they *did* have quarrels. And I consider that that was only natural under the circumstances.

I had been with Mrs Crale just over two years when Miss Elsa Greer appeared upon the scene. She arrived down at Alderbury in the summer of 19 . . . Mrs Crale had not met her previously. She was Mr Crale's friend, and she was said to be there for the purpose of having her portrait painted.

It was apparent at once that Mr Crale was infatuated with this girl and that the girl herself was doing nothing to discourage him. She behaved, in my opinion, quite outrageously, being abominably rude to Mrs Crale, and openly flirting with Mr Crale.

Naturally Mrs Crale said nothing to me, but I could see that she was disturbed and unhappy, and I did everything in my power to distract her mind and lighten her burden. Miss Greer sat every day to Mr Crale, but I noticed that the picture was not getting on very fast. They had, no doubt, other things to talk about!

My pupil, I am thankful to say, noticed very little of what was going on. Angela was in some ways young for her age. Though her intellect was well developed, she was not at all what I may term precocious. She seemed to have no wish to read undesirable books, and showed no signs of morbid curiosity such as girls often do at her age.

She, therefore, saw nothing undesirable in the friendship between Mr Crale and Miss Greer. Nevertheless she disliked Miss Greer and thought her stupid. Here she was quite right. Miss Greer had had, I presume, a proper education, but she never opened a book and was quite unfamiliar with current literary allusions. Moreover she could not sustain a discussion on any intellectual subject.

She was entirely taken up with her personal appearance, her clothes, and men.

Angela, I think, did not even realize that her sister was unhappy. She was not at that time a very perceptive person. She spent a lot of time in hoydenish pastimes, such as tree climbing and wild feats of bicycling. She was also a passionate reader and showed excellent taste in what she liked and disliked.

Mrs Crale was always careful to conceal any signs of unhappiness from Angela, and exerted herself to appear bright and cheerful when the girl was about.

Miss Greer went back to London – at which, I can tell you, we were all very pleased! The servants disliked her as much as I did. She was the kind of person who gives a lot of unnecessary trouble and forgets to say thank you.

Mr Crale went away shortly afterwards, and of course I knew that he had gone after the girl. I was very sorry for Mrs Crale. She felt these things very keenly. I felt extremely bitter towards Mr Crale. When a man has a charming, gracious, intelligent wife, he's no business to treat her badly.

However, she and I both hoped the affair would soon be over. Not that we mentioned the subject to each other – we did not – but she knew quite well how I felt about it.

Unfortunately, after some weeks, the pair of them reappeared. It seemed the sittings were to be resumed.

Mr Crale was now painting with absolute frenzy. He seemed less preoccupied with the girl than with his picture of her. Nevertheless I realized that this was not the usual kind of thing we had gone through before. This girl had got her claws into him and she meant business. He was just like wax in her hands.

The thing came to a head on the day before he died – that is on Sept. 17. Miss Greer's manner had been unbearably insolent the last few days. She was feeling sure of herself and she wanted to assert her importance. Mrs Crale behaved like a true gentlewoman. She was icily polite, but she showed the other clearly what she thought of her.

On this day, Sept. 17, as we were sitting in the drawing-room after lunch, Miss Greer came out with an amazing remark as to how she was going to redecorate the room when she was living at Alderbury.

Naturally Mrs Crale couldn't let that pass. She challenged her, and Miss Greer had the impudence to say, before us all, that she was going to marry Mr Crale. She actually talked about marrying a married man – and she said it to his wife!

I was very, very angry with Mr Crale. How dared he let this girl insult his wife in her own drawing-room? If he wanted to run away with the girl, he should have gone off with her, not brought her into his wife's house and backed her up in her insolence.

In spite of what she must have felt, Mrs Crale did not lose her dignity. Her husband came in just then, and she immediately demanded confirmation from him.

He was, not unnaturally, annoyed with Miss Greer for her unconsidered forcing of the situation. Apart from anything else, it made *him* appear at a disadvantage, and men do not like appearing at a disadvantage. It upsets their vanity.

He stood there, a great giant of a man, looking as

sheepish and foolish as a naughty schoolboy. It was his wife who carried off the honours of the situation. He had to mutter foolishly that it was true, but that he hadn't meant her to learn it like this.

I have never seen anything like the look of scorn she gave him. She went out of the room with her head held high. She was a beautiful woman – much more beautiful than that flamboyant girl – and she walked like an Empress.

I hoped, with all my heart, that Amyas Crale would be punished for the cruelty he had displayed and for the indignity he had put upon a long-suffering and noble woman.

For the first time, I tried to say something of what I felt to Mrs Crale, but she stopped me.

She said:

'We must try and behave as usual. It's the best way. We're all going over to Meredith Blake's to tea.'

I said to her then:

'I think you are wonderful, Mrs Crale.'

She said:

'You don't know . . .'

Then, as she was going out of the room, she came back and kissed me. She said:

'You're such a comfort to me.'

She went to her room then and I think she cried. I saw her when they all started off. She was wearing a big-brimmed hat that shaded her face – a hat she very seldom wore.

Mr Crale was uneasy, but was trying to brazen things out. Mr Philip Blake was trying to behave as usual. That Miss Greer was looking like a cat who has got at the cream-jug. All self-satisfaction and purrs!

They all started off. They got back about six. I did not see Mrs Crale again alone that evening. She was very quiet and composed at dinner, and she went to bed early. I don't think that any one knew how she was suffering.

The evening was taken up with a kind of running quarrel between Mr Crale and Angela. They brought up the old school question again. He was irritable and on edge, and she was unusually trying. The whole matter was settled and her outfit had been bought, and there was no sense in starting up an argument again, but she suddenly chose to make a grievance of it. I have no doubt she sensed the tension in the air and that it reacted on her as much as on everybody else. I am afraid I was too preoccupied with my own thoughts to try and check her as I should have done. It all ended with her flinging a paperweight at Mr Crale and dashing out of the room.

I went after her and told her sharply that I was ashamed of her behaving like a baby, but she was still very uncontrolled, and I thought it best to leave her alone.

I hesitated as to whether to go to Mrs Crale's room, but I decided in the end that it would, perhaps, annoy her. I wish since that I had overcome my diffidence and insisted on her talking to me. If she had done so, it might possibly have made a difference. She had no one, you see, in whom she could confide. Although I admire self-control, I must regretfully admit that sometimes it can be carried too far. A natural outlet to the feelings is better.

I met Mr Crale as I went along to my room. He said goodnight, but I did not answer.

The next morning was, I remember, a beautiful day. One felt when waking that surely with such peace all around even a man must come to his senses.

I went into Angela's room before going down to breakfast, but she was already up and out. I picked up a torn skirt which she had left lying on the floor and took it down with me for her to mend after breakfast.

She had, however, obtained bread and marmalade from the kitchen and gone out. After I had had my own breakfast I went in search of her. I mention this to explain why I was not more with Mrs Crale on that morning as perhaps I should have been. At the time, however, I felt it was my duty to look for Angela. She was very naughty and obstinate about mending her clothes, and I had no intention of allowing her to defy me in the matter.

Her bathing-dress was missing and I accordingly went down to the beach. There was no sign of her in the water or on the rocks, so I conceived it possible that she had gone over to Mr Meredith Blake's. She and he were great friends. I accordingly rowed myself across and resumed my search. I did not find her and eventually returned. Mrs Crale, Mr Blake and Mr Philip Blake were on the terrace.

It was very hot that morning if one was out of the wind, and the house and terrace were sheltered. Mrs Crale suggested they might like some iced beer.

There was a little conservatory which had been built on to the house in Victorian days. Mrs Crale disliked it, and it was not used for plants, but it had been made into a kind of bar, with various bottles of gin, vermouth, lemonade, ginger-beer, etc., on shelves, and a small refrigerator which was filled with ice every morning and in which some beer and ginger-beer was always kept.

Mrs Crale went there to get the beer and I went with her. Angela was at the refrigerator and was just taking out a bottle of beer.

Mrs Crale went in ahead of me. She said:

'I want a bottle of beer to take down to Amyas.'

It is so difficult now to know whether I ought to have suspected anything. Her voice, I feel almost convinced, was perfectly normal. But I must admit that at that moment I was intent, not on her, but on Angela. Angela was by the refrigerator and I was glad to see that she looked red and rather guilty.

I was rather sharp with her, and to my surprise she was quite meek. I asked her where she had been, and she said she had been bathing. I said: 'I didn't see you on the beach.' And she laughed. Then I asked her where her

187

jersey was, and she said she must have left it down on the beach.

I mention these details to explain why I let Mrs Crale take the beer down to the Battery garden.

The rest of the morning is quite blank in my mind. Angela fetched her needle-book and mended her skirt without any more fuss. I rather think that I mended some of the household linen. Mr Crale did not come up for lunch. I was glad that he had at least *that* much decency.

After lunch, Mrs Crale said she was going down to the Battery. I wanted to retrieve Angela's jersey from the beach. We started down together. She went into the Battery – I was going on when her cry called me back. As I told you when you came to see me, she asked me to go up and telephone. On the way up I met Mr Meredith Blake and then went back to Mrs Crale.

That was my story as I told it at the inquest and later at the trial.

What I am about to write down I have never told to any living soul. I was not asked any question to which I returned an untrue answer. Nevertheless I *was* guilty of withholding certain facts – I do not repent of that. I would do it again. I am fully aware that in revealing this I may be laying myself open to censure, but I do not think that after this lapse of time any one will take the matter very seriously – especially since Caroline Crale was convicted without my evidence.

This, then, is what happened.

I met Mr Meredith Blake as I said, and I ran down the path again as quickly as I could. I was wearing sandshoes and I have always been light on my feet. I came to the open Battery door, and this is what I saw.

Mrs Crale was busily polishing the beer bottle on the table with her handkerchief. Having done so, she took her dead husband's hand and pressed the fingers of it on the beer bottle. All the time she was listening and on the alert. It was the fear I saw on her face that told me the truth.

I knew then, beyond any possible doubt, that Caroline Crale had poisoned her husband. And I, for one, do not blame her. He drove her to a point beyond human endurance, and he brought his fate upon himself.

I never mentioned the incident to Mrs Crale and she never knew that I had seen it.

Caroline Crale's daughter must not bolster up her life with a lie. However much it may pain her to know the truth, truth is the only thing that matters.

Tell her, from me, that her mother is not to be judged. She was driven beyond what a loving woman can endure. It is for her daughter to understand and forgive.

End of Cecilia Williams's Narrative.

Dear M. Poirot,

I am keeping my promise to you and have written down all I can remember of that terrible time sixteen years ago. But it was not until I started that I realized how very little I *did* remember. Until the thing actually happened, you see, there is nothing to fix anything by.

I've just a vague memory of summer days – and isolated incidents, but I couldn't say for certain what summer they happened even! Amyas's death was just a thunderclap coming out of the blue. I'd had no warning of it, and I seem to have missed everything that led up to it.

I've been trying to think whether that was to be expected or not. Are most girls of fifteen as blind and deaf and obtuse as I seem to have been? Perhaps they are. I was quick, I think, to gauge people's moods, but I never bothered my head about what *caused* those moods.

Besides, just at that time, I'd suddenly begun to discover the intoxication of words. Things that I read, straps of poetry – of Shakespeare – would echo in my head. I remember now walking along the kitchen garden path repeating to myself in a kind of ecstatic delirium 'under the glassy green translucent wave' . . . It was just so lovely I had to say it over and over again.

And mixed up with these new discoveries and excitements there were all the things I'd liked doing ever since I could remember. Swimming and climbing trees and eating fruit and playing tricks on the stable boy and feeding the horses.

Caroline and Amyas I took for granted. They were the central figures in my world, but I never *thought* about them or about their affairs or what they thought and felt.

I didn't notice Elsa Greer's coming particularly. I thought she was stupid and I didn't even think she was good-looking. I accepted her as someone rich but tiresome, whom Amyas was painting.

Actually, the very first intimation I had of the whole thing was what I overheard from the terrace where I had escaped after lunch one day – Elsa said she was going to marry Amyas! It struck me as just ridiculous. I remember tackling Amyas about it. In the garden at Handcross it was. I said to him:

'Why does Elsa say she's going to marry you? She couldn't. People can't have two wives – it's bigamy and they go to prison.'

Amyas got very angry and said: 'How the devil did you hear that?'

I said I'd heard it through the library window.

He was angrier than ever then, and said it was high time I went to school and got out of the habit of eavesdropping.

I still remember the resentment I felt when he said that. Because it was so *unfair*. Absolutely and utterly unfair.

I stammered out angrily that I hadn't been listening – and anyhow, I said, why did Elsa say a silly thing like that?

Amyas said it was just a joke.

That ought to have satisfied me. It did – almost. But not quite.

I said to Elsa when we were on the way back: 'I asked Amyas what you meant when you said you were going to marry him, and he said it was just a joke.'

I felt that ought to snub her. But she only smiled.

I didn't like that smile of hers. I went up to Caroline's room. It was when she was dressing for dinner. I asked her then outright if it were possible for Amyas to marry Elsa.

I remember Caroline's answer as though I heard it now. She must have spoken with great emphasis.

'Amyas will only marry Elsa after I am dead,' she said.

That reassured me completely. Death seemed ages away from us all. Nevertheless, I was still very sore with Amyas about what he had said in the afternoon, and I went for him violently all through dinner, and I remember we had a real flaming row, and I rushed out of the room and went up to bed and howled myself to sleep.

I don't remember much about the afternoon at Meredith Blake's, although I *do* remember his reading aloud the passage from the Phædo describing Socrates' death. I had never heard it before. I thought it was the loveliest, most beautiful thing I had ever heard. I remember that – but I don't remember when it was. As far as I can recall now, it might have been any time that summer.

I don't remember anything that happened the next morning either, though I have thought and thought. I've a vague feeling that I must have bathed, and I think I remember being made to mend something.

But it's all very vague and dim till the time when Meredith came panting up the path from the terrace, and his face was all grey and queer. I remember a coffee cup falling off the table and being broken – Elsa did that. And I remember her running – suddenly running for all she was worth down the path – and the awful look there was on her face.

I kept saying to myself: 'Amyas is dead.' But it just didn't seem real.

I remember Dr Faussett coming and his grave face. Miss Williams was busy looking after Caroline. I wandered about rather forlornly, getting in people's way. I had a nasty sick feeling. They wouldn't let me go down and see Amyas. But by and by the police came and wrote down things in notebooks, and presently they brought his body up on a stretcher covered with a cloth.

Miss Williams took me into Caroline's room later. Caroline was on the sofa. She looked very white and ill.

She kissed me and said she wanted me to go away as soon as I could, and it was all horrible, but I wasn't to worry or think about it any more than I could help. I was to join Carla at Lady Tressillian's because this house was to be kept as empty as possible.

I clung to Caroline and said I didn't want to go away. I wanted to stay with her. She said she knew I did, but it was better for me to go away and would take a lot of worry off her mind. And Miss Williams chipped in and said:

'The best way you can help your sister, Angela, is to do what she wants you to do without making a fuss about it.'

So I said I would do whatever Caroline wished. And Caroline said: 'That's my darling Angela.' And she hugged me and said there was nothing to worry about, and to talk about it and think about it all as little as possible.

I had to go down and talk to a Police Superintendent. He was very kind, asked me when I had last seen Amyas and a lot of other questions which seemed to me quite pointless at the time, but which, of course, I see the point of now. He satisfied himself that there was nothing that I could tell him which he hadn't already heard from the others. So he told Miss Williams that he saw no objection to my going over to Ferriby Grange to Lady Tressillian's.

I went there, and Lady Tressillian was very kind to me. But of course I soon had to know the truth. They arrested Caroline almost at once. I was so horrified and dumbfounded that I became quite ill.

I heard afterwards that Caroline was terribly worried about me. It was at her insistence that I was sent out of England before the trial came on. But that I have told you already.

As you see, what I have to put down is pitiably meagre. Since talking to you I have gone over the little I remember painstakingly, racking my memory for details of this or that person's expression or reaction. I can remember nothing consistent with guilt. Elsa's frenzy. Meredith's grey worried face. Philip's grief and fury – they all seem natural enough. I suppose, though, someone *could* have been playing a part?

I only know this, *Caroline did not do it.*

I am quite certain on this point, and always shall be, but I have no evidence to offer except my own intimate knowledge of her character.

End of Angela Warren's Narrative.

BOOK III

CHAPTER I

Conclusions

Carla Lemarchant looked up. Her eyes were full of fatigue and pain. She pushed back the hair from her forehead in a tired gesture.

She said:

'It's so bewildering all this.' She touched the pile of manuscripts. 'Because the angle's different every time! Everybody sees my mother differently. But the facts are the same. Everyone agrees on the facts.'

'It has discouraged you, reading them?'

'Yes. Hasn't it discouraged you?'

'No, I have found those documents very valuable – very informative.'

Poirot spoke slowly and reflectively.

Carla said:

'I wish I'd never read them!'

Poirot looked across at her.

'Ah – so it makes you feel that way?'

Carla said bitterly:

'They all think she did it – all of them except Aunt Angela and what she thinks doesn't count. She hasn't got any reason for it. She's just one of those loyal people who'll stick to a thing through thick and thin. She just goes on saying: "Caroline couldn't have done it."'

'It strikes you like that?'

'How else should it strike me? I've realized, you know, that if my mother didn't do it, then one of these five people must have done it. I've even had theories as to why.'

'Ah! That is interesting. Tell me.'

'Oh, they were only theories. Philip Blake, for instance. He's a stockbroker, he was my father's best friend – probably my father trusted him. And artists are usually careless about money matters. Perhaps Philip Blake was in a jam and used my father's money. He may have got my father to sign something. Then the whole thing may have been on the point of coming out – and only my father's death could have saved him. That's one of the things I thought of.'

'Not badly imagined at all. What else?'

'Well, there's Elsa. Philip Blake says here she had her head screwed on too well to meddle with poison, but I don't think that's true at all. Supposing my mother had gone to her and told her that she wouldn't divorce my father – that nothing would induce her to divorce him. You may say what you like, but I think Elsa had a bourgeois mind – she wanted to be respectably married. I think that then Elsa would have been perfectly capable of pinching the stuff – she had just as good a chance that afternoon – and might have tried to get my mother out of the way by poisoning her. I think that would be quite *like* Elsa. And then, possibly, by some awful accident, Amyas got the stuff instead of Caroline.'

'Again it is not badly imagined. What else?'

Carla said slowly:

'Well, I thought – perhaps – *Meredith*!'

'Ah – Meredith Blake?'

'Yes. You see, he sounds to me just the sort of person who would do a murder. I mean, he was the slow dithering one the others laughed at, and underneath, perhaps, he resented that. Then my father married the girl he wanted to marry. And my father was successful and rich. And he did make all those poisons! Perhaps he really made them because he liked the idea of being able to kill someone one day. He had to call attention to the stuff being taken, so as to divert suspicion from himself. But he himself was far the most likely person to have taken it. He might, even, have liked getting Caroline hanged – because she turned him down long ago. I think, you know, it's rather fishy what he says in his account of it all – how people do things that aren't characteristic of them. Supposing he meant *himself* when he wrote that?'

Hercule Poirot said:

'You are at least right in this – not to take what has been written down as necessarily a true narrative. What has been written may have been written deliberately to mislead.'

'Oh, I know. I've kept that in mind.'

'Any other ideas?'

Carla said slowly:

'I wondered – before I'd read this – about Miss Williams. She lost her job, you see, when Angela went to school. And if Amyas had died suddenly, Angela probably wouldn't have gone after all. I mean if it passed off as a natural death – which it easily might have done, I suppose, if Meredith hadn't missed the coniine. I read up coniine, and it hasn't got any distinctive post-mortem appearances. It might have been thought to be sunstroke. I know that just losing a job doesn't sound a very adequate motive for murder. But murders have been committed again and again for what seem ridiculously inadequate motives. Tiny sums of money sometimes. And a middle-aged, perhaps rather incompetent governess might have got the wind up and just seen no future ahead of her.

'As I say, that's what I thought before I read this. But Miss Williams doesn't sound like that at all. She doesn't sound in the least incompetent –'

'Not at all. She is still a very efficient and intelligent woman.'

'I know. One can see that. And she sounds absolutely trustworthy too. That's what has upset me really. Oh, *you* know – *you* understand. You don't mind, of course. All along you've made it clear it was the truth you wanted. I suppose now we've *got* the truth! Miss Williams is quite right. One must accept truth. It's no good basing your life on a lie because it's what you want to believe. All right then

'– I can take it! My mother wasn't innocent! She wrote me
that letter because she was weak and unhappy and wanted
to spare me. I don't judge her. Perhaps I should feel like
that too. I don't know what prison does to you. And I don't
blame her either – if she felt so desperately about my father
I suppose she couldn't help herself. But I don't blame my
father altogether either. I understand – just a little – how he
felt. So alive – and so full of wanting everything . . . He
couldn't help it – he was made that way. And he was a great
painter. I think that excuses a lot.'

She turned her flushed excited face to Hecule Poirot with
her chin raised defiantly.

Hercule Poirot said:

'So – you are satisfied?'

'Satisfied?' said Carla Lemarchant. Her voice broke on
the word.

Poirot leant forward and patted her paternally on the
shoulder.

'Listen,' he said. 'You give up the fight at the moment
when it is most worth fighting. At the moment when I
Hercule Poirot, have a very good idea of what really
happened.'

Carla stared at him. She said:

'Miss Williams loved my mother. She saw her – with her
own eyes – faking that suicide evidence. If you believe what
she says –'

Hercule Poirot got up. He said:

'Mademoiselle, because Cecilia Williams says she saw
your mother faking Amyas Crale's fingerprints on the beer
bottle – on the beer *bottle*, mind – that is the only thing
need to tell me definitely, once for all, that your mother did
not kill your father.'

He nodded his head several times and went out of the
room, leaving Carla staring after him.

CHAPTER II

Poirot Asks Five Questions

I

'Well, M. Poirot?'

Philip Blake's tone was impatient.

Poirot said:'

'I have to thank you for your admirable and lucid account of the Crale tragedy.'

Philip Blake looked rather self-conscious.

'Very kind of you,' he murmured. 'Really surprising how much I remembered when I got down to it.'

Poirot said:

'It was an admirably clear narrative, but there were certain omissions, were there not?'

'Omissions?' Philip Blake frowned.

Hercule Poirot said:

'Your narrative, shall we say, was not entirely frank.' His tone hardened. 'I have been informed, Mr Blake, that on at least one night during the summer, Mrs Crale was seen coming out of your room at a somewhat compromising hour.'

There was a silence broken only by Philip Blake's heavy breathing. He said at last: 'Who told you that?'

Hercule Poirot shook his head.

'It is no matter who told me. That I *know*, that is the point.'

Again there was a silence; then Philip Blake made up his mind. He said:

'By accident, it seems, you have stumbled upon a purely private matter. I admit that it does not square with what I have written down. Nevertheless, it squares better than you might think. I am forced now to tell you the truth.

'I *did* entertain a feeling of animosity towards Caroline

201

Crale. At the same time I was always strongly attracted by her. Perhaps the latter fact induced the former. I resented the power she had over me and tried to stifle the attraction she had for me by constantly dwelling on her worst points. I never *liked* her, if you understand. But it would have been easy at any moment for me to make love to her. I had been in love with her as a boy and she had taken no notice of me. I did not find that easy to forgive.

'My opportunity came when Amyas lost his head so completely over the Greer girl. Quite without meaning to I found myself telling Caroline I loved her. She said quite calmly: 'Yes, I have always known that.' The insolence of the woman!

'Of course I knew that she didn't love me, but I saw that she was disturbed and disillusioned by Amyas's present infatuation. That is a mood when a woman can very easily be won. She agreed to come to me that night. And she came.'

Blake paused. He found now a difficulty in getting the words out.

'She came to my room. And then, with my arms round her, she told me quite coolly that it was no good! After all, she said, she was a one-man woman. She was Amyas Crale's, for better or worse. She agreed that she had treated me very badly, but said she couldn't help it. She asked me to forgive her.

'And she left me. *She left me!* Do you wonder, M. Poirot, that my hatred of her was heightened a hundredfold? Do you wonder that I have never forgiven her? For the insult she did me – as well as for the fact that she killed the friend I loved better than any one in the world!'

Trembling violently, Philip Blake exclaimed:

'*I don't want to speak of it*, do you hear? You've got your answer. Now go! And never mention the matter to me again!'

'I want to know, Mr Blake, the order in which your guests left the laboratory that day?'

Meredith Blake protested.

'But, my dear M. Poirot. After sixteen years! How can I possibly remember? I've told you that Caroline came out last.'

'You are *sure* of that?'

'Yes – at least – I think so . . .'

'Let us go there now. We must be *quite* sure, you see.'

Still protesting, Meredith Blake led the way. He unlocked the door and swung back the shutters. Poirot spoke to him authoritatively.

'Now then, my friend. You have showed your visitors your interesting preparations of herbs. Shut your eyes now and think –'

Meredith Blake did so obediently. Poirot drew a handkerchief from his pocket and gently passed it to and fro. Blake murmured, his nostrils twitching slightly:

'Yes, yes – extraordinary how things come back to one. Caroline, I remember, had on a pale coffee-coloured dress. Phil was looking bored . . . He always thought my hobby was quite idiotic.'

Poirot said:

'Reflect now, you are about to leave the room. You are going to the library where you are going to read the passage about the death of Socrates. Who leaves the room first – do you?'

'Elsa and I – yes. She passed through the door first. I was close behind her. We were talking. I stood there waiting for the others to come so that I could lock the door again. Philip – yes, Philip came out next. And Angela – she was asking him what bulls and bears were. They went on through the hall. Amyas followed them. I stood there waiting still – for Caroline, of course.'

'So you are quite sure Caroline stayed behind. Did you see what she was doing?'

Blake shook his head.

'No, I had my back to the room, you see. I was talking to Elsa – boring her, I expect – telling her how certain plants must be gathered at the full of the moon according to old superstition. And then Caroline came out – hurrying a little – and I locked the door.'

He stopped and looked at Poirot, who was replacing a handkerchief in his pocket. Meredith Blake sniffled disgustedly and thought: 'Why, the fellow actually uses *scent!*'

Aloud he said:

'I am quite sure of it. That was the order. Elsa, myself, Philip, Angela and Caroline. Does that help you at all?'

Poirot said:

'It all fits in. Listen. I want to arrange a meeting here. It will not, I think, be difficult . . .'

III

'Well?'

Elsa Dittisham said it almost eagerly – like a child.

'I want to ask you a question, madame.'

'Yes?'

Poirot said:

'After it was all over – the trial, I mean – did Meredith Blake ask you to marry him?'

Elsa stared. She looked contemptuous – almost bored.

'Yes – he did. Why?'

'Were you surprised?'

'Was I? I don't remember.'

'What did you say?'

Elsa laughed. She said:

'What do you think I said? After *Amyas* – Meredith?

It would have been ridiculous! It was stupid of him. He always was rather stupid.'

She smiled suddenly.

'He wanted, you know, to protect me – to "look after me" – that's how he put it! He thought like everybody else that the Assizes had been a terrible ordeal for me. And the reporters! And the booing crowds! And all the mud that was slung at me.'

She brooded a minute. Then said:

'Poor old Meredith! Such an ass!' And laughed again.

IV

Once again Hercule Poirot encountered the shrewd penetrating glance of Miss Williams, and once again felt the years falling away and himself a meek and apprehensive little boy.

There was, he explained, a question he wished to ask.

Miss Williams intimated her willingness to hear what the question was.

Poirot said slowly, picking his words carefully:

'Angela Warren was injured as a very young child. In my notes I find two references to that fact. In one of them it is stated that Mrs Crale threw a paperweight at the child. In the other that she attacked the baby with a crowbar. Which of those versions is the right one?'

Miss Williams replied briskly:

'I never heard anything about a crowbar. The paperweight is the correct story.'

'Who was your own informant?'

'Angela herself. She volunteered the information quite early.'

'What did she say exactly?'

'She touched her cheek and said: "Caroline did this when I was a baby. She threw a paperweight at me.

Never refer to it, will you, because it upsets her dreadfully."'

'Did Mrs Crale herself ever mention the matter to you?'

'Only obliquely. She assumed that I knew the story. I remember her saying once: "I know you think I spoil Angela, but you see, I always feel there is nothing I can do to make up to her for what I did." And on another occasion she said: "To know you have permanently injured another human being is the heaviest burden any one could have to bear."'

'Thank you, Miss Williams. That is all I wanted to know.'

Cecilia Williams said sharply:

'I don't understand you, M. Poirot. You showed Carla my account of the tragedy?'

Poirot nodded.

'And yet you are still –' She stopped.

Poirot said:

'Reflect a minute. If you were to pass a fishmonger's and saw twelve fish laid out on his slab, you would think they were all real fish, would you not? But one of them might be stuffed fish.'

Miss Williams replied with spirit:

'Most unlikely and anyway –'

'Ah, unlikely, yes, but not impossible – because a friend of mine once took down a stuffed fish (it was his trade, you comprehend) to compare it with the real thing! And if you saw a bowl of innias in a drawing-room in December you would say that they were false – but they might be real ones flown home from Baghdad.'

'What is the meaning of all this nonsense?' demanded Miss Williams.

'It is to show you that it is the eyes of the mind with which one really sees . . .'

Poirot slowed up a little as he approached the big block of flats overlooking Regent's Park.

Really, when he came to think of it, he did not want to ask Angela Warren any questions at all. The only question he did want to ask her could wait . . .

No, it was really only his insatiable passion for symmetry that was bringing him here. Five people – there should be five questions! It was neater so. It rounded off the thing better.

Ah well – he would think of something.

Angela Warren greeted him with something closely approaching eagerness. She said:

'Have you found out anything? Have you got anywhere?'

Slowly Poirot nodded his head in his best China mandarin manner. He said:

'At last I make progress.'

'Philip Blake?' It was halfway between statement and a question.

'Mademoiselle, I do not wish to say anything at present. The moment has not yet come. What I will ask of you is to be so good as to come down to Handcross Manor. The others have consented.'

She said with a slight frown:

'What do you propose to do? Reconstruct something that happened sixteen years ago?'

'See it, perhaps, from a clearer angle. You will come?'

Angela Warren said slowly:

'Oh, yes, I'll come. It will be interesting to see all those people again. I shall see *them* now, perhaps, from a clearer angle (as you put it) than I did then.'

'And you will bring with you the letter that you showed me?'

Angela Warren frowned.

'That letter is my own. I showed it to you for a good and

207

sufficient reason, but I have no intention of allowing it to be read by strange and unsympathetic persons.'

'But you will allow yourself to be guided by me in this matter?'

'I will do nothing of the kind. I will bring the letter with me, but I shall use my own judgement which I venture to think is quite as good as yours.'

Poirot spread out his hands in a gesture of resignation. He got up to go. He said:

'You permit that I ask one little question?'

'What is it?'

'At the time of the tragedy, you had lately read, had you not, Somerset Maugham's *The Moon and Sixpence*?'

Angela stared at him. Then she said:

'I believe – why, yes, that is quite true.' She looked at him with frank curiosity. 'How did you know?'

'I want to show you, mademoiselle, that even in a small unimportant matter, I am something of a magician. There are things I know without having to be told.'

CHAPTER III

Reconstruction

The afternoon sun shone into the laboratory at Handcross Manor. Some easy chairs and a settee had been brought into the room, but they served more to emphasize its forlorn aspect than to furnish it.

Slightly embarrassed, pulling at his moustache, Meredith Blake talked to Carla in a desultory way. He broke off once to say: 'My dear, you are very like your mother – and yet unlike her, too.'

Carla asked: 'How am I like her and how unlike?'

'You have her colouring and her way of moving, but you are – how shall I put it – more *positive* than she ever was.'

Philip Blake, a scowl creasing over his forehead, looked out of the window and drummed impatiently on the pane. He said:

'What's the sense of all this? A perfectly fine Saturday afternoon –'

Hercule Poirot hastened to pour oil on troubled waters.

'Ah, I apologize – it is, I know, unpardonable to disarrange the golf. *Mais voyons*, M. Blake, this is the daughter of your best friend. You will stretch a point for her, will you not?'

The butler announced: 'Miss Warren.'

Meredith went to welcome her. He said: 'It's good of you to spare the time, Angela. You're busy, I know.'

He led her over to the window.

Carla said: 'Hallo, Aunt Angela. I read your article in *The Times* this morning. It's nice to have a distinguished relative.' She indicated the tall, square-jawed young man with the steady grey eyes. 'This is John Rattery. He and I – hope – to be married.'

Angela Warren said: 'Oh! – I didn't know . . .'

Meredith went to greet the next arrival.

'Well, Miss Williams, it's a good many years since we met.'

Thin, frail and indomitable, the elderly governess advanced up the room. Her eyes rested thoughtfully on Poirot for a minute, then they went to the tall, square-shouldered figure in the well-cut tweeds.

Angela Warren came forward to meet her and said with a smile: 'I feel like a schoolgirl again.'

'I'm very proud of you, my dear,' said Miss Williams. 'You've done me credit. This is Carla, I suppose? She won't remember me. She was too young . . .'

Philip Blake said fretfully: 'What *is* all this? Nobody told me –'

Hercule Poirot said: 'I call it – me – an excursion into the past. Shall we not all sit down? Then we shall be ready when the last guest arrives. And when she is here we can proceed to our business – to lay the ghosts.'

Philip Blake exclaimed: 'What tomfoolery is this? You're not going to hold a *séance*, are you?'

'No, no. We are only going to discuss some events that happened long ago – to discuss them and, perhaps, to see more clearly the course of them. As to the ghosts, they will not materialize, but who is to say they are not here, in this room, although we cannot see them. Who is to say that Amyas and Caroline Crale are not here – listening?'

Philip Blake said: 'Absurd nonsense –' and broke off as the door opened again and the butler announced Lady Dittisham.

Elsa Dittisham came in with that faint, bored insolence that was a characteristic of her. She gave Meredith a slight smile, stared coldly at Angela and Philip, and went over to a chair by the window a little apart from the others. She loosened the rich pale furs round her neck and let them fall back. She looked for a minute or two about the room, then at Carla, and the girl stared back, thoughtfully appraising the woman who had wrought the havoc in her parents' lives. There was no animosity in her young earnest face, only curiosity.

Elsa said: 'I am sorry if I am late, M. Poirot.'

'It was very good of you to come, madame.'

Cecilia Williams snorted ever so slightly. Elsa met the animosity in her eyes with a complete lack of interest. She said:

'I wouldn't have known *you*, Angela. How long is it? Sixteen years?'

Hercule Poirot seized his opportunity.

'Yes, it is sixteen years since the events of which we are to speak, but let me first tell you why we are here.'

And in a few simple words he outlined Carla's appeal to him and his acceptance of the task.

He went on quickly, ignoring the gathering storm visible on Philip's face, and the shocked distaste on Meredith's.

'I accepted that commision – I set to work to find out – the truth.'

Carla Lemarchant, in the big grandfather chair, heard Poirot's words dimly, from a distance.

With her hand shielding her eyes she studied five faces, surreptitiously. Could she see any of these people committing murder? The exotic Elsa, the red-faced Philip, dear, nice, kind Mr Meredith Blake, that grim tartar of a governess, the cool, competent Angela Warren?

Could she – if she tried hard – visualize one of them killing someone? Yes, perhaps – but it wouldn't be the right kind of murder. She could picture Philip Blake, in an outburst of fury, strangling some women – yes, she *could* picture that . . . And she could picture Meredith Blake, threatening a burglar with a revolver – and letting it off by accident . . . And she could picture Angela Warren, also firing a revolver, but not by accident. With no personal feeling in the matter – the safety of the expedition depended on it! And Elsa, in some fantastic castle, saying from her couch of oriental silks: 'Throw the wretch over the battlements!' All wild fancies – and not even in the wildest flight of fancy could she imagine little Miss Williams killing anybody at all! Another fantastic picture: 'Did you ever kill anybody, Miss Williams?' 'Go on with your arithmetic, Carla, and don't ask silly questions. To kill anybody is very wicked.'

Carla thought: 'I must be ill – and I must stop this. Listen, you fool, listen to that little man who says he knows.'

Hercule Poirot was talking.

'That was my task – to put myself in reverse gear, as it were, and go back through the years and discover what really happened.'

Philip Blake said: 'We all know what happened. To pretend anything else is a swindle – that's what it is, a bare-faced swindle. You're getting money out of this girl on false pretences.'

Poirot did not allow himself to be angered. He said:

'You say, *we all know what happened.* You speak without reflection. The accepted version of certain facts is not necessarily the true one. On the face of it, for instance, you, Mr Blake, disliked Caroline Crale. That is the accepted version of your attitude. But anyone with the least flair for psychology can perceive at once that the exact opposite was the truth. You were always violently attracted towards Caroline Crale. You resented the fact, and tried to conquer it by steadfastly telling yourself her defects and reiterating your dislike. In the same way, Mr Meredith Blake had a tradition of devotion to Caroline Crale lasting over many years. In his story of the tragedy he represents himself as resenting Amyas Crale's conduct on *her* account, but you have only to read carefully between the lines and you will see that the devotion of a lifetime had worn itself thin and that it was the young, beautiful Elsa Greer that was occupying *his* mind and thoughts.'

There was a splutter from Meredith, and Lady Dittisham smiled.

Poirot went on.

'I mention these matters only as illustrations, though they have their bearing on what happened. Very well, then, I start on my backward journey – to learn everything I can about the tragedy. I will tell you how I set about it. I talked to the Counsel who defended Caroline Crale, to the Junior Counsel for the Crown, to the old solicitor who had known the Crale family intimately, to the lawyer's clerk who had been in court during the trial, to the police officer in charge of the case – and I came finally to the five eye-witnesses who had been upon the scene. And from all of these I put together a picture – a composite picture of a woman. And I learned these facts:

'*That at no time did Caroline Crale protest her innocence* (except in that one letter written to her daughter).

That Caroline Crale showed no fear in the dock, that she showed, in fact, hardly any interest, that she adopted throughout a thoroughly defeatist attitude. That in prison she was quiet and serene. That in a letter she wrote to her sister immediately after the verdict, she expressed herself as acquiescent in the fate that had overtaken her. And in the opinion of everyone I talked to (with one notable exception) *Caroline Crale was guilty.*'

Philip Blake nodded his head. 'Of course she was!'

Hercule Poirot said:

'But it was not my part to accept the verdict of *others*. I had to examine the evidence for *myself*. To examine the facts and to satisfy myself that the psychology of the case accorded itself with them. To do this I went over the police files carefully, and I also succeeded in getting five people who were on the spot to write me out their own accounts of the tragedy. These accounts were very valuable for they contained certain matter which the police files could not give me – that is to say: A, certain conversations and incidents which, from the police point of view, were not relevant; B, the opinions of the people themselves as to what Caroline Crale was thinking and feeling (not admissible legally as evidence); C, certain facts which had been deliberately withheld from the police.

'I was in a position now to judge the case for *myself*. There seems no doubt whatever that Caroline Crale had ample motive for the crime. She loved her husband, he had publicly admitted that he was about to leave her for another woman, and by her own admission she was a jealous woman.

'To come from motives to means, an empty scent bottle that had contained coniine was found in her bureau drawer. There were no fingerprints upon it but hers. When asked about it by the police, she admitted taking it from this room we are in now. The coniine bottle here also had her fingerprints upon it. I questioned Mr Meredith Blake as to the order in which the five people left this room on that day – for it seemed to me hardly conceivable that *any one* should be able to help themselves to the poison whilst five people were in the room. The people left the room in this order – Elsa Greer, Meredith Blake, Angela Warren and Philip Blake, Amyas Crale, and lastly Caroline Crale. Moreover, Mr Meredith Blake has his back to the room whilst he was waiting for Mrs Crale to come out, so that it was impossible for him to see what she was doing. She had, that is to say, the opportunity. I am therefore satisfied that she did take the coniine. There is indirect confirmation of it. Mr Meredith Blake said to me the other day: 'I can remember standing here and smelling the jasmine through the open window.' But the month was September, and the jasmine creeper outside that window would have finished flowering. It is the ordinary jasmine which blooms in June and July. But the scent bottle found in her room and which contained the dregs of coniine had originally contained jasmine scent. I take it as certain, then, that Mrs Crale decided to steal the coniine, and surreptitiously emptied out the scent from a bottle she had in her bag.

'I tested that a second time the other day when I asked Mr Blake to shut his eyes and try and remember the order of leaving the room. A whiff of jasmine scent stimulated his memory immediately. We are all more influenced by smell than we know.

'So we come to the morning of the fatal day. So far the facts are not in dispute. Miss Greer's sudden revealing of the fact that she and Mr Crale contemplate marriage, Amyas Crale's confirmation of that, and Caroline Crale's deep distress. None of these things depend on the evidence of one witness only.

'On the following morning there is a scene between husband and wife in the library. The first thing that is overheard is Caroline Crale saying: 'You and your women!' in a bitter voice, and finally going on to say, 'Some day I'll kill you.' Philip Blake overheard this from the hall. And Miss Greer overheard it from the terrace outside.

'She then heard Mr Crale ask his wife to be reasonable. And she heard Mrs Crale say: 'Sooner than let you go to that girl – I'll kill you.' Soon after this Amyas Crale comes out and brusquely tells Elsa Greer to come down and pose for him. She gets a pullover and accompanies him.

'There is nothing so far that seems psychologically incorrect. Every one has behaved as they might be expected to behave. But we come now to something that *is* incongruous.

'Meredith Blake discovers his loss, telephones his brother; they meet down at the landing stage and they come up past the Battery garden, where Caroline Crale is having a discussion with her husband on the subject of Angela's going to school. Now that does strike me as very odd. Husband and wife have a terrific scene, ending in a distinct threat on Caroline's part, and yet, twenty minutes or so later, she goes down and starts a trivial domestic argument.'

Poirot turned to Meredith Blake.

'You speak in your narrative of certain words you overheard Crale say. These were: "It's all settled – I'll see to her packing." That is right?'

Meredith Blake said: 'It was something like that – yes.'

Poirot turned to Philip Blake.

'Is your recollection the same?'

The latter frowned.

'I didn't remember it till you say so – but I do remember now. Something *was* said about packing!'

'Said by Mr Crale – not Mrs Crale?'

'Amyas said it. All I heard Caroline say was something about its being very hard on the girl. Anyway, what does all this matter? We all know Angela was off to school in a day or two.'

Poirot said: 'You do not see the force of my objection. Why should *Amyas Crale* pack for the girl? It is absurd, that! There was Mrs Crale, there was Miss Williams, there was a housemaid. It is a woman's job to pack – not a man's.'

Philip Blake said impatiently:

'What does it matter? It's nothing to do with the crime.'

'You think not? For me, it was the first point that struck me as suggestive. And it is immediately followed by another. Mrs Crale, a desperate woman, broken-hearted, who has threatened her husband a short while before and who is certainly contemplating either suicide or murder, now offers in the most amicable manner to bring her husband down some iced beer.'

Meredith Blake said slowly: 'That isn't odd if she was contemplating murder. Then, surely, it is just what she *would* do. Dissimulate!'

'You think so? She has decided to poison her husband, she has already got the poison. Her husband keeps a supply

216

of beer down in the Battery garden. Surely if she has any intelligence at all, she will put the poison in one of *those* bottles at a moment when there is no one about.'

Meredith Blake objected.

'She couldn't have done that. Somebody else might have drunk it.'

'Yes, Elsa Greer. Do you tell me that having made up her mind to murder her husband, Caroline Crale would have scruples against killing the girl too?

'But let us not argue the point. Let us confine ourselves to facts. Caroline Crale says she will send her husband down some iced beer. She goes up to the house, fetches a bottle from the conservatory where it was kept and takes it down to him. She pours it out and gives it to him.

'Amyas Crale drinks it off and says: "Everything tastes foul today."

'Mrs Crale goes up again to the house. She has lunch and appears much as usual. It has been said of her that she looks a little worried and preoccupied. That does not help us – for there is no criterion of behaviour for a murderer. There are calm murderers and excited murderers.

'After lunch she goes down again to the Battery. She discovers her husband dead and does, shall we say, the obviously expected things. She registers emotion and she sends the governess to telephone for a doctor. We now come to a fact which has previously not been known.' He looked at Miss Williams. 'You do not object?'

Miss Williams was rather pale. She said: 'I did not pledge you to secrecy.'

Quietly, but with telling effect, Poirot recounted what the governess had seen.

Elsa Dittisham moved her position. She stared at the drab little woman in the big chair. She said incredibly:

'You actually saw her do *that*?'

Philip Blake sprang up.

'But that settles it!' he shouted. 'That settles it once and for all.'

Hercule Poirot looked at him mildly. He said: 'Not necessarily.'

Angela Warren said sharply: 'I don't believe it.' There was a quick hostile glint in the glance she shot at the little governess.

Meredith Blake was pulling at his moustache, his face dismayed. Alone, Miss Williams remained undisturbed. She sat very upright and there was a spot of colour in each cheek.

She said: 'That is what I saw.'

Poirot said slowly: 'There is, of course, only your word for it . . .'

'There is only my word for it.' The indomitable grey eyes met his. 'I am not accustomed, M. Poirot, to having my word doubted.'

Hercule Poirot bowed his head. He said:

'I do not doubt your word, Miss Williams. What you saw took place exactly as you say it did – and because of what you saw I realized that Caroline Crale was not guilty – could not possibly be guilty.'

For the first time, that tall, anxious-faced young man, John Rattery, spoke. He said: 'I'd be interested to know *why* you say that, M. Poirot.'

Poirot turned to him.

'Certainly. I will tell you. What did Miss Williams see – she saw Caroline Crale very carefully and anxiously wiping off fingerprints and subsequently imposing her dead husband's fingerprints on the beer bottle. On the beer *bottle*, mark. But the coniine was in the glass – not in the bottle. The police found no traces of coniine in the bottle. There had never been any coniine in the bottle. *And Caroline Crale didn't know that.*

'She who is supposed to have poisoned her husband didn't know *how* he had been poisoned. She thought the poison was in the bottle.'

Meredith objected: 'But why –'

Poirot interrupted him in a flash.

218

'Yes – *why*? Why did Caroline Crale try so desperately to establish the theory of suicide? The answer is – must be – quite simple. Because she knew who *had* poisoned him and she was willing to do anything – endure anything – rather than let that person be suspected.

'There is not far to go now. Who could that person be? Would she have shielded Philip Blake? Or Meredith? Or Elsa Greer? Or Cecilia Williams? No, there is only one person whom she would be willing to protect at all costs.'

He paused: 'Miss Warren, if you have brought your sister's last letter with you, I should like to read it aloud.'

Angela Warren said: 'No.'

'But, Miss Warren –'

Angela got up. Her voice rang out, cold as steel.

'I realize very well what you are suggesting. You are saying, are you not, that I killed Amyas Crale and that my sister knew it. I deny that allegation utterly.'

Poirot said: 'The letter . . .'

'That letter was meant for my eyes alone.'

Poirot looked to where the two youngest people in the room stood together.

Carla Lemarchant said: 'Please, Aunt Angela, won't you do as M. Poirot asks?'

Angela Warren said bitterly: 'Really, Carla! Have you no sense of decency? She was your mother – you –'

Carla's voice rang out clear and fierce.

'Yes, she was my mother. That's why I've a right to ask you. I'm speaking for *her*. I *want* that letter read.'

Slowly, Angela Warren took out the letter from her bag and handed it to Poirot. She said bitterly:

'I wish I had never shown it to you.'

Turning away from them she stood looking out of the window.

As Hercule Poirot read aloud Caroline Crale's last letter, the shadows were deepening in the corners of the room. Carla had a sudden feeling of someone in the room,

219

gathering shape, listening, breathing, waiting. She thought: '*She's* here – my mother's here. Caroline – Caroline Crale is *here* in this room!'

Hercule Poirot's voice ceased. He said:

'You will all agree, I think, that that is a very remarkable letter. A beautiful letter, too, but certainly remarkable. For there is one striking omission in it – it contains no protestation of innocence.'

Angela Warren said without turning her head: 'That was unnecessary.'

'Yes, Miss Warren, it was unnecessary. Caroline Crale had no need to tell her sister that she was innocent – because she thought her sister knew that fact already – knew it for the best of all reasons. All Caroline Crale was concerned about was to comfort and reassure and to avert the possibility of a confession from Angela. She reiterates again and again – *It's all right, darling, it's all right.*'

Angela Warren said: 'Can't you understand? She wanted me to be happy, that's all.'

'Yes, she wanted you to be happy, that is abundantly clear. It is her one preoccupation. She has a child, but it is not that child of whom she is thinking – that is to come later. No, it is her sister who occupies her mind to the exclusion of everything else. Her sister must be reassured, must be encouraged to live her life, to be happy and successful. And so that the burden of acceptance may not be too great, Caroline includes that one very significant phrase: "*One must pay one's debts.*"

'That one phrase explains everything. It refers explicitly to the burden that Caroline has carried for so many years ever since, in a fit of uncontrolled adolescent rage, she hurled a paperweight at her baby sister and injured that sister for life. Now, at last, she has the opportunity to pay the debt she owes. And if it is any consolation, I will say to you all that I earnestly believe that in the payment of that debt, Caroline Crale did achieve a peace and serenity greater than any she had ever known. Because of her belief that she was paying that debt, the ordeal of trial and condemnation could not touch her. It is a strange thing to say of a condemned murderess – but she had everything to make her happy. Yes, more than you imagine, as I will show you presently.

'See how, by this explanation, everything falls into its place where Caroline's own reactions are concerned. Look at the series of events from her point of view. To begin with, on the preceding evening, an event occurs which reminds her forcibly of her own undisciplined girlhood. Angela throws a *paperweight* at Amyas Crale. That, remember, is what she herself did many years ago. Angela shouts out that she wishes Amyas was dead. Then, on the next morning, Caroline comes into the little conservatory and finds Angela tampering with the beer. Remember Miss Williams's words: "Angela was there. She looked guilty . . ." Guilty of playing truant, was what Miss Williams meant, but to Caroline, Angela's guilty face, as she was caught unawares, would have a different meaning. Remember that on at least one occasion before Angela had put things in Amyas's drink. It was an idea which might readily occur to her.

'Caroline takes the bottle *that Angela gives her* and goes down with it to the Battery. And there she pours it out and gives it to Amyas, and he makes a face as he tosses it off and utters those significant words: "Everything tastes foul today."

'Caroline has no suspicions then – but after lunch she goes down to the Battery and finds her husband dead – and she has no doubt at all but that he has been poisoned. *She* had not done it? Who, then, has? And the whole thing comes over her with a rush – Angela's threats, Angela's face stooping over the beer and caught unawares – guilty – guilty – guilty. Why has the child done it? As a revenge on Amyas, perhaps not meaning to kill, just to make him ill or sick? Or has she done it for her, Caroline's sake? Has she realized

221

and resented Amyas's desertion of her sister? Caroline remembers – oh, so well – her own undisciplined violent emotions at Angela's age. And only one thought springs to her mind. How can she protect Angela? Angela handled that bottle – Angela's fingerprints will be on it. She quickly wipes it and polishes it. If only everybody can be got to believe it is suicide. If Amyas's fingerprints are the only ones found. She tries to fit his dead fingers round the bottle – working desperately – listening for someone to come . . .

'Once take that assumption as true, and everything from then on fits in. Her anxiety about Angela all along, her insistence on getting her away, keeping her out of touch with what was going on. Her fear of Angela's being questioned unduly by the police. Finally, her overwhelming anxiety to get Angela out of England before the trial comes on. Because she is always terrified that Angela might break down and confess.'

CHAPTER IV

Truth

Slowly, Angela Warren swung round. Her eyes, hard and contemptuous, ranged over the faces turned towards her.

She said:

'You're blind fools – all of you. Don't you know that if I had done it I *would* have confessed! I'd never have let Caroline suffer for what I'd done. Never!'

Poirot said:

'But you did tamper with the beer.'

'I? Tamper with the beer?'

Poirot turned to Meredith Blake.

'Listen, monsieur. In your account here of what happened, you describe having heard sounds in this room, which is below your bedroom, on the morning of the crime.'

Blake nodded.

'But it was only a cat.'

'How do you know it was a cat?'

'I – I can't remember. But it was a cat. I am quite sure it was a cat. The window was open just wide enough for a cat to get through.'

'But it was not fixed in that position. The sash moves freely. It could have been pushed up and a human being could have got in and out.'

'Yes, but I know it was a cat.'

'You did not *see* a cat?'

Blake said perplexedly and slowly:

'No, I did not see it –' He paused, frowning. 'And yet I know.'

'I will tell you *why* you know presently. In the meantime I put this point to you. Someone could have come up to the house that morning, have got into your laboratory, taken

223

something from the shelf and gone again without your seeing them. Now if that someone had come over from Alderbury it could not have been Philip Blake, nor Elsa Greer, nor Amyas Crale nor Caroline Crale. We know quite well what all those four were doing. That leaves Angela Warren and Miss Williams. Miss Williams was over here – you actually met her as you went out. She told you then that she was looking for Angela. Angela had gone bathing early, but Miss Williams did not see her in the water, nor anywhere on the rocks. She could swim across to this side easily – in fact she did so later in the morning when she was bathing with Philip Blake. I suggest that she swam across here, came up to the house, got in through the window, and took something from the shelf.'

Angela Warren said: 'I did nothing of the kind – not – at least –'

'Ah!' Poirot gave a yelp of triumph. '*You have remembered*. You told me, did you not, that to play a malicious joke on Amyas Crale you pinched some of what you called "the cat stuff" – that is how you put it –'

Meredith Blake said sharply:

'Valerian! Of course.'

'Exactly. *That* is what made you sure in your mind that it was a cat who had been in the room. Your nose is very sensitive. You smelled the faint, unpleasant odour of valerian without knowing, perhaps, that you did so – but it suggested to your subconscious mind "Cat". Cats love valerian and will go anywhere for it. Valerian is particularly nasty to taste, and it was your account of it the day before which made mischievous Miss Angela plan to put some in her brother-in-law's beer, which she knew he always tossed down his throat in a draught.'

Angela Warren said wonderingly: 'Was it really that day? I remember taking it perfectly. Yes, and I remember getting out the beer and Caroline coming in and nearly catching me! Of course I remember . . . But I've never connected it with that particular day.'

'Of course not – because there was no connection *in your mind*. The two events were entirely dissimilar to you. One was on a par with other mischievous pranks – the other was a bombshell of tragedy arriving without warning and succeeding in banishing all lesser incidents from your mind. But me, I noticed when you spoke of it that you said: "I pinched, etc., etc., *to put it* in Amyas's drink." You did not say you had actually *done* so.'

'No, because I never did. Caroline came in just when I was unscrewing the bottle. Oh!' It was a cry. 'And Caroline thought – she thought it was *me* –!'

She stopped. She looked round. She said quietly in her usual cool tones: 'I suppose you all think so, too.'

She paused and then said: '*I didn't kill Amyas*. Not as the result of a malicious joke nor in any other way. If I had I would never have kept silence.'

Miss Williams said sharply:

'Of course you wouldn't, my dear.' She looked at Hercule Poirot. 'Nobody but a *fool* would think so.'

Hercule Poirot said mildly:

'I am not a fool and I do not think so. *I know quite well who killed Amyas Crale.*'

He paused.

'There is always a danger of accepting facts as proved which are really nothing of the kind. Let us take the situation at Alderbury. A very old situation. Two women and one man. We have taken it for granted that Amyas Crale proposed to leave his wife for the other woman. But I suggest to you now *that he never intended to do anything of the kind*.

'He had had infatuations for women before. They obsessed him while they lasted, but they were soon over. The women he had fallen in love with were usually women of a certain experience – they did not expect too much of him. But this time the woman did. She was not, you see, a woman at all. She was a girl, and in Caroline Crale's words,

225

she was terribly sincere . . . She may have been hard-boiled and sophisticated in speech, but in love she was frighteningly single-minded. *Because* she herself had a deep and overmastering passion for Amyas Crale she assumed that he had the same for her. She assumed without any question that their passion was for life. She assumed without asking him that he was going to leave his wife.

'But why, you will say, did Amyas Crale not undeceive her? And my answer is – the picture. He wanted to finish his picture.

'To some people that sounds incredible – but not to anybody who knows about artists. And we have already accepted that explanation in principle. That conversation between Crale and Meredith Blake is more intelligible now. Crale is embarrassed – pats Blake on the back, assures him optimistically the whole thing is going to pan out all right. To Amyas Crale, you see, everything is simple. He is painting a picture, slightly encumbered by what he describes as a couple of jealous, neurotic women – but neither of them is going to be allowed to interfere with what to him is the most important thing in life.

'If he were to tell Elsa the truth it would be all up with the picture. Perhaps in the first flush of his feelings for her he did talk about leaving Caroline. Men do say these things when they are in love. Perhaps he merely let it be assumed, as he is letting it be assumed now. He doesn't care what Elsa assumes. Let her think what she likes. Anything to keep her quiet for another day or two.

'Then – he will tell her the truth – that things between them are over. He has never been a man to be troubled with scruples.

'He did, I think, make an effort not to get embroiled with Elsa to begin with. He warned her what kind of a man he was – but she would not take warning. She rushed on her Fate. And to a man like Crale women were fair game. If you had asked him he would have said easily that Elsa was young – she'd soon get over it. That was the way Amyas Crale's mind worked.

'His wife was actually the only person he cared about at all. He wasn't worrying much about her. She'd only got to put up with things for a few days longer. He was furious with Elsa for blurting out things to Caroline, but he still optimistically thought it would be "all right". Caroline would forgive him as she had done so often before, and Elsa – Elsa would just have to "lump it". So simple are the problems of life to a man like Amyas Crale.

'But I think that that last evening he became really worried. About Caroline, not about Elsa. Perhaps he went to her room and she refused to speak with him. At any rate, after a restless night, he took her aside after breakfast and blurted out the truth. He had been infatuated with Elsa, but it was all over. Once he'd finished the picture he'd never see her again.

'And it was in answer to that that Caroline Crale cried out indignantly: "You and your women!" That phrase, you see, put Elsa in a class with others – those others who had gone their way. And she added indignantly: "Some day I'll kill you."

'She was angry, revolted by his callousness and by his cruelty to the girl. When Philip Blake saw her in the hall and heard her murmur to herself, "It's too cruel!" it was of Elsa she was thinking.

'As for Crale, he came out of the library, found Elsa with Philip Blake, and brusquely ordered her down to go on with the sitting. What he did not know was that Elsa Greer had been sitting just outside the library window and had overheard everything. And the account she gave later of that conversation was not the true one. There is only her word for it, remember.

'Imagine the shock it must have been to her to hear the truth, brutally spoken!

'On the previous afternoon Meredith Blake has told us

227

that whilst he was waiting for Caroline to leave this room he was standing in the doorway with his back to the room. He was talking to Elsa Greer. That means that she would have been *facing* him and that *she* could see exactly what Caroline was doing over his shoulder – and that she *was the only person who could do so*.

'She saw Caroline take that poison. She said nothing, but she remembered it as she sat outside the library window.

'When Amyas Crale came out she made the excuse of wanting a pullover, and went up to Caroline Crale's room to look for that poison. Women know where other women are likely to hide things. She found it, and being careful not to obliterate any fingerprints or to leave her own, she drew off the fluid into a fountain-pen filler.

'Then she came down again and went off with Crale to the Battery garden. And presently, no doubt, she poured him out some beer and he tossed it down in his usual way.

'Meanwhile, Caroline Crale was seriously disturbed. When she saw Elsa come up to the house (this time really to fetch a pullover), Caroline slipped quickly down to the Battery garden and tackled her husband. What he is doing is shameful! She won't stand for it! It's unbelievably cruel and hard on the girl! Amyas, irritable at being interrupted, says it's all settled – when the picture is done he'll send the girl packing! *"It's all settled – I'll send her packing. I tell you."*

'And then they hear the footsteps of the two Blakes, and Caroline comes out and, slightly embarrassed, murmurs something about Angela and school and having a lot to do, and by a natural association of ideas the two men judge the conversation they have overheard refers to *Angela*, and "I'll send her packing" becomes "I'll see to her packing."

'And Elsa, pullover in hand, comes down the path, cool and smiling, and takes up the pose once more.

'She has counted, no doubt, upon Caroline's being suspected and the coniine bottle being found in her room. But Caroline now plays into her hands completely. She brings down some iced beer and pours it out for her husband.

'Amyas tosses it off, making a face and says: "Everything tastes foul today."

'Do you not see how significant that remark is? *Everything* tastes foul? Then there has been something else *before* that beer that has tasted unpleasant and the taste of which is *still in his mouth*. And one other point. Philip Blake speaks of Crale's staggering a little and wonders "if he has been drinking." But that slight stagger was the *first sign of the coniine working*, and that means *that it had already been administered to him some time before Caroline brought him the iced bottle of beer*.

'And so Elsa Greer sat on the grey wall and posed and, since she must keep him from suspecting until it was too late, she talked to Amyas Crale brightly and naturally. Presently she saw Meredith on the bench above and waved her hand to him and acted her part even more thoroughly for his behalf.

'And Amyas Crale, a man who detested illness and refused to give in to it, painted doggedly on till his limbs failed and his speech thickened, and he sprawled there on that bench, helpless, but with his mind still clear.

'The bell sounded from the house and Meredith left the bench to come down to the Battery. I think in that brief moment Elsa left her place and ran across to the table and dropped the last few drops of the poison into the beer glass that held that last innocent drink. (She got rid of the dropper on the path up to the house – crushing it to powder.) Then she met Meredith in the doorway.

'There is a glare there coming in out of the shadows. Meredith did not see very clearly – only his friend sprawled in a familiar position and saw his eyes turn from the picture in what he described as a malevolent glare.

'How much did Amyas know or guess? How much his conscious mind knew we cannot tell, but his hand and his eye were faithful.'

Hercule Poirot gestured towards the picture on the wall.

'I should have known when I first saw that picture. For it is a very remarkable picture. It is the picture of a murderess painted by her victim – it is the picture of a girl watching her lover die . . .'

CHAPTER V

Aftermath

In the silence that followed – a horrified, appalled silence, the sunset slowly flickered away, the last gleam left the window where it had rested on the dark head and pale furs of the woman sitting there.

Elsa Dittisham moved and spoke. She said:

'Take them away, Meredith. Leave me with M. Poirot.'

She sat there motionless until the door shut behind them. Then she said: 'You are very clever, aren't you?'

Poirot did not answer.

She said: 'What do you expect me to do? Confess?'

He shook his head.

Elsa said:

'Because I shall do nothing of the kind! And I shall admit nothing. But what we say here, together, does not matter. Because it is only a question of your word against mine.'

'Exactly.'

'I want to know what you are going to do?'

Hercule Poirot said:

'I shall do everything I can to induce the authorities to grant a posthumous free pardon to Caroline Crale.'

Elsa laughed. She said: 'How absurd! To be given a free pardon for something you didn't do.' Then she said: 'What about me?'

'I shall lay my conclusion before the necessary people. If they decide there is the possibility of making out a case against you then they may act. I will tell you in my opinion there is not sufficient evidence – there are only inferences, not facts. Moreover, they will not be anxious to proceed against any one in your position unless there is ample justification for such a course.'

Elsa said:

'I shouldn't care. If I were standing in the dock, fighting for my life – there might be something in that – something alive – exciting. I might – enjoy it.'

'Your husband would not.'

She stared at him.

'Do you think I care in the least what my husband would feel?'

'No, I do not. I do not think you have ever in your life cared about what any other person would feel. If you had, you might be happier.'

She said sharply:

'Why are you sorry for me?'

'Because, my child, you have so much to learn.'

'What have I got to learn?'

'All the grown-up emotions – pity, sympathy, understanding. The only things you know – have ever known – are love and hate.'

Elsa said:

'I saw Caroline take the coniine. I thought she meant to kill herself. That would have simplified things. And then, the next morning, I found out. He told her that he didn't care a button about me – he *had* cared, but it was all over. Once he'd finished the picture he'd send me packing. She'd nothing to worry about, he said.

'And she – was sorry for me . . . Do you understand what that did to me? I found the stuff and I gave it to him and I sat there watching him die. I've never felt so alive, so exultant, so full of power. I watched him die . . .'

She flung out her hands.

'I didn't understand that I was killing *myself* – not him. Afterwards I saw her caught in a trap – and that was no good either. I couldn't hurt her – she didn't care – she escaped from it all – half the time she wasn't there. She and Amyas both escaped – they went somewhere where I couldn't get at them. But they didn't die. *I* died.'

Elsa Dittisham got up. She went across to the door. She said again:

'*I died . . .*'

In the hall she passed two young people whose life together was just beginning.

The chauffeur held open the door of the car. Lady Dittisham got in and the chauffeur wrapped the fur rug round her knees.

Penguin Books
The Overcrowded Barracoon

V. S. Naipaul was born in 1932. He is the
author of *The Mystic Masseur* (1957; John
Llewelyn Rhys Memorial Prize), *The Suffrage of
Elvira* (1958), *Miguel Street* (1959; Somerset
Maugham Award), *A House for Mr Biswas* (1961),
The Middle Passage (1962), *Mr Stone and the
Knights Companion* (1963; Hawthornden Prize),
An Area of Darkness (1964) and *The Mimic Men*
(1967). *A Flag on the Island* (1967) is a collection
of his short stories. His latest books are *The Loss of
El Dorado* (1969), *In a Free State* (1971; Booker
Prize) and *Guerrillas* (1975).

V. S. Naipaul

The Overcrowded Barracoon
and other articles

Penguin Books

Penguin Books Ltd,
Harmondsworth, Middlesex, England
Penguin Books Inc.,
7110 Ambassador Road, Baltimore, Maryland 21207, U.S.A.
Penguin Books Australia Ltd,
Ringwood, Victoria, Australia
Penguin Books Canada Ltd,
41 Steelcase Road West, Markham, Ontario, Canada
Penguin Books (N.Z.) Ltd,
182–190 Wairau Road, Auckland 10, New Zealand

First published by André Deutsch 1972

Published in Penguin Books 1976

Made and printed in Great Britain by
Hazell Watson & Viney Ltd,
Aylesbury, Bucks
Set in Linotype Baskerville

Contents

I

An Unlikely Colonial

London

The Times Literary Supplement, 15 August 1958

For me the problem of mass communication is still only an academic problem. I have written three books in five years and made £300 out of them. The Americans do not want me because I am too British. The public here do not want me because I am too foreign. But I have been lucky in other ways. After only five years I am just able to make a living by writing. Many people here still feel that writing is an amateur activity and deserves gratuities rather than payment; but this is better than the attitude in say, Trinidad, where it is felt that writing is its own reward. But for how long can I continue to live in London and continue writing?

I live in England and depend on an English audience. Yet I write about Trinidad, and more particularly the Indian community there. Few novels have been written about Trinidad and I cannot deny that this gives me some advantages. There is the additional advantage that Trinidad society is so far unformed; ambitions are not uniform; the class structure is so fluid as to be almost non-existent; there is a vague urge to respectability, but this can express itself in startling ways.

Superficially, because of the multitude of races, Trinidad may seem complex, but to anyone who knows it, it is a simple colonial philistine society. Education is desirable because it may lead to security, but any unnecessary acquaintance with books is frowned upon. The writer or the painter, unless he wins recognition overseas, preferably in England, is mercilessly ridiculed. This is only slowly changing. Respectability and class still mean very little.

Money means a good deal more, and the only non-financial achievements which are recognized are those connected with sport and music. For these reasons Trinidadians are more recognizably 'characters' than people in England. Only a man's eccentricities can get him attention. It might also be that in a society without traditions, without patterns, every man finds it easier 'to be himself'. Whatever the reason, this determination of people to be themselves, to cherish their eccentricities, to reveal themselves at once, makes them easy material for the writer.

I have often heard people in this country deploring the disappearance of 'characters'. A well-known humorist once drove me twenty miles on a Sunday morning to meet a man in a country pub. He was recognizably, absurdly, a character, a cross between Mr Pickwick and a Giles old man. He was holding court when we arrived. To appreciate his remarks one had to know much of what he had said in the past; he had his punch lines, which were coaxed out of him and received with roars of laughter. The humorist listened with awe, appreciation and a deepening depression. He was positively gloomy when we left. 'Great character,' he said. 'Very few of them left nowadays.' A few words about the welfare state and the degeneracy of the country followed.

In *The Acceptance World* Anthony Powell gets to the heart of the problem:

I began to brood on the complexity of writing a novel about English life, a subject difficult enough to handle with authenticity even of a crudely naturalistic sort, even more to convey the inner truth of the things observed. Those South Americans sitting opposite, coming from a continent I had never visited, regarding which I possessed only the most superficial scraps of information, seemed in some respects easier to conceive in terms of a novel than most of the English people sitting round the room. Intricacies of social life make English habits unyielding to simplification, while understatement and irony –

in which all classes of this island converse – upset the normal emphasis of reported speech. How, I asked myself, could a writer attempt to describe in a novel such a young man as Mark Members, for example, possessing so much in common with myself, yet so different? ... Viewed from some distance off, Members and I might reasonably be considered almost identical units of the same organism, scarcely to be differentiated even by the sociological expert.

Might it not be because of this that English writers are depending more and more on 'gimmicks' – sex, snobbery, religion, anger?

It is a formidable problem and one which I do not have to face. My material is abundant, new and easily grasped. I need no gimmicks. But I have certain handicaps. The social comedies I write can be fully appreciated only by someone who knows the region I write about. Without that knowledge it is easy for my books to be dismissed as farces and my characters as eccentrics. There can also be misunderstanding: the critic of the *Observer* thinks I get my dialect from Ronald Firbank. And there can be simple exasperation: the critic of the *Yorkshire Post* says she is just fed up with Trinidad and Trinidad dialect. This, from Yorkshire! It isn't easy for the exotic writer to get his work accepted as being more than something exotic, something to be judged on its merits. The very originality of the material makes the work suspect. And the exotic humorous writer is in a particularly delicate position. Consider this comment on my first novel in a weekly paper, now justly defunct: 'His whole purpose is to show how funny Trinidad Indians are.' The *Daily Telegraph* says I look down a long Oxford nose at the land of my birth. The *Evening Standard*, however, thinks that I write of my native land with warm affection. None of these comments would have been made about a comic French or American novel. They are not literary judgments at all. Imagine a critic in Trinidad writing of *Vile Bodies*: 'Mr Evelyn Waugh's whole purpose is to show how funny English people are. He looks down his nose at the land of his birth. We hope that in future he writes of his native land with warm affection.'

But – the English writer does not write for Trinidad. And I write for England. And for me the regional barrier is much more difficult than it is, say, for someone from Yorkshire. People are used to reading about Yorkshire, used to the dialect. I am much more used to it than the critic of the *Yorkshire Post* is used to the Trinidad dialect.

And it isn't only that the dialect is new. People have been used to reading about non-Europeans through European eyes. India, with the vision of Kipling or Forster of J. R. Ackerley or John Masters, is best-selling territory. But what happens when R. K. Narayan writes about it? He has invention, warmth, humour, truth, a miraculous lightness of touch. Yet he remains comparatively unknown to the library reader. The alien, customary vision is missing.

There is, too, the prejudice of the European against the non-European. Forty years ago Sinclair Lewis was protesting against the indifference of English readers to American books. 'I do think,' Hugh Walpole wrote in 1922, 'that it has been the fault of some of the newer American writers that, clever though they are, they have presented American life to us in so ugly a fashion – ugly in speech, in background, in thought.' The ugliness remains, but today publishers fly over regularly to the United States to buy books. Is there, then, a political reason for interest in books from other countries? Does it depend on the size and power of the country one writes about? If this is so, Narayan may yet have a best-selling future. And I never will if I continue to write about Trinidad.

It is an odd, suspicious situation: an Indian writer writing in English for an English audience about non-English characters who talk their own sort of English. The Americans at least had their own audience. I cannot help feeling that it might have been more profitable for me to appear in translation. It would have been necessary then for the critic of the *Yorkshire Post* to do her job rather than express her exasperation; and there would have been no talk about the degree of affection with which I regarded my native land.

Most reviewers have judged me fairly. Some have been generous. I comment on those who have made political rather than literary judgments because I feel they represent the attitude of the reading public.

Yet there are writers in my position who have overcome public indifference. I have studied them closely and find that, apart, of course, from plain merit, there are three devices I can employ.

Sex, first of all. Sex, even in St Kitts, leaps through every barrier. But I cannot write Sex. I haven't the skill, or the wide experience which is necessary if one's work is to have variety. And then I would be embarrassed even at the moment of writing. My friends would laugh. My mother would be shocked, and with reason. Here are the publishers' notes about two successful books by Caribbean writers: one is described as a 'boy's lust for women in the South American jungle'; the chief attraction of the other is its 'quick-to-strip heroines'.

Another device is to introduce an English or American character and write the story around him. This is the device used by British film-makers who put American characters in the most English setting. It is good business, but bad art.

Then there is Race. I wonder that no one has yet done a study of the reasons for the perennial popularity of books about racial discrimination. I believe they give a certain sadistic pleasure, a vicarious sense of power. The Sunday newspapers that serialize stories of oppression and humiliation by the oppressed and the humiliated are not going to try to lose their readers by attempting to uplift them: they respect them too well. To be successful, these chronicles of oppression must have clear oppressors and clear oppressed. This is not easy for an Indian. The most he can manage is something like Mulk Raj Anand's *Untouchable*. And for an Indian from an easy-going multi-racial society it is almost impossible. Oppressors and oppressed change so quickly. Even if I had any inclination to write that sort of book, eight years in England have shown me that the race issue is too complicated to be dealt with at best-seller, black-and-white level. It was unfortunate, for instance, that the *Manchester Guardian* should have carried a warm article by a Sinhalese about race discrimination in America at a time when his countrymen were killing Tamils in Ceylon.

These are the three ways open to me. I have to reject them all.

The only way out is to cease being a regional writer. People who wish me well have urged me to do so before it is too late. They say I have lived long enough in England to write about England. I would like nothing better. But there are difficulties.

The English writer benefits by travel but the foreign writer who comes to England benefits less. A few years ago I read that Simenon had come to England on a holiday and was dividing his time between Glasgow and Birmingham and Leeds. It sounded like a working holiday, but I don't believe anything came out of it.

It is a matter of climate. In a warm country life is conducted out of doors. Windows are open, doors are open. People sit in open verandas and cafés. You know your neighbour's business and he knows yours. It is easy for the visitor to get to know the country. He is continually catching people in off-duty positions. In England everything goes on behind closed doors. The man from the warm country automatically leaves the door open behind him. The man from the cold country closes it: it has become a point of etiquette. The moment the warm weather comes here the BBC urges people to turn down their radios: the open window is an event. The men of Muswell Hill, shopping on a Saturday morning, wear their summer clothes self-consciously, like a new uniform. And when pub doors are wedged open and people lounge in front gardens in shirt-sleeves what a disorderly, Southern, un-English aspect comes over this country!

And I feel I know so little about England. I have met many people but I know them only in official attitudes – the drink, the interview, the meal. I have a few friends. But this gives me only a superficial knowledge of the country, and in order to write fiction it is necessary to know so much: we are not all brothers under the skin. It might have been possible for me, at the end of my first year here, to write about England. First impressions, reinforced by what one reads in the newspapers, are often enough to give authenticity 'of a crudely naturalistic sort'. But now I feel I can never hope to know as much about people here as I do about Trinidad Indians, people I can place almost as soon as I see them.

The privacy of the big city depresses me. There are no communal pleasures in London. Between the activity and the response there is always the barrier of self-consciousness. You go to a restaurant or a night-club, you eat, you watch, you pay, you come out and look for a bus, feeling you have wasted your money. The theatre is a disappointment. There seems to be no complete communication between the actor and the audience, nothing to weld the audience together. You watch, you come out in the interval to smoke or have a drink, you watch again, and it is all over. You might have been at home, before the television set. However gay the musical or farce, however good the acting, you come out alone into the cold streets, private, sitting in a bus full of grim people who have left their pleasure behind them in the theatre. I like Spanish dancing but I do not care to see it in London. Something is missing; the communal element is not there; all you have is a remote spectacle. It isn't that the dances have been vulgarized – whole-hearted vulgarity is at least vigorous. They have been sterilized, by the audience. I have sat for half an evening in a cinema in the Kilburn High Road, watching Spanish dancing, wondering whether this was really the thing I liked in Spain. Then some Spaniards in the audience, who could bear it no longer, began shouting at the dancers – encouragement, raillery, a little abuse. By looks and action the dancers responded; the rest of the audience responded; for just that moment they had ceased to be individuals who had paid the price of their seat to witness a spectacle which was socially and culturally approved but with which they were not involved.

This may be a futile complaint. How can things be otherwise when London is so big and audiences so sophisticated? But that doesn't lessen my disappointment with the theatre in London. I get more pleasure from going to a cinema in Trinidad. As for the little theatres, the dedicated and dead hand of uplift and culture rests on their efforts. It is hard to imagine Pepys writing of a play today: 'It was so mean a thing as, when they came to say it would be acted again tomorrow, both he that said it, Beeson, and the pit fell a-laughing.'

My disappointment with the theatre symbolizes the barrenness of my life in London. The profession I follow may be partly responsible for this. Perhaps the fault is wholly mine. But after eight years here I find I have, without effort, achieved the Buddhist ideal of non-attachment. I am never disturbed by national or international issues. I do not sign petitions. I do not vote. I do not march. And I never cease to feel that this lack of interest is all wrong. I want to be involved, to be touched even by some of the prevailing anger.

And yet I like London. For all the reasons I have given it is the best place to write in. The problem for me is that it is not a place I can write about. Not as yet. Unless I am able to refresh myself by travel – to Trinidad, to India – I fear that living here will eventually lead to my own sterility; and I may have to look for another job.

Cricket

Encounter, September 1963

'Who is the greatest cricketer in the world?' The question came up in a General Knowledge test one day in 1940, when I was in the fourth standard at the Tranquillity Boys' School in Port of Spain. I saw it as a trap question. Though I had never seen him play, and he was reported to live in England, no cricketer was better known to me than Learie Constantine. Regularly in the *Trinidad Guardian* I saw the same picture of him: sweatered, smiling, running back to the pavilion bat in hand. To me the bat was golden: Constantine, in a previous General Knowledge test, had proved to be 'the man with the golden bat' as, earlier, he had been 'the man with the golden ball'. But now – the greatest cricketer? I wrote 'Bradman'. This was wrong; the pencilled cross on my paper was large and angry. 'Constantine' was the answer to this one too.

The teacher was a Negro, brown-skinned, but this is a later assessment and may be wrong: to me then, and for some time afterwards, race and colour were not among the attributes of teachers. It is possible now to see his propaganda for Constantine as a type of racialism or nationalism. But this would be only part of the truth. Racial pride pure and simple in the victories of Joe Louis, yes. But the teacher's devotion to Constantine was more complex. And it is with the unravelling of this West Indian complexity that C. L. R. James, politician, pamphleteer, historian, former cricket correspondent for the *Manchester Guardian*, is concerned. He has done his job superbly.

Beyond a Boundary, like Nirad Chaudhuri's *Autobiography of an Unknown Indian*, is part of the cultural boomeranging from the former colonies, delayed and still imperfectly understood. With one or two exceptions, a journalistic reaction to his material – cricket – has obscured the originality of Mr James's purpose and method.

Since 1950 the newspapers have perhaps made us too familiar with calypsos at Lord's. For West Indians, as one cricket writer says, the game is a carnival. But what a game to choose for a carnival! It is leisurely, intricate, difficult to appreciate, its drama often concealed or curtailed; and the players stop for tea. Soccer, swift, short and brutal, would have been more suitable; or baseball, or bullfighting. But cricket has been chosen; and the conclusion must be that we are dealing with more than the picturesque. Consider just what cricket means to the West Indian: in Trinidad, with a population of 800,000, 30,000 can go to a test match on one day. Consider the mixed population. Here is Mr James describing the cricket field of his school in the 1910s:

> We were a motley crew. The children of some white officials and white business men, middle-class blacks and mulattoes, Chinese boys, some of whose parents still spoke broken English, Indian boys, some of whose parents could speak no English at all, and some poor black boys who had won exhibitions or whose parents had starved and toiled on plots of agricultural land and were spending their hard-earned money on giving the eldest boy an education. Yet rapidly we learned to obey the umpire's decision ... We learned to play with the team.

Racial generalizations – about certain people being good at ball games – won't help. There has been no West African cricketer; the only Chinese cricketers of standing have come from Trinidad; and, though the fact is seldom noticed, white West Indians have produced more first-class players per thousand of their population than any other community anywhere. Consider now the history of the islands: slavery until 1834, indentured labour until 1917. And then consider the cricket code: gentlemanliness, fair play, teamwork. The very words are tired and, in the West

Indian situation, ridiculous, irrelevant. But they filled a need. In islands that had known only brutality and proclaimed greed, cricket and its code provided an area of rest, a release for much that was denied by the society: skill, courage, style: the graces, the very things that in a changed world are making the game archaic. And the code that came with the game, the code recognized by everyone, whatever his race or class, was the British public-school code:

I learned and obeyed and taught a code, the English public-school code. Britain and her colonies and the colonial peoples. What do the British people know of what they have done there? Precious little. The colonial peoples, particularly West Indians, scarcely know themselves as yet.

Twenty years ago the colonial who wrote those words might have been judged to be angling for an O BE or M BE. But Mr James, who is over sixty, has a background of Marxism (he was a prominent follower of Trotsky) and African nationalism. He was the first of the emigrant West Indian writers; and his first book, published in 1933, was *The Case for West Indian Self-Government*. Self-government has more or less come to the West Indies; Sir Learie Constantine is now the Trinidad High Commissioner in London. The West Indies, captained for the first time by a black man, did great things in Australia in 1960–1. A quarter of a million people came out into the streets of Melbourne to say goodbye to the cricketers: West Indian cricket's finest moment, which Mr James sees as something more. 'Clearing their way with bat and ball, West Indians at that moment had made a public entry into the comity of nations.' It is a success story, then, that Mr James has to tell, but an odd one, since it is also the story of the triumph of the code. To Mr James, Frank Worrell is more than the first black West Indian captain: 'Thomas Arnold, Thomas Hughes and the Old Master himself would have recognized Frank Worrell as their boy.'

This is the last sentence of Mr James's book, and this is his astounding thesis. To dismiss it would be to deny the curious position of the West Indies and West Indians in the Commonwealth, to fail to see that these territories are a unique imperial creation, where people of many lands, thrown together, 'came to maturity within a system that was the result of centuries of development in another land, was transplanted as a hot-house flower is transplanted and bore some strange fruit'. Stollmeyer, Gomez, Pierre, Christiani, Tang Choon, Ramadhin; the names of West Indian cricketers are sufficient evidence. To be a nationalist, Mr James says elsewhere, you must have a nation. The African in Africa had a nation; so had the Asian in Asia. The West Indian, whatever his community, had only this 'system'; and my fourth standard teacher could only grope towards some definition of his position in the world by his devotion to Constantine.

It is part of the originality and rightness of Mr James's book that he should have combined the story of his development within the system with his view of West Indian political growth, and combined that with sketches of West Indian cricketers he knew and watched develop. In the islands the cricketers were familiar to many; they were as much men as cricketers. So they emerge in Mr James's pages, but even so they remain touched with heroic qualities, for their success, as with Constantine or Headley, was the only type of triumph the society as a whole knew. And their failure, as with Wilton St Hill who, achieving nothing in England in 1928, remained all his life a clerk in a department store, bitter tragedy.

How did Mr James become part of this 'system'? He was born in a small Trinidad country town at the turn of the century. His father was a teacher. Yet slavery had been abolished only seventy years before, and 'Cousin Nancy, who lived a few yards away, told many stories of her early days as a house-slave'. Already, then, the slave society had been transformed, its assumptions destroyed; and this rapid transformation must be regarded as part of the West Indian good fortune. The family was not rich, but for the young James, as for every boy in the island, there was a narrow way out. Every year the government offered four exhibitions to one of the two secondary schools. There a boy could get a Senior Cambridge Certificate, which would ensure a modest job in the civil service. He could do more: he could win one of the three annual scholarships. With this he could get a profession in England, come back to Trinidad, make money and achieve honour. The form of promising boys was studied as carefully as that of race-horses; the course, from exhibition to scholarship, aroused island-wide interest and excitement.

James won his exhibition. He came from a house with books. Preparing for his exhibition, he became a 'British intellectual long before I was ten, already an alien in my own environment'. But he was ready for the public-school code of the Queen's Royal College, staffed for two generations by Oxford and Cambridge men. 'Our masters, our curriculum, our code of morals, *everything* began from the basis that Britain was the source of all light and learning, and our business was to admire, wonder, imitate, learn.' It was not hard. The colony might be ruled autocratically by Englishmen, but there was as yet no National Question and, within the school, no race question. 'If the masters were so successful in instilling and maintaining their British principles as the ideal and norm it was because within the school, and particularly on the playing field, they practised them themselves . . . They were correct in the letter and in the spirit.' They were also not competing with any other system. Today, he says, these teachers with their 'bristling Britishness' would be anachronisms. But was it possible to reject them then? Was it possible for Mr James, forty years later, at a public meeting in Manchester, to accept Mr Aneurin Bevan's sneers at public-school morality? As it was, however, the playing fields of Queen's

Royal College undid Mr James. Cricket possessed him; he did not win the scholarship. But he had educated himself 'into a member of the British middle class'. In 1932, with the encouragement and help of Learie Constantine, he came to England. And he has been a wanderer ever since.

To me, who thirty years later followed in his path almost step by step – but I only watched cricket, and I won the scholarship – Mr James's career is of particular interest. Our backgrounds were dissimilar. His was Negro, Puritan, fearful of lower-class contamination; mine was Hindu, restricted, enclosed. But we have ended speaking the same language; and though England is not perhaps the country we thought it was, we have both charmed ourselves away from Trinidad. 'For the inner self,' as Mr James writes, 'the die was cast.'

In our absence the static society we knew has altered. Secondary education is free. Not three, but more like thirty, scholarships are given each year. With the new nationalism and confidence, the public-school code has become as anachronistic as the masters who taught it. What new code will be developed in a society so clearly British-made? Cricket is no longer a substitute for nationalism. Has it then served its purpose, and will it die in the West Indies as it has died (in spite of Dexter, in spite of the Lord's test) in England? Trinidad, we must remind ourselves, has produced no major player since Ramadhin, discovered in 1950. It would be interesting to have Mr James's views. In the meantime let us rejoice over what he has given us. *Beyond a Boundary* is one of the finest and most finished books to come out of the West Indies, important to England, important to the West Indies. It has a further value: it gives a base and solidity to West Indian literary endeavour.

Jasmine

The Times Literary Supplement, 4 June 1964

One day about ten years ago, when I was editing a weekly literary programme for the BBC's Caribbean Service, a man from Trinidad came to see me in one of the freelances' rooms in the old Langham Hotel. He sat on the edge of the table, slapped down some sheets of typescript and said, 'My name is Smith. I write about sex. I am also a nationalist.' The sex was tepid, Maugham and coconut-water; but the nationalism was aggressive. Women swayed like coconut trees; their skins were the colour of the sapo-dilla, the inside of their mouths the colour of a cut star-apple; their teeth were as white as coconut kernels; and when they made love they groaned like bamboos in high wind.

The writer was protesting against what the English language had imposed on us. The language was ours, to use as we pleased. The literature that came with it was therefore of peculiar authority; but this literature was like an alien mythology. There was, for instance, Wordsworth's notorious poem about the daffodil. A pretty little flower, no doubt; but we had never seen it. Could the poem have any meaning for us? The superficial prompting of this argument, which would have confined all literatures to the countries of their origin, was political; but it was really an expression of dissatisfaction at the emptiness of our own formless, unmade society. To us, without a mythology, all literatures were foreign. Trinidad was small, remote and unimportant, and we knew we could not hope to read in books of the life we saw about us. Books came from afar; they could offer only fantasy.

To open a book was to make an instant adjustment. Like the medieval sculptor of the North interpreting the Old Testament stories in terms of the life he knew, I needed to be able to adapt. All Dickens's descriptions of London I rejected; and though I might retain Mr Micawber and the others in the clothes the illustrator gave them, I gave them the faces and voices of people I knew and set them in buildings and streets I knew. The process of adaptation was automatic and continuous. Dickens's rain and drizzle I turned into tropical downpours; the snow and fog I accepted as conventions of books. Anything – like an illustration – which embarrassed me by proving how weird my own reaction was, anything which sought to remove the characters from the make-up world in which I set them, I rejected.

I went to books for fantasy; at the same time I required reality. The gypsies of *The Mill on the Floss* were a fabrication and a disappointment, discrediting so much that was real: to me gypsies were mythical creatures who belonged to the pure fantasy of Hans Christian Andersen and *The Heroes*. Disappointing, too, was the episode of the old soldier's sword, because I thought that swords belonged to ancient times; and the Tom Tulliver I had created walked down the street where I lived. The early parts of *The Mill on the Floss*, then; chapters of *Oliver Twist, Nicholas Nickleby, David Copperfield*; some of the novels of H. G. Wells; a short story by Conrad called 'The Lagoon': all these which in the beginning I read or had read to me I set in Trinidad, accepting, rejecting, adapting, and peopling in my own way. I never read to find out about foreign countries. Everything in books was foreign; everything had to be subjected to adaptation; and everything in, say, an English novel which worked and was of value to me at once ceased to be specifically English. Mr Murdstone worked; Mr Pickwick and his club didn't. *Jane Eyre* and *Wuthering Heights* worked; *Pride and Prejudice* didn't. Maupassant worked; Balzac didn't.

I went to books for a special sort of participation. The only social division I accepted was that between rich and poor, and any society more elaborately ordered seemed insubstantial and alien. In literature such a society was more than alien; it was excluding, it made nonsense of my fantasies and more and more, as I grew older and thought of writing myself, it made me despairingly conscious of the poverty and haphazardness of my own society. I might adapt Dickens to Trinidad; but it seemed impossible that the life I knew in Trinidad could ever be turned into a book. If landscapes do not start to be real until they have been interpreted by an artist, so, until they have been written about, societies appear to be without shape and *embarrassing*. It was embarrassing to be reminded by a Dickens illustration of the absurdity of my adaptations; it was equally embarrassing to attempt to write of what I saw. Very little of what I read was of help. It would have been possible to assume the sensibility of a particular writer. But no writer, however individual his vision, could be separated from his society. The vision was alien; it diminished my own and did not give me the courage to do a simple thing like mentioning the name of a Port of Spain street.

Fiction or any work of the imagination, whatever its quality, hallows its subject. To attempt, with a full consciousness of established authoritative mythologies, to give a quality of myth to what was agreed to be petty and ridiculous – Frederick Street in Port of Spain, Marine Square, the districts of Laventille and Barataria – to attempt to use these names required courage. It was, in a way, the rejection of the familiar, meaningless word – the rejection of the unknown daffodil to put it no higher – and was as self-conscious as the attempt to have sapodilla-skinned women groaning like bamboos in high wind.

With all English literature accessible, then, my position was like that of the maharaja in *Hindoo Holiday*, who, when told by the Christian lady that God was here, there and everywhere, replied, 'But what use is that to *me*?' Something of more pertinent virtue was needed, and this was provided by some local short stories. These stories, perhaps a dozen in all, never published outside Trinidad, converted what I saw into 'writing'. It was through them that I began to appreciate the distorting, distilling power of the writer's art. Where I had seen a drab haphazardness they found order; where I would have attempted to romanticize, to render my subject equal with what I had read, they accepted. They provided a starting-point for further observation; they did not trigger off fantasy. Every writer is, in the long run, on his own; but it helps, in the most practical way, to have a tradition. The English language was mine; the tradition was not.

Literature, then, was mainly fantasy. Perhaps it was for this reason that, although I had at an early age decided to be a writer and at the age of eighteen had left Trinidad with that ambition, I did not start writing seriously until I was nearly twenty-three. My material had not been sufficiently hallowed by a tradition; I was not fully convinced of its importance; and some embarrassment remained. My taste for literature had developed into a love of language, the word in isolation. At school my subjects were French and Spanish; and the pleasures of the language were at least as great as those of the literature. Maupassant and Molière were rich; but it was more agreeable to spend an hour with the big Harrap French–English dictionary, learning more of the language through examples, than with Corneille or Racine. And it was because I thought I had had enough of these languages (both now grown rusty) that when I came to England to go to university I decided to read English.

This was a mistake. The English course had little to do with literature. It was a 'discipline' seemingly aimed at juvenile antiquarians. It by-passed the novel and the prose 'asides' in which so much of the richness of the literature lay. By a common and curious consent it concentrated on poetry; and since it stopped at the eighteenth century it degenerated, after an intensive study of Shakespeare, into a lightning survey of minor and often severely local talents. I had looked forward to wandering among large tracts of writing; I was presented with 'texts'. The metaphysicals were a perfect subject for study, a perfect part of a discipline; but, really, they had no value for me. Dryden, for all the sweet facility of his prose, was shallow and dishonest; did his 'criticism' deserve such reverential attention? *Gulliver's Travels* was excellent; but could *The Tale of a Tub* and *The Battle of the Books* be endured?

The fact was, I had no taste for scholarship, for tracing the growth of schools and trends. I sought continuously to relate literature to life. My training at school didn't help. We had few libraries, few histories of literature to turn to; and when we wrote essays on *Tartuffe* we wrote out of a direct response to the play. Now I discovered that the study of literature had been made scientific, that each writer had to be approached through the booby-traps of scholarship. There were the bound volumes of the Publications of the Modern Language Association of America, affectionately referred to by old and knowing young as PMLA. The pages that told of Chaucer's knowledge of astronomy or astrology (the question came up every year) were black and bloated and furred with handling, and even some of the pencilled annotations (*No, Norah!*) had grown faint. I developed a physical distaste for these bound volumes and the libraries that housed them.

Delight cannot be taught and measured; scholarship can; and my reaction was irrational. But it seemed to me scholarship of such a potted order. A literature was not being explored; it had been codified and reduced to a few pages of 'text', some volumes of 'background' and more of 'criticism'; and to this mixture a mathematical intelligence might have been applied. There were discoveries, of course: Shakespeare, Marlowe, Restoration comedy. But my distaste for the study of literature led to a sense of being more removed than ever from the literature itself.

The language remained mine, and it was to the study of its development that I turned with pleasure. Here was enough to satisfy my love of language; here was unexpected adventure. It might not have been easy to see Chaucer as a great imaginative writer or to find in the *Prologue* more than a limited piece of observation which had been exceeded a thousand times; but Chaucer as a handler of a new, developing language was exciting. And my pleasure in Shakespeare was doubled. In Trinidad English writing had been for me a starting-point for fantasy. Now, after some time in England, it was possible to isolate the word, to separate the literature from the language.

Language can be so deceptive. It has taken me much time to realize how bad I am at interpreting the conventions and modes of English speech. This speech has never been better dissected than in the early stories of Angus Wilson. This is the judgment of today; my first responses to these stories were as blundering and imperfect as the responses of Professor Pforzheim to the stern courtesies of his English colleagues in *Anglo-Saxon Attitudes*. But while knowledge of England has made English writing more truly accessible, it has made participation more difficult; it has made impossible the exercise of fantasy, the reader's complementary response. I am inspecting an alien society, which I yet know, and I am looking for particular social comment. And to re-read now the books which lent themselves to fantastic interpretation in Trinidad is to see, almost with dismay, how English they are. The illustrations to Dickens cannot now be dismissed. And so, with knowledge, the books have ceased to be mine.

It is the English literary vice, this looking for social comment; and it is difficult to resist. The preoccupation of the novelists reflects a society ruled by convention and manners in the fullest sense, an ordered society of the self-aware who read not so much for adventure as to compare, to find what they know or think they know. A writer is to be judged by what he reports on; the working-class writer is a working-class writer and no more. So writing develops into the private language of a particular society. There are new reports, new discoveries: they are rapidly absorbed. And with each discovery the society's image of itself becomes more fixed and the society looks further inward. It has too many points of reference; it has been written about too often; it has read too much. Angus Wilson's characters, for instance, are great readers; they are steeped in Dickens and Jane Austen. Soon there will be characters steeped in Angus Wilson; the process is endless. Sensibility will overlay sensibility: the grossness of experience will be refined away by self-awareness. Writing will become Arthur Miller's definition of a newspaper: a nation talking to itself. And even those who have the key will be able only to witness, not to participate.

All literatures are regional; perhaps it is only the placelessness of a Shakespeare or the blunt communication of 'gross' experience as in Dickens that makes them appear less so. Or perhaps it is a lack of knowledge in the reader. Even in this period of 'internationalism' in letters we have seen literatures turning more and more inward, developing languages that are more and more private. Perhaps in the end literature will write itself out, and all its pleasures will be those of the word.

A little over three years ago I was in British Guiana. I was taken late one afternoon to meet an elderly lady of a distinguished Christian Indian family. Our political attitudes were too opposed to make any discussion of the current crisis profitable. We talked of the objects in her veranda and of the old days. Suddenly the tropical daylight was gone, and from the garden came the scent of a flower. I knew the flower from my childhood; yet I had never found out its name. I asked now.

'We call it jasmine.'

Jasmine! So I had known it all those years! To me it had been a word in a book, a word to play with, something removed from the dull vegetation I knew.

The old lady cut a sprig for me. I stuck it in the top buttonhole of my open shirt. I smelled it as I walked back to the hotel. Jasmine, jasmine. But the word and the flower had been separate in my mind for too long. They did not come together.

East Indian

The Reporter, 17 June 1965

It was about thirteen or fourteen years ago. In those days
Air France used to run an Epicurean Service between
London and Paris. The advertisements taunted me.
Poverty makes for recklessness, and one idle day in the
long summer vacation I booked. The following morning
I went with nervous expectation to the Kensington air
terminal. There was another Indian in the lounge. He
was about fifty and very small, neat with homburg and
gold-rimmed spectacles, and looking packaged in a three-
piece suit. He was pure buttoned-up joy: he too was an
Epicurean traveller.

'You are coming from –?'

I had met enough Indians from India to know that this
was less a serious inquiry than a greeting, in a distant land,
from one Indian to another.

'Trinidad,' I said. 'In the West Indies. And you?'

He ignored my question. 'But you look Indian.'

'I am.'

'Red Indian?' He suppressed a nervous little giggle.

'East Indian. From the West Indies.'

He looked offended and wandered off to the bookstall.
From this distance he eyed me assessingly. In the end
curiosity overcame misgiving. He sat next to me on the
bus to the airport. He sat next to me in the plane.

'Your first trip to Paris?' he asked.

'Yes.'

'My fourth. I am a newspaperman. America, the United
States of America, have you been there?'

'I once spent twelve hours in New York.'

'I have been to the United States of America three times. I also know the Dominion of Canada. I don't like this aeroplane. I don't like the way it is wibrating. What sort do you think it is? I'll ask the steward.'

He pressed the buzzer. The steward didn't come.

'At first I thought it was a Dakota. Now I feel it is a Wiking.'

The steward bustled past, dropping white disembarkation cards into laps. The Indian seized the steward's soiled white jacket.

'Steward, is this aircraft a Wiking?'

'No, sir. Not a Viking. It's a Languedoc, a French plane, sir.'

'Languedoc. Of course. That is one thing journalism teaches you. Always get to the bottom of everything.'

We filled in our disembarkation cards. The Indian studied my passport.

'Trinidad, Trinidad,' he said, as though searching for a face or a name.

Before he could find anything the Epicurean meal began. The harassed steward pulled out trays from the back of seats, slapped down monogrammed glasses and liquor miniatures. It was a short flight, which perhaps he had already made more than once that day, and he behaved like a man with problems at the other end.

'Indian,' the Indian said reprovingly. 'and you are drinking?'

'I am drinking.'

'At home,' he said, sipping his aperitif, 'I *never* drink.'

The steward was back, with a clutch of half-bottles of champagne.

'Champagne!' the Indian cried, as though about to clap his tiny hands. 'Champagne!'

Corks were popping all over the aircraft. The trays of food came.

I grabbed the steward's dirty jacket.

'I am sorry,' I said. 'I should have told them. But I don't eat meat.'

Holding two trays in one hand, he said, 'I am sorry, sir. There is nothing else. The meals are not prepared on the plane.'

'But you must have an egg or some fish or something.'

'We have some cheese.'

'But this is an Epicurean Service. You can't just give me a piece of cheese.'

'I am sorry, sir.'

I drank champagne with my bread and cheese.

'So you are not eating?'

'I am not eating.'

'I enwy you.' The Indian was champing through meats of various colours, sipping champagne and crying out for more. 'I enwy you your wegetarianism. At home I am *strict* wegetarian. No one has even boiled an egg in my house.'

The steward took away the remains of my bread and cheese, and gave me coffee, brandy, and a choice of liqueurs.

The Indian experimented swiftly. He sipped, he gulped. The flight was drawing to a close; we were already fastening our seat belts. His eyes were red and watery behind his spectacles. He stuck his hat on at comic angles and made faces at me. He nudged me in the ribs and cuffed me on the shoulder and giggled. He chucked me under the chin and sang: '*Wege-wege-wegetarian! Hin-du wege-tar-ian!*'

He was in some distress when we landed. His hat was still at a comic angle, but his flushed little face had a bottled-up solemnity. He was in for a hard afternoon. Even so, he composed himself for a farewell speech.

'My dear sir, I am a journalist and I have travelled. I hope you will permit me to say how much I appreciate it that, although separated by many generations and many thousands of miles of sea and ocean from the Motherland, you still keep up the customs and traditions of our religion. I *do* appreciate it. Allow me to congratulate you.'

I was hungry, and my head was heavy. 'No, no, my dear sir. Allow me to congratulate you.'

To be a colonial is to be a little ridiculous and unlikely, especially in the eyes of someone from the metropolitan country. All immigrants and their descendants are colonials of one sort or another, and between the colonial and what one might call the metropolitan there always exists a muted mutual distrust. In England the image of the American is fixed. In Spain, where imperial glory has been dead for so long, they still whisper to you, an impartial outsider, about the loudness of *americanos* – to them people from Argentina and Uruguay. In an Athens hotel you can distinguish the Greek Americans, *back for a holiday* (special words in the vocabulary of immigrants), from the natives. The visitors speak with loud, exaggerated American accents, occasionally slightly flawed; the stances of the women are daring and self-conscious. The natives, overdoing the quiet culture and feminine modesty, appear to cringe with offence.

Yet to be Latin American or Greek American is to be known, to be a type, and therefore in some way to be established. To be an Indian or East Indian from the West Indies is to be a perpetual surprise to people outside the region. When you think of the West Indies you think of Columbus and the Spanish galleons, slavery and the naval rivalries of the eighteenth century. You might, more probably, think of calypsos and the Trinidad carnival and expensive sun and sand. When you think of the East you think of the Taj Mahal at the end of a cypress-lined vista and you think of holy men. You don't go to Trinidad, then, expecting to find Hindu pundits scuttling about country roads on motor-cycles; to see pennants with ancient devices fluttering from temples; to see mosques cool and white and rhetorical against the usual Caribbean buildings of concrete and corrugated iron; to find India celebrated in the street names of one whole district of Port of Spain; to see the Hindu festival of lights or the Muslim mourning ceremony for Husein, the Prophet's descendant, killed at the Battle of Kerbela in Arabia thirteen hundred years ago.

To be an Indian from Trinidad is to be unlikely. It is, in addition to everything else, to be the embodiment of an old verbal ambiguity. For this word 'Indian' has been abused as no other word in the language; almost every time it is used it has to be qualified. There was a time in Europe when everything Oriental or everything a little unusual was judged to come from Turkey or India. So Indian ink is really Chinese ink and India paper first came from China. When in 1492 Columbus landed on the island of Guanahani he thought he had got to Cathay. He ought therefore to have called the people Chinese. But East was East. He called them Indians, and Indians they remained, walking Indian file through the Indian corn. And so, too, that American bird which to English-speaking people is the turkey is to the French *le dindon*, the bird of India.

So long as the real Indians remained on the other side of the world, there was little confusion. But when in 1845 these Indians began coming over to some of the islands Columbus had called the Indies, confusion became total. Slavery had been abolished in the British islands; the Negroes refused to work for a master, and many plantations were faced with ruin. Indentured labourers were brought in from China, Portugal, and India. The Indians fitted. More and more came. They were good agriculturalists and were encouraged to settle after their indentures had expired. Instead of a passage home they could take land. Many did. The indenture system lasted, with breaks, from 1845 until 1917, and in Trinidad alone the descendants of those immigrants who stayed number over a quarter of a million.

But what were these immigrants to be called? Their

name had been appropriated three hundred and fifty years before. 'Hindu' was a useful word, but it had religious connotations and would have offended the many Muslims among the immigrants. In the British territories the immigrants were called East Indians. In this way they were distinguished from the two other types of Indians in the islands: the American Indians and the West Indians. After a generation or two, the East Indians were regarded as settled inhabitants of the West Indies and were thought of as West Indian East Indians. Then a national feeling grew up. There was a cry for integration, and the West Indian East Indians became East Indian West Indians.

This didn't suit the Dutch. They had a colony called Surinam, or Dutch Guiana, on the north coast of South America. They also owned a good deal of the East Indies, and to them an East Indian was someone who came from the East Indies and was of Malay stock. (When you go to an Indian restaurant in Holland you don't go to an Indian restaurant; you go to an East Indian or Javanese restaurant.) In Surinam there were many genuine East Indians from the East Indies. So another name had to be found for the Indians from India who came to Surinam. The Dutch called them British Indians. Then, with the Indian nationalist agitation in India, the British Indians began to resent being called British Indians. The Dutch compromised by calling them Hindustanis.

East Indians, British Indians, Hindustanis. But the West Indies are part of the New World and these Indians of Trinidad are no longer of Asia. The temples and mosques exist and appear genuine. But the languages that came with them have decayed. The rituals have altered. Since open-air cremation is forbidden by the health authorities, Hindus are buried, not cremated. Their ashes are not taken down holy rivers into the ocean to become again part of the Absolute. There is no Ganges at hand, only a muddy stream called the Caroni. And the water that the Hindu priest sprinkles with a mango leaf around the sacrificial fire is not Ganges water but simple tap water. The holy city of Benares is far away, but the young Hindu at his initiation ceremony in Port of Spain will still take up his staff and beggar's bowl and say that he is off to Benares to study. His relatives will plead with him, and in the end he will lay down his staff, and there will be a ritual expression of relief.*

It is the play of a people who have been cut off. To be an Indian from Trinidad, then, is to be unlikely and exotic. It is also to be a little fraudulent. But so all immigrants become. In India itself there is the energetic community of Parsis. They fled from Persia to escape Muslim religious persecution. But over the years the very religion which they sought to preserve has become a matter of forms and especially of burial forms: in Bombay their dead are taken to the frighteningly named Towers of Silence and there exposed to vultures. They have adopted the language of the sheltering country and their own language has become a secret gibberish. Immigrants are people on their own. They cannot be judged by the standards of their older culture. Culture is like language, ever developing. There is no right and wrong, no purity from which there is decline. Usage sanctions everything.

And these Indians from Trinidad, despite their temples and rituals, so startling to the visitors, belong to the New World. They are immigrants; they have the drive and restlessness of immigrants. To them India is a word. In moments of self-distrust this word might suggest the Taj Mahal and an ancient civilization. But more usually it suggests other words, fearfully visualized, 'famine', 'teeming millions'. And to many, India is no more than the memory of a depressed rural existence that survived in Trinidad until only the other day. Occasionally in the interior of

---

*Cremation is now permitted; ashes are scattered in the Caroni; and Ganges water is now imported.

the island a village of thatched roofs and mud-and-bamboo walls still recalls Bengal.

In Bengal lay the great port of Calcutta. There, from the vast depressed hinterland of eastern India, the emigrants assembled for the journey by sail, often lasting four months, to the West Indies. The majority came from the provinces of Bihar and eastern Uttar Pradesh; and even today – although heavy industry has come to Bihar – these areas are known for their poverty and backwardness. It is a dismal, dusty land, made sadder by ruins and place names that speak of ancient glory. For here was the land of the Buddha; here are the cities mentioned in the Hindu epics of three thousand years ago – like Ayodhya, from which my father's family came, today a ramshackle town of wholly contemporary squalor.

The land is flat, intolerably flat, with few trees to dramatize it. The forests to which reference is often made in the epics have disappeared. The winters are brief, and in the fierce summers the fields are white with dust. You are never out of sight of low mud-walled or brick-walled villages, and there are people everywhere. An impression of tininess in vastness: tiny houses, tiny poor fields, thin, stunted people, a land scratched into dust by an ever-growing population. It is a land of famine and apathy, and yet a land of rigid caste order. Everyone has his place. Effort is futile. His field is small, his time unlimited, but the peasant still scatters his seed broadcast. He lives from hand to mouth. The attitude is understandable. In this more than feudal society of India, everything once belonged to the king, and later to the landlord: it was unwise to be prosperous. A man is therefore defined and placed by his caste alone. To the peasant on this over-populated plain, all of India, all the world, has been narrowed to a plot of ground and a few relationships.

Travel is still not easy in those parts, and from there a hundred years ago the West Indies must have seemed like the end of the world. Yet so many left, taking everything – beds, brass vessels, musical instruments, images, holy books, sandalwood sticks, astrological almanacs. It was less an uprooting than it appears. They were taking India with them. With their blinkered view of the world they were able to re-create eastern Uttar Pradesh or Bihar wherever they went. They had been able to ignore the vastness of India; so now they ignored the strangeness in which they had been set. To leave India's sacred soil, to cross the 'black water', was considered an act of self-defilement. So completely did these migrants re-create India in Trinidad that they imposed a similar restriction on those who wished to leave Trinidad.

In a more energetic society they would have been lost. But Trinidad was stagnant in the nineteenth century. The Indians endured and prospered. The India they re-created was allowed to survive. It was an India in which a revolution had occurred. It was an India in isolation, unsupported; an India without caste or the overwhelming pressures towards caste. Effort had a meaning, and soon India could be seen to be no more than a habit, a self-imposed psychological restraint, wearing thinner with the years. At the first blast from the New World – the Second World War, the coming of Americans to the islands – India fell away, and a new people seemed all at once to have been created. The colonial, of whatever society, is a product of revolution; and the revolution takes place in the mind.

Certain things remain: the temples, the food, the rites, the names, though these become steadily more Anglicized and less recognizable to Indians; or it might be a distaste for meat, derived from a Hindu background and surviving even an Epicurean flight between London and Paris. Certainly it was odd, when I was in India two years ago, to find that often, listening to a language I thought I had forgotten, I was understanding. Just a word or two, but they seemed to recall a past life and fleetingly they gave that sensation of an experience that has been lived before. But fleetingly, since for the colonial there can be no true return.

In a Delhi club I met an Indian from Trinidad. I had last seen him fifteen years before. He was an adventurer. Now he was a little sad. He was an exile in the Motherland, and fifteen years had definitely taken him past youth; for him there were to be no more adventures. He was quiet and subdued. Then a worried, inquiring look came into his eyes.

'Tell me. I think we are way ahead of this bunch, don't you think?'

'But there's no question,' I said.

He brightened; he looked relieved. He smiled; he laughed.

'I'm *so* glad you think so. It's what I *always* tell them. Come, have a drink.'

We drank. We became loud, colonials together.

2
India

In the Middle of the Journey

The Illustrated Weekly of India, 28 October 1962

Coming from a small island – Trinidad is no bigger than Goa – I had always been fascinated by size. To see the wide river, the high mountain, to take the twenty-four-hour train journey: these were some of the delights the outside world offered. But now after six months in India my fascination with the big is tinged with disquiet. For here is a vastness beyond imagination, a sky so wide and deep that sunsets cannot be taken in at a glance but have to be studied section by section, a landscape made monotonous by its size and frightening by its very simplicity and its special quality of exhaustion: poor choked crops in small crooked fields, undersized people, undernourished animals, crumbling villages and towns which, even while they develop, have an air of decay. Dawn comes, night falls; railway stations, undistinguishable one from the other, their name-boards cunningly concealed, are arrived at and departed from, abrupt and puzzling interludes of populousness and noise; and still the journey goes on, until the vastness, ceasing to have a meaning, becomes insupportable, and from this endless repetition of exhaustion and decay one wishes to escape.

To state this is to state the obvious. But in India the obvious is overwhelming, and often during these past six months I have known moments of near-hysteria, when I have wished to forget India, when I have escaped to the first-class waiting-room or sleeper not so much for privacy and comfort as for protection, to shut out the sight of the thin bodies prostrate on railway platforms, the starved dogs licking the food-leaves clean, and to shut out the whine of the playfully assaulted dog. Such a moment I knew in Bombay, on the day of my arrival, when I felt India only as an assault on the senses. Such a moment I knew five months later, at Jammu, where the simple, frightening geography of the country becomes plain – to the north the hills, rising in range after ascending range; to the south, beyond the temple spires, the plains whose vastness, already experienced, excited only unease.

Yet between these recurring moments there have been so many others, when fear and impatience have been replaced by enthusiasm and delight, when the town, explored beyond what one sees from the train, reveals that the air of exhaustion is only apparent, that in India, more than in any other country I have visited, things are happening. To hear the sounds of hammer on metal in a small Punjab town, to visit a chemical plant in Hyderabad where much of the equipment is Indian-designed and manufactured, is to realize that one is in the middle of an industrial revolution, in which, perhaps because of faulty publicity, one had never really seriously believed. To see the new housing colonies in towns all over India was to realize that, separate from the talk of India's ancient culture (which invariably has me reaching for my *lathi*), the Indian aesthetic sense has revived and is now capable of creating, out of materials which are international, something which is essentially Indian. (India's ancient culture, defiantly paraded, has made the Ashoka Hotel one of New Delhi's most ridiculous buildings, outmatched in absurdity only by the Pakistan High Commission, which defiantly asserts the Faith.)

I have been to unpublicized villages, semi-developed and undeveloped. And where before I would have sensed only despair, now I feel that the despair lies more with the observer than the people. I have learned to see beyond the dirt and the recumbent figures on string beds, and to look for the signs of improvement and hope, however faint: the brick-topped road, covered though it might be with filth; the rice planted in rows and not scattered broadcast; the degree of ease with which the villager faces the official or the visitor. For such small things I have learned to look: over the months my eye has been adjusted.

Yet always the obvious is overwhelming. One is a traveller and as soon as the dread of a particular district has been lessened by familiarity, it is time to move on again, through vast tracts which will never become familiar, which will sadden; and the urge to escape will return.

Yet in so many ways the size of the country is only a physical fact. For, perhaps because of the very size, Indians appear to feel the need to categorize minutely, delimit, to reduce to manageable proportions.

'Where do you come from?' It is the Indian question, and to people who think in terms of the village, the district, the province, the community, the caste, my answer that I am a Trinidadian is only puzzling.

'But you look Indian.'

'Well, I am Indian. But we have been living for several generations in Trinidad.'

'But you look Indian.'

Three or four times a day the dialogue occurs, and now I often abandon explanation. 'I am a Mexican, really.'

'Ah.' Great satisfaction. Pause. 'What do you do?'

'I write.'

'Journalism or books?'

'Books.'

'Westerns, crime, romance? How many books do you write a year? How much do you make?'

So now I invent: 'I am a teacher.'

'What are your qualifications?'

'I am a BA.'

'Only a BA? What do you teach?'

'Chemistry. And a little history.'

'How interesting!' said the man on the Pathankot–Srinagar bus. 'I am a teacher of chemistry too.'

He was sitting across the aisle from me, and several hours remained of our journey.

In this vast land of India it is necessary to explain yourself, to define your function and status in the universe. It is very difficult.

If I thought in terms of race or community, this experience of India would surely have dispelled it. An Indian, I have never before been in streets where everyone is Indian, where I blend unremarkably into the crowd. This has been curiously deflating, for all my life I have expected some recognition of my difference; and it is only in India that I have recognized how necessary this stimulus is to me, how conditioned I have been by the multiracial society of Trinidad and then by my life as an outsider in England. To be a member of a minority community has always seemed to me attractive. To be one of four hundred and thirty-nine million Indians is terrifying.

A colonial, in the double sense of one who had grown up in a Crown colony and one who had been cut off from the metropolis, be it either England or India, I came to India expecting to find metropolitan attitudes. I had imagined that in some ways the largeness of the land would be reflected in the attitudes of the people. I have found, as I have said, the psychology of the cell and the hive. And I have been surprised by similarities. In India, as in tiny Trinidad, I have found the feeling that the metropolis is elsewhere, in Europe or America. Where I had expected largeness, rootedness and confidence, I have found all the colonial attitudes of self-distrust.

'I am craze phor phoreign,' the wife of a too-successful contractor said. And this craze extended from foreign food to German sanitary fittings to a possible European wife for her son, who sought to establish his claim further by announcing at the lunch table, 'Oh, by the way, did I tell you we spend three thousand rupees a month?'

'You are a tourist, you don't know,' the chemistry teacher on the Srinagar bus said. 'But this is a terrible country. Give me a chance and I leave it tomorrow.'

For among a certain class of Indians, usually more prosperous than their fellows, there is a passionate urge to explain to the visitor that they must not be considered part of poor, dirty India, that their values and standards are higher, and they live perpetually outraged by the country which gives them their livelihood. For them the second-rate foreign product, either people or manufactures, is preferable to the Indian. They suggest that for them, as much as for the European 'technician', India is only a country to be temporarily exploited. How strange to find, in free India, this attitude of the conqueror, this attitude of plundering – a frenzied attitude, as though the opportunity might at any moment be withdrawn – in those very people to whom the developing society has given so many opportunities.

This attitude of plundering is that of the immigrant colonial society. It has bred, as in Trinidad, the pathetic philistinism of the *renonçant* (an excellent French word that describes the native who renounces his own culture and strives towards the French). And in India this philistinism, a blending of the vulgarity of East and West – those sad dance floors, those sad 'western' cabarets, those transistor radios tuned to Radio Ceylon, those Don Juans with leather jackets or check tweed jackets – is peculiarly frightening. A certain glamour attaches to this philistinism, as glamour attaches to those Indians who, after two or three years in a foreign country, proclaim that they are neither of the East nor of the West.

The observer, it must be confessed, seldom sees the difficulty. The contractor's wife, so anxious to demonstrate her Westernness, regularly consulted her astrologer and made daily trips to the temple to ensure the continuance of her good fortune. The schoolteacher, who complained with feeling about the indiscipline and crudity of Indians, proceeded, as soon as we got to the bus station at Srinagar, to change his clothes in public.

The Trinidadian, whatever his race, is a genuine colonial. The Indian, whatever his claim, is rooted in India. But while the Trinidadian, a colonial, strives towards the metropolitan, the Indian of whom I have been speaking, metropolitan by virtue of the uniqueness of his country, its achievements in the past and its manifold achievements in the last decade or so, is striving towards the colonial.

Where one had expected pride, then, one finds the spirit of plunder. Where one had expected the metropolitan one finds the colonial. Where one had expected largeness one finds narrowness. Goa, scarcely liberated, is the subject of an unseemly inter-State squabble. Fifteen years after Independence the politician as national leader appears to have been replaced by the politician as village headman (a type I had thought peculiar to the colonial Indian community of Trinidad, for whom politics was a game where little more than PWD contracts was at stake). To the village headman India is only a multiplicity of villages. So that the vision of India as a great country appears to be something imposed from without and the vastness of the country turns out to be oddly fraudulent.

Yet there remains a concept of India – as what? Something more than the urban middle class, the politicians, the industrialists, the separate villages. Neither this nor that, we are so often told, is the 'real' India. And how well one begins to understand why this word is used! Perhaps India is only a word, a mystical idea that embraces all those vast plains and rivers through which the train moves, all those anonymous figures asleep on railway platforms and the footpaths of Bombay, all those poor fields and stunted animals, all this exhausted plundered land. Perhaps it is this, this vastness which no one can ever get to know: India as an ache, for which one has a great tenderness, but from which at length one always wishes to separate oneself.

Jamshed into Jimmy

New Statesman, 25 January 1963

'You've come to Calcutta at the wrong time,' the publisher said. 'I very much fear that the dear old city is slipping into bourgeois respectability almost without a fight.'

'Didn't they burn a tram the other day?' I asked.

'True. But that was the first tram for five years.'

And really I had expected more from Calcutta, the 'nightmare experience' of Mr Nehru, the 'pestilential behemoth' of a recent, near-hysterical American writer, a city which, designed for two million people, today accommodates more than six million on its pavements and in its *bastees*, in conditions which unmanned the World Bank Mission of 1960 and sent it away to write what the *Economic Weekly* of Bombay described as a 'strikingly human document'.

Like every newspaper-reader, I knew Calcutta as the city of tram-burners and students who regularly 'clashed' with the police. A brief news item in *The Times* in 1954 had hinted memorably at its labour troubles: some disgruntled workers had tossed their manager into the furnace. And during my time in India I had been following the doings of its Congress-controlled Corporation, which, from the progressive nationalist citadel of the twenties, has decayed into what students of Indian affairs consider the most openly corrupt of India's multitudinous corrupt public bodies: half the Corporation's five hundred and fifty vehicles disabled, many of them stripped of saleable parts, repair mechanics hampered, accounts four years in arrears, every obstacle put in the way of 'interference' by

State Government, New Delhi and a despairing Ford Foundation.

At every level I found that Calcutta enjoyed a fabulous reputation. The Bengali was insufferably arrogant ('The *pan*-seller doesn't so much as look at you if you don't talk to him in Bengali'); the Bengali was lazy; the pavements were dyed red with betel-juice and the main park was littered with used sanitary towels ('very untidy people', had been the comment of the South Indian novelist). And even in Bombay, the seat of gastro-enteritis, they spoke of Calcutta's inadequate (thirteen out of twenty-two Corporation tubewells not working) and tainted water supply with terror.

I had therefore expected much. And Howrah station was promising. The railway officials were more than usually non-committal and lethargic; the cigarette-seller didn't look at me; and in the station restaurant a smiling waiter drew my attention to a partly depilated rat that was wandering languidly about the tiled floor. But nothing had prepared me for the red-brick city on the other bank of the river which, if one could ignore the crowds, the stalls, the rickshaw-pullers and the squatting pissers, suggested, not a tropical or Eastern city, but central Birmingham. Nothing had prepared me for the Maidan, tree-dotted, now in the early evening blurred with mist and suggesting Hyde Park, with Chowringhee as a brighter Oxford Street. And nothing had prepared me for the sight of General Cariappa in the Maidan, dark-suited, English-erect, addressing a small relaxed crowd on the Chinese invasion in Sandhurst-accented Hindustani, while the trams, battleship-grey, with wedge-shaped snouts, nosed through the traffic at a steady eight miles an hour, the celebrated Calcutta tram, ponderous and vulnerable, *bulging* at entrances and exits with white-clad office workers, the neon lights beyond the Maidan gay in the mist: the invitations to espresso bars, cabarets, air travel. Here, unexpectedly and for the first time in India, one was in the midst of the big city, the recognizable metropolis, with street names – Elgin, Allenby, Park, Lindsay – that seemed oddly at variance with the brisk crowds, incongruity that deepened as the mist thickened to smog and as, travelling out to the suburbs, one saw the factory chimneys smoking among the palm trees.

And where in that bright heart, forgetting the pissers, were the piles of filth and refuse I had been told about, and the sanitary towels? In fact, as the publisher said, I had come to Calcutta at the wrong time. The city had recently been subjected to a brief and frenzied clean-up by the 'volunteers' of the new Chief Minister of Bengal; it had been hoped that this would fill the Corporation's professionals with 'enthusiasm'. An 'Operation Bull' had sought to clear the main streets of bulls which the devout Hindu releases into central Calcutta to service the holy cow. The idea was that the cows would follow the bulls. As it turned out, the cows had stayed; the bulls were returning. And no inhabitant of Calcutta doubted that with the withdrawal of the volunteers, and with so many things in India suspended because of the Emergency – suspension and prohibition being the administration's current substitute for action – the filth too would return. But for the moment some of the unfamiliar gloss remained.

All the four main cities in India were developed by the British, but none has so British a stamp as Calcutta. Lutyens's New Delhi is a disaster, a mock-imperial joke, neither British nor Indian, a city built for parades rather than people, and today given a correctly grotesque scale by the noisy little scooter-rickshaws that scurry about its long avenues and endless roundabouts. Madras, though possessing in Fort St George one of the finest complexes of eighteenth-century British architecture outside Britain, is elsewhere lazily colonial. Bombay owes much to its Parsi community, enterprising, civic-minded, culturally ambiguous; the hysterical American already quoted speaks of Bombay's 'bandbox architecture', and indeed this city, the best-run in India, is cosmopolitan to the point of characterlessness. Calcutta alone appears to have been created in the image of England, the British here falling, unusually, into the imperialist practice of the French and the Portuguese. And what has resulted in Calcutta is a grandeur more rooted than that of New Delhi: 'the city of palaces' they called Calcutta, the palaces, Indian or British, built in a style which might best be described as Calcutta Corinthian: Calcutta, for long the capital of British India, the second city of the British Empire.

In India the confrontation of East and West was nowhere more violent than in Calcutta, and two buildings, both now regarded as monuments, speak of this violence: the Mullick Palace and the Victoria Memorial. Decaying now, with servants cooking in the marble galleries, the Mullick Palace still looks like a film set. It is dominated by tall Corinthian columns; Italian fountains play in the grounds; its excessively chandeliered marble rooms are crowded out with the clutter of a hundred nineteenth-century European antique shops, this dusty plaster cast of a Greek nymph hiding that faded, unmemorable painting of red-coated soldiers repulsing some native attack. In the courtyard four marble figures represent the major continents; and on the lower floor the monumental statue of a youthful Queen Victoria makes a big room small. None of the dusty treasures of the Mullick Palace is Indian, save perhaps for a portrait of the collector: the original Bengali babu, anxious to prove to the supercilious European his appreciation of European culture. And on the Maidan stands the Victoria Memorial, Curzon's answer to the Taj Mahal, as studiedly derivative as the Mullick Palace, here recalling the Taj, there recalling the Salute. 'Passing through the Queen's vestibule into the Queen's Hall under the dome,' says Murray's *Handbook*, which characteristically gives twice as much space to this Raj Taj as to the Kailasa Temple at Ellora, one sees the dignified statue of Queen Victoria at the age when she ascended the throne (the work of Sir Thomas Brock RA); this gives the keynote to the whole edifice.

Yet out of this confrontation there emerged something new in India, an explosive mixture of East and West, a unique culture which, however despised by the non-Calcutta Bengali as jumped-up and camp-following, gave Indian nationalism many of its prophets and heroes. The Bengali will tell you that British officials were urged to treat the South Indian as a slave, the Punjabi as a friend, and the Bengali as an enemy. But when the Bengali tells you this he is speaking as of lost glories, for today, with Independence and the partition of Bengal (in Calcutta the words are synonymous), the heart has gone out of Calcutta. It is a city without a hinterland, a dying city. Even the Hooghly is silting up, and everyone agrees that Calcutta has ceased to grow economically, however much it might spread physically. Though there are endearing vestiges of the Mullick Palace mentality in, say, the literary criticism of Professor Sadhan Kumar Ghosh (compassionately dealt with in the *New Statesman* by Malcolm Muggeridge), Calcutta is exhausted, its people withdrawn. It has Satyajit Ray, the film director; it has in Sunil Janah a photographer of world stature; Bengali typography, nervously elegant, is perhaps the best in India. But the glory lies in the past, in Tagore, in Bankim Chandra Chatterji, in the terrorists, in Subhas Chandra Bose. (1962 was a good year for the Bose legend: one libel action brought by a member of the family against an Englishwoman, and another reported reappearance, this time as a sadhu in the Himalayas.)

Calcutta remains what it always has been through growth, creative disorder, quiescence. It is still, despite the strong challenge of Bombay, India's principal commercial city, and the element of Calcutta culture which might be said to be dominant is that represented by the business buildings of Dalhousie Square and the squat business houses of Imperial Tobacco and Metal Box on Chowringhee. There in air-conditioned offices may be found the young Indian business executives, the box-wallahs, the new Indian élite. A generation ago such positions would not have been acceptable to any Indian of birth; and he almost certainly would not have been accepted. But the Indian genius for compromise is no less than that of the British. The box-wallah culture of Calcutta is of a peculiar richness, and if it has not yet been explored by Indian writers this is because they have been too busy plagiarizing, or writing harrowing stories about young girls drifting into prostitution to pay the family's medical bills and stories about young girls, poor or pretty, who inexplicably die. This culture, though of Calcutta, is not necessarily Bengali. Commerce is controlled by the British and increasingly since Independence by the Marwaris – it is almost with pride that the Bengali tells you there is no Bengali businessman worth the name. The Marwaris are Indian but are spoken of throughout India as a community even more alien than the British: the feeling against them in Calcutta is something you can cut with a knife. No one of standing wishes to be directly employed by the Marwaris. The conditions are not as good as those offered by the British who are reputable; in the public mind Marwari businessmen are associated with black-marketing and speculation. No one who works for the Marwaris can therefore properly be considered a box-wallah – your true box-wallah works only for the best British firms. ('Tell me,' they were asked at Imperial Tobacco, 'was that very large painting of the Queen put up especially for the Queen's visit?' 'No,' was the box-wallah reply. 'It is *always* there.')

No one in Calcutta is sure of the origin of the word box-wallah. It has been suggested that it comes from the street pedlar's box; but in Calcutta the word has too grand and restricted a significance, and it seems to me more likely to have been derived from the Anglo-Indian office-box of which Kipling speaks so feelingly in *Something of Myself*. Perhaps the office-box, like the solar topee (still worn with mournful defiance by those ICS officers who despair of further promotion), was a symbol of authority; and though the symbols have changed, the authority has been transferred and persists.

The Calcutta box-wallah comes of a good family, ICS, Army or big business; he might even have princely connections. He has been educated at an Indian or English public school and at one of the two English universities, whose accent, through all the encircling hazards of Indian intonation, he rigidly maintains. When he joins his firm his first name is changed. The Indian name of Anand, for example, might become Andy; Dhandeva will become Danny, Firdaus Freddy, Jamshed Jimmy. Where the Indian name cannot be adapted, the box-wallah will most usually be known as Bunty. It is a condition of Bunty's employment that he play golf; and on every golf course he can be seen with an equally unhappy Andy, both enduring the London-prescribed mixture of business and pleasure.

Bunty will of course marry well, and he knows it will be counted in his favour if he contracts a mixed marriage; if, say, as a Punjabi Hindu he marries a Bengali Muslim or a Bombay Parsi. Bunty and his wife will live in one of the company's luxury flats; they will be called Daddy and Mummy by their two English-speaking children. Their furnishings will show a happy blend of East and West (Indian ceramics are just coming in). So too will their food (Indian lunch followed by Western-style dinner), their books, their records (difficult classical Indian, European chamber music) and their pictures (North Indian miniatures, Ganymed reproductions of Van Gogh).

Freed of one set of caste rules, Bunty and his wife will adopt another. If his office has soft furnishings he will know how to keep his distance from Andy, whose furnishings are hard; and to introduce Andy, who shares an air-conditioned office with Freddy, into the home of Bunty, who has an office to himself, is to commit a blunder. His new caste imposes new rituals on Bunty. Every Friday he will have lunch at Firpo's on Chowringhee, and the afternoon-long jollity will mark the end of the week's work. In the days of the British this Friday lunch at Firpo's celebrated the departure of the mail-boat for England. Such letters as Bunty sends to England go now by air, but Bunty is conscious of tradition.

It is impossible to write of Bunty without making him appear ridiculous. But Bunty is the first slanderer of his group; and enough has been said to show how admirable, in the Indian context, he is. Where physical effort is regarded as a degradation and thick layers of fat are still to many the marks of prosperity, Bunty plays golf and swims. Where elections are won on communal campaigns, Bunty marries out of his community. Bunty is intelligent and well-read; like most educated Indians, he talks well; though he has abandoned the social obligations of the Indian joint family, he is generous and hospitable; he supports the arts. Not least of his virtues is that he keeps a spotless lavatory. East and West blend easily in him. For him, who has grown up in an independent India, Westernization is not the issue it was to his grandfather and even his father. He carries no chip on his shoulder; he does not feel the need to talk to the visitor about India's ancient culture.

Occasionally, very occasionally, the calm is disturbed. 'These damned English!' Bunty exclaims. 'When are they going to learn that 1947 really happened?' The words are like an echo from the Mullick Palace. But it is a passing mood. Soon Bunty will be out on the golf course with Andy. And golf is a game they both now love.

Indian Autobiographies

New Statesman, 29 January 1965

The dereliction of India overwhelms the visitor; and it seems reasonable to imagine that the Indian who leaves his country, and all its assumptions, for the first time is likely to be unsettled. But in Indian autobiographies* there is no hint of unsettlement: people are their designations and functions, and places little more than their names. 'We reached Southampton, as far as I can remember, on a Saturday.' This is Gandhi writing in 1925 of his arrival in England as a student in 1889. That it was a Saturday was more important to him than that he had exchanged Bombay for Southampton. He had landed in a white flannel suit and couldn't get at his luggage until Monday. So Southampton is no more than an experience of embarrassment and is never described; as later London, never described, is converted into a series of small spiritual experiences, the vows of vegetarianism and chastity being more important than the city of the 1890s. A place is its name.

London was just too big for me and the two days I spent there so overwhelming that I was glad to leave for Manchester. My brother had arranged some digs in advance so that I settled in straight away.

The Story of My Experiments with Truth, by M. K. Gandhi, translated by Mahadev Desai, 1966.

Punjabi Century, by Prakash Lal Tandon, 1963.

My Public Life, by Mirza Ismail, 1954.

A Passage to England, by Nirad Chaudhuri, 1959.

The Autobiography of an Unknown Indian, by Nirad Chaudhuri, 1951.

We are forty years beyond Gandhi, but the tone in *Punjabi Century*, the memoirs of a high business executive, remains the same. India is one place, England another. There can be no contrast, no shock in reverse. It is only near the end of *My Public Life* that Sir Mirza Ismail, after listing the recommendations he made to President Sukarno for the improvement of the Indonesian administration – he recommended four new colleges, five new stadiums and 'publication of the President's speeches in book form' – it is only after this that he observes:

The standard of living is higher in Indonesia than in India. People are better clad and better fed, although cloth is much dearer. One hardly sees the miserable specimens of humanity that one comes across in the big cities in India, as well as in rural areas.

The effect is startling, for until that moment the talk had mostly been of parks and gardens and factories, and of benevolent and appreciative rulers. We have to wait until Nirad Chaudhuri's *Passage to England*, published in 1959, for something more explicit.

I failed to see in England one great distinction which is basic in my country. When I was there I was always asking myself, 'Where are the people?' I did so because I was missing the populace, the commonalty, the masses ...

The attitude might be interpreted as aristocratic; in no country is aristocracy as easy as in India. But we are in reality dealing with something more limiting and less comprehensible: the Indian habit of exclusion, denial, non-seeing. It is part of what Nirad Chaudhuri calls the 'ignoble privacy' of Indian social organization; it defines by negatives. It is a lack of wonder, the medieval attribute of a people who are still surrounded by wonders; and in autobiographies this lack of wonder is frequently converted into a hectic self-love.

For its first half Gandhi's autobiography reads like a fairy-tale. He is dealing with the acknowledged marvels of his early life; and his dry, compressed method, reducing people to their functions and simplified characteristics, reducing places to names and action to a few lines of narrative, turns everything to legend. When the action becomes more complex and political, the method fails; and the book declines more obviously into what it always was: an obsession with vows, food experiments, recurring illness, an obsession with the self. 'Thoughts of self,' Chaudhuri writes in *The Autobiography of an Unknown Indian*,

are encouraged by a religious view of life, because it emphasizes our lone coming into the world and our lone exit from it and induces us to judge values in their relation to the individual voyager, the individual voyage, and the ultimate individual destiny.

In *Punjabi Century* Prakash Tandon seems to set out to tell the story of the transformation of the Punjab from 1857 to 1947. He barely attempts the theme. He minutely describes festivals, marriage customs, his father's engineering duties, the various family houses; and the book is transformed into a tribute to his province, his caste, his family and himself: it contains an embarrassing account of his courtship in Sweden, to which is added an injured and recognizably Indian account of his difficulties in getting a job. 'Friends not only in my own country but scattered on three continents have suggested I should write my memoirs,' Sir Mirza Ismail says.

It is not easy, however, to write about oneself, and partly for this reason, and partly in order to make the memoirs more interesting, I have quoted from letters received.

Not a few of these letters are tributes to the writer. 'You're a wonder!' writes Lord Willingdon. 'I would like to name a road after you,' writes the Maharaja of Jaipur.

An old-fashioned Muslim vizier, a modern Hindu businessman, the Mahatma: assorted personalities, but recognizably of the same culture. 'Writing an autobiography is a practice peculiar to the West,' a 'God-fearing' friend said to Gandhi on the Mahatma's day of silence. 'I know of nobody in the East having written one except amongst those who have come under western influence.' And it is in this bastard form – in which a religious view of life, laudable in one culture, is converted steadily into self-love, disagreeable in another culture – that we can begin to see the misunderstandings and futility of the Indo-English encounter.

The civilizations were, and remain, opposed; and the use of English heightens the confusion. When Gandhi came to England for the Round Table Conference in 1931 he stayed for a night at a Quaker guest-house in the Ribble Valley. The garden was in bloom. In the evening Gandhi, in sandals, dhoti and shawl, walked among the flowers. He scarcely looked at them. The story is told by Tandon, who got it from the warden.

I consoled him that it was quite characteristic of Gandhiji that though he passionately advocated a return to nature he completely lacked interest in its beauty.

But was it strictly a 'return to nature' that Gandhi advocated? Wasn't it something more complex? Was Gandhi's aim to reawaken wonder, or was it rather an unconscious striving after a symbolism acceptable to the Indian masses, a political exploitation, however unconscious, of the 'ignoble privacy' of Indian attitudes? The Gandhian concept is not easily translated. A 'return to nature' and 'patriotism': in India the concepts are linked; and the Indian concept of patriotism is unique. Tandon tells how, in 1919, the Independence movement made its first impression on his district.

These visitors spoke about the freedom of India, and this intrigued us; but when they talked in familiar analogies and idiom about the Kal Yug, we saw what they meant. Had it not been prophesied that there were seven eras in India's life and history: there had been a Sat Yug, the era of truth, justice and prosperity; and then there was to be a Kal Yug, an era of false-hood, of demoralization, of slavery and poverty ... These homely analogies, illustrated by legend and history, registered easily, but not so easily the conclusion to which they were linked, that it was all the fault of the Angrezi Sarkar.

We are in fact dealing with the type of society which Camus described in the opening chapter of *The Rebel*: a society which has not learned to see and is incapable of assessing itself, which asks no questions because ritual and myth have provided all the answers, a society which has not learned 'rebellion'. An unfortunate word perhaps, with its juvenile, romantic 1950s associations; but it is the concept which divides, not the East from the West, but India from almost every other country. It explains why so much writing about India is unsatisfactory and one-sided, and it throws into relief the stupendous achievement of Nirad Chaudhuri's *Autobiography of an Unknown Indian* which, containing within itself both India and the West, has had the misfortune of being taken for granted by both sides.

Chaudhuri's *Autobiography* may be the one great book to have come out of the Indo-English encounter. No better account of the penetration of the Indian mind by the West – and, by extension, of the penetration of one culture by another – will be or can now be written. It was an encounter which ended in mutual recoil and futility. For Chaudhuri this futility is an almost personal tragedy. Yet we can now see that this futility was inevitable. To the static, minutely ordered Indian society, with its pressures ever towards the self, England came less as a political shock than as the source of a New Learning. Chaudhuri quotes from *Rajani*, a Bengali novel by Bankim Chandra Chatterji:

He did not disclose his business, nor could I ask him outright. So we discussed social reform and politics ... The discussion of ancient literature led in its turn to ancient historiography, out of which there emerged some incomparable exposition of the classical historians, Tacitus, Plutarch, Thucydides, and others. From the philosophy of history of these writers Amarnath came down to Comte and his *lois des trois états*, which he endorsed. Comte brought in his interpreter Mill and then Huxley; Huxley brought in Owen and Darwin; and Darwin Buchner and Schopenhauer. Amarnath poured the most entrancing scholarship into my ears, and I became too engrossed to remember our business.

The astonishing thing about this novel is its date, which is 1877. Kipling's *Plain Tales* were to appear in book form just eleven years later, to reveal the absurdity of this New Learning, nourished by books alone. Between the New Learning and its representatives in Simla there was a gap. Dead civilizations alone ought properly to provide a New Learning. This civilization survived; it had grown suburban and philistine, was soon to become proletarian; and it was fitting that from 1860 to 1910, which Chaudhuri fixes as the period of the Indian Renaissance, the educated Bengali should have been an object of especial ridicule to the English, to whom the unintellectual simplicities of the blue-eyed Pathan were more comprehensible. Chaudhuri, lamenting the death of the Indian Renaissance, and the corrupting, 'elemental' Westernization that took its place, pays little attention to this aspect of the encounter.

The élite Indo-English culture of Bengal was as removed from the Anglo-Indian culture of Simla as it was removed from the culture of the Indian masses. It was a growth of fantasy; the political liberalism it bred could not last. It was to give way to the religious revivalism of a mass movement, to all the combative hocus-pocus of revived 'Vedic' traditions such as the launching of ships with coconut-milk instead of champagne, and finally to that cultural confusion which some sentences of Tandon's illustrate so well:

Gandhi rechristened India Bharat Mata, a name that evoked nostalgic memories, and associated with Gao Mata, the mother cow ... He ... spoke about the peace of the British as the peace of slavery. Gradually a new picture began to build in our minds, of India coming out of the Kal Yug into a new era of freedom and plenty, Ram Rajya.

Language has at last broken down. Gao Mata, Ram Rajya: for these there are no English equivalents. We can see 'national pride' now as an applied phrase, with a special Indian meaning. In the definition of Ram Rajya the true stress falls on 'plenty', while 'freedom' is an intrusive English *word*. Here is the futility of the Indo-English encounter, the intellectual confusion of the 'new' India. This is the great, tragic theme of Chaudhuri's book.

The Last of the Aryans

Encounter, January 1966

You don't have to wait long for the characteristic Nirad Chaudhuri note in *The Continent of Circe*. It occurs, unmistakably, almost before the book begins; yet it has the effect of a climax. There is a frontispiece with two views from the author's veranda in Delhi: one looking up to clouds, one looking down to refugee tents. The title page has a Latin device: *De rerum indicarum natura: Exempla gentium et seditionum*. The motto – 'Know Thyself' – follows, in five Indo-European languages. Seven detailed contents pages come next. And then we come to text: six pages, a chapter almost, headed 'In Gratitude'. Chaudhuri begins by thanking Khushwant Singh, 'the well-known Sikh writer, good companion, and man-about-town, for the loan of his portable typewriter'. This seems straightforward enough; but it soon becomes clear that we have to do with an incident.

It is like this. Chaudhuri is tapping away on Khushwant's machine. He is nearing the end of one of the sections of his book and his gratitude to Khushwant, as he says, is at its highest. A 'public print' comes his way. It is 'the official publication of the American Women's Club of Delhi'. It contains 'An Interview with Khushwant Singh':

INTERVIEWER: Who is the best Indian writer today?
KHUSHWANT SINGH: In non-fiction? Without a doubt Nirad Chaudhuri ... A bitter man, a poor man. He doesn't even own a typewriter. He borrows mine a week at a time.

Chaudhuri is 'struck all of a heap':

My poverty is, of course, well known in New Delhi and much

further afield, and therefore I was not prepared to see it bruited about by so august a body as the American Women's Club of Delhi.

Khushwant explains. His statement has been given the wrong emphasis. He thought he was only entertaining a lady to tea; he had no idea what her real intention was. He offers Chaudhuri a brand-new portable typewriter as a gift:

I tried to show that I bore no grudge by again borrowing the machine after the publication of the article and by most gratefully accepting the present of the new typewriter.

And a footnote adds:

Having read Pascal early in life I have always tried to profit by his wisdom: *'Si tous les hommes savaient ce quils disaient les uns des autres, il n'y aurait pas quatre amis dans le monde.'*

So much about the typewriters on which the book was written; the Americans, though, continue to receive attention for a whole page.

It is impossible to take an interest in Nirad Chaudhuri's work without becoming involved with his situation and 'personality'. This has been his extra-literary creation since the publication in 1951 of his *Autobiography of an Unknown Indian*. The book made him known. But in India it also made him disliked. Cruelly, it did not lessen his poverty; this mighty work, which in a fairer world would have made its author's fortune and seen him through old age, is now out of print. So, persecuted where not neglected, as he with some reason feels, he sits in Delhi, massively disapproving, more touchy than before, more out of touch with his fellows, never ceasing to attract either the slights of the high or the disagreeable attentions of the low.

His fellow passengers on the Delhi buses wish to know the time. Without inquiry they lift his wrist, consult his wrist-watch, and then without acknowledgement let his wrist drop. Sometimes he walks; and, in a land of 'massive staticity', where when men walk it is as if 'rooted trees were waving in the wind', he walks 'in the European manner, that is to say, quickly and with a sense of the goal towards which I am going'. Elderly people shout after him, 'Left! Right! Left! Right!' Boys call out, 'Johnnie Walker!' Sometimes they come right up to him and jeer in Hindi: *'Aré Jahny.'* It is not even the Johnnie Walker of the whisky label they refer to, but 'a caricature of him by an Indian film star':

Friends ask me why I do not go for these impertinent young fellows. I reply that I retain my common sense at least to the point of forcing myself to bear all this philosophically. But being also a naturally irascible man, I sometimes breathe a wish that I possessed a flame-thrower and was free to use it. In my conduct and behaviour, however, I never betray this lack of charity.

Indoors it is hardly less dangerous. The London Philharmonic Orchestra comes to Delhi. Chaudhuri talks music to Sir Malcolm Sargent; an English lady whispers to Mrs Chaudhuri, 'What a bold man he is!' He goes to the concert the next day; the British Council has provided tickets. He finds that he is separated from his wife by the aisle. An upper-class Indian lady claims that he is sitting on her chair. She is wrong; she objects then to his proximity; she calls the upper-class usherettes to her aid. He yields; he takes his chair across the aisle to join his wife.

The extra-literary Chaudhuri 'personality' is more than a creation of art; the suffering, however self-induced, is too real. Nearly seventy, he is a solitary, in hurtful conflict at every level with his environment.

FAILURE: it is Chaudhuri's obsession. There is the personal failure: twenty years of poverty and humiliation dismissed in a single, moving sentence in the *Autobiography*. There is the failure as a scholar, recorded in the *Autobiography* and echoed in the present book.

I shall mention the names of four men whom I regard as truly learned. They are Mommsen, Wilamowitz-Moellendorf, Harnack, and Eduard Meyer. When young and immature I cherished the ambition of being the fifth in that series. So I could not have been very modest. But a standard is a standard.

There is the failure, or rather the futility, of the nineteenth-century Anglo-Bengali culture, Chaudhuri's own, set against the larger futility of British rule. These were the interwoven themes of the monumental *Autobiography*. Now Chaudhuri addresses himself to a more encompassing failure: the failure of his country, his race, and the land itself, *Aryavarta*, the land of the Aryans.

He has called *The Continent of Circe* an 'Essay on the Peoples of India'. But his subject is really the Hindus; and his starting-point is the incomprehension, rapidly giving way to rage, which the Hindus have immemorially aroused in non-Hindus. Even E. M. Forster, Chaudhuri says, is more drawn to Muslims; and for all his pro-Indian sentiment, 'there are few delineations of the Indian character more insultingly condescending' than those in *A Passage to India*. Forster's plea for Indo-British friendship reminds Chaudhuri of the poem:

> Turn, turn thy hasty foot aside,
> Nor crush that helpless worm!
> The frame thy wayward looks deride
> Required a God to form.

'This massive, spontaneous, and uniform criticism by live minds . . . cannot be cancelled by afterthoughts which have their source in the *Untergang des Abendlandes*.' And Chaudhuri wishes to cancel nothing. He seeks only to explain. But the act of explaining frequently drives *him* to rage. Where the *Autobiography* was analytic, detached and underplayed, the Essay is strident and tendentious. Chaudhuri's sense of failure and vulnerability, that personality, comes in the way; and it is as a display of personality that *The Continent of Circe* is best to be relished. It is at its most delicious when it is most passionate; and it is most passionate when, one suspects, it is most personal: in the account, for instance, of the 'sob-chamber' of Hindu family life, where the only competition is in gloom and people can legitimately consider themselves provoked if they are told they are looking well. So, in Chaudhuri's essay as much as in the work of any uncomprehending foreigner, 'Hindu' ends by being almost a word of abuse.

Hindus pacifist? Rubbish, says Chaudhuri. Hindus are militarist, have always been; it is only their inefficiency that makes them less of a menace to the world. To prove this he gives selective historical examples and interprets the frontier conflict with China in a way that will not be faulted in Peking. Again: 'The industrial revolution in India at its most disinterested is an expression of anti-European and anti-Western nationalism.' This is possible; but it cannot be squared with what immediately follows: 'a far stronger force, in actual fact the positive force, is the Hindu's insatiable greed for money'. This, at first, seems too meaningless a statement even for simple denial. But he is making an important point; he is speaking of what some people in India call the 'pigmy mentality' of the Indian capitalist:

The American industrialist is the old European Conquistador in a new incarnation . . . But the Hindu money-maker can never be anything but his *paisa*-counting sordid self . . . His spirit is best symbolized by the adulteration of food, medicine, and whatever else can be adulterated.

So that the Indian industrial revolution, so far from being an expression of anti-Western nationalism, turns out to be a very petty, private thing indeed. Its cynicism might appear to some to be an extension of caste attitudes. And it might be expected that Chaudhuri would be critical of caste. Not at all. He asks us to keep off the caste question if we don't want to pound India to dust. Caste is the only thing that holds Indian society together. It is 'a natural compensation for man's convergent zoological evolution and divergent psychological evolution'. Caste did not suppress mobility; that came only with the *Pax Britannica*. And the Chaudhuri flourish is added:

If the system suppressed anything it was only ambition unrelated to ability, and watching the mischief from this kind of ambition in India today I would say that we could do with a little more of the caste system in order to put worthless adventurers in their place.

It might seem then that Chaudhuri, in an attempt to make a whole of Hindu attitudes, has succumbed to any number of Hindu contradictions. But I also feel that Chaudhuri, living in Delhi, enduring slights and persecution, has at last succumbed to what we might call the enemy. He sees India as too big; he has lost his gift of detachment, his world view. He seeks to expose where exposure is not really necessary. He has been taken in by the glitter of 'the diplomatic' at Delhi, the flurry of visitors, the cultural displays of competing governments. He exaggerates the importance of India and the interest taken in India. People in England, he says, 'are still longing after [India] with the docility of cattle', and the words make sad reading in London in 1965.

But this is the theme of his polemic: that tropical India is the continent of Circe, drugging and destroying those whom it attracts, and that the Aryans, now Hindus, were the first to be lured from a temperate land, 'denatured' and destroyed. Their philosophy is the philosophy of the devitalized. It is rooted in secular distress, the anguish of flesh on the Gangetic Plain, where everything quickly decomposes and leads to *tamas*, a comprehensive squalor:

The tragedy of all the systems of Hindu philosophy is that they confront men with only one choice: remain corruptible and corrupt flesh, or become incorruptible and incorrupt stone.

Be neurotically fussy about cleanliness; or – the greater

spirituality – show your indifference to the extent of being able to eat excrement. Hindus are not philosophers; nor do they reverence philosophy. 'What we respect are the sadhus, possessors of occult power.'

In Chaudhuri's argument it follows without contradiction that a people obsessed with religion, really a 'philosophy of sorrow', are obsessed with sex. It is the great anodyne. 'Defeat was on the fleshly plane ... Rehabilitation must also be in the flesh.' The sex act in Hindu sculpture is not symbolic of any sort of spiritual union, as is sometimes said: it is no more than what it appears to be. With a loss of vitality this celebration of the senses declines into the 'sex-obsessed chastity of the Hindu, which is perhaps the most despicable ethical notion ever created in the moral evolution of any people':

Their admiration of the supposed superior sexual knowledge and dexterity of the Hindus is putting ideas in the heads of a particularly depraved set of Occidentals, who are coming to India and working havoc with what sexual sanity ... we still have.

Well said; but it is on the subject of sex that Chaudhuri becomes most fanciful. Tracing the decline of vitality, he makes too much, one feels, of the emphasis in Sanskrit erotic writings on the pleasures of the *purushayita* or reversed position. Wasn't it in such a position, if one reads right, that Lucius and Fotis first came together in *The Golden Ass*?

Chaudhuri writes of India as though India has never been written about before. He pays little attention to received ideas; he mentions no authorities:

I am old, and I cannot spend the few years that are left to me tilting at theories which I have taken a lifetime to outgrow ... I must therefore be resigned to being called a fool by those who believe in ghosts ... Historical conferences in India always remind me of séances.

He places the Aryan settlement of the Gangetic Plain in

the seventh century BC. This will be offensive to those
Indians who think of India as the Aryan heartland and,
playing with millennia, like to think of Rome as a recent,
and peripheral, disturbance. He allows no civilization
worth the name to the indigenous Australoids, whom he
calls the Darks. Rigid barriers were set up against them,
and Chaudhuri – going back on some of his old views –
claims that no significant intermingling of the races took
place. The Darks, in their free or servile state, remain to
this day genetically stable; and to this day, it might be
added, the burning of a giant effigy of a Dark is the climax
of an annual Hindu pageant-play. Hindu *apartheid*
quickly gave the Darks the psychology of a subject race.
Chaudhuri retells a story from the *Ramayana*, the Hindu
epic. It is reported one day to Rama, the Aryan hero, that
the son of a brahmin has died suddenly. There can be only
one explanation: an act of impiety. Rama goes out to
have a look and, sure enough, finds that a young Dark has
been performing Aryan religious rites. The Dark is at
once decapitated and the brahmin's son comes back to
life. In later versions of the story the Dark dies happily:
death at the hands of an Aryan is a sure way to heaven.
Not even slavery created so complete a subjection.

So that, as Chaudhuri tells it, the continent of Circe has
played a cruel joke on the Hindus. The first white people
to come into contact with a black race, and the first and
most persistent practitioners of *apartheid*, they have themselves, over the centuries, under a punishing sun, grown
dark. The snow-capped Himalayas have become objects
of pilgrimage; and some Hindus, in their hysteria, look
beyond that to the North Pole, of which modern map-
makers have made them aware. There, someone will tell
you in all the blaze of Madras, there at the North Pole
lies the true home of the Hindus:

The theme of paradise lost and regained is one of the major
stories of Hindu mythology, and it must date from the Iranian
sojourn of the Indian Aryans. In the stories the gods recover

74

their heaven ... But in history paradise is lost for ever; and the curse begins to work : in sorrow shalt thou eat of it all the days of thy life.

This is the true Chaudhuri mood; and, for all Chaudhuri's fanciful flights and parenthetic rages, it must be respected : the Hindu sense of exile and loss is real. Yet the layman must ask certain questions. Chaudhuri places the Aryan settlement just two or three generations before the birth of the Buddha. Could the philosophy of sorrow and the devitalization of the Aryan have occurred so soon? Could the Aryan, even the settler in the South, have undertaken the colonization of South-east Asia a thousand years later? The reader of Chaudhuri's book, working from Chaudhuri's clues, might easily come to a different conclusion from Chaudhuri. He might feel that the Hindus, so far from being denatured Aryans, have continued, in their curious and self-willed isolation, to be close to their elemental Aryan origins. For the Aryan in India, Chaudhuri says, both sensibility and effort became parts of piety; and this surely makes many Hindu attitudes less mysterious. The attitudes remain; the gloss varies with historical circumstance. Chaudhuri writes with some sharpness of Hindus who now use European rationalism to excuse their 'irrational urges and taboos'. Yet we have seen how he himself uses a borrowed language to defend caste, a primitive institution. Hindus can be found today to defend Gandhi's assassination on the grounds that the assassin was a brahmin. This is outrageous; but it becomes intelligible and logical if we see it as an extension of the old Aryan approval of Rama's slaying of the impious, and complaisant, Dark in the *Ramayana* story.

And there is the erotic sculpture. It cannot be ignored. It cannot be talked away. It is too widespread, too casual. It is of a piece with the open sensuality of the *Rig Veda*, the earliest Hindu sacred book. This has been called the first recorded speech of Aryan man. Chaudhuri translates a sample:

He achieves not – he whose penis hangs limp between his
  thighs;
Achieves he alone whose hairy thing swells up when he lies.

It is Indrani, the Queen Goddess, who speaks; and she is
a match for her consort who, for his lechery, was punished
by the appearance all over his body of a thousand *pudenda
muliebria*. This is a camp-fire, peasant lewdness. And
when all is said and done this is what *aryan* means: he
is one who tills the soil.

Chaudhuri's plea that Hindus should turn their backs
on Asia and recover their Aryan or European personality
is, if narrowly interpreted, meaningless. Part of the trouble
is that Chaudhuri makes 'Aryan' and 'European' inter-
changeable. But 'European' surely needs to be more closely
defined, and dated. It is a developing concept; 'Aryan' is
fixed. And Chaudhuri's plea becomes very thin indeed
when we find that for *homo europaeus* in his present predominant and proliferating variety Chaudhuri has no
high regard:

The most vapid and insignificant class of human beings
which so far has been evolved in history [is] the modern urban
lower middle class of the West.

The absurd thing is that in India Aryan racial pride still
has point; in Europe it has little. Of this pride Chaudhuri's book might be seen as the latest expression. He is
not European; with his poetic feeling for rivers and cattle,
his insistence on caste, he remains Aryan.

Make a European society with India's religion. Become an
occidental of occidentals in your spirit of equality, freedom,
work, and energy, and at the same time a Hindu to the very
backbone in religious culture, and instincts.

This is not Chaudhuri. It is Vivekananda, the Vedantist,
writing at the turn of the century. A Bengali, like Chaudhuri, a reformer, a product of the Anglo–Bengali culture;
and the message, with all its imprecisions and contradictions, is like Chaudhuri's. The Anglo-Bengali culture sur-

vives. To its passionate introspection *The Continent of Circe* is a late addition, quirky, at times wild, but rich and always stimulating.

Theatrical Natives

New Statesman, 2 December 1966

The Kipling revival is curious. It seems to be mainly academic – and therefore self-perpetuating – and its interest seems to be less in the work than in the man. Kipling is more complex than his legend. It is easy for the critic to be made possessive by this discovery and to go through the work just looking for clues. It can be shown, for instance, from a story like 'The Bridge-Builders', that Kipling was not insensitive to the subtleties of Hindu iconography. The fact is interesting, but it doesn't make the story any less obscure or unsatisfactory. The fact is also awkward: it doesn't fit with other facts. And so it happens that attempts to set the legend right often end in simple tabulation, of matter and motif. This is the method of Mr Stewart's *Rudyard Kipling*, which does little more than celebrate a reading of the Kipling canon.

The legend survives. 'The Kipling that Nobody Read' – the title of Mr Edmund Wilson's essay – is still the Kipling nobody reads. Kipling revaluations are self-defeating, since they lead back more surely to the only Kipling of value, which is the Kipling of the legend. It is the legend of the brief serene decade of British India, when the Mutiny finally became a memory and nationalism was still to come: a moment of order and romance, vanishing even as it was apprehended, later to embarrass, sadden, anger and be explained away, until it became historical. The legend can be accepted now. Mr Cornell accepts it: it is one of the merits of his book. *Kipling in India* is the most balanced analysis I have read of Kipling's literary achievement. Mr Cornell says that his subject is

Kipling's apprenticeship, which contained the legendary achievement: the fixing, for all time, of that moment of British India.

It was the unlikely achievement of a very young man who took his unimportant journalistic work seriously; who abandoned the graver literary ambitions of his school-days to become a kind of club-writer; who aimed at ordinariness, and feared above all to offend. The club was at first the Punjab Club, of which Kipling became a member at seventeen. Soon it was all British India. This artificial, complete and homogeneous world did not require explanations. 'Dedication,' Mr Cornell says, 'walked hand in hand with triviality.' The triviality was the triviality of 'good-fellowship, not savage mockery'; there were limits to self-satire. Kipling followed the rules and didn't sink. Like the Lama in *Kim*, he acquired merit.

Mr Cornell is right to stress the club, for it is from his function as a club-writer that Kipling's virtues came, and especially that allusive, elliptical prose, easy but packed, which, almost one hundred years later, still seems so new. Mr Cornell's account of the development of this prose is fascinating. This is Kipling at seventeen, describing a Hindu pageant in Lahore:

To the great delight of the people, Ramachandra and his brothers, attired in the traditional costume and head-dress, were mounted aloft and held the mighty bow, the breaking of which shook the world to its centre. But it must be admitted that Sita, uncomfortably astride a broad-backed wicker-work bull, supported by an uneasy Rama, buried in tinsel and attended by bearers ... was a spectacle more comic than imposing.

This, as Mr Cornell says, is cheap, obvious and anonymous. It is without Kipling's later 'visual clarity'. It is also the work of an outsider: the Anglo-Indian was closer to the country. But two years later the tone changes. Here is another fair scene:

Presently the bolder spirits among them would put out a

horny finger, and carefully touch one of the bullocks. Then as the animal was evidently constructed of nothing more terrible than clay ... the whole hand would be drawn gently over its form; and, after an appreciative pat, the adventurous one would begin a lengthy dissertation to the bystanders at large.

The outsider has drawn closer. And sixteen months later the prose is like this:

Suddhoo sleeps on the roof generally, except when he sleeps in the street. He used to go to Peshawar in the cold weather to visit his son who sells curiosities near the Edwardes' Gate, and then he slept under a real mud roof. Suddhoo is a great friend of mine, because his cousin had a son who secured, thanks to my recommendation, the post of head-messenger to a big firm in the Station. Suddhoo says that God will make me a Lieutenant-Governor one of these days. I daresay his prophecy will come true.

This is the accomplished club-writer. He has mastered his subject and he knows his audience. He deals in an irony so private it might be missed by an outsider. To the Anglo–Indian, as Mr Cornell points out, simple phrases like 'a great friend of mine' and 'a real mud roof' would have precise meanings. On the difference between the first and last quotations, he writes:

In the earlier piece, Indian life appeared as no more than a passing show to be judged and dismissed on its aesthetic merits by a superior – and very young – English spectator. In the 1886 story, however, Kipling has penetrated to the heart of the Anglo-Indian's historical dilemma with amazing swiftness and economy.

The judgment is typical of Mr Cornell's balance and perception. He has not been tempted to make use of 'The House of Suddhoo' to amend the legend; he makes a *literary* judgment, and it is correct.

Kipling's prose was later to go beyond this. It was to become a superb instrument of narration, concise, full of flavour and speed, and wonderfully pictorial. But the club-writer always needed the club, the common points of reference; he needed the legend, which perhaps his own stories had helped to create. Kipling can best be savoured in a group of related stories: to this extent the tabulators are justified. A story by Chekhov is complete in itself; a story by Kipling isn't. It is either too slight or too long-windedly anecdotal. A legitimate delay in an Indian story would lose its point elsewhere.

There were the usual blue-and-white striped jail-made rugs on the uneven floor; the usual glass-studded Amritsar *phulkaris* draped to nails driven into the flaking whitewash of the walls; the usual half-dozen chairs that did not match, picked up at sales of dead men's effects . . . The little windows, fifteen feet up, were darkened with wasp-nests, and lizards hunted flies between the beams of the wood-ceiled roof.

'William the Conqueror', from which the passage is taken (it is quoted by Mr Stewart), is not a good story. It is pure comic-strip and – it is a love story set against a background of famine and corpses – it is horrifying to some. But details like these make it a true and acceptable part of Kipling's Indian work. In another setting comparable details would tell less. They wouldn't be as intimate; the 'usual' would have less meaning; and 'dead men's effects' would not speak of that dedication which was part of the Anglo–Indian's myth. Kipling's Anglo–Indians are always slightly embarrassing when they are on leave in England; there is a similar embarrassment, of ordinariness, it might be said, even in an Indian story like 'The Gadsbys', from which India is almost totally subtracted.

Just as in that passage detail adds to detail, and we would be without none of them, so each of Kipling's Indian stories adds to the others and is supported by them. Kipling's stories are not like Chekhov's; they are like Turgenev's hunting sketches or Angus Wilson's stories of the late forties. They make one big book; they have to be taken together. They catch – or create – a complete society at a particular moment. It is in its search for the independent, good Kipling story that Kipling criticism becomes aggressive and tabulatory. Even Mr Cornell succumbs. He notices the frequency of disguises, hoaxes and frauds in the stories; and he makes much of this. He should have ignored it. The fact would have been important if Kipling were more interested in people than in the types with whom he filled his club, never allowing himself satire, mockery or anger beyond what the club permitted. As it is, such tabulation shows up the limitations of the too homogeneous club as a source for material, and it shows up the limitations of the club-writer, whose closest literary friend, later in England, was to be Rider Haggard.

The irony, like the legend, remains. The 'long-coated theatrical natives discussing metaphysics in English and Bengali' – threats to order and romance, and therefore to be ceaselessly satirized – were to lead to a writer like Nirad Chaudhuri and a film-maker like Ray. The club has disappeared. By becoming its spokesman and jester, by brilliantly creating its legend, Kipling made the disappearance of the club certain.

A Second Visit

Daily Telegraph Magazine, 11–18 August 1967

1

TRAGEDY: THE MISSING SENSE

The raja reclines below a broken chandelier in a dark narrow room right at the back of the palace. The room is in the third courtyard, the only part of the palace that still works. The raja's armchair belongs to an extensive 'sofa-set' – English suburban, 1930 – distributed down the length of the room; the magenta upholstery is grimy. A rag-carpet completely covers the floor. It has been cut out from a more enormous piece, and is folded under where it doesn't fit. It is in a violent pattern of yellow and green that camouflages the million flies that buzz in and out of the rags. A photograph of the raja's father hangs forward from the wall; flat against the wall are a photograph of a family group, a hunting print in a rustic frame, and, at the top, in the yellowing colours of an unsuccessful reproduction process, a row of misty European landscapes.

Against this the raja sits, young, plump, cool in loose white cotton, and listens without expression to his last courtier, who sits at his feet on the rag-carpet and, holding a creased typewritten memorandum of many pages, outlines once again the complications of the inter-family litigation about the property that remains. The courtier is gaunt, his bony face finer than his master's; his clothes are dingier. He is a BA – the achievement is still fresh in his mind. He entered the service of the raja's family nearly fifty years ago, and now – his own son is dead – he has nowhere else to go.

Lunch is ordered for the visitors. The raja's younger brother, lean, elegant in movement – he is an attractive badminton player – offers to show the sights. The palace is in the nondescript Lucknow style, and not old. Most of what we see was built in the 1920s, at a cost of half a million pounds. The family's revenue then was £60,000. An oval-shaped garden in the forecourt, overgrown. Tall carved wooden doors from a provincial exhibition of 1911 (the Raj then in its glory, with at least two society magazines in Calcutta, the capital). The clock-tower courtyard, with crude roundels down the archway: an English couple between the Hindu and the Muslim: he in broad-lapelled jacket and sun-helmet, she in the loose lines of the 1920s. Beyond, the apartments, miniature palaces, of the former raja's wives: the source of the present litigation.

The raja's younger brother says there are six hundred rooms in all. The statement is disturbing. It is surely an exaggeration. Exaggeration does not belong to tragedy; it destroys the mood. And once, just twenty-five, thirty years ago, five hundred servants looked after the twenty-five members of the family. Round figures again, no doubt. But the palace had its own generating plant, stables for horses and elephants, its own zoo, its own reservoir. All this is shown from the clock-tower, the English machinery broken, the plaster broken. But the view from the clock-tower also shows no other building of consequence. It shows only the grass roofs of the bazaar settlement just outside the palace gates, and the flat scorched fields.

The eagerness of the raja's brother denies sadness. And there can be no sadness. Because there was no true grandeur. There was only excess and exaggeration, dying at the stroke of the legislator's pen that abolished large estates. The palace rose out of this dust; it expressed this dust, nothing more; it is returning to dust again; and the cycle had been unfruitful (the sofa-set, the landscape prints). Peasant, briefly prodigal, is turning to peasant again, as the kitchens of the third courtyard show. There is no vacuum; litigation totally engages the calm mind. There is no tragedy. There is, as perhaps there always has been, drabness. In this plain landscape wealth itself had been just another simplicity, an event, like decay.

This is the hoax of India. We take the country too personally. We go with a sense of tragedy and urgency, with the habit of contemplating man as man, with ideas of action; and we find ourselves unsupported.

There was a famine in Bihar. It had taken some time to prepare; and in this time the wits of Delhi had called it the 'shamine'. Now it was real: thirty million people were starving, bodies wrecked beyond redemption. But famine was never the subject of conversation; there was more about it in foreign newspapers than in Indian newspapers, which continued to be occupied with the post-election manoeuvring and speeches of politicians. The Films Division made a film about the famine; in Bombay and Delhi it was discussed as a film, a documentary breakthrough. The famine was like something in a foreign country, like the war in Vietnam. It was something you went to; it tested the originality of artists.

The civil servant in Calcutta said: 'Famine? Can that be news to us?' The editor in Delhi said: 'Famine? Can I turn that into news every day?'

It was the pattern of Indian conversation. After the frenzy, the reasoned catalogue of disasters and threats – China, Pakistan, corruption, no leaders, devaluation, no money, no food – after this the frenzy burnt itself out, and the statement was made that it didn't really matter, that it wasn't news. The young poet I met in Delhi had made the statement in a long English poem on which he had been working for months. The poem was a dialogue between historical India and spiritual India; its subject was 'the metaphysical timelessness' of India. The absurd words had a meaning. The poet was saying, with the civil servant and the editor, that there was no disaster, no news, that India was infinitely old and would go on. There was no goal and therefore no failure. There were only events. There was no tragedy.

It was what, in his own stylish way, the Maharishi Mahesh Yogi was telling the inaugural meeting of his Spiritual Regeneration Movement. The red-and-black cotton banner hung out on the Delhi Ring Road, next to the Indian Institute of Public Administration; and inside, in the shuttered gloom, the Maharishi, small, black-locked, bearded, in a cream silk gown, flowers and garlands about him, sat cross-legged before the microphone, backed on the platform by his American, Canadian and other white disciples on chairs, the men in dark suits, the women and girls in silk saris: India, it might be said, getting a dose of her own medicine from the West.

The Maharishi reproved his reverential middle-class Indian audience for running after 'isms' and failing to keep in tune with the infinite which lay below flux. No wonder the country was in a mess. The reproof was rubbed in by the glamorous figures on the platform who went one by one to the microphone, now raised, and gave witness to the powers of Indian meditation, the key to the infinite. A youngish, grey-haired Canadian was described by the Maharishi as a man who had given up drilling for oil to drill for truth. He gave his witness; and then, apparently on behalf of the world, thanked India. So that at the end it was all right. Everybody had just been talking; there was no problem; everything was as before.

The infinite, metaphysical timelessness: it always came to this. From whatever point they started – the Maharishi had even mentioned Bihar and glancingly attacked the folly of giving land to ignorant peasants, as though that would solve the food problem – there always came a moment when Indians, administrator, journalist, poet, holy man, slipped away like eels into muddy abstraction. They abandoned intellect, observation, reason; and became 'mysterious'.

It is in that very area that separates India from comprehension that the Indian deficiency lies. To see mysteriousness is to excuse the intellectual failure or to ignore it. It is to fall into the Indian trap, to assume that the poverty of the Indian land must also extend to the Indian mind. It is to deal in *Bengal Lancer* romance or *Passage to India* quaintness. It is, really, to express a simple wonder.

Because it is the simplicity of India which disappoints and in the end fatigues. There is a hoax in that quaintness. The barbaric religious rites of Hinduism are barbaric; they belong to the ancient world. The holy cow is absurd; it is, as Nirad Chaudhuri suggests in *The Continent of Circe*, an ignorant corruption of an ancient Aryan reverence. The caste-marks and the turbans belong to a people who, incapable of contemplating man as man, know no other way of defining themselves. India lies all on the surface. Once certain basic lessons are learnt, it is possible to make everything up, to chart conversations, to gauge the limit of comprehension. It was even possible for me to anticipate much of what was said at the inaugural meeting of the Spiritual Regeneration Movement. Where there is no play of the intellect there is no surprise.

The beatniks of America, Australia and other countries have now recognized India as their territory. Their instinct is true. Five years ago Ginsberg left America to make an initial exploration. He found the local Indians friendly; they were flattered by the attention of someone with a name so bright and modern; it was another tribute to the East from the West. Now the beatniks are everywhere, withdrawn, not gay, and sometimes in moving little domestic groups: papa beatnik, mama beatnik, baby beatnik, the man protected by his beard and jeans, the thin young woman more exposed, the dirt showing on her sandalled feet and on the tanned but pale skin of her bony, finely-wrinkled face. They are guests in temples (the Sikhs feed everybody); they thumb lifts on the highways and travel third on the railways; sometimes they compete with the beggars in cities; they attach themselves to the camps of holy men, like the one I heard about in Hyderabad, whose big trick was to pull a prick (I never found out whose) out of his mouth. In India they have rediscovered the wayfaring life of the middle ages.

There is a difference, of course. The maimed to the maimed, the West returning mysteriousness and negation to the East, while the humiliating deals are made in New Delhi and Washington for arms and food: it is like a cruel revenge joke played by the rich, many-featured West on the poor East that possesses only mystery. But India does not see the joke. In March the glossy *Indian Hotelkeeper and Traveller* introduced a 'Seers of India' series:

India's seers and sages have something to offer to the world outside. To some of the materially affluent but psychologically sick and spiritually rudderless foreigners from far-flung corners of the world, India's saints and sadhus provide irresistible magnets of attraction. India, steeped in spirituality, has a singularly unique facet to project to the world outside which at once commands attention and admiration.

The absurdity of India can be total. It appears to ridicule analysis. It takes the onlooker beyond anger and despair to neutrality.

We were far from the drought and famine area. But even here no rain had fallen for some time, and on the leafless trees in the administrator's compound the sharp spring sun had brought out the bougainvillaea like drops of blood. Twenty miles away hailstones destroyed a village's crops. The villagers, relishing the drama, the excuse for a journey, came in a body to report. We went to have a look. On the way we made surprise stops.

We stopped first at a primary school, a small three-room brick shelter beside a banyan tree. Two brahmins in spotless white cotton, each washed and oiled, each with his top-lock of caste, each 'drawing' ninety rupees a month, were in charge. Twenty-five children sat on the broken brick floor with their writing boards, reed pens and little pots of liquid clay. The brahmins said there were 250 children at the school. The administrator said:

'But there are only twenty-five here.'

'We have an attendance of a *hundred* and twenty-five.'

'But there are only twenty-five here.'

'What can you do, sahib?'

Beyond the road some of the children not at school rolled in the dusty fields. Even with twenty-five children the two rooms of the school were full. In the third room, protected from sun and theft, were the teachers' bicycles, as oiled and cared for as their masters.

At the next school, a few miles down the road, the teacher was asleep in the shade of a tree, a small man stretched out on his tiny teacher's table, his feet balanced on the back of the chair, so that he looked like a hypnotist's subject. His pupils sat in broken rows on strips of matting that had been soaked and pressed into the earth and was of its colour. The teacher was so soundly asleep that though our jeep stopped about eight feet away from his table he did not immediately awaken. When he did – the children beginning to chant their lessons in the Indian fashion as soon as they saw us – he said he was not well. His eyes were indeed red, with illness or sleep. But redness disappeared as he came to life. He said the school had 360 pupils; we saw only sixty.

'What is the function of a schoolteacher?'

'To teach.'

'But why?'

'To create better citizens.'

His pupils were in rags, unwashed except by snot, their hair, red from sun and malnutrition, made stiff and blond with dust.

Two or three and stop. The Hindi slogan on the walls of the family planning centre looked businesslike, but the centre itself was empty except for charts and more slogans and a desk and chair and calendar, and it was some time before the officer came out, a good-looking young man in white with a neat line moustache and a wrist-watch of Indian manufacture. He said he spent twelve days a month on family planning. He led discussions and 'motivated' people to undergo vasectomy. The administrator asked:

'How many people did you motivate last month?'

'Three.'

'Your target is one hundred.'

'The people here, sahib, they laugh at me.'

'How many discussions did you lead last month?'

'One.'

'How many people were there?'

'Four.'

'What were you doing when we came?'

'I was taking food and a little rest.'

'What did you do this morning?'

'Nothing.'

'Show me your diary.'

Loose forms for travelling expenses fell out of the diary. The diary itself hadn't been filled for two months. The young man had been holding down the job for two years; every month he drew 180 rupees.

'Try to motivate me,' the administrator said. 'Come on. Tell me why I should go in for family planning.'

'To raise the standard of living.'

'How would family planning raise the standard of living?'

It was an unfair question, because concrete, and because it hadn't been put to him before. He didn't answer. He had only the abstraction about the standard of living.

Birth control here; and, not far away, the artificial insemination centre. A peasant sat on the concrete culvert of an abandoned flower-bed, holding his white cow by a rope. In a stall at the other end of the garden was the black zebu bull. Contraception, insemination: whatever the aim, nature was taking her own way in this district. It was clear what was about to happen wasn't going to be artificial: the male villagers were gathering to watch. And the centre was well-equipped. It had a refrigerator; it had all the obscene paraphernalia of artificial insemination. But the bull, the officer said, had lost its taste for artificial stimuli; which was not surprising. The bull itself was running down. Certain potent rations had been fixed for it by the authorities, but the rations hadn't been collected. Seventy natural inseminations had taken place in the last year. But no one could tell the percentage of success, in spite of the ledgers in filing cabinets and the multi-coloured charts on the walls. It hadn't occurred to the follow-up officer that he had to follow up.

'What is the purpose of artificial insemination?'

'It allows one bull to cover many cows.'

This explained everything. The larger purpose – the gradual improvement of cattle in the district – had escaped him. Where the mind did not deal in abstractions, it dealt, out of its bewilderment, in the literal and the immediate.

To abstraction itself, then: to the district degree college, the humanities, and the Professor of Literature. He was a tiny man in a white shirt and flagrant yellow trousers belted without tightness over a gentle little paunch bespeaking total contentment. He looked very frightened now: the visit wasn't fair. His mouth was open over his projecting top teeth, which were short, fitted squarely one against the other, and made a perfect ivory arc. He said he taught the usual things. 'We begin with Eshakespeare. And –' Then he went shy.

'The Romantics?' the head prompted, turning it into a supporting inquiry.

'Yes, yes, the Romantics. Eshelley.'

'No moderns?' asked the administrator. 'Ezra Pound, people like that.'

The Professor grunted. Shoulder against the head's

table, he leaned forward over his little paunch, his mouth collapsed, his eyes terrified. But he kept up with modern writing. 'Yes, yes. I have been reading *so* much Esomerset Maugham.'

'What do you think is the point of teaching literature in a country like ours, Professor?'

'Self-culture.' He had been asked that before. 'Even if there is dirt and filth, the cultured mind, as Aristotle says, gets this purge. And this catharsis, as they call it, helps the self-culture. Because it is the cultured mind that even from all this dirt and filth gets the education the lower sort of mind cannot get.'

'Lady Chatterley?' the head interrupted. He had, mysteriously, understood.

The Professor cast him a swift look of gratitude and ended with relief, 'This is the value of literature.'

Poor Professor, poor India. Yet not poor – that was only the estimate of the onlooker. The Professor, and the other officers we had met, considered themselves successful. In the midst of insecurity, they drew their rupees. The rupees were few but regular; they set a man apart. All of India that was secure was organized on this tender basis of mutual protection; no one would apply to others the sanctions he feared might one day be applied to himself. Survival – the regularity of the rupees – was all that mattered. Standards, of wealth, nourishment, comfort, were low; and so, inevitably, were those of achievement. It took little to make a man happy and free him of endeavour. Duty was irrelevant; the last thing to ask in any situation of security was *why*. A colleague of the Professor's had said that the problems of teachers in the district were two: 'Estatus and emolument.' (But he liked alliteration; he described his pupils as 'rustics or ruffians'.)

So the abstractions and good intentions of New Delhi – the dangerous administrative capital, all words and buildings, where chatterers flourished and misinterpreted the interest of the world, where analysts who had never considered the vacuum in which they operated reduced the problems of India to the day-to-day scheming of politicians, and newspapers, which had never analysed their function, reported these schemings at length and thought they had done their duty to a country of five hundred million – so the abstractions of New Delhi remained abstractions, growing progressively feebler, all the way down. Insecurity merged with the Indian intellectual failure and became part of the Indian drabness.

And the physical drabness itself, answering the drabness of mind: that also held the Indian deficiency. Poverty alone did not explain it. Poverty did not explain the worn carpets of the five-star Ashoka Hotel in New Delhi, the grimy armchairs in the serviceless lounge, the long-handled broom abandoned there by the menial in khaki who had been cleaning the ventilation grilles. Poverty did not explain the general badness of expensive, over-staffed hotels, the dirt of first-class railway carriages and the shanty-town horror of their meals. Poverty did not explain the absence of trees: even the Himalayan foothills near the resort of Naini Tal stripped to brown, heat-reflecting desert. Poverty did not explain the open stinking sewers of the new middle-class Lake Gardens suburb in Calcutta. This was at the level of security, the rupees regularly drawn. It did not speak only of an ascetic denial of the senses or of the sands blowing in from the encroaching desert. It spoke of a more general collapse of sensibility, of a people grown barbarous, indifferent and self-wounding, who, out of a shallow perception of the world, have no sense of tragedy.

It is what appals about India. The palace crumbles into the dust of the countryside. But prince has always been peasant; there is no loss. The palace might rise again; but, without a revolution in the mind, that would not be renewal.

2
MAGIC AND DEPENDENCE

A year or so ago an Indian holy man announced that he had fulfilled an old ambition and was at last able to walk on water. The holy man was claimed by a progressive Bombay weekly of wide circulation. A show was arranged. Tickets were not cheap; they went to among the highest in the land. On the day there were film teams. The water tank was examined by distinguished or sceptical members of the audience. They found no hidden devices. At the appointed time the holy man stepped on the water, and sank.

There was more than embarrassment. There was loss. Magic is an Indian need. It simplifies the world and makes it safe. It complements a shallow perception of the world, the Indian intellectual failure, which is less a failure of the individual intellect than the deficiency of a closed civilization, ruled by ritual and myth.

In Madras State the Congress had been overthrown in the elections. The red-and-black flags of the Dravidian party were out everywhere, and it was at first like being in a colony celebrating independence. But this was a victory that could be fully understood only in Hindu terms. It was the revenge of South on North, Dravidian on Aryan, non-brahmin on brahmin. Accounts had been squared with the Hindu epics themselves, sacred texts of Aryan victory: no need now to rewrite them from the Dravidian side, as had been threatened.

The students of a college held a meeting to 'felicitate' – the Indian English word – a minister-designate. 'The evening is cool and mild winds are tickling us,' a student said in his speech of welcome. He was heckled; the evening was hot. But we had moved away from reality already: the student was inviting the minister-designate to drown the audience 'in the honey of his oration'. The minister-designate responded with pieces of advice. A cunning man never smiled; at the same time it was wrong for anyone to keep on laughing all the time. Some people could never forget the loss of a small coin; others could lose six argosies on the ocean and be perfectly calm. Reality was now destroyed, and we were deep in the world of old fairy-tale: the folk-wisdom, the honey, that was the satisfying substitute, even among politically active students, for observation, analysed experience and inquiry.

The national newspaper that reported this reception also reported a religious discourse:

MEDITATION ON GOD ONLY WAY TO REDEMPTION

Madras, 9 March
Even an exceptionally intellectual and astute person is likely to falter and indulge in a forbidden act and perform a suicidal act under the influence of destiny. One has to suffer the consequences of his errors in previous life ...

This, in South India, was still news. There had been an election, though, a process of the twentieth century. And here, on the main news page of another newspaper, were post-election headlines:

MASSES MUST BE EDUCATED TO MAKE DEMOCRACY
A SUCCESS
– Prof. Ranga
PAST MISTAKES RESPONSIBLE FOR CURRENT PROBLEMS
– Ajoy Mukherjee
CONGRESS REVERSES ATTRIBUTED TO LACK OF
FORESIGHT

A nation ceaselessly exchanging banalities with itself: it was the impression Indians most frequently gave when they attempted analysis. At one moment they were expressing the old world, of myth and magic, alone; at another they were interpreting the new in terms of the old.

There is an 1899 essay, *Modern India*, in which Swami Vivekananda, the Vedantist, takes us closer to the Indian bewilderment and simplicity. Vivekananda came from

Bengal, the quickest province of India. He was pained by the subjection of his country and his own racial humiliation. He was also pained by the caste divisions of Hinduism, the holy contempt of the high for the low, the 'walking carrion' of Aryan abuse. Vivekananda himself was of the Kayastha caste, whose status is still in dispute. In religion Vivekananda later found compensation enough: he exported the Vedas to the West itself, and found admirers. *Modern India* can be seen as a link between Vivekananda's political distress and its religious resolution. It is an interpretation of Indian history in apocalyptic Hindu terms which barely conceal ideas borrowed from the West.

Every country, Vivekananda states axiomatically, is ruled in succession by the four castes of priests, warriors, merchants and *shudras*, the plebs. India's top castes have decayed. They have failed in their religious duties, and they have also cut themselves off from the source of all power, the *shudras*. India is therefore in a state of '*shudra*-hood', which perfectly accommodates the rule of the *vaishya* or merchant power of Britain. *Shudra* rule, though, is about to come to the West; and there is the possibility, in India as well as in the West, of a 'rising of the *shudra* class, *with their* shudra-*hood*'. The emphasis is Vivekananda's; and from his curious position he appears to welcome the prospect, while saying at the same time that *shudra*-hood can be rejected by India, just as 'Europe, once the land of *shudras* enslaved by Rome, is now filled with *kshatriya* [warrior] valour'.

So, out of mock-Western historical inquiry, out of borrowed ideas and personal pain, Vivekananda reduces the condition of his country to a subject for simple, though slightly distorted, Hindu religious contemplation. Failure was religious; redemption can come only through religion, through a rediscovery by each caste of its virtuous duty and – at the same time – through a discovery by India of the brotherhood of all Indians.

Modern India is part of the unread but steadily re-printed literature of Indian nationalism. It is not easy to read. It wanders, is frequently confused, and is full of the technicalities of Hindu metaphysics. It could never have been easily understood. But with Indian sages like Vivekananda, utterance is enough; the message is not important. A nation exchanging banalities with itself: it cannot be otherwise, when regeneration is believed to come, not through a receptiveness to thought, however imperfect, but through magic, through reverential contact with the powerful, holy or wise. The man himself is the magic.

There is a whole department of the Central Government at work on The Complete Works of Mahatma Gandhi; they have an entry, under that name, in the Delhi telephone directory. But *The Hindu* newspaper of Madras reported in March that 90 per cent of high-school students in one district knew nothing of Gandhi except that he was a good man who had fought for independence. In a southern city I met a twenty-year-old Dravidian student. He was a product of independence, privileged; and we met at, of all twentieth-century things, an air show. The uncertain native, of Jabalpur or Gerrard's Cross, seeks to establish his standing in the eyes of the visitor by a swift statement of his prejudices. And all this student's social attitudes were anti-Gandhian. This was news to him. He reverenced the name. It was the name alone, the incantatory magic, that had survived.

Mind will not be allowed to play on the problems of India. It is part of the Indian frustration.

But now Indians have a sense of wrongness. They have begun to feel, like the Spaniards, that they are an inadequate people; and, like the Spaniards, they feel they are inadequate only because they are uniquely gifted. 'Intelligent' is the word Indians use most often to describe themselves, and the romantic view is gaining ground that they might be intelligent to the point of insanity. In India self-examination is abortive. It ends only in frenzy or in generalities about the Indian 'character'.

The humanities are borrowed disciplines that always turn discussions about famine or bankruptcy into university tutorials. There can be no effective writing. The ritual of Indian life smothers the imagination, for which it is a substitute, and the interpretation of India in the Indian novel, itself a borrowed form, is at a low, unchanging level. 'I don't wait for another *novel*,' Graham Greene says of the Indian writer he admires; he waits for an encounter with another stranger, 'a door on to yet another human existence'. The Delhi novelist R. Prawer Jhabvala has moved away from the purely Indian themes with which she started; she feels unsupported by the material.

In such a situation the novel is almost part of autobiography, and there have been many Indian autobiographies. These – always with the exception of the work of Nirad Chaudhuri – magnify the Indian deficiency. Gandhi drops not one descriptive word about London in the 1880s, and even Mr Nehru cannot tell us what it was like to be at Harrow before 1914. The world in these books is reduced to a succession of stimuli, and the re-acting organism reports codified pleasure or pain: the expression of an egoism so excluding that the world, so far from being something to be explored, at times disappears, and the writers themselves appear maimed and incomplete. All Indian autobiographies appear to be written by the same incomplete person.

So the sense of wrongness remains unresolved. But it is possible now for the visitor to raise the question and at times to tease out a little more, especially from men under thirty-five. At a dinner party in Delhi I met a young businessman who had studied in America and had felt himself at a disadvantage. He said, 'I felt that intellectually' – the Indian pride! – 'they were far below me. But at the same time I could see they had something which I didn't have. How shall I say it? I felt they had something which had been *excised* out of me. A sort of motivational drive, you might call it.'

The jargon was blurring, but I felt that, for all his businessman's adventurousness, he was like the peasants I had met some hundreds of miles away. It was a late afternoon of dust and cane-trash, and golden light through the mango trees. The peasants were boiling down sugar-cane syrup into coarse brown sugar. The bullocks turned the mill; a black cauldron simmered over a fire-pit. A bare-backed, well-built young man scraped up sugar from the shallow brick trough level with the ground and pressed it into balls. His father chewed *pan* and watched. He said, just giving information, that his son had to write an examination in the morning. He would fail, of course; another son had written an examination six months before and had failed. In his mind, and perhaps in his son's mind, there was no link between failure and this labour in the fields. The peasants were Kurmis, a caste who claim Rajput ancestry. The British-compiled gazeteers of the last century are full of praise for the Kurmis as diligent and adaptable cultivators; they are praised in exactly the same way by Indian officials today. But they have remained Kurmis, demanding only to have their Rajput blood acknowledged.

What had been excised out of the Kurmis had been excised out of the businessman: 'motivational drive', that profound apprehension of cause and effect, which is where magic ends and the new world begins.

Causation: it was the theme of the Buddha 2,500 years ago in the distressed land of Bihar. It was the theme 150 years ago of Raja Rammohun Roy, the first British-inspired Indian reformer. It is the necessary theme to-day. It is depressing, this cycle of similar reform and similar relapse. Reform doesn't alter; it temporarily revives. Ritual and magic forever claim the world, however new its structure.

The process of relapse can be charted in our own time in the work of Vinoba Bhave, the Gandhian land-reformer of Bihar, who fifteen years ago made the cover of *Time* magazine. 'I have come,' *Time* reported him saying, 'to loot you with love.' His programme was simple: he would ask landowners to give away land to the landless. It was the spiritual way of India. 'We are a people wedded to faith in God and do not give ourselves to the quibblings of reason. We believe in what our Rishis [sages] have taught us. I have the feeling that the present-day famines and other calamities are all due to our sins.' It was not therefore his business to think in any practical way of the food problem or of creating economic units of land. 'Fire merely burns; it does not worry whether anyone puts a pot on it, fills it with water and puts rice into it to make a meal. It burns and that is the limit of its duty. It is for others to do theirs.'

With this there went ideas about education. 'Human lives are like trees, which cannot live if they are cut off from the soil . . . Therefore, everyone must have the opportunity to tend the soil . . .' Agricultural work will also keep the population down, because it takes the mind off sex. Care has to be taken in choosing a craft for a school, though. Fishing, for example, wouldn't do, because 'I have to show (the children) how to deceive the fish'; poultry-keeping is better. Literature should not be neglected. 'It is a fault in the Western system of education that it lays so little stress on learning great lines by heart.' But the best education is the one Krishna, the mythological-religious figure, received. 'Shri Krishna grazed cattle, milked them, cleaned the cowshed, worked hard, hewed firewood . . . ; later, as Arjuna's charioteer, he not only drove his horses but also cared for them.'

It isn't only that so much of this is absurd, or that Bhave was taken seriously until recently. It is that Bhave's sweetness adds up to a subtle but vital distortion of the Mahatma's teaching. The stoic call to action and duty becomes, with Bhave, an exercise in self-perfection, an act of self-indulgence and holy arrogance. He will not see his responsibility through to the end; it is the duty of fire only to burn. He separates, in a way the Mahatma never did, the private religious act from its social purpose. He misapplies the doctrine of bread-labour by which the Mahatma hoped to ennoble all labour, including that of the untouchables. Bhave says that the untouchables do work which is 'not worthy of human dignity'; they must become tillers and landowners. He leaves them, in effect, where he finds them. And he does nothing to solve the food problem which, in India, is related to the ignorant use of land.

Bhave goes back again and again to the scriptures: their rediscovery becomes an end in itself. So, in the name of reform, the Mahatma and goodness, Bhave slips into reaction. The old world claims its own.

Indians are proud of their ancient, surviving civilization. They are, in fact, its victims.

Reform this time will be more brutal. China presses; Pakistan threatens; non-alignment collapses and America drives hard bargains. The new world cannot be denied. Incapable of lasting reform, or of a correct interpretation of the new world, India is, profoundly, dependent. She depends on others now both for questions and answers; foreign journalists are more important in India than in any other country. And India is fragmented; it is part of her independence. This is not the fragmentation of region, religion or caste. It is the fragmentation of a country held together by no intellectual current, no developing inner life of its own. It is the fragmentation of a country without even an idea of a graded but linked society.

There is no true Indian aristocracy, no element that

preserves the graces of a country and in moments of defeat expresses its pride. There have been parasitic landowners, tax-farmers; there have been rulers. They represented a brute authority; they were an imposed element on a remote peasantry; in moments of stress they have – with exceptions – proclaimed only their distance. They are the aptly named 'native princes'; and though here and there their brute authority, of money or influence, has been reasserted, they have disappeared and nothing marks their passing. In Hyderabad you wouldn't have known that the Nizam had just died, that a dynasty older than Plassey had expired. Every Indian, prince or peasant, is a villager. All are separate and, in the decay of sensibility, equal.

There are contractors and civil servants in Delhi, where a 'society lady' is usually a contractor's wife. There are business executives in Calcutta, which still has an isolated, ageing set with British titles. There are the manufacturers and advertising men and film people of Bombay, where 'suave', 'sophisticated' and 'prestigious' are words of especial approval. But these are trade guilds; they do not make a society. There is an absence of that element, to which all contribute and by which all are linked, where common standards are established and a changing sensibility appears to define itself. Each guild is separate. Even the politicians, with the state withering away for lack of ideas, are sterilized in their New Delhi reserve. And each trade – except the entertainment trade – is borrowed.

Every discipline, skill and proclaimed ideal of the modern Indian state is a copy of something which is known to exist in its true form somewhere else. The student of cabinet government looks to Westminster as to the answers at the back of the book. The journals of protest look, even for their typography, to the *New Statesman*. So Indians, the holy men included, have continually to look outside India for approval. Fragmentation and dependence are complete. Local judgment is valueless. It is even as if, without the foreign chit, Indians can have no confirmation of their own reality.

But India, though not a country, is unique. To its problems imported ideas no longer answer. The result is frenzy. The journals of revolt are regularly started; they are very private ventures, needing almost no readership and having responsibility to no one; within weeks they are exhausted and futile, part of the very thing they are revolting against. Manners deteriorate. Each Indian wishes to be the only one of his sort recognized abroad: like Mr Nehru himself, who in the great days was described, most commonly, by visiting writers as the lonely Indian aristocrat – his own unexplained word – presiding over his deficient but devoted peasantry. Each Indian, looking into himself and discovering his own inadequacy, attributes inadequacy to every other Indian; and he is usually right. 'Charlatan' is a favourite word of Indian abuse. The degree of this self-destructive malice startles and depresses the visitor. 'The mutual hatred of men of their own class – a trait common to *shudras*': the words are Vivekananda's: they describe a dependent people.

This dependent frenzy nowadays finds its expression in flight. Flight to England, Canada, anywhere that lets Indians in: more than a flight to money: a flight to the familiar security of second-class citizenship, with all its opportunities for complaint, which implies protection, the other man's responsibility, the other man's ideas.

It was written, of course. It was the price of the independence movement.

The movement, as it developed under Gandhi, became a reforming religious movement, and it was in the Indian tradition that stretched back to the Buddha. Gandhi merged the religious emphasis on self-perfection in the political assertion of pride. It was a remarkable intuitive achievement. But it was also damaging. It was not concerned with ideas. It committed India to a holy philistinism, which still endures.

At the beginning of the nineteenth century Raja Rammohun Roy had said that forty years of contact with the British would revivify Indian civilization. He spoke before the period of imperialist and racialist excess; the technological gap was not as wide as it later became; the West, to the forward-looking Indian, was then less the source of new techniques than the source of a New Learning. But the gap widened and the mood changed. The independence movement turned away, as it had to, from people like Roy. It looked back to the Indian past. It made no attempt to evaluate that past; it proclaimed only glory. At the same time the imaginative probing of the West was abandoned. It has never been resumed. The fact escapes notice. The West, so much more imitable today than in 1800, might be pillaged for its institutions and technology; its approval is valuable. But the political–religious– philistine rejection still stands. The West is 'materially affluent but psychologically sick'; the West is a sham. No Indian can say why. But he doesn't need to; that battle has been won; independence is proof enough.

A scholar in Delhi reminded me that Macaulay had said that all the learning of India was not worth one shelf of a European library. We had been talking of aboriginal Africa, and Macaulay was brought in to point out the shortsightedness of a certain type of obvious comment. Later it occurred to me, for the first time, that Macaulay had not been disproved by the Indian revolution. He had only been ignored. His statement can be re-affirmed more brutally today. The gap between India and the West is not only the increasing gap in wealth, technology and knowledge. It is, more alarmingly, the increasing gap in sensibility and wisdom. The West is alert, many-featured and ever-changing; its writers and philosophers respond to complexity by continually seeking to alter and extend sensibility; no art or attitude stands still.

India possesses only its unexamined past and its pathetic spirituality. The Indian philosopher specializes in exegesis; the holy man wishes to rediscover only what has been discovered; in 1967 as in 1962 the literary folk squabble like schoolmen, not about writing, but about the proprieties of translation from all their very ancient languages. India is simple; the West grows wiser.

Her revolution did not equip India for a twentieth-century independence. When that came, it existed within an assumption of a continuing dependence: an accommodating world, of magic, where Indian words had the power Indians attributed to them. The bluff had to be called; the disaster had to come.

One by one India has had to shed ideas about herself and the world. Pain and bewilderment can no longer be resolved by the magical intervention of a Vivekananda, a Gandhi, a Nehru, a Vinoba Bhave. Fifteen years ago Bhave said, more or less, that his aim was the withering away of the state. He called it 'the decentralized technique of God'; and even the pious dismissed him as a dreamer. The state has now withered away. Not through holiness; it is just that the politicians, homespun villagers in New Delhi, no longer have an idea between them. Magic can no longer simplify the world and make it safe. India responds now only to events; and since there can be no play of the mind each disagreeable event – the Chinese attack, the Pakistan war, devaluation, famine and the humiliating deals for food with the United States – comes as a punishing lesson in the ways of the real world. It is as if successive invasions, by the reaction they provoked, that special Indian psychology of dependence, preserved an old world which should have been allowed to decay centuries ago; and that now, with independence, the old world has at last begun to disintegrate.

The crisis of India is not political: this is only the view from Delhi. Dictatorship or rule by the army will change nothing. Nor is the crisis only economic. These are only aspects of the larger crisis, which is that of a decaying civilization, where the only hope lies in further swift decay. The present frenzy cannot be interpreted simply as a decline from stability. That was the stability of a country ruled by magic, by slogans, gestures and potent names. It was the stability of a deficient civilization that thought it had made its peace with the world and had to do no more. The present mood of rejection has dangers. But it alone holds the possibility of life. The rejection is not religious, even when its aims are avowedly the protection of a religion. It does not attempt reform through self-perfection. The *mode* is new, and of the new world.

It may be that I exaggerate; that I forget the holy man putting his thumb in his mouth and pulling out a prick, to applause; that I forget the pious who, in a time of famine, pour hundreds of gallons of milk over a monumental idol while an Air Force helicopter drops flowers. But magic endures only when it appears to work. And it has been proved that man, even in India, can no longer walk on water.

The Election in Ajmer

Sunday Times Magazine, 15–22 August 1971

1

Whom to vote for? the English-language poster in New Delhi asked. And when, in mid-February, a fortnight before the first polling day, I went south to Ajmer in Rajasthan, it seemed that the half a million voters of this Indian parliamentary constituency, part urban, part rural, part desert, had a problem. The Congress had won freedom for India, and for more than twenty years, through four election victories, it had ruled. Now the Congress had split. The split had led to this mid-term election. But both sides continued to use the name. *Kangrace ko wote do*, the posters of both sides said: Vote Congress. And the same saffron, white and green flag flew from rival campaign jeeps: the jeep the favoured campaign vehicle, authoritative and urgent in the dusty streets of Ajmer, among the two-wheeled tonga carriages, the battered buses, bicycles by the hundred, handcarts and bullockcarts.

Both sides would have liked to use the old election-winning Congress symbol of the pair of yoked bullocks. But the courts had decided that the yoked bullocks shouldn't be used at all; and both sides had devised complicated and naturalistic symbols of their own. A cow licking a sucking calf: that was the Congress that was with Mrs Gandhi, the Prime Minister. A full-breasted woman at a spinning-wheel (the fullness of the breasts always noticeable, even in stencilled reproductions): that was the old or Organization Congress, that had gone into opposition. Both symbols, in India, were of equal weight. The spinning-wheel was Gandhian, the cow was sacred. Both symbols proclaimed a correct, Congress ancestry.

It was in some ways like a family quarrel, then. And, as it happened, for this Ajmer seat the candidates of the two Congresses were related. There were five candidates in all. Three were independents and of no great consequence. 'They are only contesting by way of their hobby,' a man from the Election Department said. 'They will put down their security of 500 rupees. They will get a few thousand votes and forfeit their deposit and sit quietly, that is all. It is only their hobby.'

The main candidates were Mr Mukut Bharvaga and Mr Bishweshwar Bhargava. Mr Mukut was standing for the old Congress and all its opposition associates. He was the uncle of Mr Bishweshwar, who was defending his seat for the Indira Congress. And here – a local reflection of the national quarrel about legitimacy – was the first issue in Ajmer: who was morally in the wrong? The uncle, for fighting the nephew? Or the nephew, for fighting the uncle?

Mr Mukut, the uncle, was sixty-eight years old, a lawyer, and blind. He was famous in Rajasthan for his prodigious memory and his skill in matters of land revenue. His fees were said to be as high as 1,000 rupees a day, about £50; his earnings were put at two lakhs a year, about £10,000. But Mr Mukut was also known for his free services to peasants, who still came to Ajmer to look for 'the lawyer without eyes'. Mr Mukut was an old Congressman and freedom fighter and he had gone to jail in 1942. His political career since independence had been unspectacular, but steady and without blemish: he was perhaps best known for his campaign to have clarified butter easily distinguishable from its groundnut-based substitute. He had won the Ajmer seat for Congress in 1952, 1957 and 1962. In 1967, at the age of sixty-four, he had retired, handing over the Ajmer seat to his thirty-six-year-old nephew and protégé, Mr Bishweshwar. Now, with the Congress split, Mr Mukut wanted his seat back; and, to get it, he had allied himself with all his old political enemies. Was Mr Mukut right? Was Mr Bishweshwar wrong, for resisting?

The answer, overwhelmingly, was that Mr Bishweshwar was wrong. He should have withdrawn; he should not have fought his uncle, to whom he owed so much. It was what Mr Mukut's son, who was Mr Mukut's election agent, said; and it was what Mr Bishweshwar's agent said. Mr Mukut himself always spoke of the contest with a sense of injury. 'The State Congress chose the meanest weapon,' he said, 'setting my own nephew to fight me. They know I'm a man of strong family feeling and they were hoping *I* would withdraw.' The Maharana of Udaipur, who was supporting Mr Mukut, told an election meeting, 'The Indira Congress is dividing the country, and not only ideologically. They are breaking up families.' And the Rajput village headman, loyal to his Maharana, agreed. 'A nephew who cannot love the members of his own family, how can he love the public?'

But wasn't the uncle also wrong to try to pull down his nephew? 'I didn't want my father to fight this election,' Mr Mukut's son said. 'I said, "Bapuji, you are old now, you are disabled." But then I was overwhelmed by his answer. It brought tears to my eyes. He said, "This is a time for sacrifice." '

Sacrifice: it wasn't a claim Mr Bishweshwar could make, and for much of the campaign he looked harassed and uncertain and sometimes hunted. Unlike his uncle, who always spoke freely, even elaborately, Mr Bishweshwar had little to say; and his manner discouraged conversation. He stared blankly through his glasses, like a man alerted not to say anything that might be used against him. Once he said, 'I cannot understand how my uncle can go against all those principles I imbibed from him.' It was the only comment on his uncle I heard him make, and it was spoken very quickly, like a prepared line.

Mr Bishweshwar wasn't a popular man. He suffered from all comparisons with his uncle. Mr Mukut was small

and lean and brown, an ascetic politician of the old
school, with a jail-record. Mr Bishweshwar was as tall and
plump as a film star. He was a post-independence politician, an organization man. People in his own party said
of him: 'Politics is his profession.' And: 'If politics were
taken away from him he would hardly be having two
square meals a day.' And: 'His uncle massacred hundreds
of party workers for him.' But that wasn't held against the
uncle; that was held against Mr Bishweshwar.

'I'm not working for Bishweshwar,' his campaigners
said. 'I'm working for Indira.' And this was what they said
even on polling day, waiting in the brightly coloured party
tents for voters. 'The people aren't voting for Bishweshwar. They're voting for Indira.'

Which, as everybody said, was what the election was
about: Indira, Mrs Gandhi, that formidable lady in New
Delhi, who had done a de Gaulle on the Congress and
taken over, who had abolished the old consensus politics
of the Congress. She had declared war on privilege; her
appeal was to the poor, the untouchables, the minorities.
She had nationalized the banks; she had 'de-recognized'
the princes; and, to deprive the princes of their privy
purses, she intended to change the constitution.

Indiscipline, people like old Mr Mukut said, grieving
for all those old members of the party who had fallen.
Indira Hatao, the opposition posters said: Remove Indira. And on the other side: *Garibi Hatao*, Remove
Poverty. The rich, the poor: the wonder was that, in
India, this basic division had taken such a long time to be
politically formulated. The socialists and communists
hadn't done that: they offered theologies. And this was
the first election in Ajmer in which the parties had issued
manifestoes.

Rich and poor. But there was a regional complication.
Rajasthan is a land of princes. Ajmer itself, though in the
centre of Rajasthan, hadn't been a princely state and had

no maharaja. But the Ajmer constituency was vast: two hundred miles, mainly of desert, rock and jagged brown hills, between Ajmer and Char Bazaar: more than six hours in a jeep. Two of its districts belonged to the former state of Udaipur; and the Maharana of Udaipur, who had supported Mr Bishweshwar at the last election, had declared for Mr Mukut in this. The princes of Rajasthan, 'de-recognized' by the government, their privy purses threatened, were in their different ways up in arms against the government. And they could take their case to the people and get a hearing, because they were princes.

For other people in the opposition, supporters of Mr Mukut, it wasn't so easy. Mr Kaul, an old Congressman of Mr Mukut's age, was now a member of the Indian Upper House. Mr Kaul ate only one meal a day and he said he had acquired the habit during his time in jail in 1932. But there was no jail-taint to him now; the post-independence years of power, honour and politicking had worn him smooth; and Mr Kaul thought that personal canvassing should be banned.

'We issue our manifestoes. Why should we go to the people personally? By canvassing the way is found for bribing them. Our people are poor; they don't understand what we are fighting for. Their ignorance is being exploited. The Indira Congress is spending crores of rupees, spoiling them, the peasants, the villagers, the uneducated and the labour classes. Giving them slogans. All slogans. It's our national character.'

I asked him about the national character.

'Our people don't think in terms of country first.'

'What do they think of?'

'*Nothing.*' He laughed. 'Haven't you noticed? They're indifferent.'

And on that first day in Ajmer the election seemed far away. The tongas carried advertisements for the Apollo Circus; walls everywhere were painted with family-planning slogans in Hindi. It was a Tuesday, the day of the weekly service at the Hanuman temple; and monkeys from the temple hopped from tree to tree on the nearby Circuit House hill. At the top of the hill there was a view of the clear lake beside which Ajmer is built, the water a surprise after the dust of the streets. On the black rocks at the lake-edge scores of washermen were beating the cotton clothes of the poor to death, swinging the twisted wet hanks with a steady circular motion and grunting competitively at every blow.

The sun rose higher. The brown mist lifted over the brown hills. The washermen spread out their lengths of cotton, white and coloured, and went away. Hawks hovered over the lake, at whose margin clouds of midges swirled and thinned like cigarette smoke in a wind, and then re-formed. From the flat-roofed white-and-ochre town below there came the sound of a loudspeaker: cinemas announcing their attractions. In the late afternoon there was music: a wedding procession.

The Ajmer calendar was full. On Saturday there was the eighty-ninth prize-giving of Mayo College, one of India's important English-style public schools, founded for the education of the sons of princes. Three days later came the Hindu festival of Shivratri and the opening of the Ajmer Flower Show. So, quickly, after the disorder of the main street – the mixed traffic, the cows, the rubble, the dust, the exposed food-stalls – Ajmer revealed itself as excessively ordered. There was the railway town with its great locomotive workshops and its severely graded housing. There was the medieval, narrow-laned town around the famous Muslim shrine, an object of pilgrimage. There were the newer residential areas; there was the bazaar, an extension of the disorder of the main street; and there were the ordered acres of Mayo College, where only the servants' quarters spoke of India.

Beyond the brown hills were the smaller towns and the thousand villages that made up the constituency, each village as fragmented and ordered as Ajmer itself: every man in his caste, his community, his clan: divisions not strictly racial and not strictly social: more as if, in an English village, where everyone more or less looked alike, spoke the same language and had the same religion, every man yet remembered that he was a Dane or Saxon or Jute and stuck to his kind. Cow-and-calf, spinning-wheel: poor and rich, left and right: how could these divisions apply?

In the evening I went to the Honeydew, one of the three recognizable cafés that Ajmer, with a population of 300,000, just about supports. It was air-conditioned and dim and the waiters were in white. A young man I fell in with told me that the Honeydew was for the young and 'modern' of Ajmer. He spoke sardonically but he too wanted it known that he was modern. 'My father was a semi-literate. He joined the Railways in 1920 and retired thirty-seven years later. Then he died. At the end of his life he was making 300 rupees a month. For my father it was his luck, his *karma*. What he had sown in a past life he was reaping in this. I am not like that. I am only making 400. But let people look at my suit and tie and see me spending in the Honeydew and think I'm rich.'

A cup of Honeydew coffee cost about three pennies. You could ask the waiter for a cigarette; he would place an open packet on your table and you paid only for those you took. Luxuries were small in India and little gestures were fundamental acts of defiance. To wear a tie, when money was immemorially scarce, to have a coffee in the Honeydew: that was more than extravagance. That was to deny one's *karma*, to challenge the basis of one's father's faith.

And it was of defiance that Mr Desai, once Mrs Gandhi's Deputy Prime Minister, now in the opposition and supporting Mr Mukut, was speaking in Naya Bazaar that evening. In the bazaar lanes the narrow shops, raised on platforms, glittered with electric light, tempting custom.

In the wide open area of Naya Bazaar itself, beyond the heads of the crowd, beyond the flags and bunting and posters strung across the street, and at the end of two little colonnades of fluorescent tubes, there was another platform, very clean and very bright, and there – with Mr Mukut and Mr Kaul and others no doubt sitting at his feet – Mr Desai, not looking his seventy-four years, was talking about 'the Indira psychosis', nationalization and the danger to the constitution.

At first it seemed, to use the Indian word, 'sophisticated'. But an election address, in that street, before that crowd, without an analysis of the distress that was so visible, without a promise for the future! An election address, about economic and legal matters, cast in terms of personal injury! And when Mr Desai was talking of nationalization he was talking of more than an economic issue. He was talking of an act of defiance, a threat to order and *dharma*, an impious shaking of the world. In the place of that defiance he was offering himself: his Gandhi-cap, his white homespun, his simple brown waistcoat, his well-known asceticism, his Gandhian habit of spinning: all his personal merit built up through many years of service. Religion, *dharma*, the Hindu 'right way' given a political expression: the crowd was in tune with what was being said. They listened respectfully; there was even some slight applause.

Garibi Hatao, Remove Poverty: it was possible to understand why no one before Mrs Gandhi had raised this simple political slogan. And it was also possible to understand why it was said in Ajmer that the issues of the election – Remove Poverty, Remove Indira – were too abstract and remote. There would have been more interest, people said, in elections for the State Assembly, when the politicians could play on the more immediate issues of caste and community and offer tangible rewards: a tarred road, a water-tank, electricity.

But that evening, less than twenty miles away, on

the Jaipur road, the forty-six-year-old Maharaja of
Kishangarh, politically active on the opposition side, a
member of the State Assembly, was murdered.

Kishangarh was part of the neighbouring constituency.
It is one of the lesser names of princely Rajasthan – the
state, as it existed in 1947, was just over 650 square miles
– but the Maharaja was linked by blood to the great
houses. He was well known in Ajmer. He played badminton at the Ajmer Club and tennis on the Mayo College
courts.

That evening he and the Maharani were going to a
wedding. They were about to leave when the telephone
rang. Kishangarh took the call himself. Then he told
the Maharani he had to go out for a little and would be
back in ten minutes. When he left the palace, driving himself in a little Indian-made Fiat, he had a revolver and
many rounds of ammunition; he also had about 1,500
rupees. A few miles from the palace, on a straight stretch
of the Jaipur–Ajmer road, the car stopped or was made
to stop; and Kishangarh was shot in the right ear. His
revolver was taken; his money wasn't touched.

This was the story that broke the next morning. And it
was strange, at eleven, in the bright desert light, neem trees
and cactus beside the road, thorn trees scattered about the
dug-out brown land, to see the little 'champagne-green'
Fiat, not princely or tragic, not a dent anywhere, not a
window cracked, only a finger-wipe of blood on the driving
door, at rest on the sandy verge with its front bumper
against a tall clump of the *ker* shrub, by whose red flowers
the strength of the monsoon can be foretold. The princely
licence-plate, white on red, said: *Kishangarh No. 11.*
A line of stones marked the course of the car as it had
come off the road. On the other side of the road were the
jeeps of the district police and a crowd of dhoti-clad, tur-
banned peasants.

Some local politicians were also there, among them Mr

Makrana, small and fat and grim, with dusty trousers, a worn green pullover and a very white muslin turban the size and shape of a scooter tyre. 'I am a Marwari,' he said, 'and we Marwaris wear these turbans, white or khaki, at sad deaths, funerals.' Mr Makrana was a member of the State Assembly and the whip of the party to which the Maharaja had belonged. 'The Maharaja was having a very nice influence for us. Some big person is behind this killing.' Once Mr Makrana had owned about 2,500 acres of land. 'I lost my land when the *jagir* system went out.' Under this system his tenants used to give him a third or a half of what they made. 'With that percentage we used to manage our establishment. Now I am in the marble business. I couldn't survive if I had to depend on politics. I live from the marble. Politics is only my hobby.' And, leaving me, he began again to walk up and down the road before the still peasants, his plump face set and petulant, his white turban on his head, very visibly mourning a member of his party.

The Ajmer District Magistrate, in a suit, and two senior police officers, in khaki, came in a black saloon which flew a blue police pennant. The peasants watched; Mr Makrana himself stopped to watch. A smiling, green-bereted sub-inspector from the Jaipur Dog Squad arrived and reported. And then Mr Kaul, the member of the Indian Upper House, turned up. He scrambled briskly out of his car – tight trousers stylishly creased, long brown coat – and hurried across the road to the officials, like a man used to being well received everywhere; and then gravely, as though looking at the corpse itself, he examined the Fiat.

Mr Kaul wasn't a man for white turbans and country mourning. His manner was of New Delhi; and very soon he was to issue a statement, in English: '... dastardly murder ... general atmosphere of lawlessness and violence ... leaders of the Ruling Party from the Prime Minister downwards ... using such derogatory epithets against the so-called capitalist, industrialist and feudal order ... inciting the feelings and sentiments of the masses, particularly of the Youth of the lower rungs of Society ...'

In Kishangarh the shops were shut, but the streets were full of people, stunted, thin-limbed peasants from the interior who, as soon as the news had broken that morning, had begun to make their way on foot or cycle to the palace. It was a ramshackle Indian country town, the new concrete buildings all balconies and balustrades at the top, slum at road-level, with rough additional lean-tos roofed with canvas or thatch. The asphalt road was like an irregular black path through dust and dung, unpaved sidewalks, heaps of rubble and old gravel. Then, unexpectedly, there was a lake, and in the centre of the lake an old stone building, possibly a summer pavilion; and at the end of the lakeside road the high walls of Kishangarh fort and the old town.

Inside, the procession had started to the cremation ground and the waiting pyre, prepared with sandalwood and other scents. The road and the city walls were packed, ablaze with the colours of peasant Rajasthan, red and orange and saffron. The open jeep with the body came out of the palace gate. The relations of the dead Maharaja were in white. White here the terrible colour of mourning.

In the middle of the afternoon the Fiat was still where it had been, against the *ker* bush. Some of the marker stones had been scattered. No one watched now. Some distance away two or three peasants sat in the shade of a thorn tree. The brown hills were pale in the glare. The private tragedy was over. Mr Mukut and Mr Kaul had already addressed a condolence meeting.

The Kishangarh affair had upset Mr Bishweshwar's schedule, and when I went to his house only his wife was there. The house was in an open area at the end of a dirt lane where Mr Mukut also had his law office. The ambiguous Congress flag hung limp in the little garden where flowers and shrubs grew out of bald earth.

I had been told that Mr Bishweshwar lived simply. The trellis-enclosed veranda where I sat first of all had a dark, tarnished, homely air, with rough-and-ready furniture and a strip of dirty matting. The small terrace upstairs was even less formal, with a plain concrete floor, and local five-rupee basket chairs brought out as required. A servant squatted on the floor in a small room near the steps and scoured dishes. A Hindu country interior: there was nothing, except perhaps the telephone, to suggest that this was one of the rising political households of Rajasthan and that Mrs Bishweshwar's father had been in his time a famous politician, so fierce in faction fights against Mr Kaul that Mr Nehru had had to intervene.

Mrs Bishweshwar was a pretty woman of thirty-three, pale and slightly pinched, with her head covered modestly with a dark-red sari. At first she spoke only in Hindi. She said she couldn't speak English well; but later she relented, and it turned out that she spoke English impeccably. She had been educated in a pastoral institution that her father had founded. There she had studied Indian classical music and had learned to spin. Later she took her BA in music and English and Hindi literature. She still spun. 'I believe in Gandhiji's teachings.' But she had let the literature go. 'I don't like modern literature. I can't understand it. I don't like Hindi modern literature either. I like Shakespeare, Browning, Shelley.'

She didn't like political life. 'My husband is not a politician. He is a worker.' It was the Gandhian word: a doer of good works. 'I too am an ardent believer in improving the lot of the downtrodden. But I want to work silently. I don't want publicity for myself. But I would like a lot more for my husband. People should recognize his ability. If he is a sincere and hardworking man, people should know.'

Mr Bishweshwar arrived, tall and plump, in trousers

and a brown sports shirt. He looked harassed and winded and had clearly been rattled by the Kishangarh affair. He had also missed a meeting at a village called Saradhna; and it was for Saradhna that we immediately started, accompanied – perhaps for luck on this unlucky day, perhaps for reasons of piety – by a small, energetic sadhu clad from top to toe in saffron. The sadhu seemed about to chatter with cold; it was the effect of his saffron head-dress, which was cunningly tied from one piece of cotton and looked like a cross between a mitre and a jester's cap, with flaps over the ears.

The Rajasthan village huddles together, a solid built-up mass where space is suddenly scarce. Saradhna was like this. We stopped near the two tea-shacks, their fires glowing in the dark. There was no one to receive us and we walked around to the other side of the village. Then, at a great pace, Mr Bishweshwar began to walk through the village, kicking up dust, the rubber-sandalled sadhu running at his heels, ear-flaps sticking out. We raced past stripped trees, over piles of rubble, past broken court-yards, over runnels of filth. The narrow lane twisted and turned and opened abruptly into miniature squares. We passed a group of smokers sitting peaceably in the thick warm dust around a brass plate with their smoking things; and then we were out of the village and near the tea-shacks again.

Some men came to Mr Bishweshwar then and whispered. *Unanimous, unanimous*: the English word was quite clear in all the Hindi. Not far away a man squatted in the dust, cooking some mess in a tiny black pot over an enormous straw blaze.

Mr Bishweshwar said, 'They held their own meeting. The whole village has decided to support me.'

'*Unanimous*,' a black-capped villager said, shaking his head from side to side.

It was hard to push the matter any further; and our business was therefore, quite unexpectedly, over.

As we were driving back to Ajmer it occurred to me that Mr Bishweshwar's trousers and shirt were unusual for a campaigning Congress politician. I said, 'So you don't wear homespun?'

He thought I was criticizing. He plucked at the sleeve of his brown sports shirt and said, 'This is homespun. Sometimes I wear trousers for the convenience. But I often wear the dhoti. I like the dhoti.'

So he was only out of uniform. He wasn't, as I had thought, the new-style politician, matching Mrs Gandhi's new-style campaign. He was a Congressman, aspiring after the old style; he had, as he had said, imbibed his principles from his uncle. When the Congress had split, leaving Mrs Gandhi at the head of a minority government, the leaders of the local State Congress had hesitated about which side to join; and Mr Bishweshwar, as he admitted, had hesitated with them. When they had declared for Mrs Gandhi, he had gone along with them. The new-style politics was Mrs Gandhi's, and Mrs Gandhi's alone. In Rajasthan the Congress organization, the whole structure of Congress control, remained what it was. It was Mrs Gandhi who had appeared to turn this party, ruling since independence, into the party of protest.

But for Mr Bishweshwar it remained a gamble. In 1967 he had got 145,000 votes; his main opponent, from the party known as the Jan Sangh (The National Party) had got 108,000. But in 1967 Mr Bishweshwar had had the support of Mr Mukut and the Maharana of Udaipur. Now Udaipur and the Jan Sangh were supporting Mr Mukut. Udaipur could take away Rajput votes from Mr Bishweshwar; the Kishangarh affair could have the same effect.

Mr Bishweshwar was going that evening on a two-day country tour. In his campaign headquarters – the ground floor of a villa: a stripped central room with an empty fireplace, high blue walls with little oblong windows just below the ceiling, worn rugs on the cracked concrete floor, small side rooms enclosed by latticework and wire netting

– among his workers, some paid (40 rupees a month, £2, for two hours a day), some minor politicians in their own right, whose rustic manner belied the revolutionary promises of the posters sent out from New Delhi, among the barefoot boys sitting on the floor and pasting *Vote Bishweshwar* posters on cardboard, he looked very harassed indeed.

But Mr Mukut had his problems too. Officially he was the candidate of the opposition or Organization Congress. But the Organization Congress had no organization in Ajmer. Mr Mukut was depending on the organization of the Jan Sangh; and Mr Mukut and the Jan Sangh had until recently been enemies. The central executives of the opposition parties had formed an alliance; they had agreed on a division of seats; and Ajmer had gone to the Organization Congress and Mr Mukut.

The Jan Sangh in Ajmer had been planning to put up their own man. Now they had to support Mr Mukut; and Mr Sharda, the president of the local Jan Sangh, who had contested the seat in 1967, didn't like it. He said, 'This is a Jan Sangh seat and some Jan Sangh man should have contested. I would have been a better candidate than the man they chose. Have you seen him? He's an old man of sixty-eight, blind, can't see. All the time our people come to me asking why Jan Sangh is not contesting, why I am helping this blind old man.'

And it was an unusual alliance. The Jan Sangh, founded in 1951, had grown in strength, Mr Sharda said, because the Congress was corrupt; but for most of this time Mr Mukut was the ruler of the Congress in Ajmer. It wasn't only for its opposition to Congress corruption that the Jan Sangh was known, though. The Congress was non-sectarian; Mr Mukut had a good record as a defender of Muslim rights. The Jan Sangh had come into prominence in North India as the militant Hindu party of the right, rallying Hindus against Muslims, and, within the Hindus, the Aryan, Hindi-speaking north against the Dravidian south. It spoke of the pampering of minorities; its slogan was 'Indianization'. Latterly, scenting parliamentary power, the Jan Sangh had softened its communal, Aryan line; it had decided that the enemy was Communism; but its communal reputation remained its strength.

'We don't want to take ideas from Russia and Kosygin,' Mr Sharda said. 'We have a heritage, a culture. We have the Vedas, the first book of the human race. With the Vedas' light other people have developed their cultures. So when we have got such an old heritage we believe that our race is great, is noble. My grandfather, Harbilas Sharda, has written a book called *Hindu Superiority*. In the 1930s. He has given all the facts and figures to show how the Hindu race is superior to others.'

Mr Sharda was in his fifties, small, compactly built, in a striped brown suit. He wore tinted glasses; for all his aggrieved talk of the 'blind old man' his own eyes were not too good. Eye trouble, in fact, had made him give up the practice of law and go into business as a commission agent dealing in cement and cloth. He lived in a new concrete bungalow at the bottom of the Circuit House hill, opposite a rock wall plastered with drying cow-dung cakes. He had a glass case of knick-knacks in his drawing-room; bits of vine grew out of whisky bottles, one brown, one green. On the white wall there was a portrait, like a tinted photograph, of Harbilas Sharda, the author of *Hindu Superiority*: a gentle old brahmin with a drooping moustache, in British days an elected member of the Central Legislative Assembly, given the title of Dewan Bahadur (one step below the knighthood), and famous in India as the author of the Child Marriage Restraint Act (still known as the Sharda Act), which in 1930 had banned child marriage.

'My family were the first to revolt against the social evils of the country,' Mr Sharda said. But his party was now committed to the protection of the sacred cow, as it was committed to the creation of an Indian nuclear armoury. There was no inconsistency. Like parties of the extreme right elsewhere, the Jan Sangh dealt in anger, simplified scholarship and, above all, sentimentality. It spoke of danger and distress – 'Our civilization is in danger,' Mr Sharda said – and from present impotence it conjured up a future of power, as pure as the mythical Hindu past, before the British conquest, before the Muslim invasions.

'We want nuclear bomb for the safety of the country. But this is a matter of our all-India policy. I don't talk too much about it to our villagers.' The cow was different. 'We feel that cow is a very important animal in our country, being an agricultural country, and as such should not be slaughtered. There is a candidate in Delhi, Mr Ram Gopal Shalwala, is fighting only on that. Government should give protection and give good bulls to have a better type of animal. Good arrangements of fodder should also be made, because generally there is famine in this area and thousands of animals die of famine.'

He didn't think Muslims would object. 'Muslims who live in villages and are agriculturalists like to live as Hindus do. It is only the educated fanatics who want to create this gulf of Hindus and Muslims for their own selfish motives.' But later, when we were talking about the way the 40,000 Muslim votes would go, Mr Sharda said in his direct, unrancorous way, 'They will be divided. But generally most of the Muslim votes do not go to Jan Sangh.'

As I was leaving, a barefoot servant in a torn dhoti brought in the up-country edition of *The Motherland*, the new English-language Jan Sangh daily published in Delhi. The Kishangarh story, and the charge of political murder, was still big on the front page.

The Muslim votes wouldn't go to the Jan Sangh. But Mr Mukut thought they would go to him personally, for his past services. This was on a day of exaltation when, after an evening of well-received speeches, he seemed to think that by allying himself with his former enemies he had left almost no votes for the other side.

We were driving in one of the campaign jeeps from Ajmer to the military town of Nasirabad, through country that had been stripped almost to desert by eight successive years of drought. Between the driver and myself Mr Mukut sat or half-reclined, small, frail, easily tossed about, in a dhoti and a black waistcoat, with his fine head thrown back, his sightless eyes closed, his delicate hands occasionally clutching at air. Sometimes, between sentences, his wide, expressive mouth opened and closed wordlessly, and he was then like a man gasping for breath. His gentle manner and fragility imposed gentleness on all who came near him; and I occasionally felt, as I leaned close to catch his exalted words, that I was rushing a garrulous invalid to hospital, and not racing with one of Rajasthan's master-politicians to a hard day's campaigning.

A leaflet had appeared in Ajmer calling on Jan Sangh supporters to boycott Mr Mukut. Mr Mukut said this was another trick of Mr Bishweshwar's party; he had, he said, been astonished by the loyalty of his Jan Sangh workers. Mr Mukut spoke, not quite as one who had seen the error of his Congress ways, but as someone who was at last able to speak of the errors of the Congress. The Jan Sangh said that the Congress was corrupt. It was true, Mr Mukut said. 'The power corrupted us. Our politicians became Gandhian only in name.' But he himself had been helpless; he had never been a minister. And now he saw no moral or political complication in his alliance with the Jan Sangh. His position was simple: it was as a Gandhian that he was fighting the Indira Congress, which was illegitimate, Communistic and westernizing.

'Gandhiji's ideology was quite different from the ideology of Western politicians. The foundation of his political tactics is that means should be as fair as the end.'

He didn't think this could be said of Mrs Gandhi. He was also concerned about nationalization. 'It will ruin the country. All our state-owned enterprises are so badly run.' His support of private enterprise brought him close to the hard anti-Communist line of the Jan Sangh. But Mr Mukut didn't appear to be concerned either about efficiency or capitalism. His opposition to nationalization was embedded in an over-riding Gandhian doubt about the machine age. The machine had destroyed the West, as Mr Mukut had heard; the machine would destroy India. 'What I particularly admired about Gandhiji was that he went to Buckingham Palace in 1931 in a dhoti.'

I asked why that was admirable.

'Because he put the picture of poor India before the world.'

'Mr Nehru said that the danger in a country as poor as India was that poverty might be deified.'

'Did he say that?' Mr Mukut paused. The idea was new, 'western' and perhaps intellectually unmanageable. 'I never heard him say that.' He opened and closed his mouth wordlessly; and again, head thrown back, eyes closed, he was like a gasping invalid.

We passed the new Shiva temple, still with its bamboo scaffolding, that the peasants had built to celebrate the end of the eight-year drought. It stood white in a desolation of young thorn bushes. Once there had been woodland here; but towards the end of the drought, at a time of famine, the trees had been cut down for charcoal. And then we were in the military area: barracks old and new in the stripped land, soldiers with rifles on their shoulders running in groups of two or three on the asphalt road.

The main street of Nasirabad was brilliant with stalls of fruit and vegetables. Here we stopped. Many reverential hands helped Mr Mukut out of the jeep and led him, limp-shouldered, limp-armed, between the vegetable-stalls and across the narrow pavement to a dark little office, over the front door of which, on the outside, were dusty framed diplomas from Lucknow University and, on the inside, brightly coloured Hindu religious prints. It was a lawyer's office, with a whole glass-cased wall of Indian law books covered in brown paper, the frame of the case painted yellow, with each section roughly labelled in red.

Mr Mukut said to me, 'He's one of my disciples.'

The lawyer, a middle-aged man in a chocolate-purple sports shirt, said very loudly, as though addressing the street, 'Everything I am I owe to Mr Mukut.'

They made Mr Mukut sit on a basket-chair. They brought him tea and a large, fly-infested *cachoree*, a local fried delicacy.

The lawyer said, 'Mr Mukut made me what I am. He has served many people here without payment. The people of Nasirabad remember these things.'

And Mr Mukut, leaning back, his slender legs drawn up onto the seat, his hands fumbling for the *cachoree* that had been broken for his convenience into little pieces, Mr Mukut opened and closed his mouth, like a man about to sigh.

But the lawyer had pointed the weakness of Mr Mukut's campaign. Some of the people in the office were linked to Mr Mukut by interest. The others were Jan Sangh and they for the most part were small shopkeepers. Even the forbidding, kohl-eyed young man in a cream-coloured suit and pointed black shoes, even he, who was a teacher, came from a shopkeeping family. The Jan Sangh was an urban party; it had no organization in the villages. The only party with a village organization was the Congress. It was that village organization that had to be captured; and Mr Mukut's only weapon was his influence. Mr Bishweshwar's strength was that he belonged to the ruling party; a ruling party had its ways of exerting pressure.

'I will tell you how they won the last State Assembly by-election,' the lawyer said. 'At that time this area was affected by famine. Rural people were jobless. The government machinery opened famine works in a number of places. And these famine-relief workers were given one slogan: "If you vote for the other side, famine-relief work will be closed down." ' And now the ruling party was again up to their old tricks, this time with the untouchables or Harijans, whom they were bribing in all sorts of ways and especially with loans from the nationalized banks.

A prominent Christian in Ajmer had complained to me that as a result of all the political attention the Harijans were getting out of hand. They were being 'brought up' too fast, before they had a proper 'footing'; there had been strikes. 'I am even afraid to speak harshly to some of them now,' the Christian said. I thought that the lawyer might be trying to say something like this in an indirect, un-Christian way. So I asked him, 'They're behaving badly then, these scheduled castes?'

'Badly?' The lawyer didn't understand my question. He was a Hindu; he didn't have the Christian social sense; he couldn't share the Christian's resentment. Caste was not class. No one, however successful, denied his caste, however low, or sought to move out of it; no one tried to 'pass'; no one's caste-security was threatened by any other caste. So the lawyer floundered. 'No,' he said at last, 'they are not *behaving* badly. It's just that they're being fooled.'

But what did Mr Mukut have to offer? How was he going to balance this powerful appeal of the other side? Was he campaigning, for instance, for cow-protection? Mr Mukut was astonished that I should ask. Everyone in Ajmer knew his record. During his time in parliament he hadn't only campaigned for a ban on cow-slaughter and the punishment of cow-killers; he had also campaigned for free grazing for cows anywhere.

'We are too western-oriented,' Mr Mukut said. He was sitting up now, small and neat and cross-legged in his basket-chair. 'Go to the villages. Everybody in the village now wants to wear jacket and tie. Look at our own *ayurveda* medicine. It was only after a long fight that we managed to get it accepted, these remedies that are much cheaper than any modern drugs. And then there are the pipelines.'

I said, 'Pipelines, Mr Mukut?'

'Even in the villages. The pipelines in the villages is going too far. It's all right in the cities. But in villages the healthy water from the well is good enough. But they are taking piped water now to many villages. For our women-folk this going to the well and drawing water was one of the ways in which their health was maintained. They now have got no substitute exercise for the women. Similarly, we have our own indigenous *chakki* [a quern] for grinding grain on the floor. Now they have substituted these mills run by electric power or oil-fired machines. So now the whole village sends its grain to these mills, with the result that the women are missing this exercise as well. Previously even in cities this grinding with *chakki* was done by small families. But now everything is being westernized. It is morally bad because it tells upon the health and habits of our womenfolk. And unless some alternative employment is found for them it naturally makes them sluggish.'

In a famine area! From an election candidate! But Mr Mukut could go into the villages to ask for votes because he was a Gandhian who knew that his own merit was high. He had achieved merit through service and sacrifice. Service for its own sake, sacrifice for its own sake. 'Since Mr Kaul and I left the Congress,' Mr Mukut said, 'there is no one there with a record of service. Mr Kaul was in jail; I was in jail.' Democracy, the practice of the law, the concern with rights: one set of virtues had been absorbed into another, into a concept of *dharma*, the Hindu right way; and the distortion that resulted could sometimes be startling.

2

Kishangarh was murdered on Tuesday evening. On Friday evening All-India Radio announced that the police had 'worked out' the case and arrested a student. On Saturday the details of the arrested man's 'confession' were all over Ajmer, and in the afternoon there were Hindi leaflets in the streets:

LOVE STORY: A POLITICAL OPERA

Bhim Jat, the killer of the Maharaja of Kishangarh, has confessed, and the whole affair is crystal clear. The Maharaja had a farm a few miles from Kishangarh. Bhim Jat and his beautiful sister worked for the Maharaja on this farm. The Maharaja took advantage of the girl's poverty and for a long time had illicit relations with her. Bhim Jat, a youth of nineteen, could not stand this looting of his sister's honour. He took the law into his own hands and with his country-made pistol shot the Maharaja dead.

But politics corrupts the truth and deals in lies. Some politicians immediately called a meeting to mourn the Maharaja's death and with a great show of sorrow tried to tell the voter to take his revenge by defeating the Indira Congress.

Would you vote for a party which plays with the honour of your daughter or sister? There should be rejoicing not tears at the death of these rajas–maharajas whose only princely habit is that they know how to take advantage of the poverty of young girls. Rise and utterly crush these debauched people so that never again will they come to you for votes with the name of Gandhi on their lips . . .

Has Mr Mukut no shame, to be sitting in the lap of the Jan Sangh, who were once his bitter enemies? The election should be fought on policies. Mr Mukut shouldn't be misleading the voters for his own selfish purposes. Mr Mukut has used the Maharaja's funeral-pyre to cook himself a meal of votes.

Other versions of the story were no less sad. Bhim Jat's sister had left her husband to become Kishangarh's mistress; and Bhim Jat had been ostracized by his caste for the dishonour his complaisance had brought on them all. Kishangarh had given Bhim a house on the farm; he was paying for Bhim's education; he had promised Bhim the farm itself. But then a well on the farm gushed water. In the desert water was money; and Kishangarh, worried about his 'de-recognition' and the possible loss of his privy purse, had sought to go back on his promise.

Kishangarh was the name of an eighteenth-century school of painting. Now it was linked with a peasant woman, a farm, a well: a peasant drama, far removed from the princely pageantry of the prize-giving at Mayo College that afternoon. Kishangarh was remembered there, in the obituary section of the headmaster's speech, as a distinguished and popular old boy, like the late Maharaja of Jaipur, 'who died in the UK, where he had gone to play polo, his favourite sport'.

The boys were exquisite in tight white trousers, long black coats and pink long-tailed Rajput turbans. They sat on the steps of the Mogul-style Bikaner Pavilion, with a view of the cricket field, the blank score-board, the college grounds and, in the distance, the sunlit brown hills of Ajmer. The guest of honour was the Canadian High Commissioner. Prominent among the visitors on the lower steps of the pavilion were some of the princes of Rajasthan: the Maharaja of Kotah, a couple from the house of Jodhpur, and the Maharana of Udaipur, whose ancestor had been the first to respond to an appeal of the Viceroy, Lord Mayo, for funds for a princely public school and had, a hundred years ago, almost to the day, given a lakh of rupees, then worth about £10,000.

In the open area at the foot of the pavilion were the parents, many of them box-wallahs, business executives, some from as far away as Calcutta. All week they had been gathering in Ajmer: India's modest middle class, products of the new industrial society, as yet with no common traditions or rooted strength, still only with the vulnerability of the middle classes of all very poor countries. In the poverty of India their ambition was great, but their expectations were small; they were really very easily pleased. India always threatened to overwhelm them – (those servants at the edge of the cricket field) – as the desert and the peasants and the new politics had overwhelmed Kishangarh and his ancient name.

But the Maharana of Udaipur hadn't come to Ajmer only for the prize-giving. He had been campaigning hard against Mrs Gandhi and her party in a princely freelance way, offering his services wherever they were needed; and he was in Ajmer to give Mr Mukut a hand. He had come in an open dark-green 1936 Rolls-Royce with a chauffeur, an Election Secretary and two bodyguards. He proved his worth almost at once. That very evening, while the Mayo College boys were doing *A Midsummer Night's Dream*, Udaipur addressed a meeting in the bazaar area. His name was like magic. Fifteen thousand people came to hear him.

The next day, Sunday, was the big day. Udaipur was going with Mr Mukut and Mr Sharda on a tour of those districts of the constituency that had belonged to the former Udaipur State. The little convoy started from the red-brick King Edward VII Guest House on Highway 8, not far from the mock-Mogul Queen Victoria Golden Jubilee clock-tower.

It was such an unlikely alliance. There was Mr Sharda, 'western' and businesslike in his suit, but with his pastoral Jan Sangh dream of an untouched Hindu world; he was in a jeep, packed at the back with bedding and other supplies. Mr Mukut, the Gandhian and old-time Congressman, but now formally dressed in tight white trousers and a long cream-coloured coat, was in a grey saloon. Udaipur was in his open Rolls, a man in his forties, of medium height and build, with a black beret, dark glasses and dark-blue nylon windcheater. The thirty-six-year-old

Election Secretary, very tall, with a paunch, a corrugated beard and glinting black locks, was all in loose white cotton and looked like a holy man. At the back of the Rolls the two khaki-uniformed, orange-turbanned bodyguards sat up high with their rifles: it was like a proclamation of the danger in which, in Rajasthan, princes now lived.

Udaipur was the star. That was accepted. And so briefly did Mr Mukut speak at Nasirabad, our first stop, that by the time my own jeep, after a wrong turning, had got to the meeting-place, he had finished and was sitting cross-legged on the improvised platform, eyes closed, good and quiet and patient at Udaipur's suede-shod feet, like a man accepting his own irrelevance. But Udaipur remembered him. 'People ask me, "But isn't Mr Mukut a blind man?" I say, "He is blind on the outside, not on the inside. When you go to a temple, mosque or church you close your eyes to pray. You can't see, but you aren't blind on the inside." '

Mr Mukut sat as still as a man meditating in a temple. But a packed day lay ahead. Suddenly – no speech from Mr Sharda – the meeting was over and the mood of meditation and repose vanished. So quickly did Udaipur and Mr Mukut scramble off the platform, so quickly did they bolt for their vehicles, that I lost them almost at once and didn't catch up with them again until Beawar, thirty miles away.

After Beawar it was desert; and it was desert after Bhim. No irrigated green patches, no trees, no peasants on bicycles; just rock and sometimes cactus, and the empty road. Sometimes a camel, sometimes a peasant in rags with patched leather sandals and a home-made gun: bandit country. But regularly in this wilderness little Rajput groups ran out into the road to stop the convoy and to look for the Maharana they had never seen (a Maharana of Udaipur had last been here in 1938). When Udaipur stood up in the Rolls drums beat and sometimes, unexpectedly, a trumpet sounded.

They garlanded him and dabbed his forehead with sandalwood paste; they sprinkled him with red or purple water (he had dressed for this). Ceremoniously, as though he were a god in a temple (and his dark glasses gave him a suitable inscrutability), they circled his face with fire (a blazing lump of camphor in a brass plate). Once a woman fed him some substance with her hand. Here Udaipur was more than a prince. Here he was *Hinduon ka suraj*, the Hindu Sun, an ancient title of Rajput chivalry that had merged into religion. At one stop a man cried out, 'You are our god!' And Udaipur was quick to reply, correctly, 'The God that is, is the same for you and me.'

Mr Mukut wasn't forgotten. When the Rolls moved on, the Rajputs surrounded the grey saloon. Mr Sharda always waved me on then in his impatient way and so I couldn't tell whether the men of the desert weren't exacting some tribute from Mr Mukut for their devotion to their Maharana.

Early in the afternoon we reached the walled town of Deogarh. There was pandemonium at the main gate; in the middle of the crowd a white horse with a white sheet on its back was waiting for Udaipur. The loudspeaker-man in our convoy became frenzied. 'Your Maharana has come. For 1,400 years you have known Maharanas. Now he has come, the Hindu Sun. You have longed for him as you have longed for clouds and rain. Now your Maharana has come.' But already, as in some spectacular film, the walled town was emptying; and men and women in bright turbans and saris were hurrying across the desert to the temple of Karni Devi, goddess of the town, where Udaipur was to speak.

Mr Sharda, who was, I thought, a little buttoned-up in the company of his two old political enemies, Mr Sharda whispered to me, 'Jan Sangh. All organized by Jan Sangh.'

And soon to his desert audience – bright turbans and smiling faces against a background of sand, the walled city and fort, the jagged hills faint in the haze – Udaipur was talking about Mrs Gandhi's threat to democracy and the constitution. Mr Mukut sat cross-legged on the canopied platform. The bodyguards were dusting down the Rolls in the shade of a thorn tree.

Udaipur had changed his beret for a Rajput turban. One man, so many roles. But Udaipur was a good speaker because he accepted all his roles – god, Rajput, democrat – and made them fit together. 'I am not a god. I am just a sort of representative. We are all worshippers of Lord Shiva, *Ek Ling Nath*.' He was not a politician; he wanted no man's vote. 'I am not a supporter of the Jan Sangh. I am a supporter of freedom.' The Rajputs applauded that. 'We have no policemen here and we need none. We are not like the Indira Congress. There is love between us, because we are one and the same.' They laughed at the political hit and applauded the definition of the basis of their Rajput loyalty.

Afterwards, leaving Mr Mukut to the electorate, we went to have lunch in the bare and run-down palace of Udaipur's vassal. Here the election was as if forgotten. The vassal and his infant son glittered in Rajput court costume. A red carpet lay across the dusty courtyard. Drums beat; a smiling doorkeeper took the swords of guests; in an inner room women sang. A bright-eyed old retainer came and recited ancient verses about the duties of kings. Other smiling people – everyone was smiling – came to make obeisance and offer token tributes of one rupee and five rupees.

'You see,' Udaipur said in English, his face still stained red and purple, 'how *unpopular* we are.'

The newspapers were being gloomy about Mrs Gandhi's chances, and the success of Udaipur's tour disheartened many people on Mr Bishweshwar's side. They had no comparable glamour figure. The visit of Mr Chavan, one of Mrs Gandhi's most able ministers, had been a failure;

Mrs Gandhi herself wasn't coming. All that Mr Bishweshwar's people could look forward to was the visit, on Tuesday, of Mr Bishweshwar's political patron, the Rajasthan Chief Minister. He was hardly glamorous. He was very much the local party boss, and he was coming less to make speeches than to settle certain internal party disputes which had begun to threaten Mr Bishweshwar's campaign.

The Ajmer Congress was famous for its faction fights. In 1954, when Mrs Bishweshwar's father was politically active, the administration had virtually stalled; and Mr Nehru had written a long and impatient 'note' about the local party: '... giving us continuous headaches ... The government cannot be considered to be an efficient government ... The Community Project Scheme in Ajmer was one of the least successful. In fact, for a long time practically nothing was done there.' That was the tradition. And after all its further years in power the local party was full of people who thought they had been badly treated and were taking advantage of the election to sulk. Mr Bishweshwar, aiming at independence, and trying to free himself of old intrigues by 'creating' new men of his own, had made matters worse. One aggrieved man said, 'Mr Bishweshwar is in the position of a man who has stopped believing in the loyalty of his honest wife and has begun to believe the protestations of loose girls.'

So now I heard that Mrs Gandhi hadn't come to Ajmer because she disapproved of Mr Bishweshwar, that she remembered how he had hesitated at the time of the party split, and that she was now letting him sweat it out. Other people, with memories of Mrs Bishweshwar's father, said that Mr Bishweshwar's heart wasn't in the election and that he had only been pushed into it by his wife. Everybody agreed that Mr Mukut's workers were more selfless and less mercenary and less given to sabotage. There was a lot of talk of sabotage. One man high in the party told me that of all Mr Bishweshwar's workers, paid and unpaid, 30 per cent were saboteurs.

And it was only then that I heard about the Rawats. The Rawats were originally a caste of animal-skinners. They had been advancing for some time into agriculture, the army and the police. In Jodhpur the Maharaja had decreed twenty-five years before that they were to be considered a Rajput caste. But in Ajmer the Rawats were still low, almost untouchable. They should therefore have been solidly behind the Indira Congress and Mr Bishweshwar. But there had been a crisis. Some weeks before a young Rawat wife in the Nasirabad area had been enticed away by a Rawat Christian convert. The community had been doubly dishonoured, by the adultery (in India an offence punishable with rigorous imprisonment), and by the fact that the enticer was a Christian. There had been complaints to the police, but nothing had been done; and some Rawats felt that Mr Bishweshwar and some of his Christian supporters had connived at the inactivity of the police. A leaflet had been distributed in Rawat areas: RAWATS, BROTHERS! THE INDIRA CONGRESS CANDIDATE BISHWESHWAR NATH BHARGAVA TRIFLES WITH THE HONOUR OF OUR WIVES AND DAUGHTERS. BEWARE OF HIM!

There were 50,000 Rawat voters. Kishangarh, Udaipur, Rajputs, Rawats, and sabotage: Mr Bishweshwar seemed to be in trouble all round that Monday. And this, very roughly, was the assessment of the Ajmer situation that appeared in the *Times of India*. A day or two later a large 'human-interest' photograph of Mr Mukut – a blind candidate – made the front page of the New Delhi *Hindustan Times*.

It was from Mr Kudal that I heard about the Rawats. Mr Kudal was a Congressman of fifty and he had a modest ambition: he wanted to be Mr Bishweshwar's Election Agent. The appointment was to be made on Tuesday, when the Chief Minister came; but when I saw Mr Kudal, late on Monday evening, he had heard nothing at all and was in a state of some nerves. He said, 'I very much fear that the intelligentsia is being cleverly weeded out all over India from political life.'

Mr Kudal was a lawyer. He lived in a lavatorial lane off Highway 8, in a large three-storeyed house built in the Rajasthani style with galleries around a central court-yard, and with an iron grille at the top to keep out in-truders. Narrow enclosed concrete steps took you up past his law offices and his servants' rooms to the flat roof and his pink-and-red sitting-room. Upholstered chairs were pushed against three walls and there was a glass case with figures made from shells, plastic models of Hindu deities, and other knick-knacks. It was a little like a waiting-room, with all the chairs, but Mr Kudal had many visitors. He kept in touch with the constituency; he had prepared himself for the job of Election Agent.

He was worried about the Rawats. He was less worried by Udaipur's tour. 'These public meetings are just *tamashas,* excitements. Nothing.' Elections were won with votes, and vote-getting required work. 'By work I mean the direct approach to the voters. Taking them out of the houses and sending them to the booths. I will tell you as a zealous worker that all will depend on the work we put in in the last two or three days.' And in that lay Mr Kudal's promise and his threat.

He said, 'I could swing the election in certain districts without leaving this room. It would take me a week. If I went out on the road it would take me two or three days.'

I asked him how.

'I am a man of the masses.' It was something he had worked at. He was a brahmin and a townsman and he said he had wasted a lot of time on bridge and chess before he had thought of service to the poor. He had gone out then 'among the lowest sections of the community – the Harijans and the serpent-charmers'. Not many people had done that; and it was well known in Ajmer that Mr Kudal had a lot of influence in certain low quarters. 'That is why people get worried when they hear that Kudal has joined the fray.'

So on this last evening Mr Kudal rehearsed his case, and his slightly desperate attitude was that, ready as he was to serve, he was also perfectly prepared to let Mr Bishweshwar stew in his own juice, that if the Chief Minister and Mr Bishweshwar wanted his services, if they cared at all about things like the snake-charmer vote, they would have to seek him out the next day. Mr Kudal himself intended to do absolutely nothing the next day. It was the festival of Shivratri; he was a devotee of Shiva; for him it was to be a day of temple, prayer and meditation.

Early in the morning, too early, Mr Bishweshwar came to the Circuit House to look for the Chief Minister. He looked even more harassed than I remembered. He was with a gang of rustics in dusty dhotis, brown waistcoats and Gandhi-caps. Pointlessly, like a swarm of midges, they bustled back and forth about the spacious lounge, following Mr Bishweshwar's nervous lead. When Mr Bishweshwar stood still, they all settled down on the carpet, the way the Circuit House servants did when they thought no one was about. After some fearful jabbering, four or five people speaking at once, the same things said again and again, they decided that the Chief Minister wasn't in the Circuit House and was probably somewhere else. And suddenly they all swarmed out again.

But the Chief Minister did come. And he must have had a hard day. He was still at the Circuit House at 7.30 that evening, when he should have been down in the city addressing a meeting at Kesarganj. It was just as well. Shivratri, the weekly service at the Hanuman temple, the Flower Show and the illuminations in Shah Jehan's lakeside gardens had drawn the holiday crowds; and there were only three or four hundred people – government officers, Muslims, people proving their loyalty – at Kesarganj. For an hour we were deafened by music, songs and election jingles. The crowd grew. And when at last the Chief Minister arrived, with all his party notables, I was glad to see that Mr Kudal had been called out of his retreat and was with them.

After a day spent on personality squabbles the Chief Minister now dealt only in principles. *Garibi Hatao*: nothing about Rajputs and Rawats; not a word against Mr Mukut; hardly anything about Mr Bishweshwar. Mr Bishweshwar didn't speak. Like the figure of the wife in some Egyptian sculpture, small at the feet of her lord, like Mr Mukut at the feet of Udaipur, Mr Bishweshwar sat still and modest at the feet of the Chief Minister. He leaned back on his arms; his paunch showed to advantage; and I thought I had never seen him so relaxed.

'He has every reason to look relaxed,' Mr Kudul said, as we drove to Nasirabad with some of his workers the following afternoon. 'Yesterday at 9.30 a.m., after he saw the Chief Minister he came and surrendered before me. He and his wife and his sister, his wife with tears in her eyes. I told him, "But you, Bishweshwar, must know that I was always helping you, because I believe in the principles of Mrs Gandhi, and not because of any affection I bear to you." ' So, indirectly, Mr Kudal announced that he was the Election Agent. Then he added, 'Now is the time for onslaught.'

But first we stopped at the new Shiva temple, and Mr Kudal, grateful devotee of Shiva, paid his respects to the lingam, which was set in the ground in the centre of a concrete lotus with a serrated rim. The yellow clothes of the images were damp with a sweet substance and black with sated, drugged flies.

'Here at Nasirabad,' Mr Kudal said, when we were on the road again, 'I will introduce you to Mr Mukut's and Mr Bishweshwar's staunchest supporters. They are both my closest friends and they will both offer you a cup of tea. Sometimes I contest these elections like sports.'

'Like a hobby,' a worker in the back of the jeep said.

And at Nasirabad the news was as bad as Mr Kudal could have wished. Mr Jain, the plump little jeweller ('High Class Military Novelties and Gold Ornaments') who was also the Treasurer of the Ajmer Rural District Congress Committee, seated us against bolsters on his porch, in the cosy little space – at once his office and his day-bed – between the showcase and the front wall, gave us tea and *cachoree*, and told us that the way things were going Mr Bishweshwar would be lucky to get thirty-five per cent of the town vote and fifty per cent of the village vote. 'They are neglecting the old workers. The new workers they've brought in drink and go to hotels and abuse the opposition and they think they're winning votes.'

The lawyer who was Mr Mukut's Nasirabad man – his office was just across the road – gave the same figures. 'Oh yes,' the lawyer said in his booming voice. 'Things are going right for Mr Mukut. Because of somebody. You can say it is because of me. And the Jan Sangh. And Mr Mukut – he's a great asset. And the poor personality of the opponent. All these things have combined.'

We left Nasirabad and drove off into the desert.

'Depressed?' Mr Kudal said. 'I'm a warrior who knows no defeat.'

A worker in the jeep said, 'Mr Kudal can turn the tables.'

'I'm a man of the masses,' Mr Kudal said. 'I will take you now to a village where very few people go. The Harijans there have built a Shiva temple and dedicated it to me. When I went to work among them they were an alcoholic community. I made them take the pledge. It wasn't easy. It took months.'

Sunset in the desert: neem trees and Australian dogwood black against the ochre sky. And then, on an eminence, a walled village, a high gateway, a dusty road, a temple, and a crowd around the jeep shouting, *'Indira Gandhi ki jai!* Long live Indira Gandhi!' It was as Mr Kudal had said: he was known here. Babies were shown to him, children re-introduced; boys read out the inscription on the temple gateway to show how well they could read now. And Mr Kudal, tall, bald, one of his legs shorter than the other, walked among the Harijans with his awkward gait, blinking fast behind his glasses. Without any Gandhian trappings, he was a dedicated man; and it was moving.

We went on in the dark to a village where Mr Kudal said he wanted to do 'some CID work'. I recognized the village as Saradhna. I had been there with Mr Bishweshwar and I remembered that he had been promised 'unanimous' support. But Mr Kudal doubted whether Mr Bishweshwar would get forty per cent of the vote. Saradhna was a village of Jats; a Jat political party had recently emerged, hostile to Mrs Gandhi; and the previous evening Mr Mukut and some of the leaders of the Jat party had held a meeting at Saradhna.

'CID, CID,' Mr Kudal said to his workers when we stopped. They went to the tea-stalls and we sat silent in the jeep. Our presence couldn't have been all that secret, though. Cups of tea were brought out to us. A villager came and whispered that only seventy-five per cent of the village was for Mr Bishweshwar. 'He is only giving me butter,' Mr Kudal said in Hindi. But another villager came and whispered that Mr Bishweshwar couldn't expect more than ninety per cent; and the workers, coming back from the tea-stalls, said eighty per cent.

So it seemed that the caste-appeal hadn't worked at Saradhna. And I began to wonder whether Mrs Gandhi hadn't simplified Mr Kudal's labours; whether she hadn't lifted this mid-term election high above the local politics Mr Kudal understood and enjoyed; whether in Ajmer the choice wasn't between Mrs Gandhi and the Jan Sangh in some areas, between Mrs Gandhi and Udaipur in other areas, and between Mrs Gandhi and poor old Mr Mukut everywhere else.

No drama on the road, then, for Mr Kudal. But when we got back to Ajmer we found that someone had been distributing leaflets accusing Mr Kudal of sabotage.

Mr Kudal had said that Friday was going to be a hard day. But by the time all our workers had come and we had ordered food from the bazaar it was half past eleven; and when we got to our first village it was time to eat. We sat in the rough little council-hall in the middle of a million furious flies. The workers ate off newspaper, Mr Kudal and myself off dry peepul-leaves; and the kulaks, the local vote-catchers, who had been waiting for us, waited on us. Their manner was penitential, and Mr Kudal hinted that he had come to rebuke them. They received their rebukes in private, after we had lunched.

The lunch had been heavy; the new famine road – part of the network built during the famine – was smooth. Mr Kudal fell asleep. We passed a village. Mr Kudal woke up and said he was sorry he had missed it, but he would send some of his workers there by bus that evening. We came to another village. A water-channel, freshly dug in the sand, barred our path; and Mr Kudal decided to leave that village as well to his night workers.

'Well,' he said later, 'you're seeing the Nasirabad district. You've heard the assessments of both sides. So when the results come out you will know it is entirely the result of this' – he waved at the road and the boundless desert – 'this movement. The result of this onslaught.'

At the next village – more a little town: a low-caste wedding procession in the dusty main street, a brass band in spectacularly tattered uniforms – we had cardamom tea in a cloth-seller's shop and Mr Kudal talked to the Muslim village headman. Nothing more was needed, Mr Kudal said; by evening everyone would know that Kudal was out campaigning for Indira and Mr Bishweshwar. 'They know

that after the election they will still have to come to me.'
The statement worried him, and some time later he said,
'I have helped these people. I have handled their cases for
them without fee.'

At the village after that we didn't leave the jeep. People
saw us arrive, but the only man who came to us was a
quarry-owner in a jacket and pullover. He said to Mr
Kudal in English, 'The people need *guidance*.'

'He is not for us,' Mr Kudal said afterwards. 'He em-
ploys a lot of labour and he is going to spoil thirty per
cent of the vote. But I don't argue with people three days
before an election.'

Public meetings were to end in Ajmer at five on Saturday afternoon. But canvassing and private meetings could
continue; and I heard from Mr Mukut's son, who was also
Mr Mukut's election agent, that Mr Mukut and Mr Bishweshwar were to debate that evening before the Rotary
Club of Beawar. A Rotary Club seemed an unlikely thing
for a place like Beawar to have. But Beawar also had a
Communist group. And it also, as I now learned, had
one of India's most famous astrologers, Professor B. C.
Mehta. Professor Mehta was a 'commercial' astrologer:
he specialized in market fluctuations. His cable address
was MEHTA.

I heard all this from Professor Mehta's thirty-year-old
lawyer son while we were waiting that afternoon for Mr
Mukut at his campaign headquarters. Professor Mehta,
being only a commercial astrologer, hadn't issued any
statement about the Ajmer election. But young Mr Mehta
was so confident of Mr Mukut's victory and was so
obviously welcome at campaign headquarters – 'His
father's an astrologer,' Mr Mukut's son said, introducing
him – I felt there could have been no astrological discour-
agement. And Mr Mukut, when he appeared in spotless
white dhoti and koortah, with a black woollen waistcoat, was like a man touched with glory. The gentleness

which he imposed on all who approached him now also held a little awe.

It was a long drive to Beawar. We got there at nightfall and found that nobody knew anything about a Rotary Club debate. Somebody said that Mr Bishweshwar had got cold feet; but sabotage was sabotage, and all we could do was sit in the front room of the local hotel and drink coffee. I asked about Professor Mehta. The young hotel-owner said the Professor was not only his adviser but also a personal friend. He went out to telephone and came back with the news that the Professor was coming over as soon as he had finished his supper.

'From the beginning I've had faith in astrology,' Mr Mukut said. 'Every year I have a reading on my birthday. On the 30th of January I entered my sixty-ninth year and I had a reading then.'

He wouldn't say what he had been promised. And when I asked whether Professor Mehta was his astrologer he gave his crooked long-lipped smile and didn't reply.

He became reflective. 'An election has three stages. There's the excitement of the campaign. Then there's the tension. Then the reaction, whatever the result.'

'What are you prepared for?'

He opened his sightless eyes. '*Anything.*'

But then he was restless; he wanted to leave; and he was led out to his car.

Professor Mehta was a small fat clean-shaven man of sixty in trousers and shirt. He had the distant manner of an overworked physician who has heard everything. He was unwilling to speak. As soon as he understood what I wanted he began to write, very fast, on a foolscap sheet: *Mrs Indira will win her own election by more than 50,000 votes. But she won't be able to get full majority in Centre ...*

I feel that after the busyness of the headquarters, and after the excitement of the drive, the mood of Mr Mukut's men changed there, in the stuffy little room of the Beawar hotel, when Mr Mukut's face clouded at the thought of the sabotaged evening.

On Sunday morning some of his supporters had premonitions of defeat. They came to me, as to an impartial witness, with stories that Mr Bishweshwar's men were distributing liquor in two wards of the city, and with the warning that the next day there would be leaflets, purporting to come from Mr Mukut, saying that he had withdrawn, that he had all along been for Mrs Gandhi.

Premonitions of defeat. And in the morning the disaster was clear. Outside every polling booth on the road to Nasirabad there was a decorated Indira Congress tent, where young men sat with electoral rolls and waited to receive voters. At half past ten, the sun already blazing, some of Mr Mukut's tents were only just going up; and in some places there were no tents and sometimes not even tables. Mr Mukut's son, defeat on his face, spoke of sabotage. Outside one booth two of Mr Mukut's workers stood forlorn, separate from the crowd; one of them shrugged and said, 'Harijan area.'

In Nasirabad one young man was close to tears. The Congress had ruled in Rajasthan for as long as he could remember; it was rotten and corrupt and had at last seemed about to wither away; now Mrs Gandhi had preserved it. 'You've won, you've won,' he said to Mr Kudal; and Mr Kudal, sympathetic to the young man's pain, blinked fast.

The Congress had not withered away. Its organization had remained intact and was behind Mrs Gandhi and Mr Bishweshwar. The Congress hadn't really split. There had only been defections, sufficient to provide acclamation and crowds (deceptive in a constituency with half a million voters) and what Mr Kudal had called *tamashas*, excitements. In Ajmer the Opposition or Organization Congress, on whose behalf Mr Mukut was standing, was a phantom party.

But Mr Mukut also had the Jan Sangh. The Jan Sangh was strong in Ajmer City, and a bonus was that the poll there was usually high, 70 per cent as against 50 per cent in the rural areas. With a good majority in Ajmer City – dependent on a good poll – Mr Mukut might still be in the fight. But it was in the Jan Sangh areas of the city that Mr Mukut's disaster was most plain. In Naya Bazaar, the area of small traders, a Jan Sangh stronghold, the poll at one o'clock was under 40 per cent; and Mr Mukut's election tent, without a table (and the formality that imposes), only with a long bench, was overrun by small children and already looked abandoned.

The Jan Sangh voters were abstaining. It was the possibility Mr Mukut had always discounted. By allying itself with other parties, by supporting Mr Mukut, its old enemy, by softening its racial–communal Hindu line, the Jan Sangh had compromised its right-wing purity. It had ceased to be a crusade; in the eyes of its supporters it had become as 'political' and tricky as any other party. And later that afternoon, when the news everywhere was that Mr Mukut was losing, some of those Jan Sangh abstainers were to go out and vote against him.

At half past four, half an hour before the booths closed, there were three people in Mr Mukut's campaign headquarters: a wizened old secretary at a table with a telephone that was now idle, a thin black-capped accountant in a dhoti who sat with his legs drawn up on a straight-backed chair, and a boy. Someone came in with a bill. The black-capped accountant, without changing his posture, considered the bill and spiked it. I stretched out an inquisitive hand towards the spike. Wordlessly, the accountant spun the spike away from me to the boy, who put it in a corner of the paper-littered floor.

Mr Bishweshwar, surrounded by his workers, sat in a basket-chair on the open concrete porch of his villa headquarters. He was in a state of great, laughing excitement and he was shouting into a telephone. Most of his workers were in trousers, shirts and pullovers. But Mr Bishwesh-war was in his politician's costume of homespun dhoti and koortah, the white panoply that spoke of Gandhian merit and, now, of its political rewards, all the things that went with being a member of parliament: the flat in New Delhi, the two free telephones, 51 rupees a day dur-ing parliamentary sittings, free first-class rail travel throughout India (with priority in reservations), and 500 rupees a month.

It was some time before I saw that Mrs Bishweshwar was also there, still and withdrawn, standing on the open porch as on a stage, draped in a dark-green sari, her head bowed and modestly covered in the presence of so many men: like a sorrowing classical figure, a symbol of down-trodden Indian womanhood.

Ten days later, after the remoter districts had voted, the count took place. The weather had turned, the heat was beginning; and on Highway 8 there were handcarts with little conical heaps of green and red powder for the gaieties of the Festival of Spring on the following day. The counting was done in a marquee in the Collectorate yard. Neither Mr Bishweshwar nor Mr Mukut was there. 'The commander-in-chief doesn't have to be at the front,' a counter said.

And Mr Mukut was spending this, the longest day of his political career, in his flat. It was going to be worse for him than we had expected. In Ajmer City – the counting was done district by district – he had only got 19,000 votes; Mr Bishweshwar had 43,000.

I said to Mr Mukut's son, 'So Professor Mehta advised you wrongly?'

'He didn't *advise* us wrongly. His calculations were wrong.'

Mr Bishweshwar was at his campaign headquarters. He was used now to his victory; he was at peace, but tired. The election had been a strain; he didn't share Mr Kudal's delight in the 'sports' side. He had suffered at that moment when important people had seemed about to defect. He had been badly frightened by the Rawats, and he hadn't forgiven that damaging leaflet. 'I'm going to sue. Let them apologize and so on. There's a lakh or two there.'

But he had suffered mostly because of Mr Mukut, in whose shadow he had lived for so long. I asked whether he thought they might now have broken for good. He said, 'I don't know. I went to see him yesterday. He didn't talk to me.' And Mr Bishweshwar was anxious to show that he too, though young, had a record of service and sacrifice. He hadn't been to jail, like Mr Mukut; but because of his social work he hadn't found time to marry until he was thirty-two. 'From the beginning I was interested in social service. I was scoutmaster in Government College. I don't know why, the poorer sections always attracted me. Since 1952 I have devoted myself to the peasantry.'

He made it sound like a hobby. He had modelled himself on his uncle; he too was half Gandhian, half politician, and claimed the right to exercise political power because he had earned religious merit. And Mr Bishweshwar might so easily have been on the other side, against Mrs Gandhi. 'It was a testing time for me,' he said, speaking of the Congress split, 'the choice between principle and personality.' In the end he had managed to combine both: Gandhian principle and Mrs Gandhi's personality.

All afternoon his lead lengthened. At last it reached 66,000. Mr Mukut, in the days of his glory, had never had such a majority. The caste issues had nowhere mattered. The Kishangarh affair hadn't mattered; nor had the Rawat enticement. Only Udaipur's tour had had some effect. In that remote district, where he was a god, Udaipur had cut Mr Bishweshwar's lead to just over 3,000. The electorate had everywhere voted for Mrs Gandhi and *Garibi Hatao*; they had voted out of their common distress and need.

At about half past three Mr Bishweshwar and his wife

came to the Collectorate. They were both in homespun, he in white, she in blue. He was smiling quite helplessly; she was abashed and delicate. As they walked up the middle of the marquee all of us at the District Magistrate's table rose. Someone ran up with a garland of gold and silver tinsel: it was for Mr Kudal, the triumphant election agent. The second garland, of marigold and white champa flowers, was for Mr Bishweshwar.

Outside, the crowd grew. And when, just before the results were announced, Mr and Mrs Bishweshwar left, going out the way they had come, the counters, who hadn't saluted their arrival, stood up with palms joined in the gesture of greeting and respect. The brass band, waiting outside, struck up *Colonel Bogey*. There was a float with the cow and calf in white. Men in a packed jeep scattered coloured powder on the crowd: the Festival of Spring, occurring one day early. And copies were being distributed of a one-sheet 'extra' of the Hindi *Rajasthan Patrika*:

BISHWESHWAR GETS HUGE MAJORITY
Nephew Crushes Uncle

I thought I would go to Mr Mukut.

'I will come with you,' Mr Kudal said. And when we were in the car he said, 'I must come with you. Terrible. A man who has controlled the destinies of this district for two decades, to be defeated now by his nephew, his own creature.'

In the top floor flat the unlined curtains were drawn in the front room and Mr Mukut sat cross-legged and still on his narrow bed. His eyes were closed and his head was held to one side. He was in clean white cotton, and the white was momentarily shocking, like the colour of death and grief. Half a dozen men, among them the black-capped accountant, were sitting silent on a spread on the terrazzo floor. Mr Kudal didn't speak; he went and sat on the floor with the others.

Mr Mukut's son came out and offered me a chair. He bent over his father, said, 'Bapuji,' and gave Mr Kudal's name and mine. At first Mr Mukut didn't move. Then, abruptly, he turned his head to face the room and, in a terrible gesture of grief, beat the back of his open hand hard on the bed.

No one spoke.

Mr Mukut's son brought out tea. He pulled the curtain open a little way: the barred, wire-netted window, the sunlight on the white wall of the terrace, the brown hills. He hung a brown waistcoat on his father's shoulders and the effect of the white was softened.

'They were canvassing votes for Indira,' Mr Mukut said, 'not for the candidate. Nowhere was the candidate in the picture.' He hadn't yet accepted his defeat; he still dealt in the politics of personal merit. I asked whether he and Mr Bishweshwar might be friends again. He said, 'I don't know. He came here yesterday. But he didn't say a word to me.' He turned on the transistor and the six o'clock English news from Delhi was of Mrs Gandhi's landslide victory all over the country, of the defeat everywhere of old Congressmen who had miscalculated like Mr Mukut.

'There are no morals now,' Mr Mukut said. 'The Machiavellian politics of Europe have begun to touch our own politics and we will go down.'

Mr Kudal stood up.

'As election agent I have to make an appearance in the procession,' Mr Kudal said, when we were outside. 'Otherwise my absence will be misinterpreted.'

We caught up with the procession in the bazaar. Men in open lorries were pelting everybody with little balls of coloured powder. 'Give me seven minutes,' Mr Kudal said, and disappeared into the crowd. When he came back his clothes and hair and face were satisfactorily stained with red. Red the colour of spring and triumph, and sacrifice.

3
Looking Westward

Mr Matsuda's Million-Dollar Gamble

Daily Telegraph Magazine, 14 July 1967

In June 1966 Mr Morihiro Matsuda, in his own words 'a petty citizen of Japan, uneducated and anonymous', made history of a sort when he took four pages of The Times *and* New York Times *for a 'personal message' to the world. Mr Matsuda said – among many other things – that he had a plan for bringing about peace in Vietnam in a day or, at the outside, three days. He would not reveal his plan until he had 'unrestricted power of attorney, on a blank sheet of paper' from the President, Secretary of State and Defence Secretary of the United States and from the Prime Ministers of Japan and Great Britain. 'Please give me, Morihiro Matsuda, any and every authority to conduct world politics for just one day.' It was expensive to advertise, Mr Matsuda said; it would take him ten years to save up again the £10,000 he had spent; but it was his duty to express his thoughts. He wanted no one's charity or 'goodwill money'. 'The important thing is, it is a mistake to send £1 or £5 to Matsuda and expect him to do all the work to realize world peace ... Peace must be earned by courage and effort of everyone's conscience.' Four months later Mr Matsuda advertised again.*

His two four-page advertisements in *The Times* and *New York Times* last year – *Idea for Peace in Vietnam* – were not Mr Morihiro Matsuda's first extended writings. In 1963 he published, also at his own expense, but only in Tokyo, his *Bible of Wisdom*. This book, about 60,000 words, is what its title says. It is an attempt at a personal scripture, the work of a sage or aspirant-sage who is as yet without disciples or an amanuensis. Many of the ideas in *Bible of Wisdom* were restated in the advertisement. These ideas – about happiness, neutrality, the MM (Morihiro Matsuda) method of fasting, the merit of meditation in one's coffin, the construction of a profit-making Paradise – crowded out the Vietnam issue, and suggested that Mr Matsuda was aiming at more than the cessation of a single war.

The English version of the MM *Bible* is typewritten and offset and looks like the annual report of a small company. On the back of the title page, below the copyright notice, there are comments from 'men of distinction': 'the keenest pleasure', 'nonsense', 'clamour', 'Bible of Bible', 'threshold for culture'. All these comments were composed by Mr Matsuda himself. *Bible* was offered to the public, in Japan and abroad, with the assurance that 'if this book zooms into best-sellerdom I should like to use all the profits for the establishment of the Paradise'. The Paradise is to be a mixture of holiday camp, monastery and factory. Mr Matsuda estimated its construction costs at £10,700,000. The selling price of *Bible* was seven shillings. In four years not a copy has sold anywhere.

Mr Matsuda feels he has done better with the advertisements. Most Japanese periodicals have written about him – he had the file out to show. Some have been hostile, but Mr Matsuda doesn't mind. He expected greater sympathy abroad, and he feels he has got it. *Epoca* magazine in Italy gave him five pages – Mr Matsuda's copy was worn from his brisk, flat-handed turning of the pages. *Life* gave him only two pages; but they called him a saviour.

And the letters. Mr Matsuda jumps up, making the small room smaller, and slides back a frail wall panel. He is a body-built five foot nine – he was in the body-building business until recently – and his gestures are as abrupt and large as his voice is deep. He takes out bundles of letters from a cupboard and dumps them all together over the magazines on the low table. Six hundred letters, each still in its envelope, each envelope neatly guillotined: another detail that reminds us of a fact which is obvious but not easy to grasp: that in spite of the setting, the low ceiling, the mats, the low table, the fragile partitions, all the daintiness of the Japanese house of school geography books, Mr Matsuda comes from an industrial city and is a businessman, a natural user of office equipment.

He looks on the letters as trophies. The number pleases him, but he hasn't read them all. It was news to him that one encouraging letter, on Claridge's paper, was from a Russian princess. He gave two deep grunts of pleasure when he heard, and held his head on one side. Then he recovered and said that the nobility couldn't really understand his ideas.

He has received little money. Just after the first advertisement American readers of the *New York Times* sent him 250 dollars. But there was a report in a Japanese weekly that Mr Matsuda was hoping to get a dollar from each reader of the *New York Times*; and Mr Matsuda refused the 250 dollars. He said he wasn't a beggar. Since then he has been sent only 300 dollars. He has kept this money, and intends now to keep whatever he gets. It won't be much. Over the months the letters have grown fewer; now he gets no more than one or two a week. But two Chicago newspapers have invited him to the United States. This was the call Mr Matsuda was waiting for. Once he is in America and suitably sponsored, he thinks he will make a million dollars.

Mr Matsuda is a businessman. He wouldn't say he has gambled; he would say he has invested. The advertisements cost £23,000. To find the money, he has had to sell his house and his block of fifteen flats. To give himself time for his movement, he has made over his mail-order body-building business to his former employees. They loan him £100 a month; this keeps him going for the time being. He lives now in a £25-a-month rented house in a muddy new road almost at the eastern limit of Tokyo. The houses here, in varying shades of blue, are diminutive and choked together; they have tile roofs and walls of finely corrugated tin; even the blossom gives no grace.

Mr Matsuda has no regrets. As a sage, his subject is happiness; as a businessman, he knows he has done the right thing. His routine has not greatly changed. His fishing tackle lies in the outer, mat-less room of his house, in a clutter of toys, cardboard boxes and body-building catalogues. This fishing is an aspect of his routine he has publicized; in his advertisement he even dramatized himself as someone with 'the brand of the simple fisherman'. In fact, he took up the hobby when his *Bible* failed; and in spite of difficulties – more and more barbed-wire fences – he continues to fish for four or five hours every morning on the Edo river. He has also maintained his sexual activity. Sexual vigour is one of the bonuses of his fasting; he says he enjoys sex 'just in the way that children play'.

To ask whether he thinks he has behaved fairly towards his two children or – sexual activity apart – towards his wife, his seventh, who reportedly disapproves, is to raise an irrelevant moral question. Mr Matsuda says he hasn't done a good thing or a bad thing. He has simply invested; and his sacrifice, or the fact of his sacrifice, now as widely reported as he expected, is part of that investment.

Mr Matsuda needs money. Without money he will not be able to do anything. He certainly won't be able to stop the Vietnam war. It comes from his theory of neutrality: once every man's interests are recognized, disputes vanish. It must be recognized, for instance, that the Vietnam war is kept going by American industrialists. But it must also be recognized that these industrialists have a point. Their fear of a recession if the war ends must be taken seriously. This fear must be allayed. Mr Matsuda thinks he can do it. He will protect Wall Street; he will develop America.

That, no less, is his present aim. But first he must make a million dollars.

This is how he will do it. He will go to Chicago, to deal with the newspapers that have invited him. Then he will give lectures to the university about happiness and the seven degrees of beauty. He might also make a model of his indestructible motor car – no more deaths in road accidents – and sell the development rights. From Chicago he will go to New York. He will rent a room in the Time–Life building. Then he will go to the Patent Office and register his ten patents. He has a genius-creator or logic-trainer from which he expects much; he also thinks he will do well with a *go*-game, a type of Chinese chess. His rights established, he will return to the Time–Life building, take the lift to his room, and settle down to work. He might begin with a fast. The normal MM fast lasts for thirty days. In New York he will give them one of thirty-five days. The fast will startle America; it will be taken up by newspapers and his name will be known.

Then he will launch his necklace scheme. He will have necklaces manufactured in quantity and he will get the banks to distribute them. The necklaces will be sold for 10, 50, 100, 1,000 dollars. If the Vietnam war ends through his efforts in one hundred days, these necklaces can be returned and the buyers will get three times what they paid. So he will get America to invest in peace. If the war doesn't end – well, people will have their necklaces. Mr Matsuda calculates that he will make a million dollars from the sales of the MM necklace. All this money he will use for the cause, to advertise, to develop, to reassure Wall Street.

Mr Matsuda is not taken seriously in Tokyo. He is uneducated, a self-confessed black marketeer of the late 1940s, and he is Korean. In Japan the Koreans are immigrants, and immigrant stories attach to them. Their appearance is different, their faces being flatter and less accented than the Japanese; their food is different; they have a reputation for boisterousness and violence; and it is said that a Korean can be recognized by his smell alone. This – being a Korean – is not the only category Mr Matsuda falls into. In Japan, a land still of order, where class, character and mood are printed on the face for all to read, Mr Matsuda can also be recognized as the uneducated businessman. The main characteristic of this type is that it is made illogical by easy success. The grasp of cause and effect is weakened, and is replaced by a belief in good fortune and the rightness of decisions made under its influence. 'It is essential,' *Bible* says, 'to start or invest in business when one's own fortune is strong . . . See the waves on the sea. There are no similar waves because energies come from various directions.' The successful businessman, energized, lifted above his fellows, can even say: 'Show me the map of the country now and I will tell you where to drill for oil and where to dig for gold.' His confidence is total and business becomes confused with the religious impulse in a breathless exaltation. The businessman on whose shoulder the god of good fortune sits can cry with Mr Matsuda: 'I am my own lord and master throughout heaven and earth.'

Mr Matsuda's face can be read as honest, open, generous. Although in *Bible* he says that it is part of the highest wisdom, he is not such a master of the 'reverse meaning' of words as he thinks. In both his advertisements he threatened to burn himself. But he wasn't serious; he wanted only to make a sensation. In the second advertisement he said he had been offered a job as a writer at 500 dollars a month. But that was only to appease the *New York Times* who, in their concern for Mr Matsuda, might otherwise have turned down his advertisement. In both cases the deceit is transparent. Mr Matsuda is no writer. And death – especially if accidental, and if imposed by man on man – is the one thing he hates and fears.

He wants to conquer death. He wants to live one hundred years. He wants to leave some memorial of his passage. Through all the reverse meanings of words and all the confused thinking, this is the impulse that can be discerned. This is what he has compounded with his business instincts and raised to religion. 'I think I will die a painful and fearful death. I wonder why I alone must be tormented with such thoughts . . . To me my death is the most sorrowful thing in this universe.'

Now the fear is in the background. America and a million before him: a spectacular and much-ridiculed investment prospering: the god sits with Mr Matsuda. And he has conquered death. Every year for the last ten years he has done a thirty-day fast. It is his custom then and at other times as well to meditate in his coffin. It is a plain coffin of expensive Japanese cedar; ten years ago it cost £80. It is not equipped with the winking lights Mr Matsuda would like, to remind him of the pyre. But his imagination supplies that. So he keeps in touch with his fear and his private victory, which is also his luck.

It is with a vision of this victory that *Bible* begins. The detail is cinematic; the chapter is unlike anything else that Mr Matsuda has written.

The narrator – unidentified, but he is Mr Matsuda – finds himself in a group of a hundred students of the Juvenile Classification Office at Ueno railway station, the terminus in Tokyo of trains from the north. The students board a train and after an agreeable lunch get off at a country station. An hour's drive in a waiting bus takes them to a building marked 'Goseiin Headquarters'. In the information office there are five cameras behind the counter; in front of the counter, facing each camera, there is a chair. Each student pays, sits, and is photographed. Each student is then given a gown of white silk and shown a casket. The caskets are more than six feet long but weigh less than five pounds; they are made of corrugated cardboard and printed paper scented with Japanese cypress. Each student shoulders his casket and the white procession begins to climb the hill to the temple. From time to time the students put down their caskets and refresh themselves with orange juice. It is dusk when they get to the temple. They are perspiring and hungry; they place their caskets in a designated place and in that very place, seated on cushions, they are fed. Then they take off their white robes. In the valley below lights flicker. Like the evening lights of childhood, the narrator thinks: the lights of lonely farmhouses, fireflies, lights bringing to mind tales of ghosts. But these are the lights of industrial Japan, of automobiles and motor-cycles in the rush-hour.

The temple bell sounds four times. The students from the Juvenile Classification Office hurry to the stage in the main temple. Below a chandelier sits a man they know well. He is Mr O, a millionaire and a powerful politician. He wears a white gown and is flanked by lighted candles; before him, on a low table, two black-framed photographs of himself are set face to face. Incense burns before the photographs, and there is a dish of sacrificial rice.

'Please put on your white gowns again,' Mr O says. 'And get into your caskets.'

Waiting, Mr O studies his photographs.

The narrator gets into his casket and once more smells the cypress-scented paper. The electric lights of the temple go out. Only the candles on either side of Mr O continue to burn.

'These caskets await all of you,' Mr O says. 'Even if you live for fifty years more. Deduct one third as sleeping time and another third as working time. That leaves you only six thousand full days. You cannot then say that you have girl friends or children or parents. The casket will be waiting. You cannot then say that you were not loved by your parents or that they were poor and other people were more fortunate or that your life was spoiled by treachery. There is only calcium in the urn. There is no such article as affection. You say you were born. I say a puppy was also born; the cause is the same. Do not think that your parents are divine. Learn the attitudes of the West. They are right to think of you Japanese as senti-mental twelve-year-olds. Learn non-attachment. The youth of the West do not seek assistance from their parents. Learn independence. See the nobility of work rather than its burden. Get off the merry-go-round of avarice. Now please get out and burn your caskets and white gowns.'

The lights go on. The air is frosty. The caskets and gowns are set ablaze, and the temple bell sounds ten times. The blaze dies down. Dying, it is reflected in the little mirrors hung on the surrounding trees. The narrator thinks he has never experienced anything more sublime; and he sees how foolish he has been to ignore death out of his fear of it.

'Please polish with the ashes the thing you were hold-ing.'

The narrator picks up the brass casket-knobs from the warm ashes and polishes them until they glitter.

'That part of you which was idle and pointless has been burnt away,' Mr O says. 'That part of you that knows death, and is meaningful, survives.'

When the narrator goes back to the main temple he finds his own photograph, also in a black frame, on the same table as the photographs of Mr O – the millionaire, the politician.

The framework of the vision is perhaps derived – a Japanese photographer who read a draft of this article was certain that it was – but Mr Matsuda denies any in-spiration and even denies that he is dealing in fantasy. The vision came to him, complete, one day in 1957 when he was meditating in his coffin during a fast. It passed through his mind; it existed. It is personal. So it no doubt is. The meditation on death is a Japanese commonplace; but Mr Matsuda's conclusions were needed by him alone. If death is the final futility, it also mocks affections and ren-ders painful relationships painless. It ridicules complaint and excuse. Death lifts a man out of himself and his affections. If death is the equal end of all, then it touches human achievement with true grandeur. The true futility, the puppy-existence, is the life of the man who at the end can only say that he has raised a family. Death makes achievement urgent. Death, so far from darkening the future, enhances it. It is the past that death abolishes.

The name Morihiro Matsuda, the repeating initials of which Mr Matsuda has turned into a flourish, is Japanese. Mr Matsuda took it when the Japanese Government, as an integration measure, required Koreans in Japan to take Japanese names. Mr Matsuda's original name was Sun Tokwan. He was born forty-five years ago in a riverside village some 200 miles north of Pyongyang. His father worked as a labourer for a timber company and earned about 65 sen a day (100 sen make a yen and a yen was then worth about 2s). There were four children, and the whole family lived in a hut less than ten feet square. They ate pickled meat and pickled fish every day at every meal, with the cheapest sort of Tibetan wheat as an occasional extra.

Mr Matsuda was not strong as a child and wasn't sent out to work like his brothers. He went to the church school. He liked the church better than the school. The boys teased and beat him. He didn't fight back; he had no friends or protectors; and when he got home there was no one to console him. His mother was out most of the day, looking for food for the pigs she kept; she managed to sell three or four a year. There were fights at home, too, when Mr Matsuda's father came home drunk. But his father never beat him; his father always handled him gently. It might have been because he was weak or because he looked exactly like his father. More frightening than school or drunken father was the picture of hell-fire in the house of the Roman Catholic priest next door.

Mr Matsuda's interest in Roman Catholicism faded as he grew older. He read a fair amount; he especially liked

Resurrection by Tolstoy and Gide's *La Porte Etroite*. When he was twenty he thought he would go to Japan and try to get into a college. One brother, who was now running his own iron foundry, gave him 100 yen for the journey; his other brother, who had already emigrated, met him at Tokyo Central Station. Mr Matsuda failed two entrance examinations. He was an uncompromising candidate. He thought of himself as a 'unique existence' and didn't see why he should learn foreign languages. He laid aside the black student's uniform, the only clothes he had brought from Korea, and became a labourer.

He remained a labourer all through the war. But later, in occupied Japan, there were opportunities for a Korean citizen. An acquaintance urged him to go into black-marketing. It turned out to be simple. His first deal was in sugar. He took a taxi to the barracks of the 7th Cavalry Division and loaded up with 500 yen's worth. Within hours he had sold the sugar for 900 yen. After six months of trading he had made 100,000 yen, at a time when a house could be built for 1,000 yen.

'Adequate food and clothing make people learn graces' – the observation is in Mr Matsuda's first advertisement – and now he gave himself a holiday. He went to an inn in the Chiba Prefecture, which adjoins Tokyo, and idled in luxury for a year. When the money was exhausted he began dealing in soap and rubber on the black market in Hokkaido. He used the profits to start a *sushi* (raw fish) shop in Asakusa in downtown Tokyo. He employed a woman in the shop. She was ten years older than he. She became his first woman, and they lived together for three years. Then he began to manufacture pin-ball machines. He lost his money, the *sushi* shop and the woman.

But it didn't matter now. From now on money was easy to the Korean labourer's son, himself a labourer; and women were easy, to the man with the 'foolish Korean face' who had had his first sexual experience at twenty-three in a brothel. The miracle had occurred: good fortune had come to Mr Matsuda, proof of what he had known for some time: that he was a 'unique existence'.

He had used the words in his first advertisement, and they interested me. They held less and more than simple arrogance; they were a description of the man of destiny, the man who felt himself marked. I wanted Mr Matsuda to go back to his first apprehension of this fact about himself, back to his childhood, the boy in straw shoes in the Korean winter when the river froze over.

I had spoken too quickly. I was misinterpreted.

'Yes,' Mr Matsuda said. 'I was born without the sense of smell. And I was born with one breast missing.'

The interpreter broke off. Mr Matsuda continued to talk. He put his hand on his gabardine windcheater, over his breast, and made a gesture; his face was twisted with remembered pain. But now I had misinterpreted. He was still answering a question about his childhood. But he had gone beyond his defects; the look of pain was for his first experience of beauty, when he was five. His mother wanted him to wear a kimono with buttons – it was the modern style. He had rejected the buttons; he had insisted on ribbons.

Thirty years passed before he had a second experience of beauty. Then he was experimenting with fasts and the coffin, defeating death; and it was during a fast that his eyes had been caught by a Japanese sign. His breast ached at the beauty of that sign and in his delirium he found himself playing with the size of the characters, now making them tiny, now making them enormous. Out of this experience arose his theory of beauty, which is in *Bible*. The beautiful is the manageable; to be beautiful, terror has first to be tamed.

We had been talking for almost four hours. The interpreter and the stenographer were tired; I was tired. Mr Matsuda was still fresh. His wife brought in glasses of Coca-Cola. Mr Matsuda ignored her and she looked at

no one. I tried to read her face, especially for that dis-
approval about which I had heard. But her face told me
nothing; and Japanese to whom I later showed her photograph said it was a Korean baby-face, characterless.

Presently, putting on our shoes in the outer room, we
went outside ourselves. It was still raining. In the muddy
road there were groups of heavy-thighed schoolboys coming back from school: black peaked caps, black Prussian
uniforms, thick-soled white canvas shoes. Mr Matsuda led
us over boards laid on the mud in his yard to the unpainted corrugated-iron shed just at the back of his house.
We went past the kitchen; in the open doorway an
aproned woman stared expressionlessly at us.

'The wife?' someone in our party asked in a whisper.

'No. She was wearing a green dress, if you remember.'

The coffin was in the shed, with much household junk.
It was unvarnished; it stood on its end on a stack of
scantlings. It had stain marks and looked old; at the top
of the lid there were two roughly-made panels that swung
out on hinges. Mr Matsuda lifted the lid away and was
anxious to get in, to give us a photograph.

Later he drove us back to central Tokyo in his Japanese
estate car. It was a new car – a replacement for a Buick, as
I understood: part of the advertisement sacrifice – but
it had been casually handled. The seats were grubby and
there was litter on the carpets. As he drove he spoke, and
now he didn't even wait for the interpreter. Leaning back
in the driving seat, he spoke without pause; his harsh
voice rose and rose. He was speaking of his American trip
again, outlining all his plans and hopes. Traffic was heavy.
Beyond our closed windows, fog, fumes and rain: eastern
Tokyo a worse-than-Midland townscape, in tin.

Mr Matsuda wanted our second meeting to be at the
Tokyo Press Club. He knew it well; he had spoken there
twice. But I also knew that he was on the look-out for a
press agent for his American trip, and I said it would be

better if we met at my hotel. He said he would bring his wife to drive him back home. He might want to do some drinking, and in Japan the police are fierce about people who drink and drive. In *Bible* Mr Matsuda describes himself as a drunkard; sage-like, he makes a fuss about what he considers his unlikely addiction. In the end his wife didn't come; but he had a beer. He brought the copies of *Epoca* and *Life* with him, and the letter he was sending off to the princess in Claridge's.

I wanted to hear about the necklace scheme again. I didn't think I had got it right. But I had. I said I thought he would sell more necklaces if he promised to pay up if he *didn't* stop the war. He didn't agree. Americans had contributed millions for the cause of peace; and if *Life* and *Time* and the *Reader's Digest* publicized his mission, he was sure he would do well. The necklace scheme, besides, wasn't his idea. It was *Life*'s. They wanted to sell necklaces and they had asked him to help. But he didn't want to be employed by *Life*. He just wanted to sell the M M necklace; he thought *Life* would cooperate. I said it was more likely that there would soon be two new necklaces on the American necklace market. He laughed, and added independently, in English, shaking his head over his beer, 'America many, many money.'

'What will you do if you fail, Mr Matsuda?'

It was a foolish question.

'I can't fail.'

So far, in the unfamiliar hotel, he had been subdued. But the beer reanimated him. He jumped up, walked to the bookstall and bought the latest issue of *Life*; his attitude to that magazine was already proprietorial. He came back to the table and, reading my face, said to the interpreter, 'I see I have astonished him. But let him think of Columbus and the egg.' It is one of his favourite stories; it occurs twice in *Bible*.

Admiration assists Mr Matsuda's misconception of the

West he proposes to save by conquest. In *Bible* Mr Matsuda even attributes to the West the attainment of the Hindu–Buddhist ideal of non-attachment. He can find philosophical balance in the protest demonstrations of 'English gentlemen'. As *Bible* says, 'They never denounce the policeman crying severally "Damn tax-eaters!" On the contrary, they are taking pleasant lunches sitting and singing with placards putting erect.' This idealism is to be admired; it also appears as something that might be exploited. It has led Mr Matsuda into absurdity. But he is too removed for comedy. Equally, there is no tragedy or pathos in his present adventure. His situation – a favourite English word in Japan – holds its own cure.

I asked a middle-aged Japanese, a man of culture, what he thought would happen to Mr Matsuda.

'Our businessmen of the Matsuda type and at the Matsuda stage,' he said, 'are not crazy in any medical sense. They just feel they are bound to win. But if they fail and fail and fail again, they can take the hint. They will know when good fortune has left them. Then they usually become ordinary again.'

Mr Matsuda will die.

In 1970 Time Magazine *reported that Mr Matsuda – now separated from his wife – was working as a lorry-driver in Yokohama.*

Steinbeck in Monterey

Daily Telegraph Magazine, 3 April 1970

A writer is in the end not his books, but his myth. And that myth is in the keeping of others.

Cannery Row in Monterey, the one John Steinbeck wrote about, disfigures a mile of pretty Californian coastline. The canneries used to can sardines; but the sardines began to disappear from Monterey Bay not long after Steinbeck published his book in 1945; and today all but one of the canneries have closed down. The cannery buildings remain, where they have not been destroyed by fire: white corrugated-iron buildings, as squat and plain as warehouses, backing out into the sea over a low cliff, braced by timber and tons of concrete which now only blasting can remove. Some are abandoned and show broken windows; some are warehouses; some have been converted into restaurants, boutiques, gift-shops.

The old Row has gone: the stink of fish and fish-fertilizer, the cutters and packers who could work up to sixteen hours a day when a catch was in, the winos, the derelicts who slept in pipes in empty lots, the whores. It was what Steinbeck wrote about but transmuted. What remains is like a folk-memory of community, wine, sex and talk. The tourists come for the memory. The name, Cannery Row, was made official in 1958, long after the sardine went away; before that it was Ocean View Avenue. And today, in Ring's Café next door to the Steinbeck Theatre in Steinbeck Circle – the whole complex on the site of a former cannery – the new shop-keepers and business people of the Row are meeting to talk about what they might do to get the tourists in in 1970.

1970 is the bicentennial of the founding of Monterey by the Spaniards. Some people in Ring's remember the centennial of 1947; that was the centennial of the American seizure. The main street of Monterey (today a wasteland, awaiting renewal) was painted gold and there was dancing in the streets. History in the Monterey Peninsula is this sort of fun. Steinbeck wrote angrily of Indian servitude and American land-grabbing; but there is a mixed-up myth here of a gay and gracious Mexican past, of heroic Spanish missionary endeavour, and numerous Indian slaves, all converts, happily accepting the whip for religious misdemeanours. In the dereliction of Monterey every adobe from Mexican times is preserved and labelled; there is even a movement to have the first Spanish missionary, 'the first Californian', canonized. The American seizure is celebrated on the Fourth of July with a costume pageant devised by the Navy League and the Monterey History and Art Association: old-time señoritas and Yankees listening companionably to the proclamation of annexation.

Ring's café has been in Monterey for some time, but on the Row for just over a year. Like many new places on the Row, Ring's honours the fishing past with a fishing net in its windows and wooden fish caught in the net. The proprietor is an old advertising man; from his café he publishes *The Monterey Foghorn*, a four-page satirical sheet whose cause is Cannery Row, gaiety and youth. Ring's offers 'beer, skittles and vittles'; it says it is 'under no management' and has 'the world's cuisiest cuisine'. There are paintings; the Peninsula is full of artists. At the top of the inner wall a *trompe-l'œil* painting continues the braced timber ceiling of the cannery. And above the bar, among other posters, is one advertising 'Doc's Birthday'.

This was an event that Ring's staged last year, to bring to life and perhaps to perpetuate something in the book. 'Doc' was the marine biologist in *Cannery Row*, the educated man around whom the others idled. Mack and the boys gave a party for Doc's birthday, and the party went predictably wild. Doc was a real person on the Row, Doc Ricketts; *Cannery Row* is dedicated to him. Steinbeck lent him money to buy the low unpainted wooden lab which is squashed between two cannery buildings and will now, as a men's club, be preserved. In 1948 a Southern Pacific locomotive ran into Doc's motor-car one evening on the level-crossing just above the Row, and Doc was killed. On the bar of Ring's, below glass, is a large photograph of the accident: Doc on a stretcher in the grass, the wrecked Ford, the locomotive, the crowd.

Fact, fiction, folk-lore, death, gaiety, homage: it is unsettling. But it is how myth is made. Doc as the tallest 'character' on the Row: it is as unquestioned now as the myth of gaiety. No one in Ring's can say why Doc was such a character. He was nice to everybody, they say; he drank a lot; he liked the girls. It is the book, of course, and Steinbeck. But the book itself recedes.

There are about thirty people in Ring's. Solid bald men; younger men in dark glasses; middle-aged ladies in suits; an intense young woman in a check suit and matching deerstalker cap; a mother of two, with the yawning two; a Chinese lady. The solemn young man with steel-rimmed glasses, drooping moustache, leather waistcoat and patched jeans is one of the Peninsula's artists; he and his wife run an ambitious boutique called Pin Jabs. He used to cycle up to the Row from Monterey in the old days. But most of the people here are new. Many have read *Cannery Row* and say they adore it; but some have not read any more Steinbeck.

The chairman, a gentle, slow-speaking sculptor of sixty-four, is one of the few people now on the Row who knew Steinbeck. He is a long-time Californian and knew Steinbeck in the 1930s, in the days of failure and poverty, when 'if you didn't know about his background you wouldn't have known he was a writer'. Steinbeck never spoke about his work; he was, outwardly, like the people he mixed with and wrote about. But the sculptor remembers the writing of the last page of *The Grapes of Wrath*. The novel ends in a black night of flood, when, the world a void, her own baby born dead, her family scattered, Rose of Sharon offers her breast to a lost and starving old man.

'I happened to be in his house that night. A little house he had then in Los Gatos. It was about three o'clock. I'd gone to bed and I heard him call out, "I've got it! I've got it!" I got up, everybody else got up, and he read out this last piece. The only piece I ever heard him read out.'

The sculptor is willing to forget Steinbeck's later books; for the early, Californian books, 'when he was like in his own place', he feels the deepest affection; and his attitude to Steinbeck comes close to piety.

He rises now, calls the meeting to order, and asks for ideas for Cannery Row pageants or 'projects' that might get financial support from the Monterey Bicentennial Committee and so get the tourists in next year.

'The only project we have so far is getting perhaps one of the old tanks and making a little house of it and having explanatory material there about the family that lived there.' The Malloys of *Cannery Row* set up house in an old locomotive boiler, crawling in through the fire-door; they rented out subsidiary pipes to lodgers; but then Mrs Malloy began to cry for curtains and nagged her husband away. 'Only thing we have so far. We need projects. I sure need your help.'

'I've just finished *Cannery Row*,' a young woman says. After such a flourish, what? She suggests 'a little kind of walking tour. With a map. Have the different spots, like Doc's place, what was there then, what's there now . . .'

'I suppose some kind of designation on the buildings.'

'We don't want to get too historical.'

The girl in the deerstalker suggests a tour of the surviving cannery.

'You mean the sequence of the machinery. Where the fish came in, where they went out . . .'

'What we want is a brochure like the Hearst Castle –'

'This isn't a Hearst Castle. This is spread out a little.'

'– simultaneously bringing out the historical aspect.'

Speech is slow, lingering. The ideas come slowly, linger, fade. A Steinbeck film festival. Steinbeck plays. The hiring of a 'colourful character' to wander about the Row. Each shop featuring one Steinbeck book.

'If there could be a trade fair,' the girl from Pin Jabs says.

'We have a lot of vacant lots. A lot of the action of the book took place in vacant lots, and –'

'Things happen in the vacant lot, and we get no activity at the other end. We want something that will give *complete* activity from A to Z.'

'Something more like Doc's Birthday. Let Cannery Row be Cannery Row, and downtown be downtown.'

'You're talking about something that's got to have some life going in it for three, four months.'

'. . . dancing in the streets.'

'For three, four months?'

'. . . in the empty lots. Every two hours have a different band.'

'Trouble is, we talk about sunny California. But it gets pretty cold at nights.'

'They could have like a pass to Cannery Row. It could cost five dollars and they could get a drink in the different places. A pass. The Gold Key of Cannery Row.'

'You don't want to scare off the elderly.'

The mother of the two rises with the two, now quite stupefied. She says she has to go. But she wants to say one thing. She is a mother of two, plump and pretty and perfectly serious; she gets respectful attention. They've got to raise money for the advertising, she says; and she has a couple of suggestions. 'Like have a carnival down here or something. Whole day.' She loses her audience. She suggests auctions. 'The restaurant people could auction a meal.' The restaurant people don't twitch. 'The other people could auction –'

There is a decent pause after she and the two leave.

'We're talking about auctions and things. We're talking about nickels and dimes.'

They are not tycoons, these people who have invested in the Cannery Row name; they are a little like people infected by the atmosphere which they are promoting. They call themselves 'the little people'. The big people are off-stage: the owners of the cannery buildings, investors in real estate, to whom the rents and a percentage of the profits go. Older, non-tourist businesses might go on. Like the Natural Science Establishment, which for more than a decade has been offering embalmed cats, among other things. 'We can make immediate shipment of any quantity. All our embalmed cats are shipped in waterproof plastic bags.' But for the last six or seven years the little people have been coming and going with their boutiques and batiks. Where is yesterday's 'Den of Antiquity'? Can 'Anti-macassar Factory and Psychedelic Tea Cozies' depend on its sense of fun? Not all ventures on the Row last; at least one sculptor has hanged himself.

In fifteen years, when the leases begin to run out, the high-rise hotels will go up on this reclaimed bit of pretty Californian coastline. But by that time the Cannery Row myth, which the busy little people have created, will have grown hard.

Myths grow fast here. California, of the sun and the fruit and the cool Pacific shore, is where Americans go when they have been weakened by America. And the twenty-five or thirty square miles of the Monterey Peninsula are special. 'It seems,' says Wesley Dodge, one of the new 'big people' of the Row (he's made eighty times his investment in cannery buildings and machinery), 'it seems like there's always been a group or something here that's anti to what the mass is interested in.' There have been beatniks and hippies. ('Hippies have money,' the girl from Pin Jabs says, with respect and hope.) In the old days it was the bums with their 'bindles', riding the freight cars to the Peninsula from all parts of the country.

And not only bums and beatniks. Many years ago a visiting Hindu yogi reported that the vibrations at Pacific Grove, to the west of Monterey – it begins where Cannery Row ends – were as good as anything he had found in the Himalayas. The leading bookshop in Monterey, among the restaurants and gift-shops on Fisherman's Wharf, is mystically inclined. And something of mystic exhilaration remains in the ordered pinewoods and timber lodges of Asilomar, a noted conference centre, where even on this Fourth of July weekend they are gathering for a Philosophical Roundtable.

Bang! Boom! With AURAS *flashing, sparkling and colorful as Fourth of July skyrockets, here we are* CELEBRATING *our latest Conference series get-together.* WELCOME EACH AND EVERYONE! ! *We think we've a joyous and full-filled* PROGRAM, *so once again please write down those* DREAMS, VISIONS, IMPRESSIONS *and share them with all of us along with that* SPECIAL PAST LIFE COSTUME *for our* BIG PARTY NIGHT JUBILEE.

The Roundtable's cause is reincarnation. But the thin young girl from San Diego, whose sister was in it first, says that the aim is 'to bring back like the people to God'. Her eyelids are coloured green; her painted eyebrows slant upwards in a waving line. The weekend costs 45 dollars.

Pacific Grove also has a famous festival in honour of the Monarch butterfly; a legend has been worked out which involves a lost princess and her sorrowing Indian subjects. Just to the south of the vibrations and the butterflies is an area of golf courses and country clubs dedicated to *Treasure Island*. Stevenson came to Monterey as a young man and used the topography of part of the Peninsula in that book; everything is appropriately named. And then there is Carmel-by-the-Sea.

If Monterey, just two miles away, is Mexican, then Carmel is English. Everything in Carmel is small. The houses are small, the signs are small, the shops are small and their windows display the littlest things. The smallness goes on and on; it becomes tininess, it becomes grand; it is tininess on the American scale. On a main street a cluster of rustic doll's houses with geraniums outside the tiny windows turns out to be an expensive motel. There are crooked little roofs, crooked little gates. A shop is called Hansel and Gretel, a house The Wooden Shoe.

Steinbeck called them 'the Pixie people of Carmel'. There was a vogue here in the 1920s for doll's houses for real people. There are no street lights in Carmel, no postal deliveries; the houses have no numbers; and there is a fiercely protective city council. The whole elfin English thing has become confused with an ideal not so much of literature and art as of the literary and artistic life, of culture flourishing in a certain 'atmosphere' and expressing itself in a separateness from commercial America. The place is a raging commercial success. Four million tourists come every year; people come back again and again. There are 150 shops and boutiques. Every block of the rustic shopping centre is cross-hatched, sometimes on more than one level, with arcades, each with its directory of linked wooden slabs hanging from a wrought-iron standard.

Carmel deals, above all, in art. In galleries that look like those in Bond Street, in glass-fronted studios that are like film-sets, answering every concept of the glamour of the artistic life, waves break on rocks in sunlight and moonlight, at sunrise and sunset; Monterey cypresses bend before the wind in every twentieth-century idiom. 'Verdult Art Gallery presents a showing of Dutch Master Paintings by William Verdult.' 'The immediate acceptance of her work by the public brought her to the decision that the painting profession was to be hers and her speciality in the art field was to be the ever present challenge of an ever changing sea.' 'While in high school, Garcia worked ... for Ed Ricketts, the noted marine biologist and true-life model for "Doc" in John Steinbeck's novel, *Cannery Row* ... Although primarily an impressionist, Garcia's style has ranged from realism to abstraction.'

In the setting, it is the quantity of this art, the confidence of it all, and again the quantity, that unsettle the visitor. It is as though, at its geographical limits, a culture is parodying itself: rich middle America, middle in everything, paying its holiday tribute to art, the idea of artists and freedom, and buying prettiness.

At Seaside the blacks are starting a boycott of something. At Fort Ord, just a couple of miles away, soldiers in green fatigues are training for Vietnam. Beyond that, the endless level lettuce-fields of Salinas, the bitter landscape of stoop-labour. But America ends where the Monterey Peninsula begins. On the Peninsula all is fairyland.

To be received into fairyland: it is a strange fate for Steinbeck, the novelist of social conscience, the angry man of the 1930s, the propagandist for the unions, the man who always scoffed at the myth-making capacity of his Peninsula. Probe among the shopkeepers and you find that Steinbeck didn't care, after Doc's death, what happened to Doc's lab. Look up the files of the *Monterey Peninsula Herald* and you find that in 1957, when there was some talk of preservation, Steinbeck, writing from Manhattan, where he had moved, was for pulling the whole Row down.

Or perhaps, he wrote, the canneries 'should be kept as a monument to American know-how. For it was this forward-looking intelligence which killed all the fish, cut all the timber, thereby lowering the rainfall. It is not dead either. The same know-how is lowering the water-table with deep wells so that within our lifetime California will be the desert we all look forward to.'

This is the sort of anger Monterey forgives and forgets. It is true that during the war the annual sardine catch suddenly doubled, to nearly a quarter of a million tons. But it is better for legend that the fish of Monterey should be as mysterious as the butterflies of Pacific Grove. It is better to say, as the lady from Carmel said, that 'the sardines just *flipped* their tails and went away'.

Steinbeck himself bears some responsibility. His sentimentality, when prompted by anger and conscience, was part of his strength as a writer. Without anger or the cause for anger he writes fairytales. He has the limitations of his Peninsula. He yielded to the success of *Cannery Row*; he wrote a sequel, *Sweet Thursday*. He parodied his charm; he turned the Row into fairyland.

Don Westlake's mother worked in a cannery from 1936 until 1950. Westlake himself began to work part-time in the cannery cafeteria when he was twelve. He graduated from the local high school in 1952; he is now in his early thirties. Westlake's mother and stepfather, Californian for five generations, left Monterey for Oregon last year. Westlake himself now lives in San Francisco and is a public relations man for a pharmaceutical firm.

He is tall and lean, easy of manner, the image of the healthy, educated Californian; and his Cannery Row background comes as a surprise. But it is Cannery Row that has driven him, as, he says, it has driven many of the sons of those 'Okies' who worked in the Row.

'They weren't all Italians and Poles. Many people don't know that. Okie: that was the worst insult in the world. It was to be just next to an animal. But you have to be careful nowadays. The sons of those people are the leaders of California. You use the word in distinguished company and you notice strange looks.' Not all broke away. 'Some of the boys I knew fell into their parents' way of life. Some have been to jail. As far as I'm concerned they could burn the whole Row down. It's all right for the tourists. But they and Steinbeck are romanticizing something that wasn't there. Living in pipes and boilers. That wasn't funny. Those people were human derelicts. They had no-where else to live.'

Westlake talks less with anger than with distress. He talks like a man who will never exorcize a personal hurt.

'And the place used to *stink*. Not only the fish. The heads and tails they cut off and turned into fertilizer. Every cannery had its fertilizer plant. The fish came in in the morning. There were no sonic devices in those days. You could tell where the sardines were only by the phos-phorescence at night. Every cannery had a special whistle, and when the catch came in the cannery would blow one whistle for their cutters and a later one for their packers. When you heard your whistle you would get up and drive down to the Row. We lived at Seaside; it was always the lower-class, working area.

'The girls would stand at a long trough, in front of what looked like a tractor-tread. They would drop one sardine in each tread. You would start at three in the morning and go on for twelve, fourteen, sixteen hours, until the packing was finished. In the thirties the girls were paid by the can. Sometimes they got no more than twenty-five dollars a week. During the war, when the unions came in, they were paid by the hour.

'Something you don't hear much about now is the fish poisoning. The pilchard sardine has a toxin to which some people are allergic. The hands then become red and raw and pitted and scaled like a fish. Blood poisoning can make the hands red right up the arm. Some people lost fingers through the gangrene. In those days the only cure for this fish poisoning was to soak your hands in epsom salts. My mother never had it badly. But you would see these frightened people soaking their hands in epsom salts. They were frightened because if their hands went bad they wouldn't get any more work for the rest of the season. And when the season was over there was no work for anyone. It was a boon to Monterey when the canneries were forced to close down and the people who were being exploited were forced to leave. Though most of those refugees from Monterey are still in packing. Fruit packing, in the valleys.'

The only place Westlake remembers with affection is the Bear Flag, the brothel Steinbeck wrote about, one of six on the Row at its wartime peak.

'It was my favourite hang-out when I was five. Some nights my stepfather and I would drive up to meet my mother and we would have to wait until the packing was finished. The girls would take me in then from the car. I can't remember what they looked like. All I remember is they were big motherly types. I was always warm and comfortable when I was there.'

'Sentimental?' says Wesley Dodge, the post-cannery millionaire on the Row. 'You going to be sentimental about whores? They're talking about things I didn't participate in. I didn't participate in the whores.'

Dodge is a fat, pink man with glasses. He is sixty-four and says he is too old to be happy; but he smiles easily. His office, in a converted cannery, is where the women's lavatories used to be. 'Twenty on that side, twenty on this side.' The purchase of this particular cannery was one of his coups. 'Flause was asking 240,000 dollars. I said, "Mr Flause, I don't want to give you a price. We are too far away. Mr Flause, all I will give you is 70,000 dollars." I called on the man every day for two years. I never mentioned price again. I would go around the cannery with him, inspecting the machinery. And he would turn the motors on, just to keep everything in order. One day he put his foot on a pump and it fell over and he said, "Dodge, you've just bought yourself a cannery." I paid a deposit, and as I sold the machinery, I paid him.'

If the idle canneries had come up for sale all at once, Dodge and his associates mightn't have been able to buy the 70 per cent of Cannery Row they did buy. But the cannery owners held on, hoping that the sardine might come back. For a time some canned anchovies, labelling them 'sardine-type'. 'The canneries dropped over nine years. One by one.'

It was as a dealer in second-hand machinery that Wesley Dodge came to the dying Row. A Fresno man, one-eighth Cherokee, self-educated, used from youth to working 'from can till can't', he had already made and lost two fortunes, in fruit in the 1930s, in a private airline in the 1940s. His knowledge of the second-hand machinery business came from his own love of machines and from 'watching other nationalities', mainly Jews. 'I am one of the few Gentiles in second-hand machinery.' The secret is to buy well. 'Everybody in America is a salesman. I learned to be a buyer. If you buy right, selling's no problem.' He sold Cannery Row machinery all over the world. 'Apple-canning, fish-reduction, tallow plants which take chicken waste. I didn't necessarily sell back to the fish business.' They sometimes got more from the machinery than they paid for the cannery.

And there was Dodge's interest in ocean property. 'All my life I wanted to own ocean property. There's no ocean in Nebraska. Does that mean anything to you? No ocean in Oklahoma. There's an Atlantic Ocean, there's a Pacific Ocean. In between there's no ocean. In my commercial life anyone that's owned ocean property had it made.'

There was a stripped cannery to be seen, the last. We drove there in his Cadillac.

'It's air-conditioned,' he said, as I fumbled with the car window.

It was almost dark in the cannery building; the corru-gated-iron roof looked higher inside. Small motors with fresh grey paint on their casings covered half the concrete floor. On the other side, no longer in sequence, under poly-thene, were the big, complicated machines. Moving lightly, he undraped, touched, felt, explained. Here, still looking new after twenty idle years, were the 'tractor-treads' into which the girls – now scattered, and always women –

dropped the sardines one by one, for hours; here was the sardine gut-sucker; here were metal arms so finely balanced that only full cans would depress them to that track which led to the capping machine.

'There's about 80,000 dollars here,' Dodge said. 'I live this machinery. Machinery isn't difficult if you *live* it.'

It was time for a drink. Dodge himself, after many years of whisky, eighteen to twenty shots a day, now drinks only orange juice and Seven-Up. We went to the Outrigger. It was on the sea side of a converted cannery, past gift-shops whose walls dripped pink bougainvillaea. Three gas jets on tall metal poles flared at the entrance. A spotlight picked out rocks in the sea. We entered a carpeted green grotto, of Polynesian atmosphere, with a waterfall, and stepped out into openness: the old cannery pier, carpeted, re-timbered and glassed-in. We were on water, in the middle of the bay, the lights of Seaside and Monterey curving far to the right. After the desolation of the Row, the beauty of rock and water was abrupt. It was the future.

'The square-foot value of the property will be many times greater than when Steinbeck was here,' Dodge said. He pointed to where a basket-like metal frame rose out of the sea. 'The old hopper. That's where they unloaded the fish. They were pumped in through a pipe into the cannery.'

From the high-rise, resort future of Cannery Row Dodge has withdrawn. For two million dollars, paid in cash, he and his associates have sold out to a San Francisco millionaire. 'He is seventy-five, but he has a different idea of his life than I have of mine.' Dodge feels he has had a full business life; even while on the Row he went back into fruit, where he had failed thirty years before, and 'made a lot there, a lot'. Dodge, who has no children of his own, is interested now in educating the children of his relatives and friends. He would like to support a hospital or some kind of research; but he is concerned to make his money work. 'You don't get the true value of your dollar with a foundation. You are just paying the salaries of the top men.'

Later, driving down the Row back to the centre of Monterey, he slowed down beside an empty, fenced-in lot. 'Frank Raiter's place. A real Cannery Row character. Over eighty, worth several millions. His cannery burned down two years ago. But every morning he comes here and sits in his – not a Cadillac, the one next to a Cadillac, I forget – and reads the *Wall Street Journal* for a couple of hours.'

The Row bent and straightened again. It was just here that Doc Ricketts died in 1948 – the scene under glass in Ring's café. Dodge talked about Steinbeck. He never met him; he spoke to him once, on the transatlantic telephone, to get permission to use his name for the Steinbeck Theatre.

'He hurt California terribly. I like *Tortilla Flat*, I like *Cannery Row*. I know those paisanos without knowing them, if you know what I mean. But he wrote *The Grapes of Wrath*. I've no background of being able to say this book's better than that one, but it hurt me to read *The Grapes*. It wasn't factual enough. You know what an Okie is? They moved here in *hordes*. Thousands. Thousands a *day*. I was making five to six dollars an hour, packing fruit. When they came they worked for fifteen cents, twenty cents. Fifty cents a day. Any amount a day. And I was out of a job. We had problems in 1932. They came and compounded our problems. But Steinbeck wrote *The Grapes*. It's something that people look at us as, as Californians. And he sold a lot of books. You can't assess the damage.'

New York with Norman Mailer

Daily Telegraph Magazine, 10 October 1969

Norman Mailer always campaigned in a correct dark-blue suit. Towards the end he cut his hair short. A week or so before election day the Mailer campaign staff lost some hair as well. The hefty thirty-year-old campaign manager shaved off his little beard, and the sideboards of others were abbreviated. Angry young necks showed fresh and clean; plain dark ties closed up open shirts. The first order, the one that had got rid of the manager's beard, had come from Mailer himself; it had worked its way down; and for three or four days in this last week the candidate and his staff were partially estranged.

'There's been some degree of role-confusion,' one shorn young man said.

They were still loyal at headquarters, but they said they were loyal to the campaign, the cause, the ideas. They spoke less of 'Norman'; they spoke of 'the candidate' and they made the election sound like a day of sacrifice. Where someone had pinned up *Get Ready for the Norman Conquest* someone now chalked an anti-Mailer obscenity in red, but shyly, not using the name, only the initials.

Campaign headquarters (Senator Eugene McCarthy's last year) was a large grimy room on the second floor of a decaying building on Columbus Circle, above a couple of cafés and a sauna establishment. The lift didn't always work; it was safer to go around the corner to the staircase, where rubbish was sometimes left out on the landings in plastic sacks; New York in places is like Calcutta, with money. The headquarters room was divided into offices by low flimsy partitions, which for various reasons were knocked down one by one as the campaign progressed. The furniture was sparse, trestle tables, old folding chairs, duplicating machines; there was printed paper everywhere, on walls, floor, tables.

The helpers moved in little cliques within the larger club. Sometimes, when girls brought their babies strapped to their backs in aluminium frames, it was like a hippy encampment with its familial privacies and self-satisfied dedication. During the days of the estrangement privacies vanished; and, like amateurs miming dejection in a low-budget film, the helpers huddled round a table behind the last partition and tried with the help of some beer-cans to give the impression to correspondents – at first ignored, but then welcomed – that they were drinking heavily.

It had been an ambiguous campaign – professional-amateur, political and anti-political. *The other guys are the joke*, a Mailer campaign button said. But now it was possible to feel that the estrangement was also a cover-up for doubt, perhaps panic. A fortnight before, a New York writer, no friend of Mailer, had told me that Mailer's campaign would be as self-defeating as Goldwater's had been in 1964. Mailer, like Goldwater, was a licensed figure. The media would cheer him on, but only in this role. After a time Mailer would begin to suffer from a lack of serious attention; it would get worse as the campaign went on; and at the end Mailer's ideas, however good, would be discredited and Mailer himself would be running for cover.

It didn't work out like that. But this was the gamble Mailer was taking, at the peak of his reputation. Mailer never stopped complaining about poor press coverage; but he got a lot, and it became more and more serious. On election day 41,000 registered Democrats voted for him. A good sale for any writer; and for Mailer the seven-week politician, a triumph. The blue suit, the walking tours, the handshaking: Mailer's instincts had been right. The display of energy and campaigning orthodoxy – the politician's simple self-satire – had helped to establish Mailer's seriousness.

At the same time the campaign had never ceased to be an intellectual entertainment. Through all the repetitions and simplifications Mailer always rang true. He never lost his gift of the phrase, that made so many of his comments sound like epigrams. 'Anonymity creates boredom.' 'Crime will be on the increase as long as it's the most interesting activity.' 'You will need more and more police to keep more and more bad government in power.' To the end he was good in the direct interview. His replies then – after what looked like a flick of the tongue against the top teeth, as though a piece of chewing gum was being hidden away – were abrupt, swift and pithy. The writer's imagination, ceaselessly processing and ordering experience ('You are always writing that novel about yourself,' he told me later), could at any moment pass inspection.

'If you win the Democratic nomination, which Republican would you like to run against?'

'Marchi. He says he's a conservative. I call myself a left conservative. We could have an extraordinary discussion about the meaning of conservative principles. Many people who call themselves conservatives are right-wing reactionaries. Which is a different thing altogether.' Next question. And this was at the last press conference, when Mailer was tired with words.

He was least effective in the later, non-controversial TV tournaments, where each candidate did a one-minute joust in turn. The politicians won then. Though using words, they appeared to be dismissing words, even their own; they made it plain that they genuinely wanted power and knew what that power was. Mailer's words were part of Mailer. As a writer and politician he carried a double burden; and the ridiculous part of his gamble – so private, so public – was that irresponsibility in either role would have led to the disaster that many had seen coming.

The ideas were big – New York a dying city, alienation its major problem, a complete political reorganization the only hope, with New York as the fifty-first state, more directly controlling its own funds, and the more or less autonomous city districts developing their own life-styles. There were attractive elements of fantasy: no cars in Manhattan (the city-state ringed by a monorail), free public bicycles, and a monthly sabbath, a Sweet Sunday, trafficless, when 'nothing would fly but the birds'.

The platform was like an anguished intellectual statement, and the publicity in the beginning had been a writer's publicity: rallying approval from the *New York Times* in a ponderous, punning editorial; the prizes for *Miami and the Siege of Chicago* and *The Armies of the Night*; a reported million-dollar contract for the new book about the Apollo moonshot.

The first meeting of the campaign, in Greenwich Village, was an intellectual–social occasion. It was rowdy. From press reports it appeared that Mailer was attempting a re-make of *Armies*. A false start – this was admitted later – but a writer's false start: the new book often begins like a repeat of the one just finished. Then the campaign changed. It found – what it had lacked – a political issue. It became political; it acquired substance.

The City College of New York, CCNY, which had been having its racial troubles, formulated a dual-admission policy: half of its places would be reserved for students from disadvantaged communities. There was an uproar. The disadvantaged would be black and Puerto Rican; Jewish students would suffer; standards would be lowered. Every mayoral candidate, Democratic and Republican, spoke out against the plan. Only Mailer and his 'running mate' were for it. The campaign that had begun as an entertainment now seemed dangerous to some. 'The Jews here regard Mailer as a sinner': this was the message from a Mailer worker in the Bronx. A poll showed opinion eight to one against dual-admission; and for the next few days, for five or six more times a day, Mailer worked hard to show that what looked irresponsible had logic and was socially necessary. After a week there was a compromise; CCNY said they would take only 400 disadvantaged students, not 1,500; the issue faded. But the campaign had proved itself.

In the early days Mailer could say of a rival: 'If I didn't make a vow to use no obscene language, I would say that Wagner was full of an unmarketable commodity.' This was the Village Mailer. At the end he said of Wagner: 'He's the lead hobby horse in a wooden field.' This was funnier; it also made more political sense. On election night, the fight lost and won, the cheering crowd followed Mailer from headquarters across Eighth Avenue to his car. They were also cheering Mailer's wife and Mailer's mother, both of whom had taken part in the campaign. The politician as family man: to this extent the campaign had become orthodox.

Three weeks before, Mailer had told a television reporter that running a campaign was like writing a novel. The same confidence was required; there were analogous problems of creation. 'Your brains are working all the time. The writer works on a world, brings it to a resolution; and that world changes him. When a writer finishes a novel he is a changed man.'

If Mailer had a political base, it was his glamour as a writer. But glamour also stood in his way.

At the annual dinner of the Village Independent Democrats the two speakers were to be men who had worked with Senator Eugene McCarthy and the late Senator Robert Kennedy. McCarthy, Kennedy: these were the magic names not only of the left, the protesting, the liberal, but also of those asserting an intellectual separateness and therefore content to lose. 'I know a man who supported fourteen losing candidates,' a visitor from the Lexington Avenue Democrats said. Mailer was going to lose, but the

Lexington visitor wasn't prepared to admit Mailer as one of his losers. The ideas were good, but Mailer belonged to another area of American glamour.

Benign now, still powerfully built rather than 'unwillingly fat' (his own words), a little tired after a day spent on a campaign paper, blue eyes twinkling in a harassed, mobile face, Mailer was undeniably a presence among the Village Independent Democrats at their pre-dinner cocktails.

'I've talked to Mr Mailer,' a forty-year-old woman said. (Over severe, separating foundations, her neckline plunged and plunged.) 'And he says I can follow him around in the press car and I want to go everywhere he goes.' Her escort, led by the hand, smiled neutrally.

Banning, the campaign manager, listed the evening's engagements. They were to end about midnight.

The woman hesitated, then chose the dinner.

Schwartzman, the nineteen-year-old student on the Mailer advance staff, said, 'She probably said she was a freelance and writing a feature. You do get types like that. Now the agency girl, that's more my type of writer. A little tall, but still.'

The agency girl, blonde, tanned, cool in a flaming red sweater, had just joined the campaign. She too was writing a feature. In the car afterwards she got out her notebook.

'Why haven't you gone to Vietnam, Mr Mailer?'

'I don't want to get killed.'

'I was there for two years. I wasn't killed.'

'That is a horrible and obscene war. I would have done something. I would have got killed.'

Banning leaned over the front seat to talk of campaign plans. Mailer sat forward, and the two men discussed walking tours and the wisdom of campaigning in certain East Side bars. Mailer didn't want to campaign in bars. It would mean either doing a lot of drinking in one place or getting in the way of a voter who wanted a drink.

The agency girl said, 'Do you think you have enough of a political record, Mr Mailer?'

Mailer turned to her and smiled. 'As a man who's been married four times – take this down – I say to politicians never run on your past record.'

While her pen worked, Banning talked about an article on the campaign in *Life*. 'On Wednesday it was four pages. On Thursday it was two. On Friday it was one and a half.'

Mailer said it was hard on the writer. 'That's why *Life*'s going broke.'

'People say,' Banning said, '*Life*'s going broke because of what they're paying you for your moonshot article.'

Mailer smiled at the agency girl. 'Perhaps they're trying to rebuke me.'

'Perhaps,' the girl said, 'I should get you angry. Mr Mailer, why do you talk so much?'

It was the sort of newspaper feature the campaign was attracting.

We were in the lower East Side. A 'surviving' area, Mailer called it affectionately: decaying red-brick houses, narrow shops with dirty windows, an occasional empty lot.

'If you are Lithuanian,' a man said on the steps of the East Midtown Reform Democratic Club, 'how come your name is Mailer?'

'Lithuanian Jew,' Mailer insisted. 'On both sides.'

It was a small hall, panelled down one side and decorated with KLM posters, bunting and the Stars and Stripes. There were about forty people on folding metal chairs.

'By the look of you,' Mailer said, 'I can see you are not a soft Democratic Club. Let's have the questions. I can see that the person who asks the first question is going to be in as much trouble as me.'

The question was about the fifty-first state. 'You think the Governor of New York would let you or anybody else get away from them?'

'We all know what breaks up an unhappy marriage. It's a smart Jewish lawyer. I submit that I am the smartest Jewish attorney in town.'

The mood didn't last. A woman asked about CCNY. She sat next to a tweed-jacketed man who might have been her husband; they both looked like teachers. 'Why don't you send them all to Harvard and give them all a really *good* education?' This was the Jewish backlash; she was speaking of the blacks and Puerto Ricans.

'You know you are just giving expression to your prejudice. Harvard's my old college –'

'That's why I said it.'

'Let's assume that Harvard's going down the drain –'

'You're putting words in her mouth!' the man shouted.

'Our universities are to education what the *New Yorker* is to literature. A minor organ with a major function.' Laughter cleared the air. 'Pardon this digression. No one should trust a speaker who strays from the point.' He addressed the man: 'You recognize the unhappiness with which you speak?' It was a direct, gentle inquiry.

'I do,' the man said. His response was like a reflex; his tone was confessional.

A moment of stillness: the man and woman, for all their passion, and the respectable jauntiness of their 'budget' clothes, were older than they had first appeared.

It wasn't a perfect solution, Mailer said, exploiting the moment. But it was better that the colleges should make some adjustments rather than be destroyed altogether. If the blacks hadn't been betrayed so often, if opportunities had been given them, 'you would have had blacks as mean and as ugly as any –' His mischievousness was like the other face of anger; he was deliberately destroying the mood.

'You are asking the kids to pay for it!' the woman shouted.

'Let him talk!'

'The kids will have,' Mailer said, above the voices calling for order, 'the exhilarating existential experience of going to school with black people.'

That was the end. And, unexpectedly, there was applause, Mailer walking smartly down, arms held out wide, palms open, like a wrestler about to charge.

The next halt, a fund-raising one, was at a place called the Electric Circus in the Village. It was a good name. In the stairways and corridors blue, red and mauve neon strips reflected on walls that might have been papered with aluminium foil; and at the end of this neon fantasy was a wide white hall, packed with the young. It was a paid-up Mailer crowd. But Mailer, solitary before the microphone, appeared irritated. 'You are here to see me work, is that it?' The questions were too sympathetic. 'When we win, which would give all of us great concern –' But there was little of that. It was as though, out of his security here, Mailer had committed himself to frowns and silences and was waiting to be provoked. 'Now, listen. I'm much more conservative than most of you people here. I'll work for and support your neighbourhood, but I don't think I'll approve of it.'

After that, ten minutes at the League of Women Voters in the public library opposite the Museum of Modern Art. An anti-Rockefeller art-student demo going on outside that: a swift exchange of literature, campaign with campaign. And then a confusion of causes: Badillo, one of Mailer's rivals, coming out of the library with his staff, Mailer going in with his, everybody with leaflets for everybody else.

'Everywhere I go I see Badillo buttons. I feel Badillo's staked you guys.'

'Norman, Norman,' the Badillo supporter said. 'That's not a nice thing to say.'

A meeting with the East Side Democrats was on the schedule. But only the wife of the campaign photographer was there, in a belted pink mackintosh. She had been waiting on the pavement a long time; the club room was locked. The busy campaign, unexpectedly isolated, re-assembled; and then Banning told us to hurry over to the West Side Democrats; we were already very late for them.

'Advance did a fine job,' someone in the second car said.

'I've been talking to taxi-drivers,' a foreign reporter said (he had joined us at the Electric Circus). 'They may know about *The Naked*. But they don't always know who the author is.'

'I was talking to an old Jew in Brooklyn yesterday. I told him about Mailer. He said, "Isn't he the guy stabbed his wife?" Nine years, and he's talking about it like he'd read it in the paper that morning.'

'He probably gets his papers late.'

They talked about the agency girl.

'You think she's for real, a writer?'

'With looks like that she could be anything. But she's a groupie. She's only going for the big man.'

We weren't late for the West Side Democrats. A dingy first-floor hall overlooking Broadway, photographs of Robert Kennedy, old Eugene McCarthy stickers, the Stars and Stripes. A mixed crowd of about fifty, some Puerto Ricans, a couple of blacks. One of Mailer's rivals was still talking.

'. . . I tell you one thing we can do real fast to get better crime control . . .' This was Congressman Scheuer, spending half a million dollars to come last in the primary, below Mailer.

Mailer entered, his hair frizzing out now. The TV lights blazed on him. Heads turned; hands were shaken.

'. . . get police out of all station-house and routine jobs . . . all non-crime-control functions . . .'

The applause wasn't for the Congressman. It was for Mailer, withdrawing after his false entry. Presently, through the mêlée, the Congressman walked out, smiling, a private figure.

But they were a dull audience, and because they were dull, Mailer tried. Irony, to begin with. CCNY was being taken over, he said, by the same Communist plot Mayor Wagner had talked about some years ago. The audience remained vacant. 'That was a joke.' He told an Irish joke in an Irish accent. Silence. 'Now that I've lost this club –' The laugh came; the audience relaxed. Mailer talked for twenty minutes; it was the best speech of the evening.

In the morning there was a story in the *New York Times*.

'Campaign' by Mailer Upstages
The Once Festival in 'Village'
... First, however, the audience at the last in the current Electric Ear series of multimedia affairs at the East Village rock hall witnessed a psychodrama of another variety, 'The Campaign', starring Norman Mailer ... While TV cameras captured the bizarre scene, Mr Mailer urged statehood ...

And at the Overseas Press Club they were gloomy. Neither the *Times* nor the *Post* nor the *News* had sent a man to the press conference that morning, when Mailer and his running mate – Jimmy Breslin, a popular columnist, a heavy, dark-haired Irishman of menacing and explosive appearance – were to present a paper on housing. Banning had brought a boxful of copies; he found only about fifteen takers, radio and TV people, who always served the campaign well, some foreign reporters, and the agency girl, now in green. The TV cameras and the lights played on her for a little. She remained cool. Out of a cross face Mailer smiled.

A reporter asked for a statement on the 'integrity' of the New York press.

'The simple statement,' Breslin said, 'is that no one's here. They'll begin to listen when they hear shotguns on Park Avenue.'

'Electric Circus,' Mailer said afterwards, looking at the *Times*, which Banning had folded over to show the story. 'I didn't like the name. I didn't like the building.'

'It was a horrible building,' Banning said.

'How much did we get out of it?'

'A couple of hundred bucks.'

'Not worth it.'

'I was talking to an A P man,' Banning said, explaining the poor attendance at the conference. 'They had a list up in the office. "These stories we will cover this morning." And another list. "These stories we will not cover this morning." We'll call *another* press conference tomorrow at the *same* time. *That's* the way to test them.'

I was beginning to recognize Banning's style in drama. It might have been his diplomatic training; he had served for some time in the American Foreign Service. Or it might have been his later work in broadcasting. ('I couldn't tell you even today,' he said after the campaign, 'whether politics or show business is my first love.')

About thirty reporters came the next day. The agency girl wore cream. The *Times* sent a man; so did the *Post*. There had been a lot on the T V networks the previous evening – the interviews, so casual, given an extra, separate reality when slotted into the news programmes on the small screen – but Mailer was still complaining.

'We have to bludgeon our way into a newspaper office to get a small piece. They are trying to make our campaign ridiculous and up to a point they have succeeded. We have made mistakes on the way; we have played into their hands.'

Tempers were shorter; there were fewer jokes. Mailer looked tired and aggressive; it was his face that suggested defeat. But he might have been acting: his face was so mobile, his moods so quick.

Two hours later, at his Wall Street rally, standing below the statue of Washington on the steps of the Old Treasury Building, he was a different man. Hands now in trouser-pockets below the buttoned jacket, now in jacket pockets, he appeared to strut, like a boxer in the new respectability of a suit, confident of his public spread out in rows on the wide steps, filling the famous narrow street below. The sound system was bad. All the words were lost, including Breslin's threat about the shotguns on Park Avenue. But the scene was dramatically right.

A stranger coming on Wall Street at that moment with a knowledge of America gained only from films would have found in the scene a familiar glamour. He would have seen the man up there as every type of American myth-figure: boxer, sheriff, bad man, mobster, even politician. It was the setting: the famous street in the famous city, the buildings, the flags, the rhetoric and history in the Washington statue. And it was also Mailer: his sense of the city, perhaps, his sense of occasion.

But when I talked to Mailer a week after the election I found that his own memories of the Wall Street rally were vague; the details of the campaign, of particular scenes and particular words, had blurred.

'You don't operate as a writer. You don't see what people are wearing. You are aware of people only as eyes, a type of response. It's more like being an actor.'

2

The day after the Wall Street rally, after many more meetings, speeches, ceremonies, questions and answers and statements, Mailer said, 'I've become duller. Steady, serious, duller. I've become a politician.'

He was in shirtsleeves in headquarters. The grimy windows were pushed open; the afternoon was thundery. He had just given a twenty-minute 'in depth' TV interview; and it was part of the wastefulness of campaigning: that excellent interview, and the events of the week, would make about five minutes on the network's Saturday news.

He had discovered, he said, that politics was hard work. Sleep was the thing he dreamt about and he understood now how sleep could be the politician's sex. 'Someone should do a Freudian analysis of this thing, being a politician. It's all a matter of orality. It's the most oral people who get along. My tongue feels like a hippopotamus's. It's all a matter of tongue and lips. It's so strange for me, so different from my practice as a writer. I used to feel that if I talked about something I had lost it. I would go out to do an article. When I came back and my wife asked me what I thought about it, I wouldn't talk. That's why I feel I couldn't do a book about this.'

'What do you think about him?' Schwartzman asked me afterwards.

It was a question Mailer sometimes asked his staff after a meeting; it was a question the staff often asked reporters they had got to know. It was the burden of glamour: Mailer's staff required him never to fail, even in a short exchange with a reporter.

'Friday's a fun day,' Banning said. 'He's going to the races at Aqueduct.'

'Fun?' I said. 'You mean no campaigning?'

'There are going to be 70,000 people there.'

The special express trains funnelled them in from Manhattan and Brooklyn; and from the platform, level with the floor of the coaches, they poured down the covered ramp to the stand, spoiling the symmetry of the arrangement only when they broke out into the sunlight – the wide car-parks glinting like the open sea – to get to the two-dollar gates. First on the covered ramp (leading to the five-dollar gates) and then in the sunlight, Mailer and his party stood, facing the rush: Breslin, the columnist, more popular than Mailer here, Mailer in light check trousers and a blazer, smiling shyly, Mailer's wife, small, an actress, in a sober olive outfit, now part of the campaign.

The crowd swirled past them. But, like pebbles on a smooth beach, the campaign party was a disturbance, and disturbance built up around them: swift handshakes, an exchange, a little crowd, enough for the cameras, and even a little sound off-camera. 'I've been thinking about this guy. I wanted to see him. He's in favour of dual-admission.' 'You haven't got a ghost of a chance, ya bum!'

Then the party, going through the five-dollar gates, were taken up the escalators to the concourse, where they were soon untraceable.

I fell in with a young man, equally lost, from Liberation News Service. He was hairy and hippyish and aggrieved. He had had to fight his way into the campaign car that morning and he hadn't even had an interview with Mailer. He showed me a transcript he had made of his conversation with Banning.

'BANNING: Look, we need coverage from you New Left nuts like a hole in the head ... You got to get votes from a lot of strange places to win in this town ... He needs support from the left like he needs a shit haemorrhage.'

'Mailer isn't offering an alternative to American politics,' the man from Liberation News said, as we walked through the crowd, looking for the campaign. 'He's offering only a distorted version of the old style.'

The bright green centre of the track was patterned with flowers; in the distance the jets rose one after the other from the permanent kerosene haze over Kennedy Airport.

'The trouble is that Mailer sees himself as an existential hero. In America, where action is frowned on among intellectuals, the existential hero would say, "The worst thing in the world is boredom. We must create drama by our own actions." Mailer creates this excitement, without giving an analysis of why that world is boring and dull. He says, "It is boring and dull, but it will be interesting if I inject myself into it." '

Existential: it was a Mailer word I was beginning to learn; it explained much of what I had felt about the campaign, its glamour and ambiguity. He was only nineteen, the Liberation News man, but the fluency of the American young no longer surprised me.

'What is most important is that when Mailer is defeated it won't be said that he's been defeated by the unworkable and corrupt New York City system. It will be said that it was his individual failure. As a critical man he will have lost a marvellous opportunity of exposing the undemocratic nature of American politics.'

It was easy to see why Banning didn't want him around. Just then, though, the Liberation News man very badly wanted to see Banning: he had forgotten a roll of exposed film in the campaign car.

We ran into one of the TV cameramen. I asked him how he assessed the day's campaigning.

'Oh, we'll make it look bigger.'

'Is that official policy?' the man from Liberation News asked.

'We make everything bigger.'

Outside the restaurant – Mailer having a slow lunch inside – we saw Banning, brisk and businesslike. His beard barely lifted; he ignored us.

'He *hates* me,' the man from Liberation News said, and looked down at his soft suede boots.

I wanted company back to Manhattan. I gave the man from Liberation News some of my notes and persuaded him to forget his exposed film. The train was full of boys and girls, red from the beach. Everyone in the Mailer campaign spoke of the sickness of the society. But to the visitor no city appeared richer in pleasure, and more organized for it. And Mailer's trip to the races made a three-column spread, with a photograph, in the *New York Times*: that was the reality of our afternoon excursion.

'The thing about this campaign,' the girl in headquarters said, 'is that it's fantastically seductive.' She was twenty-four, thin, with a sharp little nose. 'These boys here on the campaign are all like Norman. They have the same tremendous ego and this makes them fantastic to be with. They're so fantastically alive every minute. Hardly anybody else is.' She herself came from New Jersey. 'I had to leave because I was like a freak there. I am like' – she sighed, and her eyes widened behind her tinted granny glasses – 'well, a socialist.' After the campaign she was going on to do some summer work for GI Resistance. 'It'll be idealistic to say it's because I have a brother in Vietnam. It's more like, well, being addicted.'

'I don't know how the whole concept of doing your own thing became so sacred,' Banning said when the campaign was over. 'I don't know whether it's American or just youthful. I know how vicious the establishment is. I am 20,000 dollars in debt – well, say 15,000. But maybe I'm not as disillusioned as everybody else. Maybe everybody is up-tight. Notice the difference between the Kennedy kids we had and the McCarthy kids. The Kennedy people want to win. The McCarthy-oriented types are addicted not just to lost causes but to a concept of lost causes. They just want to make a statement and stand around being right. "I know what is wrong, I'm noble." This I don't buy.'

McCarthy types, Kennedy types, the New Left, the addicted, the Mailer-glamoured, the election-glamoured (bullhorns, loudspeaker cars, sticky labels): even with the heroic pattern-figure of Mailer, the wonder was that the campaign held together and looked professional, that the strains didn't show more.

The reporters came and went. The press became better and better. Dustin, who was in charge of Advance, told me that the article by the agency girl had come out. 'They must have cut a lot,' he said. There were occasional muted reports of internal trouble: a public outburst because of some carelessly displayed posters; an amateur art show not opened, Mailer's wife going instead to speak the nice words Mailer couldn't bring himself to speak. Then Banning lost his beard.

The gloomiest day in headquarters was the Friday before the election. A Harlem rally had been planned for that day. But Clarence 27x Smith, a Black Muslim of some local renown, was shot dead in a lift in the morning (New York always organized for drama, as it was for pleasure), and Mailer cancelled the rally. In headquarters they felt that Mailer had let them down; the show ought to have gone on. The cast and band of *Hair*, I was told, had been recruited and were game; black bodyguards could have been hired for a hundred dollars.

'Don't ask Banning too many questions,' I was told. 'He'll hit you like Norman.'

Banning, tie-less, jacketless, with a beer-can, was dejected and acting tough. He said there was 'an atmosphere of political death' over the campaign. I asked for the schedule. He mimicked my pronunciation. 'Stick around,' he said. 'You'll hear.' It struck me for the first time that he would have a good microphone voice.

'It isn't all Norman,' the girl from New Jersey said. 'Half of this is that it's all going to end on Tuesday and everybody on the campaign's got to go back to not having power. Everything else is going to go on. This stops on June 17, this closeness and intimacy with people who have become your whole life. And these boys, they fight with Norman, but they go to the meetings. And when Norman gets up there and tells it like it is, they all dissolve and you can tell it in their eyes. It's why they come the next day.'

Banning wasn't in the office the next day. But Dustin and his wife and some others were, and after lunch we drove through the rain to Macy's department store, where – but no one was sure – Mailer was campaigning among the shoppers. All we saw from the car were some very young volunteers offering damp leaflets; they didn't know where Mailer was.

He and Mrs Mailer were inside the store, as it turned out, until the guard asked them to campaign outside.

When we walked round the block we found them. Girl volunteers were asking people, 'Have you met Mr Mailer?' And the Mailers were shaking hands. Mailer looked worn, preoccupied, working only with his eyes; his hair, cut shorter, looked greyer. Mrs Mailer was as composed as always. 'I am an actress,' she said later. 'This is the biggest audience I've played to.' A blind man stood beside Mailer, rattling his coins in a green cup and tapping his stick; his eyelids were sealed over hollow sockets so that his face, without expression, was like a dummy's.

It was an extraordinary, smiling scene. The Mailers smiled; the people whose hands had been shaken smiled, and they waited, smiling, to see others have their turn. The girl volunteers smiled; we were all smiling.

'It's *good*,' Dustin said, his gloom vanished. 'We could win.' Dustin had been a Kennedy man.

Mailer, getting into the car, called Dustin over. A girl volunteer turned on me with big eyes. 'I'm *crazy*!' A minute ago she had been demure. 'I *love* him! I've read *all* his books. This is the first time I've *seen* him! I *love* him!' She sat down hard on the table with the campaign buttons. 'I'm *crazy*!'

Dustin came back, exultant. 'He wants a motorcade.' Dustin liked motorcades.

Later, at the Sullivan Street fair – old brick houses with fire-escapes, the street muddy and littered, remote Italian women sitting with bandaged ankles and legs beside food-stalls and toystalls, sausages grilling over charcoal – Dustin and Mailer talked again.

'Look at them,' Dustin's wife said. 'Don't you think they look a little alike, with the hair?'

On Monday, at the last press conference, Mailer bounced back to form after a tired, constricted TV appearance the previous day. Banning was there, friendly again, in a suit, stage-managing again. The four motorcade cars were wait-ing outside. A German producer said, 'The film in Ger-many is finished. It was shown Saturday night.' A girl with a foreign accent was told that press seats were reserved for the New York City press. Mailer, Mrs Mailer and Breslin sat in the third car. Banning was in the loudspeaker car at the front; he was to do the talking.

'Mailer-Breslin and the fifty-first state. You've had the rest. Choose the best.'

It was the motorcade slogan. The story was that it had been suggested to Mailer by a Negro. Banning didn't like it, but he was speaking it with conviction. On Broadway there were some waves and shouts. But Harlem, with its sullen privacies, where garishness and dereliction appeared one and indivisible, was silent. In the South Bronx the advertisements were in Spanish; and Banning – a new talent revealed –spoke in Spanish: *'... dos coches atrás, en el carro abierto....'* His accent was good. But there was no response from the pavements. The motorcade slowed down in the traffic, merged into it.

Mailer signalled from the open car. Banning ran to confer, then came to us. 'OK, we'll meet up at 50th Street and Sixth Avenue, in front of the Time-Life Building. We're just going to shake hands and cut the horseshit with the motorcade.' Banning hadn't liked the idea of the motorcade. The motorcade broke up; and in silence, without loudspeakers, the cars raced separately back to Manhattan.

The reception outside the Time-Life building was very good. Mailer, with his vision of New York as two cities, spoke passionately for the disadvantaged. But his best audience was always the middle-class, the educated, the bohemian, the people who held him in awe.

They had laid in the beer in headquarters. The TV cameras and monitors had been installed. The last partition had gone, and at the end of the room they had built a platform, against a wall decorated with the campaign posters (already souvenirs, already being taken away by collectors). The mood was good. It was a victory mood, and victory meant not coming last.

'It's been important to me,' Banning said, summing up the campaign. 'Mailer's obviously going to be important to American history. He'll either be a force for enormous destruction or he'll be one of the great builders. He clearly is going to do something more than write *The Armies of the Night*.'

In the evening the hall began filling up: the media people (the TV reporters grave, aware of the envy of the young), the volunteers from the boroughs, a number of strays. There was a girl in half-Mexican, half-Hindu hippy costume sitting on the floor before a red candle. She had missed the point; she had also underestimated the crowd. The girl from New Jersey turned up with a Negro. Banning, dashing and unexpected in a pale-blue silk neck-scarf, stood on the platform, like an actor in the lights, and repeatedly called for order. The results began to come in. They were as expected. Mailer was running above Congressman Scheuer, with five to six per cent of the votes; Breslin was doing even better in his contest for the Presidency of the Council: he was getting ten per cent. There was applause and stamping.

Banning said that the building would collapse. 'If you have the death wish, don't wish it on other people.'

They were rebels, and the moment was high. But they were also Americans, careful of the self in every way, never reckless. They began to go.

At about midnight Mailer, Mrs Mailer and Breslin came, cameras and lights preceding them. Through hand-shakes they walked to the platform.

'We can hardly claim victory,' Mailer said. It was their joke; victory was what they were celebrating. 'Listen. You've been terrific. We've run further on less. We've spent one-tenth of what Wagner spent. I've got five per cent of the vote; he's got thirty. So we've done twice as well as he.' He was mischievous, the hero restored to his followers. Banning stood beside me, dissolving; it was as the girl from New Jersey had said.

The TV lights heightened colour, deepening the beauty of Mrs Mailer. Mailer's eyes showed as the clearest blue. The posters on the wall glowed. It was a narrow hall, the platform central, and on the monitor screens the scene was like something out of a well-organized film. So that this last moment of glamour linked to that other, on the steps of the Old Treasury Building in Wall Street.

One notice hadn't been forgotten. *Anyone interested in GI Resistance work this summer please sign name* ... There had been four signatures in the afternoon; now the sheet was full.

I had lunch with Mailer a week later. He had spent a few days in Cape Cod; he had been to the Frazier-Quarry fight the evening before; he was editing a film that day; he would soon have to start working on his moonshot articles. 'That's going to be a strange assignment. The astronauts won't talk to me. They're writing their own book.' His writer's life was catching up with him again.

Politics seemed far away. But he was sensitive to the charge that he had split the liberal vote and helped the cause of the backlash. He thought that many of the people who had voted for him wouldn't have otherwise voted. He didn't think he had done well enough; he had lost some votes in the last week; not enough people had been reached. It astonished him that people who had shaken his hand and had been friendly hadn't voted for him.

He said again that, becoming a politician, he had become duller. But he understood now that politicians were serious when they spoke of 'service'. A politician had to serve, had always to give himself, to his supporters, to the public. It was his weakness, for instance, that he couldn't answer when people asked him whether he would clear their streets of garbage. He remained loyal to his ideas – the fifty-first state, power to the neighbourhoods – but he thought that perhaps another candidate, even someone very dull, might have done better politically with them.

Dull: it was the recurring word. It was as though, during the campaign, Mailer had redefined his writer's role by negatives. He couldn't assess the value of the campaign.

'If you don't win, you change very little.' Perhaps some of the ideas would survive: time alone would show. 'Or it might just be a curiosity. Perhaps four years from now, at the next election, someone might say, "Remember when that writer ran for Mayor?" '

Jacques Soustelle and the Decline of the West

Daily Telegraph Magazine, 26 January 1968

From a distance Jacques Soustelle appears to be two men. There is the exiled politician whose cause, *Algérie française*, Algeria is France, has been destroyed. And there is the ethnologist and scholar, the imaginative interpreter of ancient Aztec life, whose first book, published when he was twenty-three, was *Mexique, Terre Indienne*: Mexico is Indian, you might say. Both careers have been remarkable and both are likely to continue. In the serenity of the last two or three years of exile, Soustelle has become a prolific scholar again. *Arts of Ancient Mexico*, published in England a few months ago, has been recognized as a major work. And he is still only fifty-five: he will not be a political exile forever.

Serenity is Soustelle's own word. It is one of the unlikely things that have come to him in his exile which, when it began in 1962, was 'dreary and dangerous'. He was then on the run, a figure of newspaper melodrama, alleged to be plotting in Italy, Portugal, Vienna.

Early in his exile he was denounced to the Italian police by a newspaper reporter who spotted him in a Brescia hotel. The name Soustelle used then was Jean Albert Sénèque. It 'amused' him. (The Stoic philosopher Seneca, when he was very old, was accused of conspiring against the Emperor Nero, and was required to commit suicide.) But exile presently became less amusing. Soustelle was expelled from Italy, banned for a time by Switzerland and West Germany. After someone tried to kill de Gaulle in August 1962, French government agents became active all over Europe. During a carnival dance at a Munich hotel in

February 1963, ex-Colonel Argoud, another exile, was kidnapped; he was found in Paris the next morning, badly beaten up, in a van near Notre Dame. After this Soustelle dropped out of the news. When, a year later, he was arrested in a Lausanne hotel and expelled from Switzerland, he was using a more commonplace name: Jacques Lemaire.

'Two attempts were made to kill or kidnap me. The first time I didn't know. The second time I knew. A clumsy attempt had been made to bribe someone with $100,000. We played hide-and-seek for a few days. Then I shook him off.'

Now the pressure has lessened. France is still closed to him but he can move about freely outside. General de Gaulle is reported to have asked recently after Monsieur and Madame Soustelle and to have sent his good wishes to M. Soustelle through a common acquaintance. Mme Soustelle still lives and works in Paris. She, too, is an Aztec scholar. She and Jacques Soustelle were married in 1932, when he was nineteen; they have no children. They keep in touch; Soustelle confirms the Paris story that the language of the Aztecs is their secret language, which they use, or used, on the telephone.

Last March, Soustelle was a candidate in the French elections in his old constituency of Lyon. Election would have given him immunity. But he would have been arrested if he had entered France to campaign; in that month a traveller saw his name prominent among the list of proscribed people at Orly airport. Soustelle sent over a tape-recorded speech. He came second with 8,000 votes. Some people think that Soustelle should have gone to France then, that his arrest would have been a one-night affair. But Soustelle is cautious. Though he is open now to interviews and no longer feels he has to sit facing the main door of hotels, he still requires meetings to be arranged through his lawyer. And the lawyer sits in on all conversations. It is a remnant of the theatre that has surrounded Soustelle since his flight from Paris to Algiers in May 1958, when his aim was to use *Algérie française* to bring de Gaulle back to power. He was reported then to have escaped from Paris – where he was being watched – in the boot of a car.

He says it isn't true; and all that high adventure now seems so unlikely as, among the flowers and carpets of a grand hotel in the slack season, Soustelle breaks off to consider the wine list or to ask a solicitous waiter for a packet of Players *médium*. The pronunciation is for the waiter's benefit. Soustelle's own English is brisk, complex, colloquial. The occasional French words he uses – *éveilleur*, *acharné* – are those for which there is no ready English equivalent.

Photographs emphasize Soustelle's heaviness, his double chin, the firm set of the wide mouth, the rimless glasses and the dark pouches under the assessing eyes. But the face is mobile; eyes and lips are easily touched with humour. He knows about wine and will talk about it, but precisely: 'I know the vineyard', 'I know the owner'. He draws your attention to the cigarettes he smokes. They are Players; they hold a story. In Lyon in 1927 Soustelle won an English essay competition. The prize was a fortnight in London. He stayed in a house near Clapham Common. He travelled a lot on the Underground, and it was from a machine in an Underground station that he bought his first packet of cigarettes. They were Players; he has smoked them ever since.

His manner is like that of a university lecturer who knows his own reputation and will not be drawn beyond his own subject. 'If you have nothing to say to him,' his lawyer says, 'he has nothing to say to you.' Soustelle is not interested in ideas for their own sake. He always appears to speak from a well-prepared position; and this is more than an attribute of exile. He gives the impression that he came to terms with himself a long time ago, perhaps even in his precocious adolescence, and that his areas of interest have been defined by his experience: his scholarship, Mexico, the war, Algeria. He still seems able to survey his experience with wonder; he seems continually to process and refine this experience as it expands within its defined limits. It is the method neither of the scholar nor of the politician, but of both together; and it comes close to the method of the novelist, making art of egotism, creating a private impenetrable whole out of fragments which from a distance might appear unrelated.

Consider the Players cigarettes. Soustelle is conscious of them as a link with his adolescence, his early academic brilliance, his first trip to London – and the Elgin Marbles. In that fortnight he spent much time among them in the British Museum. They made him want to go to Athens; and it was only last spring, in the serenity of exile, that he was able to go. He was overwhelmed; he had expected Greek monuments to be on a smaller scale. And there was another surprise. He had always liked Roman monuments; he found he didn't like them as much in Athens: they seemed so crude. The visit helped him to clarify his ideas about the United States and the 'provincialization' of Europe. And these ideas have come directly from his experience as a scholar and politician.

Europe has been provincialized because she has withdrawn from the 'wide spaces' of Africa. Civilizations are limited in space as well as in time; and this withdrawal, like the Roman withdrawal from Dacia and Britain, is 'the first sign, the first wrinkles, of old age'. Rome incorporated Gaul; France ought to have incorporated Africa. Instead, France yielded to the 'idol' of decolonization and the pressures of mercantile capitalism and converted the low cultures of black Africa into a *poussière* of petty dictatorships.

'They will use what France left there to the last tractor, to the last bolt, to the last little teaspoon. After that, as in Tripolitania, they will let the goats graze where wheat formerly grew.'

True decolonization would have come from incorporation, with equal rights and an equal advance for all. But this was rejected; it was too difficult.

France has failed and has retreated across the Mediterranean into her own 'hexagonal' territory not through defeat – militarily Algeria was a French victory – but through decadence, through bourgeois selfishness, *les week-ends et les vacances d'été et d'hiver,* and through racialism: the unwillingness of the French to accept that Africans, Arabs, Berbers, and the Maltese, Spanish and Greek *colons* of Algeria might also have been made Frenchmen.

All civilizations have perished; even their ruins will go one day; there is no pattern and no goal. But it is Hegelian nonsense to say that the world's history is the world's justice; the stoic must always fight. Ideas which do not lead to action are just dreams; action without an 'ideological orientation' is only nihilistic opportunism.

So, until the serenity and release of exile, Soustelle the scholar-politician has been trapped in his dual role. The politician is only a part of Soustelle; and his political views, when separated from his experience, can be simplified and used by people to whom they give comfort. Like de Gaulle himself in 1958, Soustelle can be all things to all men.

All Soustelles must originally have come from the area around Soustelle, a hamlet in the Cevennes which today has a population of about one hundred, many of whom are named Soustelle. Jacques Soustelle was born in Montpelier and grew up in a semi-rural suburb of Lyon. He never knew his father; his mother remarried when he was ten; his stepfather, 'a very good man', was a motor mechanic and worked at his trade until recently. The family was Protestant. Jacques Soustelle was an only child in a house which at one time held a grandfather and three aunts, one of whom managed the household. During the first war his mother worked in a post office; later she worked in an office. 'We were not lumpen-proletariat. But we were proletariat.'

It was his class teacher, 'a very good man', who suggested to Mme Soustelle that her son should look beyond the *certificat d'études* and go to a *lycée*. He was the first of those teachers, those very good men, as Soustelle today remembers them all, who helped and guided and arranged the scholarship examinations which led to Paris and the Ecole Normale Supérieure when he was seventeen, the *agrégation* and the diploma in ethnology three years later. 'By the time I was twenty I had sat twelve competitive examinations. I wasn't very good in mathematics, but I came first in everything else.' In Paris he had also ghosted a Fourier anthology and some detective stories, to supplement his scholarship money; and he gave lessons.

He had always read a lot, and his interests had set early. He read natural history and history; even as a boy he liked reading about the Roman Empire in its third-century decline, 'that majestic and terrible spectacle'; and a taste for Jules Verne had led on to books of travel and books about exotic peoples. In Paris his thoughts turned naturally to ethnology after he met three scholars who were outstanding in the subject. Paul Rivet was one of these. Rivet was director of the Musée de l'Homme, then the Musée d'Ethnographie. Soustelle worked in the Musée de l'Homme for half the day, among the artefacts of the people he studied. To him these artefacts were works of art and not quaint; and through them he felt linked to the makers. He had developed the almost religious feeling that the finest and most comprehensive study was Man. About this time some dancers from New Caledonia came to Paris, and Soustelle was able to spend an evening with them. He remembers it as a privilege, part of his luck.

The peoples of Oceania – visited for the first time in 1945, when he was de Gaulle's Minister for the Colonies – were then his special interest. But Paul Rivet had visited Mexico in 1930 and had come back enthusiastic about the

Otomí tribe, about whom little work had been done. Rivet said he would send Soustelle out to Mexico, where there was a French cultural mission, if Soustelle became *agrégé*. Soustelle shifted his interest to Mexico. And Rivet was as good as his word. The *agrégation* results came out in August 1932; in October Soustelle and his wife – they had not long been married – sailed for Mexico.

The Soustelles worked among the Otomí in Central Mexico. They also worked among the very small tribe called the Lacandones in the south-east. In the rainy season the Soustelles went to Mexico City. There they fell among Mexican intellectuals; they became friendly with the painter Rivera. 'There was still something of the post-revolutionary fervour, a general awareness of the Mexican past. I remember that someone even organized a *velada*, a vigil, in honour of the old Aztec god Quetzalcoatl. On the other side there were people, sometimes of Indian ancestry, who thought that the Indian past was bloody and barbaric and should be forgotten. Of course I took the Indian side. But Mexico can be neither Indian nor Spanish. It is what it is: Indian and Spanish.'

The Aztec universe, as Soustelle has described it, was fragile and unstable. The world had been destroyed more than once before and was going to be destroyed again. Destruction could be stayed only by a continual offering of human blood. 'I never thought of human sacrifice as a barrier to my understanding of the Aztecs. I was imbued very early with the idea of the relativity of human morals.' In Soustelle's writings this sacrifice becomes the tragic, ennobling, wearying act of men determined to keep their world going. But destruction came. Between 1519 and 1521 the Spaniards smashed the head and heart of the developing civilization. If the Aztecs had been left alone, Soustelle thinks, they would have taken Mexico into the equivalent of the Meiji era in Japan. And, strangely, in his writings there is little anger at the destruction, and little regret for what might have developed. 'The Spaniards couldn't have acted otherwise. And we mustn't forget the efforts some Spaniards made to record and defend; or that they made possible the society in which Indian life was to reawaken.'

It was this Mexican experience – so large, so complete: grandeur, destruction, decadence, incorporation, new life – that Soustelle sought twenty years later to apply to Algeria: the equation of Mexican Indians, who had only Mexico, with Arab guerrillas, who could look to a vast Muslim world, which had once just failed to overrun Europe itself.

Soustelle was in Mexico, vice-president of a conference of Americanists, when the war broke out. He took a Dutch ship to Ramsgate and made his way to France to join the regiment in which he had done his military service in 1936. He had nothing to do for some months. Then he was recruited into the Ministry of Information which the Daladier government was establishing. He was sent back to Mexico and was there when France fell. He was prepared then to be an exile forever. He thought he would go to Canada and serve in a French Canadian regiment. But a friend in the British Consulate told him that there was a French general in London who was setting up an organization. Soustelle sent a cable to London; after three days he got a reply from one of de Gaulle's aides.

He was asked to stay on in Mexico for a little to organize support for the Free French from the local French community. Then, in a ship full of New Zealanders and Australians, future pilots, he went to England. 'At Liverpool, where we docked, I had a lot of trouble to prove that I wasn't a dubious character. But it was all right at Carlton Gardens. By some chance de Gaulle's ADC was an old schoolfellow of mine from Lyon. I met de Gaulle that very day. Two or three days later I was invited to dinner.' Then, as always later, de Gaulle's manner was one of icy formality. De Gaulle was fifty, Soustelle twenty-eight; it was the beginning of an association that lasted eighteen years. 'The great qualities in him which attracted me can still be seen today, but only in caricature.'

Soustelle was put in the 'foreign service' section and sent back to Latin America once again. Later, in London, he was National Commissioner for Information with the Liberation Committee. When the Allies landed in North Africa he became Secretary-General for Action in France. His job was to pool the resources of the Free French Intelligence with those of the Vichy Deuxième Bureau, which had fled to North Africa after the German occupation of Southern France; and to supply the French underground. 'We ran short of French banknotes, and in the end we were dropping little pieces of paper signed by Mendès-France promising to pay after the liberation. The winter of 1943–4 was horrible. So many people one knew disappeared, were killed or committed suicide. Such a waste of life. I don't think the underground in France would have lasted another year.'

The liberation came, and disillusionment. 'Everything just went back to what it was before. We overestimated the importance of the Resistance. You know, it was just point something per cent of the population that took part. I suppose the First World War was the beginning of the end for France. Fewer people were killed in the Second War. But France was occupied and we became hopelessly divided. We fought against one another in Syria and Dakar. And we didn't show sufficient restraint after the liberation. It would have been difficult, I know.'

General de Gaulle presently withdrew from politics. But Soustelle stayed on. His academic career continued. In 1955, the year he published his master-work, *The Daily Life of the Aztecs*, he became – with de Gaulle's blessing – Governor-General of Algeria, where, on 1 November 1954, the insurrection had broken out, with seventy separate incidents.

In time the insurrection tied down 500,000 French

troops. When it was over in 1962, the French had lost 14,000 men, the insurgents 140,000; 3,000 European civilians had been killed, 30,000 Arabs.

In the legend, which has lasted, Soustelle underwent a conversion in Algeria. The sight of a massacre, it was said, unhinged him; overnight the reforming pro-Arab liberal became a supporter of *Algérie française*; and his head was finally turned, so the legend goes, by the adulation of the *colons* among the crowd of a hundred thousand who gathered to cheer him off at the end of his two-year term. The massacre story is in Soustelle's favour, but it is the part of the legend he most vehemently rejects. His aim in Algeria had always been integration, on the Mexican pattern. To hand the country over to a terrorist faction would have been irresponsible, illiberal and stupid. Integration would not have been easy. It would have taken time and money, but he was prepared to use the newly-discovered resources of the Sahara to create this new Algeria. In 1958 integration was more than a possibility. But de Gaulle wasn't impressed. And to Soustelle all that has followed has been betrayal and destruction. 'Destruction is not a style: it is the negation of all styles.' The million *colons* have left; one Algerian dictatorship has been replaced by another. Arab Algeria sinks; an idea of France has been destroyed.

Soustelle's political career so far has been contained within two periods of exile. The scholar whose nationalism was aroused before the war by the German threat has known only political defeat. The defeats grew bigger even as his political authority grew. The fall of France has been followed by the fall of the French Empire. The vision of the Paris–Algiers–Brazzaville axis shrank to the vision of France stretching from Dunkirk to Tamanrasset, the Touareg town in the Sahara. Now there is only France. But if Algeria went yesterday, Corsica and Brittany might go tomorrow: it is the logic of bourgeois indifference and decline. The third world that France now seeks to lead is a chimera; de Gaulle's personal rule has taken France away from her friends. France, Soustelle feels, has been politically neutered. A fresh disaster is being prepared.

Dealing with defeat, the scholar, so exact in his own discipline, turns to the generalizations of emotion. He sees technical progress coinciding with moral and aesthetic decay. 'Our civilization has had no style for a century.' 'A civilization which is exhausted no longer attracts.' And his imprecise fears have now gone beyond the ruined idea of France to Western civilization itself. No capable enemy, no overwhelming external proletariat is yet visible. But that proves nothing.

These propositions are all debatable. Perhaps what is missing is a definition of the civilization that is threatened: perhaps such a definition will show that at the heart of the despair lies a patriotism that has been both nourished and wounded by defeat, as by a drug. Soustelle's main concern now is to return to his country. Inaction need not be ignoble. 'I might abstain from political life. But I can't admit being ostracized after twenty-seven years in the service of my country.' This is part of the serenity of exile and it may go when exile ends. The certainty of total defeat, the defeat that leaves no more battles to be fought, is its own dangerous solace. It can commit a man to hopeless duty and quixotic action and release him from the fear of failure.

This playing with the idea of defeat appears also to come from the Soustelle who makes art out of his experience and who now, in exile, has discovered all the consonances of this experience. The politician has known defeat; the ethnologist has studied a defeated people (a recent letter has told him that the Lacandones are in danger of extinction); the study of ethnology itself derives from a civilization that is on the defensive. The pattern, too neat, belongs to art. It is art, though, that comes close to self-indulgence. Even the stoicism is like romance: one of Soustelle's favourite historical tableaux is the second-century philosopher–emperor Marcus Aurelius holding the Germans on the Danube.

This romance, which holds the fear of the sudden unknown destroyer, can be taken beyond the scholar's discovery of the nervous Aztec world, awaiting Cortés. When he was a boy in Villeurbaine in Lyon, Soustelle liked to read the Roman histories of Ammianus Marcellinus. In a footnote in his last book, *Les Quatre Soleils*,* Soustelle retells a story from this historian. On a day in AD 241 the citizens of Antioch were at the theatre. Suddenly one of the actors broke off and said: 'Am I dreaming? Or are those Persians?' The audience turned. The archers of King Sapor stood on the topmost terrace; their bows were drawn.

* *The Four Suns*, translated by E. Ross, André Deutsch, London, 1971.

4

Columbus and Crusoe

Columbus and Crusoe

The Listener, 28 December 1967

The adventure of Columbus is like *Robinson Crusoe.* No one can imaginatively possess the whole; everything beyond the legend is tedious and complicating. It is so even in Björn Landström's book, *Columbus,* which makes the difficult adventure as accessible as it can be made. The text itself is a retelling from the usual sources. The maps and illustrations are more important. The maps make medieval ideas of geography clear. The illustrations, a true labour of love, are numerous and exact: ships, the islands, the people, the weather, the vegetation, and even the Flemish hawk's bell which delighted the natives until it became a measure of the gold dust the discoverer required them to collect.

In the legend Columbus is persecuted by many enemies; he goes back to Spain white-haired, in chains, and he dies in poverty and disgrace. It is Columbus's own picture: he had a feeling for theatre. His concern for gold exceeded his sovereign's: he expected to get a tenth of all that was found. The chains were not necessary; he was begged to take them off. He wore them for effect, just as, after the previous disaster, he had returned in the Franciscan habit. That disaster had its profitable side. He had sent back slaves, as he had always intended. He claimed, or his son claimed for him, that he had got rid of two-thirds of the natives of Hispaniola in two years; the remainder had been set to gathering gold dust. (This was an exaggeration: he had only got rid of a third). Even after his disgrace he fussed about his coat-of-arms, appropriating a red field for the castle of Castile, as on the royal coat-of-arms. He complained to the end about his poverty, but one of his personal gold shipments, again after his disgrace, amounted to 405 pounds. His father was a weaver; his sister married a cheesemonger; his son married a lady of royal blood. And at his death Spain hadn't gained very much. Mexico was thirteen years away; and the Indies, the source of his gold, where he thought he had discovered the Terrestrial Paradise, had become, largely through his example, *anus mundi*.

It is a story of extended horror. But it isn't only the horror that numbs response. Nor is it that the discoverer deteriorates so steadily after the discovery. It is the banality of the man. He was looking less for America or Asia than for gold; and the banality of expectation matches a continuing banality of perception. At the heart of the seamanship, the toughness, the avarice, the vindictiveness and the brutality, there is only this:

16 September. Here the Admiral says that on that day and all succeeding days they met with very mild breezes, and the mornings were very sweet, with naught lacking save the song of the nightingale. He adds: 'And the weather was like April in Andalusia.'

29 September. The air was very sweet and refreshing, so that the only thing lacking was the song of the nightingale; the sea was as calm as a river.

This is from *The Book of the First Voyage*, when he was at his most alert. The concrete details are deceptive. The sea and its life are observed, but mainly for signs of the nearness of land; just as, at the moment of discovery, the natives are studied, but only by a man 'vigilant' – his own word – for gold. 'Their hair is not curly . . . they are not at all black.' Not an anthropological interest, not the response of wonder – disappointment rather: Columbus believed that where Negroes were, there was gold. Beyond this vigilance the words and the perceptions fail. The nightingale, April in Andalusia: the props of a banal poetry are used again and again until they are without meaning. They are at an even lower level than the recent astronaut's 'Wow' – there is nothing like this pure cry of delight in Columbus. After the discovery, his gold-seeking seaman's banalities become repetitive, destroying romance and making the great adventure trivial. A book about Columbus needs to have pictures, and this is why Mr Landström's book is so valuable.

The medieval mind? But Queen Isabella wrote during the second voyage to find out what the climate was like. April in Andalusia wasn't enough: she wanted pictures, and the romance. Marco Polo, whom Columbus had read, dealt in romance; and Amerigo Vespucci, after whom the continent is not unfairly named. Vespucci thought it worth mentioning that the natives of the islands and the Main pissed casually into the hot sand during conversation, without turning aside; that the women were wanton and used a certain animal poison, sometimes lastingly fatal to virility, to increase the size of the male member. Perhaps he made this up; but though he too was vigilant and his own voyage ended in profitable slave-trading, he sought in the tradition of travel–romance to awaken wonder at the fact of the New World.

The facts about Columbus have always been known. In his own writings and in all his actions his egoism is like an exposed deformity; he condemns himself. But the heroic gloss, which is not even his own, has come down through the centuries. When the flagship ran aground at Haiti on the first voyage, the Indians were more than helpful: they wept to show their sympathy. Columbus was vigilant: he noted that it would be easy to subdue this 'cowardly' unarmed race. This is what he presently did. Mr Landström suggests that it was unfortunate and not really meant: it is the traditional gloss. On the third voyage Columbus thought he had discovered the Terrestrial Paradise. Mr Landström, again following the gloss, says that Columbus wasn't very well at the time. But it was just this sort of geography that had made him attempt the Ocean Sea.

In this adventure, as in today's adventures in space, the romance is something we ourselves have to supply. The discovery needs a hero; the contempt settles on the country that, in the legend, betrays the hero. The discovery – and it would have come without Columbus – could not but be horrible. Primitive people, once exposed, have to be subdued and utilized or somehow put down, in the Indies, Australasia, the United States, Southern Africa; even India has its aboriginal problems. Four hundred years after the great Spanish debate, convened by the Emperor, on the treatment of primitive people, Rhodesia is an imperial issue. The parallel is there; only the contemporary debate, conducted before a mass-electorate on one side and a dispossessed but indifferent primitive people on the other, is necessarily more debased.

There is no Australian or American black legend; there is at the most a romantic, self-flattering guilt. But the black legend of Spain will persist, as will the heroic legend of Columbus. The dream of the untouched, complete world, the thing for ourselves alone, the dream of Shangri-la, is an enduring human fantasy. It fell to the Spaniards to have the unique experience. Generosity and romance, then, to the discoverer; but the Spaniards will never be forgiven. And even in the violated New World the Spaniards themselves remained subject to the fantasy. The quest for El Dorado became like a recapitulation of the whole New World adventure, a wish to have it all over again; more men and money were expended on this in twenty expeditions than on the conquest of Mexico, Peru and New Granada.

Robinson Crusoe, in its essential myth-making middle part, is an aspect of the same fantasy. It is a monologue; it is all in the mind. It is the dream of being the first man in the world, of watching the first crop grow. Not only a dream of innocence: it is the dream of being suddenly, just as one is, in unquestionable control of the physical world, of possessing 'the first gun that had been fired there since the creation of the world'. It is the dream of total power. 'First, I made him know his name should be Friday, which was the day I saved his life. I called him so for the memory of the time. I likewise taught him to say master, and then let him know that was to be my name.' Friday is awkward about religion; Crusoe cannot answer. Power brings problems. Crusoe sees some cannibals about to kill and eat a man. He runs to liberate. But then he stops. What is his right to interfere? Is it just the gun? Some Spaniards are to be rescued. How will his freedom and power continue? How will they obey? Where do sanctions start in the empty world? They must sign a contract. But there is no pen, no paper: a difficulty as particular and irrational as in a nightmare. It is from more than a desert island that he is rescued. The issues can never be resolved.

Later Crusoe makes good, in that very New World, but in the settled, beaten-down slave society of Brazil. The horror of the discovery, of being the first totally powerful man in the world: that happened a long time before.

The Ultimate Colony

Daily Telegraph Magazine, 4 July 1969

British Honduras is the last British territory on the American mainland, and the present Governor ought to be the last. But this is uncertain. After five years of internal self-government, with a Premier and ministers, complete independence is still difficult. The problem is one of succession. Guatemala says that British Honduras is hers and should be returned to her. American mediation has failed. In British Honduras itself the Opposition has grown strong on the charge that the government is preparing to sell out to Guatemala. The government says it isn't. But it cannot act. It requires independence to prove its point, and independence will come only when the point is proved.

The Governor who is there, withdrawn, waiting to hand over, is Sir John Paul. His service before this was in West Africa, in Sierra Leone and the Gambia. British Honduras is his last colonial posting. He is fifty-three; his own future is uncertain. He is no longer a pensionable officer and he has as yet no job in England to go back to. In British Honduras he has little to do. He assents to bills in the name of the Queen; he is head of the Civil Service; he handles external affairs. His only direct responsibility is defence – there is a small British garrison – and public order – he shares control of the police with the minister concerned.

'Security and stability. Very important, but rather boring. One doesn't really have a full-time job. One tends to be a little isolated and divorced. Quite rightly: the country runs itself. One doesn't want to impinge.'

The Governor's tact is like sensibility, an expression of

a natural cool melancholy. He is a tall man, heavy but still athletic. During office hours he wears a white shirt and a tie, no jacket: the dress expressing the ambiguous formality of his job.

'So long as it's a dependent territory the Governor can't be an anomaly. But he can have damned little to do. It's even worse when you're a Governor-General. There's even less to do. I had a year of that in the Gambia. I saw that the only way of getting out was to write a republican constitution. I did so. We put it to the electorate and they rejected it.'

White water-skis and fishing rods lean against the wall of the Governor's office, airy and light. A half-open umbrella hangs from the grey steel safe. There is a wall-map: this all but empty British territory – 9,000 square miles, 100,000 people – incongruous in Latin America: Mexico the industrial giant to the north, Guatemala of the high mountains, the political assassinations, the temperate flowers and fruit, the Spanish and Mayan architectural antiquities, to the west and south. The wire-netted windows of the Governor's office show the sparse gardens of Government House, the two tall royal palms. Just beyond the garden wall is the Caribbean, not blue here, thick with catfish, restless scavengers of the waters of this city built on swampland.

The Empire here was never grand. It began as a seventeenth-century coastal intrusion on the Spanish American Empire. The territory doubled its size in the last century. But it was acknowledged as an intrusion and was never settled; it never became a land of plantations. The first interlopers came with their Negroes to cut logwood; their successors went further inland to cut mahogany. The mahogany forests have all been cut down. Bush remains, and scattered little bush communities: Maya Indians, who move among the mighty ruins of their civilization like any other degraded immigrant group; Black Caribs, transported from the West Indian island of St Vincent, considered by Negroes to be very black and ugly, with a bad smell; Spanish and mestizo refugees from Yucatan; and, in the last ten years, some thousands of Mennonites, a Bible-reading German–American sect, who have transformed many square miles of tropical bush, bought at fifteen shillings an acre, into the landscape of pioneer America. The descendants of the Negro log-cutters, now two-thirds of the population, and confirmed lovers of city life, live in the overcrowded coastal capital, Belize City.

From the air Belize City is an arbitrary white huddle at the edge of a sodden land where forests occasionally reflect the sun as a pale white disc. The coastline is untidy with drowned islets, like darker cloud shadows; during the 1961 hurricane one 'exclusive' American-owned islet, the cause of some local resentment, sank with its three cottages. Corrugated-iron latrines overhang the wide, slow canals of the city; in one night-club tourists are invited to feed the catfish.

In this city to be buried in 'a good dry hole' is to be lucky. In the late afternoons Negroes in jackets and ties – famous throughout Central America for their immunity to disease – walk behind the hearses to the cemetery just outside the town, waving white handkerchiefs. Afterwards they stand relaxed and emblematic among the higher tombstones, chatting, waving in the dusk. It is like a ceremony of bewildered farewell at the limit of the world. But they are only keeping off the mosquitoes and sandflies.

In Belize City the Union Jack is the flag of Negro protest against the Guatemalan claim. The Negroes of British Honduras were not plantation slaves. They were foresters. And though until recently some private houses in Belize City could still show their old slave punishment cells, with the original chains, the Negroes look back with pride to the days when, securely British, they fought shoulder to shoulder with their proprietors against the Spaniards.

'If you mention slavery here,' the Negro leader of the Opposition says, 'people would stare at you and wonder what you are talking about.'

The Guatemalans say jokingly that Guatemala should take back British Honduras and Britain should take back her Negroes. The Mexicans have a joke like this too: Mexico will take British Honduras, Guatemala will take the *negritos*.

The Vice-President of Guatemala, one of his country's leading intellectuals, doesn't find the joke funny. He doesn't want the Negroes, and he is frightened of Mexico. Mexico too has a claim, to a good half of British Honduras; but Mexico will act only if Guatemala does. The Guatemalan Vice-President despairs. He is an Indian and a patriot; he thinks that Guatemala has lost British Honduras, her twenty-third department, that the land has been spitefully spoiled by the British, who packed it out with Negroes and now require neither the land nor the Negroes.

'We have no Negro problem. A Negro has only to square his shoulders, and ten of our Indians will run. We are a weak race. The British brought over those Negroes from the Congo, Angola, the Sudan. They can work well in the heat; our Indians can't. Negroes don't fall ill easily. Malaria doesn't touch them. When the Negro mates with the Indian he produces the *sambo*. That is a race that quickly becomes degenerate.'

But Vice-Presidents change; the Guatemalan claim can at any time become a Guatemalan crusade. Nothing will happen, though, while British Honduras remains British; and the question of who will get the Negroes will remain academic so long as there is a Governor and the Union Jack flies over Government House, not as protest, but as a sign of a continuing order.

Government House is a white two-storeyed wooden building that looks like a large private house. It has only three – enormous – bedrooms. Its neutral style conceals its age. It was begun in 1815, and is not like the Government Houses of the later Empire. It has been neglected for periods and has been through many hurricanes. The tidal wave that followed the last, in 1961, covered the main floor and disfigured the central mahogany staircase, the building's only notable feature.

'It was all much grander in the Gambia. There had been East African governors before. They had, I think quite rightly, very strong views about how a Governor should be looked after. Most beautiful garden too. But of course this house suits the resources of the country.'

Government House costs the Government of British Honduras £11,000 a year. That covers everything: the monogrammed china and silver, bought through the Crown Agents in London; the three stewards, Lloyd, Garnett and George; Leone, the cook, Adela, the laundress; the two secretaries in the Governor's outer office; and the Governor himself. The Governor's ADC is an adjutant in the local Volunteer Guard.

'He's part-time. There's very little formality about this job now. The flag is lowered at 6.30. The police sentries do it. In the Gambia it was done with ceremony, with sounding – what do they call it – the Retreat. We did it once here and I must say I thought it was jolly impressive. We had a presentation of insignia and we had 350 to 400 guests and the flag was lowered and they beat the Retreat. But it taxed our resources so much we haven't done it since.

'We have receptions every month or so. Generally. It's the one place where everybody can meet. It's not a criticism, but people here tend to mix with their own group. My wife does the whole thing herself. I have no housekeeper. So when I am on my own the entertaining is restricted.

'We had a fine new car. It's just been smashed up. Brand-new Austin Princess, possibly a write-off. Most infuriating.

It's been sent to England for repairs. So we are reduced to a 1962 Rover.'

The Governor has a Land-Rover for touring. His tours are official, but muted and almost private: the Premier of British Honduras has made it clear that he doesn't like official public 'confrontations' with the Governor.

'He's very sensible. One can only talk piously.'

The Governor has been to the Assembly only once. He has only once seen, and can no longer remember, the locally designed costume – black coat, white lace cuffs, white cravat, long red gown – which the mace-bearer, a former stevedore, complainingly wears. The Assembly has been adjourned and adjourned: the Governor has never made a Speech from the Throne.

'Not that this concerns me,' the Governor says.

The Governor has taken up painting again. 'It keeps me out of mischief.' His Gambian watercolours – precise, meticulous, limpid – hang on the grey walls of Government House among old official photographs, a tarnished oil painting of the Berkshire downs and a view of the Thames.

'The Governor,' the Premier says, 'is like St John the Baptist. He gets smaller every day. Government House isn't Government House. Government House is the Premier's Office and the Assembly.'

Next to Government House is the Premier's official residence. It is an inelegant wooden bungalow, white with blue facings – the colours of the Premier's party – and a red tin roof.

In the dining-room there is a larger-than-life portrait of the Premier, done by a local artist from a photograph. It shows a youthful, mischievous man of fifty in glasses and wearing an open-necked shirt. The mischief is in the eyes and the mouth; the lips are welted and look bruised and parched. The artist had trouble with the mouth, and managed to hit it off only while listening to the Premier's voice on the radio. The Premier is heard every morning on the programme called *Wake up and Work*. The Premier is a man of mixed race: Maya Indian, European, some seepage of African. He looks white; this painting makes him black.

The Premier, the Honourable George Price, does not live in his official residence. He lives in his old family house in the rundown centre of Belize City. The unpainted house, on tall stilts, had been weathered black. It is blank and shuttered behind a high fence; and it has no front steps.

The Premier goes home early. He is unmarried; a neighbour cooks for him. He receives few visitors at home and he seldom takes home official papers. He reads novels – Thomas Mann is a favourite – and theological works. He says his prayers before going to bed. He is up at five and goes to Mass at 5.30. He does not worry through to political decisions; they come to him after the night of prayer and rest; and he is in his office punctually at eight. He has no grey hairs.

When he was a young man George Price studied for the priesthood – the disturbing mouth is that of a self-willed priest – and even his enemies say that neither age nor power has changed him. He is not interested in money; he is known to give away money; his outer office is always full of suppliants. His official car is a Land-Rover; he ceaselessly tours the empty country, greeting, checking. Then, abruptly every day, the public life ends.

'Mr Price is not like the rest of men,' the leader of the Opposition says. 'The rest of us have wives and families, recreations. Mr Price has a one-track mind. He wants to get rid of the British but we believe he is quite willing to replace the British by the Guatemalans.'

'This is a subtle thing,' the Premier's second-in-command says. 'The subtlety is that if Guatemala takes over, Mr Price has less to lose. Mr Price's complexion and racial make-up have given some credence to this belief.'

'It usually is a good way,' the Opposition second-in-command says, 'to parade as a religious person. Who's Price trying to kid? Price has long dreamed of a glorious Latin–Catholic Central American Empire.'

'Price doesn't look it,' the Guatemalan Vice-President says, 'but he is a Negro. If he was a Maya Indian and a patriot, as some people say, he wouldn't have got mixed up with all those Negroes over there.'

Once, when he was only a nationalist agitator, the first in British Honduras, the Guatemalan claim was useful to George Price. Now, as Premier, he is trapped by the claim; it erodes his power.

'I don't think anybody felt the life was going to come so quickly to an end. After Ghana one could do nothing about it and one wanted to do nothing about it.'

A visit to Trinidad in 1934–5 was the Governor's first glimpse of a colony. It made him think of a career in the Colonial Service.

'I liked the *ambience*, the friendliness of the people. Mark you, in those days there were far fewer opportunities for people like myself in the industrial or commercial world, for people who had – it tends to be a dirty word – a public school education.' The Governor was at Weymouth in Dorset. 'Long since defunct.'

'I applied to join the Colonial Service before the war. I was at Cambridge, came down in June 1939. Thought I might as well have a regular commission and get properly involved instead of hanging around getting pushed around. I was a prisoner most of the war. I was in the Royal Tank Corps. Captured in Calais in 1940. After the war I was seconded as ADC to Sierra Leone. When I was released from the Army I joined the Colonial Service and became a District Commissioner. I had great difficulty getting rid of my regular commission. Not because they particularly wanted me – I'm sure of that – but on principle . . .

'The work of ADC was one of the most fascinating jobs you could ever have. You were virtually on your own in those days. You got very attached to the people. We all felt a sense of participation. One talks of colonialism now ... People tend to look at Empire in the context of the last fifty or one hundred years. But I think it fair to say that without Empire over the centuries there wouldn't have been the spread of knowledge. Africa is the most contentious example, I suppose. I feel there must be something on the credit side. This is no criticism of the local people. They were prisoners of their own circumstances ...

'It was the most rewarding part of my life. You were very clearly defined. One knew exactly, in one's modest way, what one was trying to do. You weren't humbugged too much by what we used to call the Secretariat. We were alone much of the time. Pretty early evenings, no electric lights. We had small children. That kept us pretty busy. We used to read a lot. One spent a lot of time on tour. Of course, in those days one walked, seeing what was going on.'

On the stroke of eight the Land-Rover sweeps up the short drive to the portico of Government House. The Premier, tall and slender, in an open-necked braided Yucatan-style shirt, bounces out after his aide.

'Morning, Excellency!'

The Premier likes to use titles and he always appears to put them between inverted commas.

It is the day of the Premier's weekly tour; the visiting writer will go with him. The Governor, in white shirt and tie, is there to greet the Premier. The formalities are brief and urgent. The aide runs to close the Land-Rover door, and soon we are on the road.

'Marnin', Miss Virginia.'

When the Premier waves he abandons conversation and concentrates; he is like a man giving a benediction.

Nine men are standing around a small patch on the

main road. The PWD lorries have broken down again. The Premier makes a note. Later we pass PWD mounds of earth.

'Jarge Price, clean the road!' someone shouts.

We stop often.

'Marnin', marnin'.'

The Premier strides ahead in his flapping shirt, loose tan trousers and big black shoes. The aide runs, to protect the Premier against enraged dogs. The muscular young Negro driver stands beside his vehicle, chewing gum, tall, in boots, tight jeans and jersey, dark glasses.

'Marnin'. It's Jarge Price, the Premier. Lemme see your kitchen. Lemme see wa' you cook this marnin'.'

He lifts lids, examines breakfast plates, gives his benediction. And we bolt for the Land-Rover.

When George Price left the seminary, for financial reasons, he found a job with a local self-made timber millionaire. He stayed with him for fourteen years as secretary and travelling companion.

'We travelled everywhere. I remember one day at a hotel in Chicago putting a value on the people around the dining table. I made it 300 million dollars. When you mix with people like that all the time you can't feel too much envy. I very early on had the feeling of *sic transit gloria mundi*. Turton had all this money. But he was a sick man . . .

'Whenever I went into a bank I used to feel: you are entering the temple of the capitalists. I suppose I used to say it sometimes. Turton didn't always like the things I said. I was quoting to him one day from the 1931 Encyclical – I think it was *Quadragesimo Anno*. About relations between employer and worker, the living wage and so on. He listened and I thought I was getting through. At the end he said, "Jarge, the Pope doesn't know a shit about business."

'It was Turton who made me go into politics. He said,

"You will go into politics." He made me run for the Belize City Council in 1944. I lost. Now if a doctor said to me to give up politics, I wouldn't.'

But politics do not stand still. The colonial politician who is the first leader and educator is also the man who most speedily makes himself out of date. Politics as the vocation of the failed priest, the empty land as the parish: it no longer answers. The Guatemalan claim has made the politics of British Honduras artificial and static. Development, like independence itself, recedes. The Premier has been to these villages too often before; he is no longer a man with news.

'They don't seem to be looking for a messiah,' the Premier's second-in-command says. 'They seem to want participation. Or collective leadership. I think Mr Price senses this change in the country. He has recently enlarged his cabinet.'

'I am getting old,' the Premier says. 'I am not a fighter as I used to be.'

'One's career has changed quite completely from the way one envisaged it,' the Governor says. 'One of the ironies is that most of the time one's been working oneself out of a job. I've been extremely lucky. Very few left now, out of the old Colonial Service. Infinitesimal number really.'

The world intrudes. The sons of people once content with the Premier's benediction go away to study and come back and curse both parties. They talk of Vietnam and Black Power. They undermine the Negro loyalty to the slave past.

'The whites are buying up the land. English colonialism tried to condition the black man against using the land. There was a concerted effort by the English colonialists to have their black slaves remain log-cutters.

It became a sort of phallic symbol to the black to be a log-cutter.'

The politics of British Honduras have always had a racial–religious undertone: the Negro–Protestant town, the Roman Catholic country. Now race threatens to make the old politics even more irrelevant. The premier, white below his carefully maintained tan, a political vanity, is especially vulnerable.

The Governor gets a report on the latest Black Power meeting.

'They pulled in 150 last night. I must say I couldn't make head or tail of what was said.'

We are having drinks around the small new pool at the side of Government House. The sea breeze is moist.

'Do you think he'll have lunch with me?' the American Consul asks. He is concerned: the local spokesman for Black Power, who is just twenty-one, went to an American university on an American government scholarship. 'I wish someone would give me 12,000 dollars to send my son to college.'

The Consul is friendly, intelligent. He has had some experience of British colonies in transition. He 'watched' the affairs of British Guiana at a time when the Jagan government was being overthrown by Negro racist riots and an American-supported strike.

The United States has an interest: it is the true issue of imperial succession.

The Governor, anxious to be active again, thinks of his own future.

'There is no obligation on the part of the government to find another job for me. I don't know what the future holds. But we've been lucky. The big concern was the education of one's daughters, and we are more or less at the end of that tunnel.'

The Governor will leave the Colonial Service with an affection for the countries he worked in, but with no great nostalgia. He will remain concerned about the debasing effect of tourism on backward countries, and all that these countries have to do.

'Take the Gambia. You couldn't get people to go to school in some areas. Most awful waste of manpower. Those people, as of now, they've not a hope in hell, and they'll be living for, what, sixty, seventy years.'

The Governor will also be taking back a memory of the midnight handover in the Gambia: the Union Jack coming down, the lights going off and coming on again, the new Gambian flag in place, the handshakes from the Gambians, delighted but also managing in that moment to express a personal concern for the Governor.

The flag that came down that midnight is in the Governor's Hampshire cottage. It was hung out of the window to celebrate his daughters' success in the A-level examinations.

The Premier plans to build a retreat in the cool Mountain Pine Ridge region.

'Mr Price knows how to survive,' the Premier's second-in-command says. 'He's a natural politician. I don't see the demise of Mr Price.'

But in the clerical mischievousness of the Premier, which can at times be like arrogance, and in his daily routine, there is already more than a hint of withdrawal. He will fight to the end. But he also tells his supporters, 'My day will come. I will go.'

He has never cared for the things of the world. But for most of his life he has been immersed in them, and he often reflects on the strangeness of his career.

'I have this recurring dream. I am in church. Someone is saying mass – Turton, my old employer, or Pinks, one of his managers – and I wonder why I, who would so much like to be up there, am not, and that old sinner is.'

St Kitts: Papa and the Power Set

The New York Review of Books, 8 May 1969

After more than twenty years as a folk leader, one of the Negro shepherd–kings of the Caribbean, Robert Bradshaw of St Kitts – 'Papa' to his followers – is in trouble. Two years ago he became the first Premier of the three-island state of St Kitts–Nevis–Anguilla. The state had a total area of 153 square miles and a population of 57,000. It has since become smaller. Anguilla has seceded and apparently gone for good, with its own islet dependencies of Scrub Island, Dog Island, and Anguillita: a loss of thirty-five square miles and 6,000 people. There is discontent in Nevis, fifty square miles. In St Kitts itself, Papa Bradshaw's base, there is a dangerous opposition.

The opposition union is called WAM, the opposition political party PAM. WAM and PAM: it is part of the deadly comic-strip humour of Negro politics. These are still only the politics of kingship, in which there are as yet no rules for succession. It is only when leaders like Papa Bradshaw are in trouble, when they are threatened and fight back, that they become known outside their islands; and it is an irony of their kingship that they are then presented as dangerous clowns. Once Papa Bradshaw's yellow Rolls-Royce was thought to be a suitable emblem of his kingship and courage, a token of Negro redemption. Few people outside knew about the Rolls-Royce; now it is famous and half a joke.

The folk leader who has been challenged cannot afford to lose. To lose is to be without a role, to be altogether ridiculous.

'Papa Bradsha' started something,' a supporter says. 'As long as he lives he will have to continue it.'

Bradshaw prepares to continue. The opposition are not allowed to broadcast; their supporters say they do not find it easy to get jobs. Men are recruited from the other Caribbean islands for the police. The St Kitts army, called the Defence Force, is said to have been increased to 120; Papa Bradshaw is the Colonel. There are reports of a helicopter ready to police the island's sixty-eight square miles.

It has been played out in other countries, this drama of the folk leader who rules where he once securely agitated and finds that power has brought insecurity. In St Kitts the scale is small, and in the simplicity of the setting the situation appears staged.

Think of a Caribbean island roughly oval in shape. Indent the coastline: beaches here, low cliffs there. Below the sharp and bare 4,000-foot peak of a central mountain chain there is a forest. Then the land slopes green and trimmed with sugar-cane, uncluttered with houses or peasant allotments, all the way down to the sea. A narrow coast road encircles the island; it is impossible to get lost. The plantation workers live beside this road, squeezed between sugar-cane and sea. Their timber houses are among the tiniest in the world.

All the history of St Kitts is on this road. There, among those houses on low stilts, whose dirt yards run down through tangled greenery to the sea, Sir Thomas Warner landed in 1623, to found the first British colony in the West Indies. Here, in the barest opening in the sugar-cane, are two rocks crudely carved by the aboriginal Caribs, whom the English and French united to exterminate just there, at Bloody River, now a dip in the road. Sir Thomas Warner is buried in that churchyard. Not far away are the massive eighteenth-century fortifications of Brimstone Hill, once guarding the sugar-rich slave islands and the convoys that assembled in the calm water here for the run to England. The cannons still point; the site has been restored.

In the south-east the flat coastal strip broadens out into a little plain. Here, still set in the level green of sugar-cane, are the air-strip and the capital, Basseterre. There is one vertical in this plain: the tall white chimney of the island's single sugar factory.

The neatness and order is still like the order of the past. It speaks of Papa Bradshaw's failure. He hasn't changed much. His fame came early, as an organizer of the sugar workers; a thirteen-week strike in 1948 is part of the island's folk-lore. But Bradshaw's plantation victories mean less today to the young. They do not wish to work on the plantations. They look for 'development' – and they mean tourism – on their own island. The air over nearby Antigua rocks with 'Sunjets' and 'Fiesta Jets'. St Kitts only has brochures and plans; the airfield can only take Viscounts. It is unspoiled; the tourists do not come. The feeling among the young is that Papa Bradshaw has sold out to the sugar interests and wants no change.

And Bradshaw's victories were only of St Kitts. They meant little to the peasant farmers of Nevis, and nothing to the long-independent farmers and fishermen of Anguilla, seventy miles away. The Nevisians and Anguillans never voted for Bradshaw. Bradshaw didn't need their votes, but he was irritated. He said he would put pepper in the soup of the Nevisians and bones in their rice; he would turn Anguilla into a desert and make the Anguillans suck salt. That was eleven years ago.

'Gahd bless Papa Bradsha' for wa' he do.' It is only the old and the devout among the plantation Negroes in St Kitts who say that now. They remember the *ola* or trash houses, the cruel contract system, the barefoot children and the disease. Bradshaw himself worked as a young man in the Basseterre sugar factory; he carries a damaged hand as a mark of that service. Like many folk leaders, he never moved far beyond his first inspiration. It is also true that, like many folk leaders, he is responsible for the hope and the restlessness by which he is now, at the age of fifty-one, rejected.

The weatherbeaten little town of Basseterre also has a stage-set simplicity. There is a church at the end of the main street. PAM hangs its home-made board in the veranda of a rickety little house. Directly opposite is a building as rickety, but larger; this is labelled 'Masses House' and is the headquarters of the Bradshaw union. At times of tension this section of the main street is known as the Gaza Strip.

Masses House has a printery which every day runs off 1,200 copies of a ragged miniature newspaper called *The Labour Spokesman*. Even with large headlines there isn't always enough news to fill the front page; sometimes a joke, headlined 'Humour', has to be added. Sport is good for a page or two or three. A cricketer like Sobers can make the local sportswriter ambitious. 'The shy boy of seventeen, not yet lost his Mother's features on his debut against England in the West Indies in 1954, has probably rose to the pinnacle of being the greatest cricketer both of our time and the medieval age. If W. G. Grace were to twitch in his grave at the comment he would only turn over on the other side to nod his approval.'

A few doors away from Masses House is Government Headquarters, a modernistic building of three storeys. Grey air-conditioners project from its façade; a pool in the patio is visible through the glass wall. The hotel is opposite, a converted old timber house. The manager is a gentle second-generation Lebanese whose nerves have been worn fine by the harassments of his large family, his staff, untrained or temperamental, the occasional assertive Negro group, and the political situation. 'Have you seen our Premier, sir?' He supports Bradshaw but avoids controversy; he knows now he will never see Beirut.

A short side street leads to Pall Mall Square: the church, the timbered colonial–Georgian Public Library and Court, the St Kitts Club, the private houses with lower floors of masonry, upper floors shingled, white and fragile, and steep four-sided roofs. The garden is unkempt, the wire fences around the central Victorian fountain trampled down, the lamp-standards empty and rusting; but the trees and flowers and the backdrop of mountains are still spectacular. Pall Mall Square is where PAM holds its public meetings. It is also, as all St Kitts knows, the place where, among trees and flowers and buildings like these, 'new' Negroes from Africa were put up for auction, after being rested and nourished in the importers' barracoons, which were there, on the beach, not far from today's oil-storage tanks.

The past crowds the tiny island like the sugar-cane itself. Deeper and deeper protest is always possible.

At about ten every morning the guards change outside Government Headquarters. The green-bereted officer shouts, boots stamp; and the two relieved soldiers, looking quickly up and down the street, get into the back of the idling Land-Rover and are driven to Defence Force Headquarters, an exposed wooden hut on high ground near ZIZ, the one-studio radio station.

Against the soft green hills beyond Basseterre, the bright blue sea and the cloud-topped peak of Nevis, a Negro lounges in a washed-out paratrooper's uniform, thin and bandy-legged, zipped-up and tight, like a soft toy.

It seems to be drama for the sake of drama. But there are bullet marks on the inside of the hut. These are shown as evidence of the armed raid that was made on Basseterre by persons unknown in June 1967, at the beginning of the Anguillan crisis. The police station was also attacked. Many shots were fired but no one was killed; the raiders disappeared. Bradshaw added to his legend by walking the next morning from Government Headquarters to

Masses House in the uniform of a Colonel, with a rifle, bandolier, and binoculars.

The raid remains a mystery. Some people believe it was staged, but there are Anguillans who now say that they were responsible and that their aim was to protect the independence of their island by kidnapping Bradshaw and holding him as a hostage. The raid failed because it was badly organized – no one had thought about transport in Basseterre – and because Bradshaw had been tipped off by an Anguillan businessman.

Days after the raid leading members of PAM and WAM were arrested. They went on trial four months later. Defence lawyers were harassed; and Bradshaw's supporters demonstrated when all the accused men were acquitted. Ever since, the rule of law in St Kitts has appeared to be in danger. The definition of power has become simple.

> I see them:
> These bold men; these rare men –
> Above all other men that toil –
> That LIVE the truth; that suffer:
> These policemen. We love them!

The poem is from *The Labour Spokesman*. There may no longer be a danger from Anguilla, but the police and the army have come to St Kitts to stay.

I first saw St Kitts eight years ago, at night, from a broken-down immigrant ship in Basseterre harbour. We didn't land. The emigrants had been rocking for some time in the bay in large open boats. The ship's lights played on sweated shirts and dresses, red eyes in up-turned oily faces, cardboard boxes and suitcases painted with names and careful addresses in England.

In the morning, on the open sea, the nightmare was over. The jackets and ties and the suitcases had gone. The emigrants, as I found out, moving among them, were politically educated. Copies of *The Labour Spokesman* were about. Many of the emigrants from Anguilla, which had been recently hit by a hurricane, were in constant touch with God.

The emigrants had a leader. He was a slender young mulatto, going to England to do law. He moved among the emigrants like a trusted agitator; he was protective. He was a man of some background and his political concern, in such circumstances, seemed unusual. He mistrusted my inquiries. He thought I was a British agent and told the emigrants not to talk to me. They became unfriendly; word spread that I had called one of them a nigger. I was rescued from the adventure by a young Baptist missionary.

I didn't get the name of the ship-board leader then. In St Kitts and the Caribbean he is now famous. He did more than study law. He returned to St Kitts to challenge Bradshaw. He founded PAM. He has been jailed, tried, and acquitted; he is only thirty-one. He is Dr William Herbert. A good deal of his magic in St Kitts, his power to challenge, comes from that title of Doctor – obtained for a legal thesis – which he was then travelling to London to get.

He came into the Basseterre hotel dining-room one morning. As soon as we were introduced he reminded me of our last meeting. The ship, he said, was Spanish and disorganized and he was young. He was as restless and swift and West Indian-handsome as I had remembered: his five months in jail have not marked him.

'I don't want to frighten you,' he said, when he came to see me later that day. 'But you should be careful. Writers can disappear. Two soldiers will be watching the hotel tonight.'

We drove to a rusting seaside bar, deserted, a failed tourist amenity.

'Have you seen Bradshaw?'

I said that the feeling in Government Headquarters was that I might be a British agent. Mr Bradshaw wouldn't give an interview, but he had come over to the hotel one morning to greet me.

'He's an interesting man. He knows a lot about African art and magic and so on. It perhaps explains his hold, you know.'

We went to look at Frigate Bay, part of the uninhabited area of scrub and salt-ponds which is attached like a tail to the oval mass of St Kitts. The government had recently announced a £29-million tourist development plan for Frigate Bay. Some in-transit cruise passengers had been taken to inspect the site a few days before; *The Labour Spokesman* had announced is as the start of the tourist season.

'Development!' Herbert said, waving at the desolation. 'If you come here at night they shoot you, you know. It's a military area. They say we are trying to sabotage.'

On the way back we detoured through some Basseterre slum streets. Herbert waved at women and children. '*How, how, man?*' Many waved back. He said it was his method, concentrating on the women and children; they drew the men in.

Herbert is the first and only Ph.D. in St Kitts. Beside him, Bradshaw is archaic, the leader of people lifted up from despair, the man of the people who in power achieves a personal style which all then feel they share. In St Kitts and the West Indies Bradshaw is now a legend, for the gold swizzle-stick he is reputed to bring out at parties to stir his champagne, the gold brush for his moustache, the formal English dress, even the silk hose and buckle shoes on some ceremonial occasions, the vintage yellow Rolls-Royce. He has a local reputation for his knowledge of antiques and African art and for his book-reading. He is believed to be a member of several book clubs. He reads much Winston Churchill; his favourite book, his PRO told me, is *The Good Earth*; his favourite comic strip, *Li'l Abner*.

It is an attractive legend. But I found him subdued, in dress and speech. I was sorry he didn't want to talk more to me; he said he had suffered much from writers. I understood. I looked at his moustache and thought of the gold brush. He is well-built, a young fifty-one, one of those men made ordinary by their photographs. We talked standing up. His speech was precise, very British, with little of St Kitts in his accent. He stood obliquely to me; he wore dark glasses. As we walked down the hotel steps to the Land-Rover with his party's slogan, 'Labour Leads', he told me he was pessimistic about the future of small countries like St Kitts. He worked, but he was full of despair. He had supported the West Indian Federation, but that had failed. And it is true that Bradshaw began to lose his grip on St Kitts during his time as a minister in the West Indian Federal Government, whose headquarters was in Trinidad.

The Negro folk leader is a peasant leader. St Kitts is like a black English parish, far from the source of beauty and fashion. The folk leader who emerges requires, by his exceptional gifts, to be absorbed into that higher society of which the parish is a shadow. For leaders like Bradshaw, though, there is no such society. They are linked forever to the primitives who were the source of their original power. They are doomed to smallness; they have to create their own style. Christophe, Emperor of Haiti, creator of a Negro aristocracy with laughable names, came from this very island of St Kitts, where he was a slave and a tailor; the inspiration for the Citadel in Haiti came from those fortifications at Brimstone Hill beside the littoral road.

The difference between Herbert and Bradshaw is the difference between Herbert's title of Doctor and Bradshaw's title of Papa. Each man's manner seems to contradict his title. Herbert has none of Bradshaw's applied style. His out-of-court dress is casual; his car is old; the house he is building outside Basseterre is the usual St Kitts miniature. His speech is more colloquial than Bradshaw's, his accent more local. His manners are at once middle-class and popular, one mode containing the other. He never strains; he moves with the assurance of his class and his looks. To all this he adds the Ph.D.

'Tell me,' Bradshaw's black PRO asked with some bitterness, 'who do you think is the more educated man? Herbert or Bradshaw?'

It would have been too sophisticated a question to put to the young and newly educated who went to Herbert's early lectures on economics, law, and political theory in Pall Mall Square.

'Studyation is better than education,' Bradshaw said, comforting his ageing illiterates from the canefields. It became one of his *mots*.

But Herbert grew as the leader of literate protest. Everything became his cause. New electricity rates were announced: large users were to pay less per unit. Standard practice in other countries, but Herbert and PAM said the new rates were unfair to the poor of St Kitts. The poor agreed.

Bradshaw and one of his ministers became law students; Bradshaw was almost fifty. The faded notifications of their enrolment in a London Inn are still displayed in the portico of the Court in Pall Mall Square; both men were said to be eating dinners during their official trips to London. Then Anguilla seceded; PAM and WAM were as troublesome as their names; the world press was hostile. Herbert, jailed, tried, acquitted, became a Caribbean figure. Bradshaw was isolated. He appeared to be on the way out. But then he recruited a young St Kitts lawyer-lecturer as his Public Relations Officer.

This man has saved Bradshaw, and in a few months he has given a new twist to St Kitts politics. Bradshaw's tactics have changed. He is no longer the established leader on the defensive, attracting fresh agitation. He has become once again the leader of protest. It is in protest that he now competes with Herbert. The young PRO has provided the lectures and the intellectual backing. He is known to the irreverent as Bradshaw's Race Relations Officer. The cause is Black Power.

The avowed aim is the dismantling of that order which the geography of the island illustrates. The word the PRO sometimes uses is Revolution. The word has got to the white suburb of Fortlands and the Golf Club, where the little group of English expatriates is known as the Whisperers.

Someone put it like this: 'What Bradshaw now wants to do is to make a fresh start, with the land and the people.'

The politics of St Kitts today, opaque to the visitor looking for principles and areas of difference, become clearer as soon as it is realized that both parties are parties of protest, in the vacuum of independence; and that for both parties the cause of protest is that past, of slavery. What is at stake is the kingship, and this has recently been simplified. The difficult message of Black Power – identity, economic involvement, solidarity, as the PRO defines it – has become mangled in transmission. It can now be heard that Bradshaw, for all the English aspirations of his past, is a full-blooded Ashanti. Herbert is visibly mulatto.

Herbert's father was Labour Relations Officer for the sugar industry at the time of Bradshaw's famous thirteen-week strike. It was a difficult time for the Herbert family. They were threatened and abused by the strikers; and the St Kitts story is that Herbert, still a boy, met Bradshaw in the street one day and vowed to get even. Herbert says the meeting may have taken place, but he doesn't remember it.

I asked him now whether power in St Kitts was worth the time, the energy, the dangers.

'A man is in the sea,' Herbert said. 'He must swim.'

There is still a Government House in St Kitts, a modest, wide-verandaed timber house on an airy hill. The butler wears white; a lithograph of a local scene, a gift of the

Queen, hangs in the drawing-room; there is a signed photograph of the Duke of Edinburgh. The governor is a Negro knight from another island, a much respected lawyer and academic. He is without a role; he is isolated from the local politics of kingship, this fight between the lawyers, in which the rule of law may go. He has spent much of his time in Government House working on a study of recent West Indian constitution-making. It is called *The Way to Power*.

The PRO on whom Bradshaw depends, the lawyer-lecturer to whom he has surrendered part of his power, is Lee Moore, a short, slight, bearded, country-born Negro of about thirty. Moore says that when he came back to St Kitts from London he rejected the view that what was needed in St Kitts was a Negro aristocracy. But the political usefulness of Black Power was only accidentally discovered, in the excitement that followed a lecture he gave on the subject.

Now, like Herbert, Lee Moore drives around the circular St Kitts road, mixing law business with campaigning, waving, mixing gravity with heartiness. On his car there is a sticker, cut out from a petrol advertisement: *Join the Power Set*.

I made a tour with him late one afternoon. Shortly after nightfall we had a puncture. He was unwilling to use the jack; he said he didn't know where to put it. He crouched and peered; he was confused. Some cars went by without stopping. I began to fear for his clothes and dignity. Then two cyclists passed. They shouted and came back to help. 'We thought it was one of those brutes,' one of them said. A van stopped. The jack wasn't used. The car was lifted while the wheel was changed.

Moore was in a state of some excitement when we drove off again, and it was a little time before I understood that is was an important triumph.

'It's how I always change a wheel. Did you hear what

those boys on the cycles shouted? *"It's Lee Moore's car."* '

Power, the willing services of the simple and the protecting: another man of the people in the making, another Negro on the move.

After a while he said reflectively, 'If it was Herbert he would still be there, I can tell you.'

Herbert, though, might have used the jack.

Anguilla: The Shipwrecked Six Thousand

The New York Review of Books, 24 April 1969

Among the green and hilly islands of the Caribbean Anguilla is like a mistake, a sport. It is seventeen miles long and two miles wide and so flat that when Anguillans give you directions they don't tell you to turn right or left; they say east or west. It is rocky and arid. There are no palm trees, no big trees. Mangrove is thick above the beaches, which look as they must have done when Columbus came. The forests that then existed have long been cut down; and the Anguillans, charcoal-burners and boat-builders, are the natural enemies of anything green that looks like growing big.

Sugar-cane used to grow in some places, but even in the days of slavery it was never an island of plantations. In 1825, nine years before the abolition of slavery in the British Empire, there were about three hundred white people and three hundred free coloureds, people of mixed race. Between them they kept about three thousand Negroes. The Negroes were a liability. On other Caribbean islands Negroes were let off on Saturdays to work on their own plots. In Anguilla they were turned loose for half the week to forage for themselves.

Today there are only about twelve thousand Anguillans. Half of them live or work overseas, in the nearby United States Virgin Islands, in Harlem, and in Slough in Buckinghamshire, known locally as Sloughbucks. But there are houses and plots for most of them to return to; the desolate island has long been parcelled out.

In mid-December last year, when I was there, the island was filling up for Christmas. The Viscount aircraft of

LIAT, Leeward Islands Air Transport ('We fly where buccaneers sailed'), had stopped calling ever since Anguilla rebelled in 1967 and broke away from the newly independent three-island British Commonwealth state of St Kitts-Nevis-Anguilla. But the Anguillans (after chasing away an American and his DC-3) had set up three fiercely competitive little airlines of their own, Air Anguilla, Anguilla Airways, Valley Air Services, each with its own livery and its own five-passenger Piper Aztecs regularly doing the five-minute, five-dollar connecting hop from St Martin.

More than any other Caribbean community, the Anguillans have the sense of home. The land has been theirs immemorially; no humiliation attaches to it. There are no Great Houses, as in St Kitts; there are not even ruins.

For the Anguillans history begins with the myth of a shipwreck. This was how the white founders came, the ancestors of the now multi-coloured clans of Flemings, Hodges, Richardsons, Websters, Gumbs. About the arrival of the Negroes there is some confusion. Many know they were imported as slaves. But one young man was sure they were here before the shipwreck. Another felt they had come a year or two after. He didn't know how or why. 'I forget that part.' The past does not count. The Anguillans have lived for too long like a shipwrecked community.

They are not well educated. Instead, they have skills, like boat-building, and religion, which is a continual excitement. Few Anguillans act without divine guidance. The Anguillan exodus to Sloughbucks that began in 1960 had the sanction of God; and a similar certitude is behind the secession from St Kitts and the boldness of many recent Anguillan actions.

So close to God, the Anguillans are not fanatical. They have the Negro openness to new faiths. Eight years ago Mr Webster, the now deposed President, re-thought his position and, at the age of thirty-four, left the Anglicans for the Seventh Day Adventists. He would like to see more and varied missionary activity on the island. 'If the Jehovah's Witnesses or any other denomination convert one or ten souls they are doing a good job and serving the community. Because our basic plan is to keep Anguillans as pious as possible. This keeps out partial and immoral thoughts.'

The island has its own prophet, Judge Gumbs, Brother George Gumbs (Prophet), as he signs his messages to the new local weekly. He is not without honour; he is consulted by high and low. When the spirit moves him he cycles around with a fife and drum, 'a short black man with a cap' (an Anguillan description), preaching and sometimes warning. He is said to get a frenzied feeling about a particular place, a field, a stretch of road; a few days later the disaster occurs. In December, three or four days after Mr Webster said that Anguilla was going to leave the Commonwealth altogether, Judge Gumbs was out, preaching. I didn't see him, but I was told he had no news; he just asked the people to pray. No news from Judge Gumbs was good news.

Certain other reverences remain, to bind the community: certain families act or take decisions in times of crisis. The reverences follow the antique patterns, whose origins have been forgotten. Colour is accidental, and nothing angers the Anguillans more than the propaganda from St Kitts, seventy miles away, that their rebellion is the rebellion of a slave island, with the blacks loyally following the whites and browns. The reverences are of Anguilla, and the Anguillans describe themselves as Negroes. Mr Webster, who could be of any race between the Mediterranean and India, describes himself as a Negro. It is true: losing the historical sense, the Anguillans have also lost the racial sense. It isn't an easy thing to put across, especially to St Kitts, which is now playing with its own concept of Black Power.

*

Anguillans have never liked being administratively linked with St Kitts, and they have hated Robert Bradshaw, the St Kitts Premier, ever since, angered by their indifference, he said he would turn the island into a desert and make the Anguillans suck salt. They were frightened by the idea of an independent St Kitts-Nevis-Anguilla under Bradshaw's rule; and there was a riot in February, 1967, when, as part of the independence celebrations, St Kitts sent over some beauty queens to give a show in the Anguilla High School. The police used tear gas, but inefficiently. They gassed the queens and the loyal audience, not the enraged Anguillans outside. Reinforcements from St Kitts's one-hundred-man Police Force were flown in next day. Houses were searched; the Anguillan leaders took to the bush.

It was the signal for a general revolt. The Warden's house was set on fire; the Warden fled. From time to time during the next three months shots were fired at the police station at night. The hotel where the acting Warden was staying was set on fire; he too left. The next day the bank manager was attacked. Two days later several hundred Anguillans rushed the police station. The seventeen policemen offered no fight; they were put on a plane and sent back to St Kitts; and the Anguillans set up their own five-man police force.

Ten days later, fearing outside intervention (Jamaica nearly sent in troops), and guided now by that religious certitude, the Anguillans raided St Kitts and shot up the police station and Defence Force Headquarters. The raid, by twelve men, was openly planned; people went down to the wharf in the afternoon to wave as the fifty-foot cutter left for St Kitts. Five and a half hours later the cutter tied up, quite simply, at the main pier in St Kitts. Then the Anguillans discovered they hadn't thought about motorcars. They had intended to kidnap Bradshaw; they had to be content with scaring him.

Some time later there was a report that thirty-five men

from St Kitts had invaded Anguilla. The man who was the Provisional President flew over the reported landing area in an Aztec, dropping leaflets asking the invaders to surrender. But there were no invaders. The fighting was over. All that followed were words; secession was a fact. Anguilla had become the world's smallest republic.

Its status was ambiguous. It still considered itself within the Commonwealth. It looked to London for a constitutional settlement, for some sanction of its separation from St Kitts. London didn't know what to do. For more than two hundred years, in fact, no one had really wanted Anguilla or had known what to do with it. The place was a mistake.

It had its formalities. When you got off the Piper Aztec you went through Anguillan Immigration and Customs; they were both in one room of the two-roomed airport building. The Immigration man had a khaki uniform, an Anguilla badge, and an Anguilla rubber-stamp. You needed an Anguillan driving licence; it cost a dollar; you paid at the Police Station in the long low Administration Building. The five-man police force was enough; there was little crime. Women quarrelled and used four-letter words; the police visited and 'warned'; that, in the main, was the routine. There was a jail, and there was one prisoner. He had been there for a year, a St Kitts man on a charge of murder. There was no magistrate to try him. Mr Webster was hoping to deport the man as soon as the secession issue was settled.

In the Post Office you bought Anguillan stamps, designed and produced by an English firm and sold by them to overseas collectors for a fifteen per cent commission. Incoming mails were regular; Anguilla had beaten the St Kitts postal ban by having two box numbers on the half French, half Dutch island of St Martin. In the Treasury, next door to the Post Office, there was a notice about the new two per cent income tax. Other taxes, on liquor and petrol, had been lowered, to increase consumption and revenue; and it had worked. People told me there were more cars in Anguilla than ever before.

The administration, spare and efficient, had been inherited with the Administration Building. An elected fifteen-man Council ruled. This structure of government was like sophistication in a community that had for long organized itself around its own reverences. The island ran itself; it worked. After half a day the visitor had to remind himself of size and quaintness. It was there, in the new flag, designed by some Americans: a circle of three orange dolphins on white, a lower stripe of turquoise. And in the fanciful anthem, composed by a local 'group':

... An island where the golden corn is waving in the breeze! An island full of sunshine and where Nature e'er doth please.

The visitor heard that the beaches were watched every night, in case St Kitts invaded; that there were secret military exercises every fortnight; that the Anguillans had more than the four machine-guns, fifty-five rifles, fifteen shotguns, and two boxes of dynamite they had at the time of secession. There was talk of a repeat raid on St Kitts; there was even a hint of a fighter being called in. St Kitts was still claiming Anguilla and still advertising it in its tourist brochures ('Island of charm . . . for the holiday-seeker who wants to get away from it all'). But the Anguillans were secure. They knew that St Kitts had its own political dissensions, that many people in St Kitts were on their side, and that the 120-man St Kitts army had enough to do at home. The Anguillans didn't talk much about Bradshaw and St Kitts. They talked more of their own dissensions, their own politics.

Shipwrecked and isolated, the community had held together. With the quick semi-sophistication that had come with independence, the feeling that the island was quaint, famous, and tourist-precious, the old rules and reverences had begun to go. A few months before, on the quaint air-strip, the engine of a Piper Aztec had been smashed up at night with a hammer. Family rivalry was said to be the cause.

There is only one hotel with electricity in Anguilla, the Rendezvous. It is like a rough motel; and the lights go off at nine. It is owned by Jeremiah Gumbs, half-brother of Judge Gumbs, the prophet, and is run by Jeremiah's sister, who has spent many years in the United States and speaks with an American accent; the atmosphere of Negro America is strong.

I knew about Jeremiah Gumbs. He had been described to me as 'the smart Anguillan', the only one who had made good in the United States. He was a considerable local benefactor; and he was Anguilla's link-man with the bigger world. He had given a number of interviews to American newspapers, had presented Anguilla's case at the United Nations, and had led an Anguillan delegation to the OAS building (they found it closed).

He was there, assessing and formidable (I had been told in St Kitts never to laugh at Anguillans), while his sister showed me round.

'And here, young man, you can plug in your shaver. Which is more than you did this morning.'

She was very large; she was called Lady B. I recognized her as a 'character'. Characters lie on my spirit like lead; and I resolved never to shave while I was at the Rendezvous.

At lunch Jeremiah, sucking fish, began to boom across the dining-room, at first as though to himself.

'They call it a rebellion.' His accent too was American. 'Most peaceful rebellion in the world. Rebellion? It's a rebellion against years of neglect, that's all. What's wrong with being small? Why shouldn't a small country have dignity? Why shouldn't a small country have pride? Why shouldn't –'

I tried to break into his harangue. 'Gumbs. It's an old island name.'

'One man,' he said. 'One man gave this island a library. One man set up the X-ray unit in the hospital. One man did all this. What did Bradshaw do? Police, plastic bombs, tear gas, things we never saw before. Now he says *I* am the big villain, the leader of the rebels.'

I had heard no such thing.

'One man. Joe Louis. Marian Anderson. You get no more than one in a generation. It's because I care. I remember when I was a child we had four successive droughts in this island of Anguilla. I know what poverty is. I remember days in New York in the Depression when I didn't have the subway fare and had to walk one hundred blocks to school. Days when I didn't even eat an apple.'

It hadn't marked him. He was an enormous man. Fifty-five, sharp-nosed, with a moustache and thin greying hair, he was like somebody out of those Negro Westerns of thirty years ago, *Two-Gun Man from Harlem, Harlem on the Prairie*. It was the way he ate, the way he walked and talked; it was the rock and the dust outside. He was the man opening up a territory.

'You come to write something, huh?'

I said, with acute shame, that I had.

'You go ahead and write. They come all the time. They sit on the beach and write all day long.' His voice began to sing in the American way: 'Just like Nature intended.'

I resolved never to set foot on his beach.

We met that afternoon on the dusty road, he in his high jeep, a territory-opener, I in the low exposed mini-jeep I had rented from him.

'You making out all right?'

I was choking with dust and had already been lost twice (those Anguillan compass directions), but didn't tell him: he had sold me a map.

'You write and tell them. You tell them about this bunch of rebellious savages.'

*

For a short time after secession the Anguillans flew the flag of San Francisco, the gift of an editor who belonged to what is known in the island as the San Francisco Group. The Group took a whole-page advertisement in the *New York Times* in August 1967 for 'The Anguilla White Paper', which they composed.

Anguillans, the White Paper said, were not backward simply because they didn't have telephones. 'Do you know what one Anguillan does when he wants to telephone another Anguillan? He walks up the road and talks to him.' But the absence of telephones was part of the case against St Kitts; and it isn't easy to get about the island without a jeep. There are people in West End (where the people are mainly blackish, with occasional blond sports) who have never been to East End (where many of the fair people are).

Anguillans didn't 'even want one Hiltonesque hotel'; it would turn them into 'a nation of bus boys, waiters and servants'. They didn't want more than thirty 'guests' at one time; it wouldn't be polite for a guest to go away without at least lunching with the President. They didn't want 'tourists'.

The White Paper – it offered honorary citizenship for $100 – made $25,000 for Anguilla. Some Anguillans felt they had been made ridiculous by the White Paper. But Mr Webster, who signed it as Chief Executive, told me he stood by it. Jeremiah Gumbs, though, was extending his hotel; other people had put up establishments of their own of varying standards (the tourist future could still be one of rough bars and souvenir-stalls and ice-cream stands, very private enterprise); and Mr Webster himself said that he would like to see Anguilla as a tourist resort.

It was part of the Anguillan confusion. Too many people had wanted to help, finding in Anguilla an easy cause, a little black comedy. The Anguillans, never seeing the joke, always listened and then grew frightened and self-willed.

One member of the San Francisco Group was Professor Leopold Kohr of the University of Puerto Rico, a sixty-year-old Austrian who went to live in America in 1938. Kohr has long promoted the theory of the happy small society; his book, *A Breakdown of Nations*, was published in London in 1957 (it is now out of print). In 1958 Kohr addressed the Welsh Nationalist Party that wants Wales to break away from England; he is now on a year's sabbatical at the University of Swansea. Kohr feels that small communities are 'more viable economically than larger powers', and he thought Anguilla 'the ideal testing ground'. Immediately after secession the Anguillan leaders were beating up support in the nearby islands. They met Kohr and the San Francisco Group in Puerto Rico. 'My team,' Kohr says, 'was accepted within twenty-four hours.'

There appeared to be early proof of economic viability when it was rumoured that Aristotle Onassis had offered a million dollars a year for the right to use Anguilla as a flag base. The story is still current in the West Indies and Kohr still appears to believe in it. In St Kitts and Anguilla, however, it was dismissed as one of Jeremiah Gumbs's stories. Mr Webster, as Chief Executive, wrote twice to Onassis but got no reply. The commercial offers that did come from the United States were, in Kohr's words, from 'interests of all shady shades'.

A local man I met at the airport one Saturday – like market-day, then, with the cardboard boxes and baskets and parcels coming off the Aztecs, the women waiting for letters, messages, remittances from their men in the American Virgin Islands – a local man whispered to me about the Mafia and their agents among the local people. (From recent newspaper reports I feel he has been whispering to many other visitors.) I asked Mr Webster about this. He said, puzzlingly, that this whispering about the Mafia was official Anguillan policy, to keep the Mafia away. He also asked me not to pay too much attention to white 'stooges'.

At this stage I began to feel I was sinking in antique, in-bred Anguillan intrigue.

There were people, though, who, while not wishing to go back to St Kitts, had become less happy about the future than Mr Webster or Professor Kohr. They had seen no 'development' in a year of ambiguous independence and they feared what would happen if Anguilla officially declared itself outside the Commonwealth. Anguilla, like Rhodesia, would be outlawed. It would attract outlaws.

The new weekly, *The Beacon* (typewritten and offset, the equipment a gift from a Boston firm), had run an editorial warning against a unilateral declaration of independence. It had created some doubt in the island; it made independence appear a little more difficult.

'If we sell away our rights to American businessmen now,' the young electrician-editor said to me in a bar, 'we will be the laughing-stock of the Caribbean and the world. Don't get me wrong,' he added, speaking slowly while I took down his words. 'If Britain don't do nothing, then I feel we should go on our own.'

'I go put his balls through the wringer,' a young man said angrily to Mr Webster at the airstrip, showing *The Beacon*. Such violence of language was once reserved for Bradshaw of St Kitts. Mr Webster, hiding his distress – it was Saturday, his sabbath – calmed the young man down.

The frightened, the bold, 'stooges', 'Mafia': this was the rough division at which the visitor arrived, feeling his way through intrigue that appeared to follow no race or colour line. Responsibility, acquired lusts and fears now balancing the old certitude, had brought dissensions, the breaking up of that sense of isolation and community which was the point of independence.

There was the Canadian with the idea for a radio station, for which for some reason he required stretches of beach. There was Jeremiah Gumbs's plan for a Bank of Anguilla (he actually started building), which frightened many people. There was Jeremiah Gumbs's plan for a 'centre for physical medicine'. 'The trouble is, will I get my people to understand it? Or will they object to it like the American Medical Association?' I could never understand what he meant; I heard it said that he wanted to bring down an American who had a magic cure. I remembered Jeremiah's half-brother, Judge Gumbs.

The Anguillan faith in Jeremiah Gumbs as their guide to big American investment had been shaken by these projects and he had been dropped as an adviser to the Council. When I was in Anguilla I felt he was in disgrace, sulking at the Rendezvous. And his own attitude to Anguilla changed from meal to meal. Sometimes he was a patriot. 'St Kitts will be sorry if they attacked us. When we have finished with them, the British Government will have to feed them on crackers and molasses, I guess.' Sometimes he was despairing about Anguillans. 'They don't know they don't know.' He could give this a gloss. 'The trouble,' he said during one gloomy meal, 'is that colonialism has made the Anguillan a *shell*.'

His changes of mood were linked with the arrival, examination, and dismissal of another American with an idea. This man was looking for a 'fran-chise': a grant of land and, I believe, a twenty-five-year monopoly in the quarrying and block-making business. His examination by the Council and the Council's lawyer, who had flown in from Trinidad, lasted eight hours; and when he appeared at Jeremiah Gumbs's table at dinner, a young soft-bellied man in trousers of shocking Sherwood green, he looked bruised. I heard later that toward the end of his examination he was close to tears.

It was a subdued Jeremiah Gumbs who padded about the dining-room in his slippers, pouring water, offering bread, like a man still with a duty to his ranch-hands. Afterwards he led me through the wire-netting door to the open verandah. Sand-flies and mosquitoes pounced. He slapped and clapped his big hands, killing and calm.

'Who is this lawyer guy? Is he a constitutional lawyer, a company lawyer, a criminal lawyer? Does he know anything about economics? You tell Webster. He's got to have a development plan. Otherwise he's going to frighten off a lot of people. And they are not that many. They are not that many.'

In the morning the sad American left, green check jacket matching his trousers.

Jeremiah Gumbs still suffered. 'He was gonna invest plenty. He wasn't gonna make money for four years. *Then* you'll let someone *else* in? These people don't understand economics. If Webster could worry he'd be worried. He was gonna build that road, open up that whole area. Put value on people's property. Houses going up alongside the road. But these people don't understand. Look at me. *I* put this place up. *I* advertised Anguilla. Now other people have put down their little places. The tourist comes to the airport, the taxi-drivers rush him, take him this place, that place. *I* advertised.' His voice began to sing. 'It's not a way to live. I don't know. I feel there's another way to live.'

I said I felt he had done enough for Anguilla.

He said he wouldn't rest until he had done a lot more. 'I love this country. I love the people. I know what poverty is like. I know what drought is like. I care. I remember when I was a boy . . .'

On my bill there was a charge for an Anguillan flag. I told Lady B. I hadn't had one.

'You want one, young man?' She waved it at me when she gave it, and did a gigantic little mimicry of a drum-majorette. 'Anguilla, here I come.'

I put it in my pocket, the flag of the territory that Jeremiah Gumbs didn't look like opening up.

Independence, as a smooth administration: that worked. Independence as the preserver of an old community: that made sense. Independence as 'development' and quick tourist money: that, as the San Francisco Group romantically sensed, defeats itself. Anguilla was going to disappoint more of its supporters. Independence had only just come; and Anguilla already required pacification.

Pacification came, heavy-handed and absurd – but only to the outsider looking for comedy or a manageable cause. The Anguilla problem remains: the problem of a tiny colony set adrift, part of the jetsam of an empire, a near-primitive people suddenly returned to a free state, their renewed or continuing exploitation.

When I left Anguilla, Jeremiah Gumbs was giving instructions to the workmen (and a very slow, contemplative, sand-sifting workwoman) who were running up the barrack-like extension to the hotel. The other day, quite by chance, I saw him in a dark suit, his ring on the small finger of his large left hand, in the Delegates' Lounge of the United Nations. Four English journalists were taking down his grave words.

The British invasion was two days away. Jeremiah – an American citizen, his business in the United States the Gumbs Fuel and Oil Burner Service of Edison, New Jersey – was the petitioner that day for Anguilla, before the Committee on Colonialism. He spoke lucidly and without exaggeration; his tone was one of injury, familiar to me; but everything he said about the planned British invasion was true.

He was the official Anguillan spokesman again. He was back in favour in Anguilla. And it was not surprising to learn from newspaper reports that the American in green had returned to Anguilla. He had returned as a lawyer. He had no law degree, but he had 'an extensive law library'; he was given a permit to practise. He did more. He advised on the new Anguillan constitution. (The previous one, very short, had been drafted by a Harvard professor, who had somehow ceased to be important in Anguilla.) The *National Observer* gave some of the provisions of the new constitution. Businesses, foreign or local, could not be expropriated by the Anguillan government; foreign governments could not bring tax suits against Anguilla-based businesses. A judge of the Anguillan Supreme Court didn't have to be an Anguillan or a lawyer; all he needed was a permit to practise law in Anguilla, and he had to be over thirty-five. The *National Observer* also gave some details of the franchise the American had asked for in December, for his basic building-materials plant: twenty-five years tax-free, the Anguillan government to get 500 dollars a year in return.

After the British invasion the American was put on a Cessna and sent off the island.

'It may seem strange to people who have lost faith in the United Nations,' Jeremiah Gumbs said to reporters a week later, 'but on our little island the United Nations is still regarded, in spite of its imperfections, as the great hope of small nations and people of goodwill anywhere.'

It was the *New York Times* Quotation of the Day. The *Times* also presented, as news, some lines from the two-year-old Anguillan anthem. Anguilla – as cause, as comedy – appeared set for a re-run.

Power?

The New York Review of Books, 3 September 1970

The Trinidad Carnival is famous. For the two days before Ash Wednesday the million or so islanders – blacks, whites, the later immigrant groups of Portuguese, Indians, and Chinese – parade the hot streets in costumed 'bands' and dance to steel orchestras. This year there was a twist. After the Carnival there were Black Power disturbances. After the masquerade and the music, anger and terror.

In a way, it makes sense. Carnival and Black Power are not as opposed as they appear. The tourists who go for the Carnival don't really know what they are watching. The islanders themselves, who have spent so long forgetting the past, have forgotten the darker origins of their Carnival. The bands, flags and costumes have little to do with Lent, and much to do with slavery.

The slave in Trinidad worked by day and lived at night. Then the world of the white plantations fell away; and in its place was a securer, secret world of fantasy, of Negro 'kingdoms', 'regiments', bands. The people who were slaves by day saw themselves then as kings, queens, dauphins, princesses. There were pretty uniforms, flags and painted wooden swords. Everyone who joined a regiment got a title. At night the Negroes played at being people, mimicking the rites of the upper world. The kings visited and entertained. At gatherings a 'secretary' might sit scribbling away.

Once, in December 1805, this fantasy of the night overflowed into the working day. There was serious talk then of cutting off the heads of some plantation owners, of drinking holy water afterwards and eating pork and dancing. The plot was found out; and swiftly, before Christmas, in the main Port of Spain square there were hangings, decapitations, brandings and whippings.

That was Trinidad's first and last slave 'revolt'. The Negro kingdoms of the night were broken up. But the fantasies remained. They had to, because without that touch of lunacy the Negro would have utterly despaired and might have killed himself slowly by eating dirt; many in Trinidad did. The Carnival the tourist goes to see is a version of the lunacy that kept the slave alive. It is the original dream of black power, style and prettiness; and it always feeds on a private vision of the real world.

During the war an admiration for Russia – really an admiration for 'stylish' things like Stalin's moustache and the outlandish names of Russian generals, Timoshenko, Rokossovsky – was expressed in a 'Red Army' band. At the same time an admiration for Humphrey Bogart created a rival 'Casablanca' band. Make-believe, but taken seriously and transformed; not far below, perhapse even unacknowledged, there has always been a vision of the black millennium, as much a vision of revenge as of a black world made whole again.

Something of the Carnival lunacy touches all these islands where people, first as slaves and then as neglected colonials, have seen themselves as futile, on the other side of the real world. In St Kitts, with a population of 36,000, Papa Bradshaw, the Premier, has tried to calm despair by resurrecting the memory of Christophe, Emperor of Haiti, builder of the Citadel, who was born a slave on the island. Until they were saved from themselves, the 6,000 people of Anguilla seriously thought they could just have a constitution written by someone from Florida and set up in business as an independent country.

In Jamaica the Ras Tafarians believe they are Abyssinians and that the Emperor Haile Selassie is God. This is one of the unexpected results of Italian propaganda during the Abyssinian war. The Italians said then that there was a secret black society called Niya Binghi ('Death to the Whites') and that it was several million strong. The propaganda delighted some Jamaicans, who formed little Niya Binghi play-groups of their own. Recently the Emperor visited Jamaica. The Ras Tafarians were expecting a black lion of a man; they saw someone like a Hindu, mild-featured, brown and small. The disappointment was great; but somehow the sect survives.

These islanders are disturbed. They already have black government and black power, but they want more. They want something more than politics. Like the dispossessed peasantry of medieval Europe, they await crusades and messiahs. Now they have Black Power. It isn't the Black Power of the United States. That is the protest of a disadvantaged minority which has at last begun to feel that some of the rich things of America are accessible, that only self-contempt and discrimination stand in the way. But in the islands the news gets distorted .

The media cannot make the disadvantages as real as the protest. Famous cities are seen to blaze; young men of the race come out of buildings with guns; the black-gloved hands of triumphant but bowed athletes are raised as in a religious gesture; the handsome spokesmen of protest make threats before the cameras which appear at last to have discovered black style. This is power. In the islands it is like a vision of the black millennium. It needs no political programme.

In the islands the intellectual equivocations of Black Power are part of its strength. After the sharp analysis of black degradation, the spokesmen for Black Power usually become mystical, vague, and threatening. In the United States this fits the cause of protest, and fits the white audience to whom this protest is directed. In the islands it fits the old, apocalyptic mood of the black masses. Anything more concrete, anything like a programme, might become simple local politics and be reduced to the black power that is already possessed.

Black Power as rage, drama and style, as revolutionary jargon, offers something to everybody: to the unemployed, the idealistic, the drop-out, the Communist, the politically frustrated, the anarchist, the angry student returning home from humiliations abroad, the racialist, the old-fashioned black preacher who has for years said at street corners that after Israel it was to be the turn of Africa. Black Power means Cuba and China; it also means clearing the Chinese and the Jews and the tourists out of Jamaica. It is identity and it is also miscegenation. It is drinking holy water, eating pork and dancing; it is going back to Abyssinia. There has been no movement like it in the Caribbean since the French Revolution.

So in Jamaica, some eighteen months ago, students joined with Ras Tafarians to march in the name of Black Power against the black government. Campus idealism, campus protest; but the past is like quicksand here. There was a middle-class rumour, which was like a rumour from the days of slavery, that a white tourist was to be killed, but only sacrificially, without malice.

At the same time, in St Kitts, after many years in authority, Papa Bradshaw was using Black Power, as words alone, to undermine the opposition. Round and round the tiny impoverished island, on the one circular road, went the conspiratorial printed message, cut out from a gasoline advertisement: *Join the Power Set.*

Far away, on the Central American mainland, in British Honduras, which is only half black, Black Power had just appeared and was already undermining the multi-racial nature of both government and opposition. The carrier of the infection was a twenty-one-year-old student who had been to the United States on, needless to say, an American government scholarship.

He had brought back news about the dignity of the

peasant and a revolution based on land. I thought the message came from another kind of country and somebody else's revolution, and wasn't suited to the local blacks, who were mainly city people with simple city ambitions. (It was front-page news, while I was there, that a local man had successfully completed an American correspondence course in jail management.)

But it didn't matter. A message had come. 'The whites are buying up the land.' 'What the black man needs is bread.' 'It became a phallic symbol to the black to be a log-cutter.' It was the jargon of the movement, at once scientific-sounding and millenarian. It transcended the bread-and-butter protests of local politics; it smothered all argument. Day by day the movement grew.

Excitement! And perhaps this excitement is the only liberation that is possible. Black Power in these black islands is protest. But there is no enemy. The enemy is the past, of slavery and colonial neglect and a society uneducated from top to bottom; the enemy is the smallness of the islands and the absence of resources. Opportunism or borrowed jargon may define phantom enemies: racial minorities, 'élites', 'white niggers'. But at the end the problems will be the same, of dignity and identity.

In the United States Black Power may have its victories. But they will be American victories. The small islands of the Caribbean will remain islands, impoverished and unskilled, ringed as now by a *cordon sanitaire*, their people not needed anywhere. They may get less innocent or less corrupt politicians; they will not get less helpless ones. The island blacks will continue to be dependent on the books, films and goods of others; in this important way they will continue to be the half-made societies of a dependent people, the Third World's third world. They will forever consume; they will never create. They are without material sources; they will never develop the higher skills. Identity depends in the end on achievement; and achievement here cannot but be small. Again and again the protest leader will appear and the millennium will seem about to come.

Fifty years ago, writing at a moment when Spain seemed about to disintegrate, Ortega y Gasset saw that fragmented peoples come together only in order 'to do something tomorrow'. In the islands this assurance about the future is missing. Millenarian excitement will not hold them together, even if they were all black; and some, like Trinidad and Guyana and British Honduras, are only half black. The pursuit of black identity and the community of black distress is a dead end, frenzy for the sake of frenzy, the self-scourging of people who cannot see what they will have to do tomorrow.

In *We Wish to be Looked Upon*, published last year by Teachers College Press, Vera Rubin and Marisa Zavalloni report on surveys of high-school students in Trinidad they conducted in 1957 and 1961, at a time of pre-independence, messianic optimism. (Eric Williams had come to power, suddenly and overwhelmingly, in 1956.) The students were asked to write at length about their 'expectations, plans and hopes for the future'.

Black: I would like to be a great man not only in music but also in sociology and economics. In the USA I would like to marry a beautiful actress with plenty of money. I would also like to be famed abroad as one of the world's foremost millionaires.

Black: In politics I hope to come up against men like Khrushchev and other enemies of freedom. I hope I will be able to overcome them with my words, and put them to shame.

Black: I expect to be a man of international fame, a man who by virtue of his political genius has acquired so much respect from his people that he will be fully capable of living in peace with his people.

Black: I want to be a West Indian diplomat. I would like to have a magnetic power over men and a stronger magnetic power over women. I must be very intelligent and quick-witted: I must be fluent in at least seven languages. I must be very resourceful and I must say the correct thing at the correct moment. With these qualities and a wonderful foresight and with other necessary abilities which I can't foresee, I would be able to do wonders for the world by doing wonders for my nation.

East Indian: I will write a book called the *Romance of Music and Literature*. I will make this book as great as any Shakespeare play; then I will return to India to endeavour to become a genius in the film industry.

East Indian: I want to develop an adventurous spirit. I will tour the earth by air, by sea, and by land. I shall become a peacemaker among hostile people.

East Indian: When I usually awake from my daydream, I think myself to be another person, the great scientific engineer, but soon I recollect my sense, and then I am myself again.

Coloured (mulatto): Toward the latter part of my life I would like to enter myself in politics, and to do some little bit for the improvement and uplift of this young Federation of ours.

Coloured: I am obsessed with the idea of becoming a statesman, a classical statesman, and not a mere rabble-rouser who acts impulsively and makes much ado about nothing.

White: I am going to apprentice myself to a Chartered Accountant's firm and then to learn the trade. When I want to, leave the firm and go to any other big business concern and work my way up to the top.

White: I want to live a moderate life, earning a moderate pay, slowly but surely working my way in the law firm, but I don't want to be chief justice of the Federation or anything like that ... Look around. All the other boys must be writing about their ambitions to be famous. They all cannot be, for hope is an elusive thing.

White: By this time my father may be a shareholder in the company, I will take over the business. I will expand it and try to live up to the traditions that my father has built up.

Without the calm of the white responses, the society might appear remote, fantastic and backward. But the white student doesn't inhabit a world which is all that separate. Trinidad is small, served by two newspapers and two radio stations and the same unsegregated schools. The intercourse between the races is easier than inquiring sociologists usually find; there is a substantial black and East Indian middle class that dominates the professions. When this is understood, the imprecision of black and East Indian fantasy – diplomacy, politics, peacemaking – can be seen to be more than innocence. It is part of the carnival lunacy of a lively, well-informed society which feels itself part of the great world, but understands at the same time that it is cut off from this world by reasons of geography, history, race.

The sub-title of Rubin and Zavalloni's book is 'A Study of the Aspirations of Youth in a Developing Society'. But the euphemism is misleading. This society has to be more precisely defined. Brazil is developing, India is developing. Trinidad is neither undeveloped nor developing. It is fully part of the advanced consumer society of the West; it recognizes high material standards. But it is less than provincial: there is no metropolis to which the man from the village or small town can take his gifts. Trinidad is simply small; it is dependent; and the people born in it – black, East Indian, white – sense themselves condemned, not necessarily as individuals, but as a community, to an inferiority of skill and achievement. In colonial days racial deprivation could be said to be important, and this remains, obviously, an important drive. But now it is only part of the story.

In the islands, in fact, black identity is a sentimental trap, obscuring the issues. What is needed is access to a society, larger in every sense, where people will be allowed to grow. For some territories this larger society may be Latin American. Colonial rule in the Caribbean defied geography and created unnatural administrative units; this is part of the problem. Trinidad, for instance, was detached from Venezuela. This is a geographical absurdity; it might be looked at again.

A Latin American identity is also possible for Guyana and British Honduras. But local racial politics and servile prejudice stand in the way. The blacks of British Honduras, in their one lazy, mosquito-infested town, reject 'Latinization' without knowing what they are rejecting. Until Black Power came along last year, the black flag of protest against Latinization was the Union Jack; and the days of slavery were recalled with pride as the days when blacks and their English owners, friends really, stood shoulder to shoulder against the awful Spaniards. The blacks, at the end of the day, see themselves as British, made in the image of their former owners, with British institutions; Latin Americans are seen as chaotic, violent, without the rule of law.

There is an irony in this. Because in these former British territories the gravest issue, as yet unrecognized, is the nineteenth-century Latin American issue of government by consent. These Caribbean territories are not like those in Africa or Asia, with their own internal reverences, that have been returned to themselves after a period of colonial rule. They are manufactured societies, labour camps, creations of empire; and for long they were dependent on empire for law, language, institutions, culture, even officials. Nothing was generated locally; dependence became a habit. How, without empire, do such societies govern themselves? What is now the source of power? The ballot box, the mob, the regiment? When, as in Haiti, the slave-owners leave, and there are only slaves, what are the sanctions?

It is like the Latin American situation after the break-up of the Spanish Empire. With or without Black Power, chaos threatens. But chaos will only be internal. The islands will always be subject to an external police. The United States helicopters will be there, to take away United States citizens, tourists; the British High Commissions will lay on airlifts for their citizens. These islands, black and poor, are dangerous only to themselves.

The Overcrowded Barracoon

Sunday Times Magazine, 16 July 1972

Six carpenters leave the Indian Ocean island of Mauritius
to go to Swaziland in Southern Africa to work for a year,
and it is front-page news in *L'Express*, the leading Mauritius newspaper. Six mouths less to feed; six families saved,
at least for a year. Twenty-five nurses, men as well as
women, are chosen for hospitals in England. England will
swallow them up; but for the moment they are famous in
their island, with their names at the top of the front page
of the *Mauritius Times*. Perhaps 10,000 applied for those
twenty-five vacancies. That is what is believed; those are
the odds.

'Your Majesty,' a young Mauritian writes to the Principal Nursing Officer of a Scottish hospital, 'will you please
find me a seat?' The newspaper correspondent who reports the joke back, himself a Mauritian, one of the lucky
ones who got away, says that flattery like this will get
young Mauritians nowhere. The correspondent is not unsympathetic; he says he knows that the young people of
Mauritius are obsessed with the idea of escape and are
'all the time morally and physically fatigued'; but the
only ones who will succeed are those with 'a fair knowledge of up-to-date things and a (really) good character
and a love for nursing'.

But so many are qualified. Since the only Mauritians
acceptable abroad are nurses, in Mauritius they all love
nursing. They are a nation of nurses. And they hang around
the ministers' doors in Port Louis, the capital, waiting for
the call to serve. The ministers are all-powerful in Mauritius; nothing can be done except through a minister. But

what can the ministers do? Once manna fell from heaven – this is how the Foreign Minister put it – and the Germans asked for 500 nurses. But manna doesn't fall every day; the hope that the French would take 5,000 units a year remains a hope.

There is a Minister of State for Emigration, a plump, chuckling mulatto, a former motor mechanic. But he can give no figures for emigration. He says he doesn't carry these figures in his head; and, besides, he is preoccupied with a local election. 'All our energies are devoted to this by-election at Curepipe. We think that Mauritius must have a good political climate to solve our problems.'

The Minister can give no figures because there are not many figures to give. So the young men hang around, sometimes for years, waiting for their careers to begin. They meet in little clubhouses of concrete or corrugated iron, decorated with posters from the British Information Services or cut-outs from foreign magazines, and talk and talk. Some of them begin to suffer from spells of dizziness and have to stay at home. Many of them get headaches, those awful Mauritian headaches that can drive an unemployed labourer mad, interrupt the career of a civil servant, and turn educated young men into mindless invalids.

It was on Mauritius that the dodo forgot how to fly, because it had no enemies: the island, 720 square miles, was once uninhabited. Now, with more than a thousand people to the square mile, the island is overpopulated.

The Dutch attempted to settle Mauritius in the seventeenth century. They cut down the ebony forests and introduced sugar-cane. When the Dutch left – driven out, it is said, by rats – the French came. The French, mainly peasants from Brittany, stayed and continued to flourish after the British conquest in the early nineteenth century. They grew sugar-cane, depending for labour first on slaves from Madagascar and Africa, and then, when slavery was abolished, on indentured immigrants from India.

Throughout the nineteenth century labour was short, and immigration from India continued until 1917, so that today Indians make up two-thirds of the population. Even with this immigration the population held steady. In 1931 the population was more or less what it had been in 1901, just under 400,000. Then the disaster occurred. In 1949 malaria was finally eradicated. The population jumped. It is now about 820,000. Three Mauritians out of five are under twenty-one. No one knows how many unemployed or idle people there are – estimates vary from 50,000 to 80,000 – and the population grows by about 12,000 every year.

The economy, and the social structure, is still that of an agricultural colony, a tiny part of an empire: the island has been independent for only three years. The large estates, the big commission agents and the sugar factories are white (though there are many Indian landowners and there is an Indian aristocracy of sorts); rural labour is Indian; mulattoes are civil servants; Negroes are artisans, dockworkers and fishermen; Chinese are in trade.

Sugar remains the main crop and virtually the sole export. Sugar-cane covers nearly half the island, so that from the air this island of disaster looks empty and green, dotted with half-pyramids of stone that are like the relics of a vanished civilization. The stone comes from the sugar-cane fields: 'de-stoning' – and the boulders are enormous – is a recurring task. Once the de-stoning was done by hand; now it is done by bulldozers. Sugar has always been an efficient industry, and in Mauritius the efficiency shows. Lushness has been abolished; order has been imposed on the tropical landscape. The visitor who keeps to the main highways sees an island as well-kept as a lawn, monotonous except for the jagged volcanic hills, miniature green Matterhorns.

An island roughly oval in shape, 720 square miles in the Indian Ocean, far from anywhere, colonized, like those

West Indian islands on the other side of the world, only for sugar, part of the great human engineering of recent empires, the shifting about of leaderless groups of conquered peoples: to the travel writers, who have set to work on Mauritius, the island is 'a lost paradise' which is 'being developed into an idyllic spot'. It is an island which the visitor leaves with 'a feeling of peace'. To the Mauritian who cannot leave it is a prison: sugar-cane and sugarcane, ending in the sea, and the diseased coconut trees, blighted by the rhinoceros beetle.

Twenty thousand tourists came to Mauritius last year. The lost paradise already has a casino, and the casino company, in tune with the holiday tastes of these low latitudes, has also put in fruit machines in the island's leading hotels. The tourists prefer the fruit machines. In the Park Hotel in Curepipe the fat women and their fatter girls start playing the machines after breakfast; in the late afternoon, when the television also blares, conversation in the lounge of this allegedly eighteenth-century building becomes impossible.

The casino is patronized mainly by local Chinese, sitting as blank-faced here before the bright tables in the dark-red hall as they do behind their shop counters in the villages, having apparently only changed from khaki shorts and singlets into suits. The Chinese are a race apart in Mauritius, and impenetrable; it is a cause for awe that people can be so reckless with money which, in the Mauritian myth, they have made by such tedious treachery. In the myth, the Chinese shopkeeper spends a part of every working day extracting one or two matches from every box in his stock, so that out of, say, twenty boxes of matches he makes twenty-one and so picks up an extra quarter-penny of pure profit.

The casino picks up more than quarter-pennies, and many Mauritians are pleased with the success and modernity of the place. I couldn't find out what there was in the casino venture for the Mauritius Treasury or the tourist trade. To enquire was only to probe a kind of native innocence. But everyone knew that the casino employed a number of people and that the white and mulatto girls who operated the tables – their satiny old-fashioned evening-dress uniforms labelled with their first names – had until a few months before been idle and unemployed. Now, very quickly, they had acquired this difficult modern skill: in this 'adaptability' – a recurring Mauritian word – lay the hope for the future. In Mauritius it always comes to this: jobs, employment, a use of the hands, something to do.

The tourists come from the nearby French island of Réunion (technically a department of France), from Madagascar, England, India, and South Africa. Relations with South Africa are close. South Africa buys, at more than a fair price, every kilo of the somewhat flavourless tea that Mauritius produces; and to see what 'Made in South Africa' looks like in Afrikaans, all you have to do is to turn over the ash-tray in your hotel room. Mauritius is no place for the anti-apartheid campaigner. Many French Mauritians have family or business links with South Africa; and during the period of French 'over-reaction' before independence ('We always over-react here') – when the French rallied their loyal Negroes (anti-apartheid people really should stay away from Mauritius) and there were rumours of a French–South African commando takeover – during this period of over-reaction a number of French people moved to South Africa.

As visitors the South Africans are popular. And not all the South Africans who come are white. BLACKS IN SOUTH AFRICA SHOULD NOT COMPLAIN: this is the front-page headline in the *Mauritius Times* over a question-and-answer interview with a visiting South African Indian, Mr Ahmed Cajee Khan.

Q: Mr Khan, how do Indians fare in South Africa?
A: Very well economically integrated with the government... Some of our people are multi-millionaires.

Q : How did this powerful position come about?
A : It's traditional among Indians . . .
Q : Would you say that a lot of what we hear against South
Africa is incorrect?
A : . . . In Mauritius I was surprised when somebody told me
there were separate toilet facilities on board South Afri-
can Airways. This is false . . .
Q : But surely there are some inflexible situations?
A : All countries have their domestic problems.
Q : Mr Khan, there is a school of thought which believes
that the political battle in South Africa is lost. Do you
subscribe to this view?
A : Not for a minute . . .
Q : Your happiness about this régime baffles me. Would I be
right in saying that it's because you don't feel the pinch
like the blacks?
A : No! Nobody feels the pinch. Everybody has a job . . .
although we should make allowance for the eternal
grumblers.

Earlier this year Black Power slogans in French and the
local French patois appeared in many towns and villages :
*C'est beau d'être noir, Noir ene jolie couleur, Noirs au
pouvoir*. It was the idea of the Foreign Minister, Gaëtan
Duval. Duval himself isn't black. He is a brown-skinned,
straight-haired man of forty, as handsome as a pop star
and with a pop star's taste in clothes. As part of his Black
Power campaign he took to wearing black leather and
making public appearances on a black horse called Black
Beauty. For many years Duval was regarded as the leader
of the island's blacks. But then two years ago, forgetting
pre-independence disputes, he took his party into a coalition government; and since then, as the government's
popularity has gone down, so has Duval's.

Black Power was Duval's way of fighting back. It was
intended, so far as I could gather, to scare off political
poachers. It certainly wasn't intended to frighten ordinary
white people. Duval supports the idea of trade with South
Africa, and he would like to see more South African

tourists. He would like to see South Africans buying houses in special tourist developments. Statistics showed, he told me one day at lunch, that a hotel room provided employment for only two servants. A house provided employment for four.

The government recognizes a problem of unemployment. A White Paper says that 130,000 new jobs will have to be created by 1980. The government doesn't recognize a problem of over-population and discourages investigation of its effects. It disapproves of 'crude' family planning programmes on TV. Mauritius is a conservative, wife-beating society and the government doesn't want to offend anybody.

There are also good political reasons. At a seminar on unemployment, which began the day after I arrived, a spokesman for the Labour Party, the major party in the ruling coalition, said: 'We have rejected the all too facile and simple explanation that unemployment is a consequence of overpopulation and the lack of capital and investment possibilities . . . In fact it is clear that the holders of economic power, either for fear of inadequate protection of their interest or again out of a carefully elaborated political strategy, refused to be involved in the necessary political process . . . The Mauritian situation, therefore, presents a picture where the holders of political power are separated by a wide, almost unbridgeable gap from those holding economic power.'

So, by stressing unemployment and by playing down over-population, the government defends itself and seeks to remain the instrument of protest, as in colonial days. Protest against the rich, so often white, whose talents and money are yet needed; protest against the sugar-cane, the slave crop, hateful yet indispensable.

But the government is unpopular. If there were an election tomorrow the government would be overthrown, not by its old enemies, most of whom it has anyway absorbed, but by the young, those people who have grown up during the years of the population explosion.

The Prime Minister, an Indian in an island with an Indian majority, is seventy. The political party of the young, whose sudden popularity has rocked the government, was founded in 1968 by a French Mauritian student, then aged twenty-three and fresh from the events of Paris. The Prime Minister has a background of rural Indian poverty. Education and self-education, the long years in London in the 1920s, first as a student, then as a doctor, trade union work on his return to Mauritius, politics: it has been a long haul, against an almost 'settler' opposition, and his achievement has been remarkable. Over the last twelve years he has created a rudimentary welfare state in Mauritius. There are extensive social services; there is a system of 'relief work' for the unemployed (4 rupees, 30 pence, four days a week); there is a monthly allowance of 10 rupees, about 75 pence, for families with three children below the age of fourteen.

This rudimentary welfare state has saved the society from collapse; and the people who have benefited are the young. They are better educated and better fed than their parents. An excellent television service keeps them sharp and well informed. Their expectations are higher; they are no longer an uncomplaining part of the old serf society. The flaw is that this welfare state has been created, perhaps at the expense of development, within a static colonial economy where sugar is still king. The higher skills are not required in Mauritius. Elsewhere, only those with really good characters and a love of nursing need apply.

'They blame the government. Once they have the certificate in hand they never think of anything else except securing a job with government. There are organized groups in agriculture, but the bulk would like to sit behind a desk and have papers to scratch all day.' 'The government has made the people of Mauritius beggars. The thing is we had an extended family system here we could have made better use of. What has happened is that all this government relief has weakened the family system.' 'Our people have no sense of adventure.' 'People are becoming accident-conscious. Malingering. My surgery is pestered with malingerers hoping to get compensation from the government for their "accidents".'

These are middle-class comments on the Mauritius welfare state, and they are supported to some extent by a White Paper. Too many people, the White Paper says, live at the 'relief' level; too many people do 'unproductive' relief jobs (sometimes relief workers are sent to clean the beaches); and as a result 'the will to work among those employed, who see it is possible to live with less work or even without working, is being affected'.

And it is easy for the visitor to be irritated. Those well-built, well-dressed young men idling away the afternoons in the choked village lanes: they are too well drilled, too ready to be an audience and sit in rows in their club-houses. The complaints come easily. 'If you want a job they put the Riot Unit against you. This happens three times in one month.' 'Every day you will see people knocking at the deputy's door asking for a job, because everyone believes, "The deputy will give my son a job, daughter a job." ' 'To see a minister you have to pay people money. We only see the pictures of the ministers.'

So they sit and complain, and threaten. 'Change the government. Replace it by the socialist party. The government tolerates capitalism.' The socialist party is the party of the young. What will it do? How will it replace capitalism? There is no clear idea. But the government must be punished. The government is the government, and can do anything it really wants. 'The government has failed not because they are foolish or wicked but because they are selfish.'

Is this really all to their life, this hanging about in the village lane, these games of dominoes, these endless political discussions in the clubhouses? Are there no other activities, no pleasures, no festivals? 'No money, no pleasures, sir.' Rum, at 55 Mauritian cents a nip, just under four pennies, is expensive, *bien, bien cher*; all they can afford is the local banana spirit, which sells at two and a half pennies a pint. The cinema is expensive, one rupee or seven and a half pennies in the third class, two rupees twenty-five in the first. 'I haven't been to the cinema for ten years.' 'I haven't been for three years.' 'There is no pleasure for us even in Diwali [the Hindu festival of lights]. We can't buy presents for the children or give them new clothes.'

But that fat, open-mouthed, jolly boy, who is on 'relief', has just got married and is clearly the clown of the group. That handsome, stylishly dressed boy comes from a poly-gamous Muslim batch of seventeen. And that sullen man of thirty-five, with the pot-belly, has had six children in the six years he has been on relief.

But irritation is unfair. The sugar-cane, the cramped villages where the sugar workers and their families live, the little market towns: what the visitor sees is all that there is in Mauritius. There is little room for adventure, except at the top, for the French (who have always had large families), for the Chinese, for the well-to-do Indians. At the bottom, where life has been brutish, vision is more restricted, and there is only this communal sense of help-lessness and self-disgust.

The relief worker, the father of six, knows he is doing a nonsense job; he doesn't attend; he goes only to sign and get his money. The weeding gangs on the sugar estate know that they are a substitute, and a less efficient and more expensive substitute, for herbicide. Everyone knows only that once the government was good and things ap-peared to be getting better; and that now, for reasons which both government and opposition say are political, things are getting worse.

The newspapers are so full of local politics that they

have no space for foreign news. So in the village club-houses they talk politics; politics absorbs all their frenzy. Speech and elections are free; real power is unobtainable; and politics is the opium of the people.

A rainy Sunday afternoon, overcast yet full of glare, and sticky between the showers. In the gravelled back street of this new *cité*, an artisans' settlement of small concrete and corrugated-iron houses just outside the town of Curepipe, an election meeting warms up. It is only a municipal by-election, but in Mauritius an election is an election, and this one has been built up into a trial of strength between the party of Gaëtan Duval, the Foreign Minister, the Black Power man, and the party called the Mauritius Democratic Union, the UDM. Duval says the initials stand for Union des Mulâtres, the Union of Mulattoes. That is Duval's line of attack. There may be other issues; but the visitor, even after he has read all the newspapers, will not be able to detect them.

This is a UDM meeting. There is as yet no audience. Only a few Negro or mulatto boys, some in over-size jackets that belong to fathers or elder brothers; and little groups of unarmed policemen, many of them Indian, in peaked caps and slate-blue raincoats. A microphone on a lorry plays a *sega*, a Mauritian calypso in the local plantation patois.

> Femme qui fume cigarettes
> Mo' pas 'oulé.
> Li a coule la mort tabac
> Dans 'ous la gue'le.
> (Woman who smoke cigarette I don't like.
> She leaking stale tobacco in your mouth.)

More and more little boys come out. One thirteen-year-old boy in his brother's jacket (three brothers, seven sisters, father out of work, mother a cook) is against the

UDM. Another boy of mixed race (four brothers, four sisters, no father, no mother) likes the UDM meetings, *parce qu'ils redressent le pays.* This is a version of the UDM slogan: elections here, like Christmas elsewhere, wouldn't be the same without the children. The road bristles with bony little legs; it is like a schoolyard at recess. ('When I go about now,' Duval tells me later, 'it's like Gulliver in Lilliput. Small children are trying to lift me up.') The UDM *sega* continues. A game of football starts in the sodden sunken field beside the road.

A motor-car rocks down a side road and pulls up next to the lorry. Stones fly. And all at once, to shouts and curses, enraged mulattoes and blacks are fighting around the car and the lorry. The football game breaks up; the children scatter, big jackets swinging above matchstick legs, and then stop to watch. The amplified *sega* continues. The gentle policemen intervene gently, leading away angry men in different directions, each man shouting over his shoulder.

The rain, the bush, the cheap houses, the poor clothes, the mixture of races, the umbrellaed groups who have come out to watch: the hysterical scene is yet so intimate: adults fighting in front of the children, the squalor of the overcrowded barracoon: the politics of the powerless.

The disturbance clears, the car drives off. The *sega* stops. The man on the lorry coughs into the microphone and the meeting begins.

'*M. Duval le zour li Black Power, le soir li blanc.* Mr Duval is Black Power in the daytime. In the night he white.'

'Black Power?' the Negro girl in a pink blouse says. 'For me it is a joke.'

'*M. Duval na pas content créole petit chevé.* Mr Duval don't like black people crinkly head. "*Quand mo' alle côte z'aut' donne-moi manze macaroni et boire rhum blanc. Moi content manze un pé c'est qui bon.*" Hear him: "When I go by other people don't give me no macaroni to eat and white rum to drink. I like eating a lil good food." '

For the Negro girl the UDM is also a joke. 'I don't care for politicians. I come here for *distraction*. There are many like me here. Seventy-five per cent of the girls and boys here don't work. The people are becoming poorer after independence. *Travaillent moins.*'

She is twenty-one, small and thin, narrow shoulders quite square, her eyes hollow. She left school at the fifth standard in 1960. 'I have done nothing since 1960. I have my typing certificate, but no work.' But, like every other young person in Mauritius, she has a story of a job which once she nearly got. 'There was a job advertised for a clerk in a filling station. I and another Muslim girl went. The Muslim girl was selected. Why? I cannot say. I called before the Muslim girl.' She is calm now, will condemn no one; but she was angry at the time. 'I returned home and said to my mother, "But look what's happened. I didn't get the job." I had been registered for five years, the Muslim girl for five months. I think the man at the filling station was a Muslim man, but I don't know. I don't know.' The memory is fresh; but this happened three years ago, when she was eighteen. Anger is useless; she will not be angry, she will criticize no one.

Her father is a painter; her mother doesn't work. She has four sisters and three brothers. 'I am the eldest. I was hoping to be a teacher. I've been to see Gaëtan Duval many times, but he's just promised and promised.' When her father is in work he earns between twenty and thirty rupees a week, between £1.50 and £2.25. The rent of their house in the *cité* is twenty-five and a half rupees a month; electricity costs another nine rupees. 'We eat rice, curry, salt fish. Sometimes we eat rice, oil and fried onions. Salt fish is dear now, a little piece for five cents [about a third of a penny]. It is very difficult for seven children. I can stay without food, but the young ones cannot.'

Amusements? The cinema? 'For five years I haven't been

to the cinema. *On n'connaît pas. Connaît pas. Je suis dé-
couragée.*' She stays at home and reads poems; she has a
schoolbook, *A Book of Longer Poems.* 'In Mauritius there
are no boy friends.' She means that there can be no casual
encounters; she cannot go out unchaperoned to mixed
gatherings. To go out with a boy, the boy will have to
write to her parents for permission; but there can be no
boys because her family are too poor to invite anyone to
their house. 'I have a rich friend from school days. Her
father is a policeman. She invites me to parties, but I can't
go. Because my mother will not let me go alone. One day
perhaps I may get married. By chance.'

For another girl a little way up the road the prospects
are brighter. She has a job as a teacher in a junior school.
She is of mixed race – part of what, in Mauritius, is oddly
called the General Population – and she is quite striking,
with attractive, well-formed lips and almost straight hair,
her looks marred only by a slight pimpliness. Her green
pullover is tight over her little breasts; she wears a plaid
skirt and a short fawn raincoat, a proper lined raincoat
(lined because Mauritius is just outside the temperate zone
and has a winter). The spirited girl supports all this stylish-
ness on her salary of fifty rupees a month, just under four
pounds. Of course she goes to parties; of course some boy
has 'written in' for her, and has been rejected.

The sun breaks through. The election speeches continue. Whole households stand outside the small houses,
all up the road; and it is a little like a fair. This group is
eating peanuts (locally grown: a new and profitable crop,
planted between the sugar-cane rows on the big estates,
part of the attempt to 'diversify'). There are ten people in
this group, shelling peanuts, laughing at the speech, scat-
tering peanut-hulls on the wet verge. Ten who live in the
little house behind the little hedge. The tall man is out of
work. Behind the hedge, at the end of the garden path, is
the father, whom at first I couldn't believe in – couldn't
believe what I had seen. A man sitting on the threshold,

brought out for the afternoon's election entertainment, a man without arms, and with legs cut off just below the hips. Tetanus.

The symptoms of depression; dizziness, a heaviness in the head, an inability to concentrate.

The mulatto civil servant who is no longer young and no longer sure of his racial status becomes nervous about his job and his future and the future of his children. He wants to get away, to leave. But the talents that support him in Mauritius cannot support him in Australia or Canada; he has little capital; he can escape, with security, only if he gets his government pension. He can resign with the pension only if he is medically unfit. Depression, then, quite genuinely incapacitates him. In time he appears before a medical board; he is 'boarded out', out of the civil service, out of Mauritius.

The unemployed young Indian labourer or labourer's son, seeing his twenties waste away, turns to studies, making unlettered attempts at the Cambridge School Certificate – always big news in the press, the arrival of the papers from England, the arrival of the results – preparing himself for a job that doesn't exist. 'I am twenty-nine. I am not married. I passed my School Certificate in 1965. I got a third grade. I applied for several posts. I never got it. Still now I am applying. I passed my School Certificate in 1968, when I was twenty-six. I got another third grade. I now work as a relief supervisor. It is not a promising job. According to my certificate it is not sufficient. I applied for Teachers' Training College six times. I like that very much.' He is all right. But some break up. They yield to their headaches, give up the impossible goal of the Cambridge School Certificate and become horribly idle, at home or in the hospital.

The travel-writer, reporting on the happy-go-lucky island customs, will tell you that a bottle of rum will gain you admittance to a *sega* party. Local doctors will tell you that alcoholism is a serious and growing problem. Rum, at 8 rupees a bottle, 60 pence, is expensive, almost a tourist luxury; the standard drink is the local banana spirit, which sells at nine pennies a bottle. A few years ago one out of ten patients sent to the mental hospital was an alcoholic; now it is one out of seven. These figures are unverifiable; the government, perhaps correctly, disapproves of such investigations.

It is no secret, however, that many cases of mental disorder are caused by malnutrition and severe anaemia. Just as it is obvious that this very thin young woman in the family planning clinic is starved and quite withdrawn. No amount of family planning will solve her problems now. This morning she had tea; yesterday, for dinner, she had a kind of soup: boiled rice soaked in tea. With lacklustre eyes in a skeletal and already moronic face, she sits listless on the wooden bench. She wears a green sari; there is a small handkerchief in her bony hand, a trace of powder on her face. Mauritius is not India; there is no longer that knowledge of fate, *karma*, in which distress is absorbed. Everyone is responsible for himself, everyone is genteel.

Three years ago a woman of thirty-five decided to allow one of her children to starve to death, to save the others. She did so; then she fell into a depression.

For the past ten years and more economists have been visiting Mauritius and writing alarming reports, making 'projections' of population and unemployment. Disaster has always appeared to lie in the future; it is assumed that at the moment people are somehow carrying on. A Mauritian journalist told me that the common people had their own little ways and could live on 25 cents a day, two pennies. It isn't true. But how can the journalist, or anyone else who has to live in Mauritius, be blamed for not seeing that the disaster has occurred?

The Mauritius economy, a government white paper says, 'is not technically backward'. The sugar estates are as efficient as can be; they engage in continuous research and are far more efficient than the small farmers. Any plan for breaking up the estates into smaller units runs the risk of damaging efficiency, and it is uncertain whether it will actually create more jobs.

Such a fragmentation may be socially satisfying. The party of the young, the Mouvement Militant Mauricien (MMM), says in its New Left-ish manifesto: '*On ne fait bien sûr pas d'omelette sans casser d'oeufs.*' That New Left omelette again; but the MMM's analysis is not all that different from the government's. They both recognize the efficiency of the economy, and its brutality. They both speak of the need to diversify agriculture and selectively to industrialize. They would both like to separate the sugar factories from the sugar estates, to separate, that is, management and money from the land. And they both seem to recognize that, at the end of the day, they will be left with what they started with: an agricultural colony, created by empire in an empty island and always meant to be part of something larger, now given a thing called independence and set adrift, an abandoned imperial barracoon, incapable of economic or cultural autonomy.

Both the MMM and the government speak, as they must speak, of a Mauritian nation. As though immigrant nations are created by words and exhortation and not by the possibilities of the land. No one has yet devised, or attempted to devise, a political philosophy for these independent island-barracoons; and it may be that their problems defy solution. The French, with their strange imperial-linguistic dreams, have made the nearby island of Réunion a department of France. Of what country can Mauritius be a department?

The MMM talks of 'a global solution'. Faced with the problems of Mauritius, even the New Left founders, and compromises. Tourism is degrading, the MMM manifesto says; and for two well-documented pages it catalogues the disasters that have befallen some Caribbean islands. But, the manifesto concludes, the situation in Mauritius is so desperate that tourism must be developed, though of course '*un tourisme visant non la classe très riche des pays étrangers, mais la classe moyenne de ces pays*'. The M M M would like to see 300,000 tourists a year, fifteen times the present number; this is also the stated target of the government.

In the circumstances, the concrete plans that are put forward often have a Robinson Crusoe, boy-scout quality. Set the unemployed to plant trees on river banks, create a National Youth Service (to do what? to be financed by what?): these were ideas put forward by the Labour Party at the seminar on unemployment.

Mr Duval, the Black Power man, has his own *Projet Cochon*, Operation Pig. He distributes piglets to potential minders and hopes in this way to create a pig-rearing industry. A good idea, I was told, with export possibilities; and there have been some successes. But it happens that pork is the Negro's favourite food; and the Chinese of course dote on it. In an island of hungry Negroes and epicurean Chinese a piglet-distributing scheme runs certain risks. I could get no figures; but it seems that enough of the distributed piglets have been eaten for *Projet Cochon* to be known now to some people as the *cochon projet*.

The tenement stands on the site of a great house in Port Louis, the capital. The high concrete wall of the great house survives; within, the front of the yard is rubbled, with faded cigarette packets, dusty cellophane wrappers and dead leaves between the stones and crushed old masonry. In one corner, right against the wall, some boys and young men, seated on boxes, are playing cards, in the middle of this hot morning. Beyond the rubble, and below two old trees, the tenement sheds of corrugated iron and wood, much repaired and added-to, run down in two parallel lines, past the communal tap and many ancillary little sheds, to the communal lavatories. The ground is rocky here; the earth, where it shows, damp and black.

A red-tiled floor in the first room on the right, quite dark below the naked corrugated-iron roof. A bed, two tables, some boxes, a clothes-line. A *Playboy* pin-up above the bed, a little bundle on the bed: a tiny red-brown baby, ten days old. The mother went out this morning to get some milk from the Child Welfare Centre, but was sent back because she hadn't taken the correct papers. Yet the 'papers', frail with handling, are there, on the table, in a little plastic envelope. She will go again tomorrow. Her fourth child: now six sleep in that room.

Her husband, an electrician, has been out of work for ten months. Once he worked in the Fire Brigade; and his Fire Brigade belt hangs on the line, the only unnecessary object in that room. He is out on the wharf this morning, hoping to get 50 cents, three and a half pennies. Yesterday there wasn't even 50 cents; and this morning she borrowed 25 cents from a neighbour. She sent a girl to buy some food, but 25 cents couldn't buy enough for a meal. So the girl bought a loaf and some chutney for 11 cents – that loaf there – and brought back the change, 14 cents, there, on the table, next to the tin of Nivea Creme, the broken comb, the worn powder puff, the half-full bottle of Cologne Impériale (a gift to the baby from the hospital nurse), the rubber dummy, and a pencil. Possessions.

She used to do family planning. But she quarrelled with her husband once and he threw away the pills, and she didn't go back to the clinic. Her husband gets angry when there is nothing to eat. He beats her then and she goes away. But then she thinks: what can the poor man do? So she stays outside for a little, cries for a bit and then goes back. She thinks now she'll put the children in a nursery and see if she can't get a job. According to her customs – she is a Tamil – she shouldn't go out for forty days after the birth of her child. But she has already broken that rule, and she needs money. So now she will go out. She will go from house to house, asking whether there are clothes to mend or dishes to wash. She'll probably make about 3 or 4 rupees a week, between 20 and 30 pennies.

The next room is larger, brighter, lighter: pale ochre walls, lino on the floor. No kitchen area at the front: the kitchen is in an adjoining room: this is an apartment. An Indian girl, a Bihari, pale and fine-featured, lives here, with a Negro girl, a friend perhaps, who has now cast herself in the role of maid. They are both very young, about eighteen, and both very small. The black girl looks shrunken and undersized. A transparent pinkish blouse shows her brassiere and the simplicity of her bony body. No sexual intent there; there is a curious guilelessness about the black girl. She is the maid; she lives through her young mistress. The Bihari girl is perfectly proportioned, even plump-thighed as she sits on the edge of the bed, occasionally nervously rocking her knees together in the Indian way. The mistress is obviously as anaemic as the maid, and perhaps even more unwell; she has the sunken, too-bright eyes of the hysteric.

A large photograph of a sailor hangs on the wall. The Bihari girl says he is Swedish.

'Is why she take *two* rooms,' the black girl says in English. 'She cook in other room. She stay here all day.'

The Bihari girl says in patois, 'My mother is at home in Petite Rivière. She lives alone since my father disappeared. My father went mad.' It is said just like that. 'Five years ago my father stopped working. He used to work as a cane-cutter. Then he began to get headaches and went to hospital. And then he disappeared. I was fourteen. My mother did a little cleaning and washing to get some money. In December of that year I came here to Port Louis. I told my mother I was coming to Port Louis. But it was my own idea. I go to see my mother sometimes; she doesn't come here. I have two brothers in school. One does a little work in a *magasin*. Here now I just sit and read and talk.'

'She no tell you,' the black girl says. 'But she no work.

All month this man' – the man on the wall – 'give this girl money. Fifty, sixty rupees, I don't know. She have baby for this sailor. The baby die. Two years now.'

There are other photographs of men stuck in the door of the glass cabinet. All the men are Europeans.

'*No Mauritius!*' the Bihari girl says in English, seeming to shriek as she switches language. 'No have job here for man.'

On the oilcloth-covered table, a Post Office savings book.

'*Fini,*' she says. '*Fini.* All fi-neshed.'

She began to save in 1967. Twenty rupees after a year; 15 rupees after eighteen months. Then the regular monthly deposits – 10, 20, 25, even 30 rupees – until the later months of her pregnancy and the miscarriage. For six months the account bleeds, and for a year after that it seems dead. In February 1971 a miraculous transfusion: 600 rupees, £45, from an English boy, commemorated by that coloured snap in the glass cabinet: a family snap, clearly from England. Only 40 rupees remain now. She has paid off her debts. She has bought a transistor, and she has bought medicines. She feels tired. She has bought Sanatogen, for her nerves, and *Sirop des Chiens*, for her blood. All there on the table, with the savings book. Above the door, a Sacred Heart, to protect this Hindu girl and her maid.

They are free now, and independent. But the pimps and gangs of Port Louis await, and the new Chinese-run brothels at Pointe aux Sables. It was at one of those places, some days later, that I saw the two girls: the maid, very demure, keeping an eye on her mistress.

A lawyer says, 'I've seen many people going into prostitution just to give a chance in life to their eldest brother or youngest brother. The girls who go aboard the ships are from the best schools in the colony.'

The gangs started four or five years ago. They grew out of job-seeking and job-sharing street brotherhoods; they became pimping groups; they became gangs for hire. A recent gangster's job: throwing acid on the face of a manager who sacked a worker. The fee: 65 rupees, £5.

In this country court consider this gang, had up for damaging property: three black boys, brothers, and a badly mutilated young redskinned mulatto. Consider the procession of shabby youths with bright faces had up for the pettiest of petty larceny. The scene is almost domestic. Much of Mauritian official architecture is on a domestic, plantation-house scale, and the little wooden court-house is as small as a drawing-room. The magistrate sits against the back wall; there is a window on either side of his chair; and there are fruit trees just outside the windows.

The law is the law, and in Mauritius a job is a job. But the police officer is depressed by his duties. He says, 'This district is one of the poorest in the island. After the crop season they have nothing to do. They fish a little and they collect acacia seeds, for which they get 12 cents [one new penny] a pound. So life is hard. It takes a lot of acacia seeds to make one pound.'

A Muslim lawyer says, 'We were more serene in 1962. We hope this is a passing phase. But that is what everyone says: "It cannot last, it cannot go on." And now this new party, the MMM, adds to the desperation. People withdrawing their capital. Prices going up. Taxes going up. Probably once a month we say, "It is only a passing phase." '

A mulatto doctor says, 'The boy who in a richer society might have gone into another, mixed social group, in the end here, through depression and frustration, collapses into his old society and resigns himself to it. It is what is saving Mauritius, this climate of acceptance of fate, of things as they are, which the Indians irradiate to the others. We are ruled by two myths. The government; and the sugar estates, the malignant white god. The white man has become a myth. If the white man didn't exist, in Mauritius we would have to invent someone like him.'

*

A huge swastika is painted on the main road that runs through the little Indian town of Triolet. The swastika is the Indo-Aryan good-luck sign and part of the decoration of a Hindu house, but here it is used politically, the emblem of a new party called the Jan Sangh, which seeks to remind Indians of their racial loyalties. Both swastika and Mr Duval's Black Power are responses to the inter-racial, New Left MMM. Fantasy responding to fantasy: it was in Triolet that the MMM won its first election victory, but in this clubhouse, just a few weeks after the election, nothing seems to remain of MMM doctrine.

There are the standard stories of Mauritian weariness, of School Certificate people who cannot get jobs and 'just stay at home pursuing their studies. They are sick with life, tired with life.' About thirty or forty have gone to England to do nursing. 'But most of us don't get it. That depends on the minister. Sometimes he doesn't allow us to go. They give favours to their families.' There is the story of the boy – that young man just passing in the road outside – who 'drank away' the little land that was his patrimony and is now like everybody else. 'Now he is in crisis.'

And there is a version of the Mauritian legend of the missed job. This is the story of a boy who two years ago lost a government job through the trickery of a clerk: a job as a messenger, worth $5\frac{1}{2}$ rupees a day, 40 pence. Everyone in the clubhouse knows this story and has his own version; and the failed messenger, when he appears, a handsome, energetic young man, is clearly a glamour figure. His neighbour got the job. 'I am not angry with him. I leave the matter in the hands of God.' In the meantime he wears a mauve MMM shirt, to express his defiance of the government.

Someone says, 'People here help one another in cases of accident. But it's different when it comes to jobs. Then families are jealous. And the bad blood comes out when they're drinking.'

They have such a developed sense of injustice. Have

they no sense of danger? They have such confidence in their rights, their votes, the power of their opinions. They regard their independence as settled and permanent; they do not see its fragility. An internal coup, an armed take-over from outside: neither hard to imagine in this area: have they no thoughts of that?

The young men in the clubhouse say, 'The government will look after that.'

But as the afternoon fades and the traffic lessens and many radios are turned on to the Indian music pro-gramme, as the talk becomes slower and less aggressive, it becomes clear that these young men are beyond the sense of danger. They see themselves, profoundly, as victims; the enemy won a long time ago.

'Today in Mauritius there is the rhinoceros beetle which can damage a coconut tree. These beetles were introduced deliberately for the medicines to be sold. Our forefathers never knew these beetles. So they made money two ways. They destroyed our coconuts and they sold the medicines. We can't suppose that the Ministry of Agriculture did this. We can suppose that some strangers did that.'

'They uprooted our orange trees, in order to get us to buy oranges from South Africa. We suppose it. They came and told us that our orange trees had a certain fungus.'

'Day after day now we hear of our people being struck down by illnesses which we did not possess.'

'Malaria.'

It was the eradication of malaria that led to the popu-lation explosion.

'No. Malaria was common here.'

'Cholera. For example, cholera was not common here. There are other illnesses now. I cannot say their names. But people do suffer from them. We suppose that certain things happen in Mauritius.'

'Sysilis.'

He is corrected. 'Syphilis. That's on the increase, espe-cially at Port Louis. The government is taking steps to legalize prostitution. They give the girls licences nowadays.'

It is the Japanese, whose trawlers use the harbour, who have introduced a system of licensing.

'On the one side the government is fighting prostitution. On the other side it is encouraging it.'

'They are right to do so, become prostitutes. They are suffering from poverty. They should do it. As I myself know –'

'I will kill my daughter if she does that.'

'But prostitution is good for them, if it gives them money. Many students have become prostitutes, especially at Port Louis.'

'They are building a new hotel here. The government will give permits for girls to work there as prostitutes.'

The talk is gentle, slow, without anger. Outside, on the road, the swastika, emblem of threat and power, and the walls scrawled and counter-scrawled with political slogans and the initials of parties.

But some are lucky. Some get away. Like this very small twenty-year-old boy, encountered not far from the Government Buildings in Port Louis, still delicately holding his 'papers', the duplicated foolscap sheet with the precious ministerial signature and ministry stamp. He is off to England; a hospital has accepted him. He is very small and pared-down, his frailty the result of an illness when he was six. He got his School Certificate in 1968, when he was seventeen, and for the last three years he has been doing nothing, just waiting for this. He is solemn and slightly defiant, as though afraid to express pleasure and ready to defend his success. He is clearly of good character. But does he have a real love for nursing? He says that he's wanted to do nothing else, ever since he was a boy; he even joined the St John's Ambulance Brigade.

His father works in a sugar factory and earns 150 rupees a month, just over £11. He has four sisters and two brothers. Their usual breakfast is bread and butter and bananas. During his years of idleness he would help with the housework in the mornings; then he would go to the British Council library to read, returning home for a lunch of rice and vegetable curry. Sometimes he fell ill and couldn't eat. Sometimes he was just too miserable to eat. He went out walking then with his friends and they had 'nice baths by the river'. His headaches could come at any moment, especially when he was alone; and as he found it hard to sleep he would stay out on the road talking to his friends until midnight. He visited his friends a lot. They would tell one another that in a year's time they would be 'safe', they would get a job; in this way they 'inspired one another with confidence'.

Certain problems remain: the raising of the £50 surety and the 1,640-rupee fare to London, the two sums equivalent to his father's wages for fifteen months. But the bank will help, and he will be able to repay from the eight or nine pounds a week he will be getting from the English hospital. He is absolutely unconcerned about racial problems in England; it will not matter to him what people say to him or about him; and he doesn't care if he never sees Mauritius again. He and his friends have given up local politics. Politics can't help anyone in Mauritius now. The government can't help anyone now. 'The MMM is also the same. It is better to depend on yourself.'

In a bigger, richer country Gaëtan Duval, the Foreign Minister, might have been an actor or a pop star. He has the disquieting attractiveness (though, at forty, his looks have begun to go, and he is concerned about his softening waistline); he has the hair, the clothes; and he has the actor's needs. His enemies say politics provides him with a 'periodic mob-bath'; he says, as an actor might say, that he is in politics for 'the love'. 'You get people to love you and you feel love for them.' And he was especially pleased, when I met him, with his 'Black is Beautiful' campaign. 'In these few weeks I have created a psychological revolution in the mind of the black man in this country.'

But he was also advocating trade with South Africa. How was that linked with Black Power?

'They're *not*! That is the point.' And he roared with laughter, rocking back in his chair, his lace-trimmed black shirt open all down his milky-brown chest. He called, '*Madame Bell! Madame Bell!*' And when the middle-aged white receptionist-secretary came in from the outer office, he asked her for the text of the speech that had been made in his praise a fortnight before in Paris, when he had been presented with the Gold Star of Tourism by the Société des Gens de Lettres de France.

The speech was brought in, a foolscap sheet, and – though there was really no need: in the morning the text was to be in the newspapers – Duval began to read it out. '*Monsieur le Ministre, laissez-moi d'abord saluer le Ministre des Affaires Etrangères, l'Homme d'Etat, l'Ecrivain, le Penseur, l'Homme d'Action. Vous êtes le symbole de tout ce que nous aimons en l'Ile Maurice* ... That's the sort of thing that makes our Franco-Mauritians mad. That a black man should be a symbol of French culture. And I am the sort of man who rubs it in.'

Until recently, Duval said, the French believed that there were only 10,000 French-speaking people in Mauritius – the French Mauritians. Now they knew that one-third of the island, and that meant a lot of black people, spoke French. 'The French are pouring money on me. They gave me four million rupees. Another million this week. And now we've sent fifty-three workers to France. I'm fighting this election on my *foreign* policy.' But the South Africans were *slow*. 'They're slower than the old Boers.' He had asked them for a three-year supply of subsidized pig-food for his pig scheme, but so far they hadn't done anything.

Someone came into the office.

'Meet François,' Duval said. 'Factotum, friend.' We were

all going to lunch in Curepipe. As we were leaving the courtyard, Duval called out to someone, 'Good news. Germany is taking thirty-six more. Lufthansa, in Frankfurt.' Thirty-six workers.

'In addition to the hundred?'

'Yes. I will announce it at the meeting today.' And as we drove along the scenic highway (its flowering roadside shrubs and roundabout gardens maintained by relief workers) he said, 'I told the Germans when I was there that if they had anything to give me they had better give it to me before the election. Otherwise they would have to give it to somebody else . . . It doesn't matter at all whether we lose this municipal seat or not, because we have such a majority. But I create this atmosphere of tension. I can't live otherwise. I can do these things because everyone thinks I am a little mad and do not act altogether rationally . . . What do you think of these?' He passed me, from a full box, his new publicity photographs, taken especially for the election: sitting in his black leather suit on Black Beauty, sitting astride a motorcycle, and standing with crossed legs against the front of his sports car. 'They are for the women. I appeared on French television in an Indian outfit and I am still getting letters. The English don't like me, even when they try. The French are different. Do you know what they said about me in the French papers? A handsome black god.'

When we were in the restaurant in Curepipe I told him – after a glass or two of wine – that I found it hard to think of him as a politician. He said he could leave politics; he was a farmer. I said I'd heard that some of the piglets he had distributed had been eaten. He was instantly serious and offended; but then, almost at once, he said that perhaps some had been eaten, but that wasn't what he had heard.

François, factotum, friend, spoke in patois.

At the end Duval said, 'I've just been hearing a sad story. The father of all the little pigs died. Black Power.'

A waiter came and said, '*M. Duval, téléphone pour 'ous.*'

'*Qui sanne là-ça?*'

'*Consul africain.*'

'The South Africans,' Duval said.

When he came back he said, 'The consul has just had a telephone call from South Africa. They've offered a gift of fifty sows and two boars and free food for them for one year. I told him to tell Pretoria to send me a telegram.' No doubt for the meeting.

I said, 'I thought you asked for pig-food for three years.'

'That was subsidized. This is free. They're scared.'

There was a French consulate wedding party in a private room of the restaurant. A young Frenchwoman came out, became ecstatic at the sight of Duval and, ignoring the rest of us, embraced him and began to talk. Then a blue-suited man came out and said, '*Gaëtan, ils te demandent de venir les bénir.*'

'*Je n'ai pas mon collier de maire.*'

But he got up and went. He came back many minutes later. His eyes were champagne-bright and he was smiling. 'I've just heard something very funny. This girl who's got married, you see, is half Belgian and half Polish. Typically French. She was there with her brother. I said to them, "If you are Polish, why aren't you more beautiful?" And the brother said, "*Parce que nous sommes habillés.*" '

Later, in the crowded town hall, Duval had some of his supporters sing one of his campaign songs for me.

> Black Beau-tee! Black Beau-tee!
> Black is beautiful!
> Beautiful, beautiful
> Is black.

'This is going to be the uniform,' Duval said, showing some bits of material. 'Black and red. Black belts with red trousers. Black shirt. Wet look.'

The following day, when I went to the Foreign Ministry to check my notes of our lunch, Duval introduced a little Negro boy in the outer office as the composer of his campaign *sega*. The boy beat time on Madame Bell's table and sang:

> Mo' dire 'ous: la frapper.
> Laisse-mo' trappe-li,
> Laisse-mo' batte-li.
> Mo' alle condamné,
> Jamais mo' va laisser mulâtre
> Faire mari de mon endroit.
> (I tell you, hit them. Lemme catch them,
> lemme lash them. I rather go to jail than let
> a mulatto man boss me around.)

'The level of political thought here is *fantastically* low,' Paul Bérenger, the twenty-six-year-old French Mauritian founder of the MMM, said. He had been shot at a few days before from the town hall in Curepipe where Duval's men had sung the Black Beauty song for me. And now – in Port Louis, in this new air-conditioned basement restaurant, almost empty after lunch – Bérenger was with his bodyguard, a black giant called Muttur, running slightly to fat, but still famous locally as a boxer. Bérenger was in his own way as stylish as Duval, and in Mauritius as exotic. Small, slender, soft-spoken, with tinted rimless glasses, a thin handlebar moustache, and a black leather jacket hanging over his shoulders, he was like a European, of Europe. There was no trace of Mauritius in his speech or accent; and he looked what he was, a man from the Paris barricades of '68. 'A good year, if I may say so.'

He said, 'Of course the government talks only of *unemployment*. That word tends to make it only an issue of economics, to take the human and political aspects out of it ... Before 1968 in Mauritius people didn't have to think or offer serious economic or political programmes. They simply had to play the racial card. In the past the people at the top sought to take the pressure out of the situation by having the different races fight and kill each other, and they would start the same thing again if they could ... The history of this country is the history of several different struggles succeeding one another and then fighting each other. That's the drama of this place. The first struggle was the struggle of the slaves. The head of a rebellious slave, a Malagasy chief, was kept in our museum here in Port Louis for many years. Then you have the rise of the coloureds [mulattoes]. In 1911 there were riots here in Port Louis between coloureds and whites. Then the Indians. The coloureds, following the white example, became anti-Indian. Then the creoles [blacks] also fell for that. And the main agent of that change was Duval. That is the importance, the malefic importance, of Duval: bringing over the blacks on the side of the whites. Duval is a myth. He is a creation. He is King Creole. Created by the newspapers. It's a myth that's dead. But he doesn't want to die.'

Bérenger snapped his fingers. The black bodyguard brought out a paper-bag of what looked like sweets. Bérenger took one; the bodyguard took one. Bérenger said, 'Hack's Cough Drops.'

Bérenger comes from an old French Mauritian family. His father was a civil servant. Not a planter, not a landed man; and there are people in Mauritius who say that this is at the heart of Bérenger's own rebellion. In 1963, at the age of eighteen, before going to university (North Wales), he worked for a while as a sailor. 'The MMM was started during a holiday in Mauritius in 1968. Though that makes it sound more casual than it was. The government made us a present. We planned to demonstrate peacefully against Princess Alexandra's visit. The government threw eighteen of us into jail. Why Alexandra? Well, Alex's husband is Ogilvy, Ogilvy is Lonrho, and Lonrho is extremely powerful here – hotels, sugar factories, import–export. Plus the waste involved in the reception. I've been in jail four times since then ... The situation is bad. People feel it can blow up at any moment. I doubt whether we'll go past this year without the government crumbling or an uprising or general elections.'

I told him I had found no trace of MMM doctrine in Triolet. The socialism his party had expounded seemed to have been absorbed into the paranoid myth of the enemy.

He didn't answer directly. He said, 'There is always *something* behind the myth.' And then, tentatively, like a man thinking aloud, he began to talk around the subject of myth-making. 'Things can go fantastic distances in the minds of people here. I suppose the size of the island has something to do with it … There is a definite melodramatic tendency. In Port Louis, for example, I was said to have an *electric* baton. I don't know what they meant by that. In Curepipe it was a baton with a chain. And my black leather jacket is supposed to be bullet-proof. And I suppose that if as I walk past the municipality office in Curepipe I am shot at; and if there is a minister, supposedly the protector of the black, who wears black leather and sits on a black horse; then you are in a situation that can give rise to any kind of myth.

'You live with certain things; you don't put them together. There's one of our ministers – it's only now, as I am talking here, I see how extensive this myth-faculty is – this minister, on election day he wore his paratroop uniform. Ramgoolam [the Prime Minister] used to be a myth. The *chacha* or uncle of the Hindus. Very active and powerful, but somehow floating above it all. There is a biography of Ramgoolam by one of our local writers. It's a biography without a date. It's fantastic mythology and poetry and things … I believe the real depression comes when you go through our education system. There's the linguistic aspect. The language we all use is despised.' (The MMM is romantic about the local patois, which it sees as an important part of a 'national' culture.) 'The Franco-Mauritians too have their myths. When I came back the story among them was that *I* had brought de Gaulle down.

You can find it still. "If Paul brought de Gaulle down, what chance does poor old Ramgoolam have?" They all deal in fantasies. And it's rooted in the colonial situation.'

He made the two hours pass quickly. As he left with his bodyguard he smiled and said, 'I've got to go now and get some "tough guys" for the forum this afternoon.'

But the tough guys were not needed. No one tried to break up the M M M meeting that afternoon, which was in the town of Rose Hill. The hall was packed with several hundred students. A racially mixed audience, a mixed platform, ideas being treated like news: it was the brightest gathering I had seen in Mauritius. And by its very existence it was – but perhaps only in the eye of the visitor – a tribute to the liberal administration that was being rejected.

'It is an imitation,' Sir Seewoosagur Ramgoolam, the Prime Minister, says. 'They are trying to imitate Mao, Fidel Castro. Fantasy? They are not dealing in fantasy; they think their ideas will take root here. There *is* poverty. But we are trying to contain that by social services. We spend about thirty million rupees on assistance. People criticize us for that, for giving things like family allowances. My reply is: "Children are born. I cannot allow them to grow up stunted. If they are well fed, well educated, they are not a burden on society. Otherwise they will become backward, mentally."'

A different vocabulary, different concerns: a different life. The Prime Minister is nearly as old as the century; and that poetic biography Bérenger spoke about is an attempt to do justice to a subject which – though the scale is small, the setting restricted – is worthy of legend: the rise to power of a man born into a depressed and leaderless community, in an agricultural colony, in the darkest age of colonialism. Few colonial leaders have shown such courage and tenacity as Ramgoolam; few, having achieved power, have been so anxious to heal old enmities and rule humanely. But already the new state, as incomplete as it ever was, is threatened, and from more than one direction.

Bérenger says, 'This hanging around ministers' offices, people looking for jobs, this is encouraged by the ministers. Each minister is trying to succeed Ramgoolam and each is trying to play his card.'

The Prime Minister says, 'Now we have the Public Service Commission. This waiting outside the doors of ministers is a mistake. It is a relic of colonial days.'

The old enemy. And also the new: 'Colonialism is a destructive institution. It creates parasites and hangers-on. And they are still with us – people of all races who profited from the stay in this country of a foreign power. I don't know whether they've completely reconciled themselves to the changes. I think this new movement, the MMM, is a devious approach by these same people to revive themselves. I think they want to have their own back on me especially and my party.'

The Prime Minister has one bad eye, damaged by a cow's horn when he was a child. The drawing-room of his new house in Port Louis, built on the site of his old house, is full of the mementoes of his long political life: signed portraits, photographs of airport meetings, ponderous official gifts in a variety of national styles. Here, among his souvenirs, he constantly entertains. He likes informal dinner parties, conversation, chat. He would like to retire, to become his legend, to be 'above it all'.

But tranquillity recedes. The barracoon is overcrowded; the escape routes are closed. The people are disaffected and have no sense of danger.

More about Penguins and Pelicans

Penguinews, which appears every month, contains details of all the new books issued by Penguins as they are published. From time to time it is supplemented by *Penguins in Print*, which is our complete list of almost 5,000 titles.

A specimen copy of *Penguinews* will be sent to you free on request. Please write to Dept EP, Penguin Books Ltd, Harmondsworth, Middlesex, for your copy.

In the U.S.A.: For a complete list of books available from Penguins in the United States write to Dept CS, Penguin Books Inc., 7110 Ambassador Road, Baltimore, Maryland 21207.

In Canada: For a complete list of books available from Penguins in Canada write to Penguin Books Canada Ltd, 41 Steelcase Road West, Markham, Ontario.